016689

INDEPENDENCE

6 ⁵⁵

I0603650

GREAT LIVES:

THEATER

DAVID WEITZMAN

Atheneum Books for Young Readers

For Nina

Atheneum Books for Young Readers
An imprint of Simon & Schuster Children's Publishing Division
1230 Avenue of the Americas
New York, New York 10020

Copyright © 1996 by David Weitzman
Photographs courtesy of Photosearch, Inc.

All rights reserved including the right of reproduction in whole or in part in any form.

The text of this book is set in ITC Century Book

First Edition

Printed in the United States of America

10   9   8   7   6   5   4   3   2   1

Library of Congress Cataloging-in-Publication Data
Weitzman, David L.
Great lives: theater / David Weitzman.
p.   cm.
Includes bibliographic references and index.
Summary: Presents biographies of more than twenty actors and playwrights
who have left their mark on the theater, including Anton Chekhov, Edwin Booth,
Sarah Bernhardt, George Bernard Shaw, and Paul Robeson.
ISBN 0-689-80579-9
1. Dramatists—Biography—Juvenile literature. 2. Actors—Biography—
Juvenile literature. [1. Dramatists. 2. Actors and actresses.] I. Title.
PN2205.W45   1996
809.2—dc20
95-25994
CIP AC

Contents

Foreword

That enormous Past pushing us
    forward with an irresistible power
And in front of us all that enormous
    Future
breathing us in with an irresistible
    power.

—Paul Claudel

How do you write about acting? How do you describe the art? The craft is in the voice, a fleeting gesture, a sideward glance, a decisive movement across the stage, a flash of the eyes, something called presence, the chemistry of the actor and the audience. We can see the art of painters and sculptors and read the art of writers and poets. But when the echo of a voice fades and then disappears into the farthest gallery of the theater, what's left? When an expression that enchants or terrifies us flickers across the actor's face and, in an instant, is replaced by another, it is no more. When a stunning performance is over and the curtain comes down, leaving us speechless and scarcely able to get up from our seats, how can we describe that private moment that gave us a glimpse into the character's soul—and our own?

The playwright describes the setting, the costumes, blocking—the positions and movements about the stage—even something of the actors' moods and actions, but to have a performance we must have performers. The talented actor breathes life into the words written on the page, creating something marvelous and new. Memorizing the lines is only the beginning. What happens next is magic. The actor takes the words on the page and, seemingly without effort, creates a new being on the stage. And that's the art of the actor.

So how do we describe the spell an actor long ago cast upon the audience? We can never really know what it was like to watch a performance by David Garrick, Edmund Kean, or Molière, or the scene at Shakespeare's Globe Theatre. We must rely on accounts and impressions left by those who were there—on stage, in the wings, or out in the audience. As for the craft, we're fortunate that so many actors and dramatists have left delightfully detailed and candid descriptions of their day-to-day work on the stage. With some creative reading and our imaginations, we can try to relive those moments of great acting.

The inventions of recording and motion pictures in the late 1800s made it possible for the first time to hear and see performances after they happened. Edwin Booth can actually be heard on old cylinders recorded toward the end of his life. Eleonora Duse and Helen Hayes made movies, though neither considered their film performances as good as their performances on the stage.

Many actors were not interested in appearing in films. And there's a good reason for that. Stage actors pick up much of their energy from the audience, and it is immensely different—some would say impossible—to act if there are no people out front beyond the footlights.

If you've ever seen a play in the theater and then watched the same performance on television, you'll understand the difference. Something unexplainable but absolutely essential is lost when a live performance is put on film or videotape.

Still, other actors and playwrights were able to adapt their art to new media. Ethel Barrymore especially loved radio and enjoyed being in movies, as did her famous brothers. Jean-Louis Barrault, Laurence Olivier, Paul Robeson, and Ethel Waters, among others, have left us some of their finest performances on film. Olivier is credited with being the first director to successfully bring Shakespeare to the screen. Bertolt Brecht's *Threepenny Opera* first became known to American audiences in its film version. Oscar Hammerstein's musicals have been enjoyed by many more people on film than on the stage. Film and television productions of plays by Tennessee Williams, Eugene O'Neill, Lorraine Hansberry, and Luis Valdez have been made during their lifetimes—sometimes with the playwrights directing—so we can expect that these productions are reasonably true to the writers' intentions if not exactly as they would have done it.

The short biographies in this book suggest that the best way to know actors and playwrights is to understand their lives, the "enormous past" pushing them forward, the experiences they brought with them to their characters and roles. For many, acting was a birthright coming as naturally from their ancestors and parents as their facial features and the color of their hair. They went on stage as other children would enter the family business. Others decided they wanted to act or write plays after being enchanted by a performance or enthralled with an actor. And for some, acting was an escape, a chance to get away if only for a few brief hours from the pain, misery, or loneliness of their lives and into another life. It worked both ways. Some shaped their stage roles with their life experiences; some created whole lives from their roles on the stage.

You are about to learn something of the lives of a very few of the talented actors and playwrights who have enlivened stages all over the world. They were not privileged or special children. None of them was born great, although the public may have expected nothing less than greatness of a young Barry-more or Booth. There are no typical families here, except in the sense that they are all different. And there is no one kind of child who becomes an actor.

With a few exceptions, most young actors did not come out of secure, happy families; indeed the reverse seems to be true. Many of the most brilliant actors and writers came out of pitiful, miserable lives, and the stage, for them, was simply the means of survival. Some got encouragement in their love of the theater from their families, while others were forced to leave home to follow their hearts. You might even conclude, after reading a few of these biographies, that talented actors, at least tragedians, must be forged out of hungry, cold, impoverished childhoods with indifferent, if not cruel, parents. Can one act a tragic role without having suffered tragedy? Maybe not.

You may find in the real lives and the stage lives of these actors a mirror reflecting something about who you yourself are and what you might become in the enormous future.

PART I

CLASSICAL DRAMATISTS

Anton Chekhov

1860–1904 Russian novelist and playwright

In *The Theatre of Revolt* Robert Brustein quotes Anton Chekhov:

> All I wanted was to say honestly to people: "Have a look at yourselves and see how bad and dreary your lives are!" The important thing is that people should realize that, for when they do, they will most certainly create another and better life for themselves.

Anton Chekhov accomplished just this in plays like *The Seagull*, *Uncle Vanya*, *The Three Sisters*, and *The Cherry Orchard*. He used the theater not merely to entertain or dazzle, and not to dramatize or romanticize Russian life—which was in Chekhov's day quite dreary—but to show real lives and everyday joy and sadness. "I like life on the whole," he said, "but Russian provincial life, that mean, petty life, is something I detest and despise with all my strength." Chekhov brought this life, the life of the great majority of the people in the world, to the stage and in doing so created the modern introspective theater.

Although Chekhov is unblinking and realistic in his portrayal of Russian peasants, he is most of all understanding and sympathetic. He was one of them. Anton Chekhov was born on January 17, 1860, in Taganrog, in south Russia. "All the houses seem to be falling down," he recalled; "their walls have not been repaired for a long time; the roofs are unpainted, the shutters closed. . . . Taganrog was filthy, empty, lazy, ignorant and boring. There is not a single sign-board without some mistake in spelling." Among the run-down buildings

3

was his father's small shop, displaying two signs: TEA, SUGAR, COFFEE AND COLONIAL WARES, and the other: DRINKS TO BE CONSUMED ON OR OFF THE PREMISES.

Taganrog had its elegant, rich neighborhoods, but it was in poor man's Taganrog that Chekhov was born and grew up. The streets were unpaved, muddy bogs all winter and dusty ruts all summer. There were only two streets with lights, forcing the ragged peasants and dockworkers who tramped through the night from place to place to carry lanterns. Water was scarce—the Chekhovs got theirs from the rain barrel set beneath the drainpipe—and it carried cholera.

The year after Anton's birth, Russia freed the serfs, the last country in all of Europe to abolish slavery. His grandfather, Yegor Chekh, was a serf, but saved his money and bought freedom for himself, his wife, and their three sons at seven hundred rubles per "soul." Throughout his life, Chekhov would be always aware of his serf ancestors, how he had come out of slavery. In *The Cherry Orchard*, written in the last year of his life, the character Lyuba speaks Chekhov's feelings about slavery: that it doesn't go away but remains always in the landscape and in people's hearts.

Think only, Anya, your grandfather, and great-grandfather, and all your ancestors were slaveowners—the owners of living souls—and from every cherry in the orchard, from every leaf, from every trunk there are human creatures looking at you. . . . Your orchard is a fearful thing, and when in the evening or at night one walks about the orchard, the old bark on the trees glimmers dimly in the dusk, and the old cherry trees seem to be dreaming of centuries gone by and tortured by fearful visions.

So it was that Chekhov's father, Pavel Yegorovich, became a free man. Well, not entirely: His father regularly beat his children and forced them into work of his choosing. Pavel was apprenticed as a salesclerk until he was nineteen and then sent to work for a merchant in Taganrog. While a clerk, he was slapped, left hungry, and forced to sleep on the floor. But Pavel also managed some learning along the way, reading and writing from a village priest and, on his own, singing and the violin. He married Yevgenia Yakovlevna. Three years before Anton's birth, he realized his dream and opened his own grocery store.

What Chekhov remembered most vividly about his early years were the beatings. These were bitter years, remembered as a time of "torture"—"In childhood I had no childhood," he often said. He was actually surprised to find that one of his young friends was never beaten at home, for beating was the traditional Russian way of childrearing. Nor did you get it only from your parents; any adult felt the right to punish any child in sight, pulling their hair or twisting their ears for no reason other than it was good for them.

Chekhov remembers his mother as a gentle, tender woman, but passive and too weak to protect her children from their father's brutality. With six children to feed and all the clothing to be made and mended, Yevgenia had little time to herself, but she did take the time to appreciate her children. Whenever their father was gone, the whole family became immediately more relaxed, and the children would take out the games forbidden by their father. Little Anton, who was the most lively of the children, would immediately just let go, telling jokes, performing, and mimicking.

But what Chekhov recalled most lovingly were the times Yevgenia would sit with her children around her and tell stories. One of the stories she told them was about the days during the Crimean War, when British and French warships shelled Taganrog's harbor. She and Pavel and all the other villagers had been forced to leave the town and hide out in the countryside. It was there in 1855 that her first child was born, Anton's older brother Alexander. Three more sons followed, Nikolai (1858),

Anton (1860), and Ivan (1861), then a daughter, Marya (1863), and another son, Mikhail (1865).

Their favorite story, the one they asked for time and again, was the one about their mother's dreamlike odyssey across Russia. Yevgenia was then a small child and with her mother and sister had been visiting family in a village in northern Russia. One day, they received word that their father, who had been traveling on business, had died in a cholera epidemic somewhere in the area of Novocherkask, in the south, but no one knew where he had been buried.

The widow called for a carriage and, with her two little girls, set out to find her husband's grave. Yevgenia remembered every fascinating detail of the journey that went on for weeks and weeks. Her children sat spellbound as she told of the creaky old carriage clattering across the countryside, the dark forests that went on and on seemingly without end, of frightened wanderers met on deserted trails, and the fear, the most terrible fear of all, of being overtaken by highway robbers.

"What about the grave? Did you find Grandfather's grave?" Anton and his brothers and sister would ask in an excited whisper, though they had heard the answer many times.

"Never! We traveled all over Russia, from Marshansk to Taganrog. When we reached here, we found the sea, which prevented us from going any farther. My mother had friends in this town and they took us in. Little by little we grew used to it, and we stayed here. Then, one day, I met your father . . ."

Long after the last sounds of Yevgenia's voice faded into silence, the children would sit warm in their mother's love, a peaceful family—until Pavel returned home.

It wasn't that Pavel didn't love his children, for he did. But he had been brought up by a brutal despot, and he no doubt felt that this was the best way to raise children. If, at particularly brutal moments, Yevgenia protested timidly, he would answer, "This is how I was brought up and, as you can see, it hasn't hurt me too much."

Chekhov never held any grudges or felt any lasting bitterness against his father. When young, he was no doubt confused about his feelings, alternately fearing and loving the unhappy man who could only express his affection through tyranny. Later, Chekhov understood how unhappy his father must have been in the life that had been created for him by his own father. Pavel was a sensitive, artistic person, drawn to mysticism, who once dreamed of being a priest. There were not many grocers in all of Russia who, like Pavel, painted icons and played the violin so passionately. His life and the lives of his children would have been different if, somehow, he might have become a choirmaster or a member of an orchestra. Nevertheless, Chekhov appreciated him, saying often, "We get our talent from our father." From their mother, he felt, they had gotten their soul.

When Chekhov was six years old he was enrolled in school. It was not the Russian school Yevgenia preferred, but the Greek school—Pavel's choice, of course. Among the people of Taganrog was a large population of Greeks who had come to this port town as common dock hands and become millionaires. Since the Greeks had done so well, Pavel reasoned, he would send his sons to their school and maybe some of their skill and industriousness would rub off on them.

But the school turned out to be a disaster. Seventy students between the ages of six and twenty sat in five rows of desks in a dirty, dingy, dilapidated one-room school. Every day, Anton and his brother Nikolai went to school and sat on the front bench, the beginner's row, and learned nothing from the incompetent, uncaring schoolmaster. But the boys dared not complain to their father. To his credit, when he examined his sons and found that, by Christmas, they had learned nothing, Pavel relented, and announced that the boys would be sent to the state school.

Taganrog state school, a ramshackle, barrackslike building with dark corridors and dimly lit rooms, was not much better. Thousands of schools like these all over the country were the foundation of the Russian educational system. Later in his life, Chekhov looked back on his teachers and lamented how little had changed after all the years since his childhood. "We ought to realize that without a wide education of the people," he told his friend, the famous writer Maxim Gorky, "Russia will collapse, like a house built of badly baked bricks. A teacher must be an artist, in love with his calling; but with us he is a journeyman, ill educated. . . . He is starved, crushed, terrorized by the fear of losing his daily bread. We ought to be ashamed of it."

Those who could endure it spent eight years in school, studying mostly Latin, Greek, and Russian language. But Chekhov would take eleven years, until he was nineteen. He had failed the third and fourth years and had to repeat them. He was not a brilliant student, but then he had little time to study. Pavel's shop opened at five o'clock in the morning every day of the year and closed at eleven at night. Anton and his brothers were expected to spend all their time there when they weren't in school, in church, or sleeping, and sleep wasn't considered important. Often, Chekhov recalled, the children would be kept in church all night, and then, stumbling half asleep through the dark, icy streets at dawn, toward home and bed, his father would prod them toward the shop, shouting, "It's not worth going to bed. You'll have to open the shop in an hour's time!"

In Russia the fear of revolution was gripping the government, and most of the trouble seemed to be coming from students at the universities, so the first response of the government was to control education. By tightening its grip on the schools and controlling the free flow of ideas, the government hoped to produce docile citizens rather than people of independent minds. This is why much of Chekhov's education was little more than rote memory, and why students, rather than being encouraged, were actually punished for thinking.

The young Chekhov found school uninspiring and dry as toast. For this reason he grew to hate subjects that he would have enjoyed and excelled in were the school better. He learned to hate mathematics, Greek, and, sadly, the classics.

Chekhov's real school was not in the dull, lifeless classrooms where he "went to school." His real school was the streets and the people of Taganrog. Like many children who seem withdrawn and quiet, Chekhov had become a skilled observer of human nature. He was fascinated by the people he saw on the streets, especially the main street where the wealthy, elegant Europeans lived, and the beautiful women dressed in the fashion of Moscow and Paris. Nothing escaped his eye—a stiffly uniformed policeman, the amusing antics of a little dog, a funeral procession following behind an open casket, a quarrel among some longshoremen down at the wharf, young maidens and elderly women. He and his friends played in the public parks, played street games, sat out on the jetty for hours, watching the barges, swimming, fishing. During the summer they went barefoot and slept out at night in little huts they had built themselves. Chekhov spent hours reading on his own; James Fenimore Cooper's books were his favorites.

Late in the summer came the best time of all, a long journey by wagon with picnic lunches and nights spent in small country inns, on the way to visit Grandfather Yegor Mikhailovich, an overseer of a large farm. It was a happy time for the children; Father was too busy with the shop to come along and Grandfather Yegor didn't beat his grandchildren as he had their father. The visit was an adventure, and fun, but not all play. It was harvesttime and each of the grandsons was assigned a task. Anton was put in charge of a steam-powered threshing machine, which included

keeping an accurate written record of the weight of grain it processed. He loved the work, the peasant farmers, and the machines. Unknown to him then, Chekhov was storing up images of work, scents, movements, and sounds, workdays and peasant life, which would later give so much color and poignancy to his writing.

It was during summer vacation that he discovered a new game, a "game" for adults, certainly nothing he would learn about in school—the theater. One of Taganrog's few cultural assets was a theater with a high standard of acting for so provincial a town. Chekhov must have walked past the theater on Petrovskaya Street hundreds of times, but one time he stopped, looked around to see if anyone was noticing him, went in, and watched a performance of *La Belle Hélène*. Chekhov was thoroughly enchanted despite the amateur set— a blue backcloth for the sky and a big yellow ball representing the moon—and some bad acting. He returned whenever he could to see *Hamlet*, Gogol's *The Inspector General*, and an adaptation of *Uncle Tom's Cabin*. He was invited backstage and introduced to the actors. He had found a new world, an escape from everyday life.

Along the way, Chekhov found a school friend who shared his love of theater, Alexander Vishnyevsky, who

Anton Chekhov photographed in Melikhovo at the age of thirty-seven.
THE BETTMAN ARCHIVE.

would later become a member of the Moscow Art Theatre and an actor in future Chekhov plays. But the boys had a problem. It was against school rules to attend the theater, and if permission were granted it would be only on the condition that the student be accompanied by an adult. A school monitor was posted at the theater to catch any student who violated the rules. Chekhov and Vishnyevsky, in what may be their first acting roles, resorted to disguise. They smeared their faces with makeup and put on false beards and spectacles and were so successful that they were able to walk confidently past the monitor and climb up to the top gallery. As the house lights dimmed and the stage lights came up, Chekhov felt more excitement and happiness in his heart than ever before.

Chekhov soon found that it was not enough to attend the theater; he wanted to take part, to belong to the theater. At the home of a school friend, Andrei Drossi, a small theater began to take shape. The sitting room was divided by a curtain decorated with a huge firebird and parrots made of brightly colored materials. Behind the curtain was the stage; in front of it were the stalls. A cupboard held the props, costumes, wigs, and makeup. The boys, along with Chekhov's brothers and sisters, entertained family, friends, and neighbors with the young playwright's versions of plays he had seen in the theater, among them *The Inspector General.* The plays were a success, not just because everyone knew Anton, the producer/director/set designer/actor, but because they really were entertaining and funny. Chekhov played the part of the fat mayor, pillows stuffed into his shirt and multicolored cardboard medals covering his chest, driving the audience into a frenzy of laughter and applause. To his repertoire he added his own plays with hilarious caricatures of people everyone knew—the dentist, a silly old teacher, a doddering old priest, and the mayor of Taganrog.

The next year the theatrical triumphs and childhood gaiety ended. The family moved to Moscow—Pavel had gone bankrupt and was moving into a house given to him by his father—leaving Chekhov, now fourteen, entirely on his own. He was given a bed in the corner of a room by the lodger in his old house, and was expected not only to live alone but also to sell the property his family had left behind and even to help support them.

Chekhov became dangerously ill, but was nursed back to health by the school doctor. Dr. Strempf treated the boy with such care and love that a close attachment grew between them, and Chekhov decided that he wanted to become a doctor too. But for now, he needed to finish school and support himself by tutoring for a few rubles a month. He survived the cold and the illnesses that would trouble him for the rest of his life, passed his examinations creditably, obtained a scholarship of twenty-five rubles a month, and even managed to write sketches for plays. In 1879, he left Taganrog, thinking, as little Anya would say when she left her cherry orchard behind, "Good-bye, house. Good-bye, past," and went off to his family in Moscow.

It probably comes as a surprise that the man who captured Russian life so touchingly in short stories, novels, and plays actually started out to be a doctor. Arriving in Moscow, Chekhov discovered he loved the city. He enrolled in the medical school. But his heart was still filled with dreams of writing. In 1880, when he was not yet twenty, he had a story published and, most important, received an honorarium, the first money he had earned by his pen. He used it to give his mother a birthday party with a huge cake. Having tasted success, he wanted to write, write, write whenever he had spare time. He was actually able to earn a living for himself and his family with his writing.

By 1885, just a year out of medical school, Chekhov had achieved a reputation as a writer, though he still regarded himself as an amateur who enjoyed amusing people and also earning a living. He was invited to be a regular contributor to the *Novoye Vremia (New Time)*, the most respected daily newspaper in all of Russia.

Though all the world has loved Chekhov's stories, he seems to have had one goal that tantalized and beckoned him his whole life, the theater. Every chance he got, Chekhov attended plays and rehearsals and visited with actor friends backstage. It was all part of his growing awareness of himself as a dramatist, a kind of rehearsal for a life to come. "To write a play," he wrote his friend Gorky years later, "you must go to the theater, see it from close-to. By frequently attending rehearsals, you will acquire the knack more easily. Nothing enables you to understand stage conditions better than the disorder that reigns at rehearsals."

Soon Chekhov was spending more and more time at the theater, in the audience, but mostly backstage and with the actors. His early plays were failures, which discouraged him for a time, but *The Seagull* would change his life and would change forever the direction of Russian theater. It would be a new experience for the actors. "The main thing, my dears," he told them at the first rehearsal, "is not to be theatrical. Everything must be simple, completely simple. The characters are all ordinary, simple people."

British actor Paul Scofield *(second from right)* is Uncle Vanya in the 1970 production of the play at the Royal Court Theatre, London. PHOTOFEST. PHOTOGRAPH BY ZOE DOMINIC.

It was apparently a new experience for the audience as well. They jeered at one actress so heartlessly that she broke into tears. As the play went on, the audience hooted and guffawed louder and louder until the actors could not be heard. The hissing and catcalls got so loud that the most experienced theatergoers said they had never seen anything like it, even in the often rowdy Russian theater. At the end of the second act, Chekhov could stand it no longer and ran from the theater out into the street.

At first, Chekhov felt he had failed, when in fact the audience was simply unable to accept his new concept of theater. Why would anyone write a play about such dull, loutish people? Peasants! And do you call that acting? Why, you can see that sort of thing out on the streets anytime, or in one's own house. Chekhov's play had suffered the fate of anything new, some would say revolutionary.

The Seagull was a marvelous play, and if its first audience didn't quite see it that way, there were others who did. Fortunately, the play was included in the repertory of the new Moscow Art Theatre, created by two men whose vision of the theater was like that of Chekhov.

Konstantin Stanislavsky and Vladimir Nemirovich-Danchenko wished to accomplish nothing less with their theater than to bring about a complete reform of the Russian stage. Nemirovich-Danchenko admired Chekhov and understood that the failure of *The Seagull* was yet another proof of the inadequacy of the existing theater to produce and perform new plays.

The Seagull's opening night in the Moscow Art Theatre was tense, and at first there was no response at all from the audience. When the curtain fell on the first act in dead silence, the actors were stunned, certain they had failed. Olga Knipper, the lead actress, broke into hysterical sobs. But then suddenly the audience erupted into wild applause, demanding that the curtain be raised, revealing the actors too surprised to bow, calling them back again and again. Chekhov had found his theater, his audience, and a life on the stage—a short life, for he would live only another six years.

Chekhov's failing health forced him to move to Yalta and the milder climate of the south. It was during this time that he married Olga Knipper and wrote for her two of his most loved plays, *The Cherry Orchard* and *The Three Sisters*.

Many readers and theatergoers complain that Chekhov is simply too grim and depressing. Yet he was always an optimist, remembered by his friends for his gaiety and humor, always hopeful that the terrible lives of ordinary people he showed on the stage would someday change. What we mistake for pessimism is actually Chekhov's realism. Theater, for him and the generation of playwrights to follow, was not merely entertainment, all happiness and light. And it certainly wasn't about heroes and villains. In real life, Chekhov wrote:

> People do not shoot themselves, or hang themselves, or fall in love, or deliver themselves of clever sayings every minute. They spend most of their time eating, drinking, running after women or men, talking nonsense. It is therefore necessary that this should be shown on the stage. A play ought to be written in which the people should come and go, dine, talk of the weather, or play cards, not because the author wants it but because that is what happens in real life. Life on the stage should be as it really is, and the people too should be as they are and not on stilts.

Henrik Ibsen

1828–1906 Norwegian poet and dramatist

It is almost certain that before your schooling is completed you will read one of Ibsen's plays and that, most likely, it will be *A Doll's House*. It is not just another "important" play, and Ibsen is not just another "great" playwright. There are good reasons to read Ibsen, and one of them is that after the first performance of *A Doll's House*, the theater was never again the same. Playwrights after Ibsen began writing as never before and called for actors capable of new techniques to meet the demands of the new plays. Within months of the play's publication in Denmark, it was published in Germany, Finland, England, Russia, Sweden, Italy, and America and, over the years, performed on stages from Peking to New York, from Buenos Aires to Sydney.

The story of *A Doll's House*, especially one scene, profoundly shocked American audiences, indeed audiences all over the world. There were words—everyday words, nothing vulgar—that had never been spoken on the stage before with such point-blank realism. The characters were not kings and queens, or Capulets and Montagues living in some distant kingdom long ago, but a Mr. and Mrs. such as might have lived right next door. They were ordinary people like us in their ordinary parlor having a seemingly ordinary quarrel, which, of course, will come to a predictably ordinary conclusion with the wife submissively agreeing with her husband. Helmer reminds his wife sternly, "Thou art, first and foremost, wife and mother."

"That I no longer believe," replies Nora. "I believe that I am first and foremost a human being; I, as well as thou—or, in any case, that I should endeavor to become one."

The audience sits stunned. But then Nora turns her back on her husband and her children and leaves them, closing the door behind her.

That sound, the slam of that door, even more than the words, was too much for an audience in the 1870s. The theater erupted into pandemonium and shouts of protest. Men raised their fists in anger, screaming, "No! No!" at the helpless actors frozen in midsentence in their roles. Others turned their backs on the stage, gathered up their cloaks and flustered wives, and stamped indignantly up the aisle and out into the street.

Succeeding performances were disrupted by demonstrations and counterdemonstrations. Something had changed and somehow the world was not the same anymore. As the English poet John Donne wrote, " 'Tis all in pieces, all coherence gone."

In Germany, especially, and in Sweden, the climax of *A Doll's House* was met with such moral indignation that a famous actress given Nora's role refused to play it as written. She simply would not allow Nora to leave her husband and children. Ibsen finally agreed to a new ending for German audiences:

> . . . for use in an emergency . . . according to which Nora does not leave the bedroom, where they exchange two remarks and Nora collapses at the door and falls to the floor. . . . It is entirely against my wishes when it is used, but I harbor the hope that it will not be used in quite a number of German theatres.

What was all the fuss about? The "fuss" is not over yet, but it is the difference between present-day attitudes toward women and those commonly held in the 1870s. As Ibsen put it, "To love, to sacrifice all, and to forget—that is the saga of womanhood." Nora had not merely disagreed and asserted herself, not merely aspired to being a human being apart from her roles as her husband's wife and her children's mother. Nora had committed a barbaric act of violence against her family, against all of society. Worse, in a society dominated by men, she had dared to contradict her husband, to disobey the master of the house. She was in revolt.

In that shocking moment on a stage in Copenhagen, Nora was also turning her back and closing the door on the theater of the past, Greek drama, the theater of Sophocles and Shakespeare. Nora's assertion of her individuality goes against all the myths and accepted

Liv Ullmann and Sam Waterston starred in the 1975 production of *A Doll's House* at the Lincoln Center Theater in New York.
LINCOLN CENTER THEATER COLLECTION. PHOTOGRAPH BY FRIEDMAN-ABELES.

mores of the day. And yet she is not doomed by the gods or her own actions like Oedipus. Nor is she domesticated and transformed like Kate in *The Taming of the Shrew*. She fights back against unfairness and oppressive custom, not just for herself—and this is what made her so dangerous—but for all women everywhere. Through her, Ibsen had created a new kind of theater, which came to be called the Theater of Revolt.

To understand Theater of Revolt we have to look a moment at theater before Ibsen, what Professor Robert Brustein calls "theater of communion." In the old theater, traditional myths and stories are enjoyed by an audience of believers. There is sadness and even moments of terror, and new ideas appear, even important ideas, but in the end we are not left discomforted or disoriented. It all happens within the accepted customs and beliefs of the audience. Any character who violates the rules of society would, as the audience sitting in judgment expects, recant and seek forgiveness by the end of the play or be punished or even destroyed. At the end of the play, all is well that ends well and the universe remains coherent. It's like dropping a pebble in a large pond. The ripples disturb the smooth surface of the water, but only temporarily, and then they are gone, leaving the pond as calm and serene as it was before.

But Ibsen's plays are quite different. Characters express new or suppressed ideas not commonly held by the audience; indeed, they are considered dangerous. They are dangerous because they are disruptive—another word for change—and they run counter to accepted ways of doing things. What's more, there's no comfort in fantasy here; contemporary society is put right up there on the stage. Everything is real and the characters look and act like the middle-class men and women in the audience. Few if any men in the audience would have tolerated what they saw as Nora's insolence, her audacity, her defiance. She was seen as a child who had badly misbehaved, and most men would have approved of Helmer's punishing her. Few if any women in that audience—at least until that moment—could have imagined themselves acting as Nora had, even if their own marriages and their own lives were a lie. But it had happened for the first time in front of everybody. The possibility could no longer be hushed up or ignored. The pond could not return to its placid smoothness; it was now a turmoil of violent currents, vortexes, and waves.

Henrik Ibsen initiated the Theater of Revolt. He was a radical and a revolutionary, not just for his time but for all time. He believed not in step-by-step changes over many years or decades, but in immediate change, sweeping away old, established ideas. "Your changing pawns is a futile plan," he wrote in a poem. "Make a sweep of the chessboard, and I'm your man." Ibsen's "sweep" of the old theater opened up new possibilities for writing plays and new opportunities for playwrights to follow, among them August Strindberg, Anton Chekhov, Bernard Shaw, Bertolt Brecht, Luigi Pirandello, American

dramatist Eugene O'Neill, and French writers Antonin Artaud and Jean Genet. It was *A Doll's House* that inspired African-American dramatist Lorraine Hansberry to write plays.

It is easy and, at the same time, difficult to understand where this fervor for change came from, given the very primitive and traditional way that life began for Ibsen. But in his own remembrances and in the stories others tell about him there may be clues to the birth of a revolutionary. It began in Skien, a small town on the east coast of Norway.

From his father, Knud, Ibsen was descended from a line of seafarers. His earliest known ancestor was Simen Ibsen-Holst, born in Bergen in the 1570s, the first of a long line of ship's captains. The name derives from Ib, the old Danish form of Jacob and the traditional ending *sen*—son, or Jacobson. In 1777, Knud Ibsen, Henrik's father, was born into an apparently cheerful and happy family of seven boys and girls. Forsaking the sea, he became a merchant. No photograph or portrait of Knud exists, but he was remembered for his sparkling eyes and the little cap, like a beret, that he always wore. He was liked for his wit and the stories he loved to tell, but he also had a sharp tongue, which made some wary of him.

Ibsen's mother, Mariechen Cornelia Altenburg, came from a family of merchants. Her father had begun his career as a shipmaster, but had in later life become a merchant. In his brief auto-biographical notes Ibsen has said little of his mother, but in characters like Nora he may actually have been saying a lot. As a child, young wife, and mother, Mariechen was remembered as a spontaneous, lively woman, a talented artist who passed on to Henrik a love of drawing and water-color painting. She was also a fine pianist and loved to sing. There was no chance, of course, for her to be an artist; even to dream about such a possibility then would have been painfully futile. She had a passionate interest in the theater. When traveling Danish players came to town, she would slip out evening after evening to the performances. Some found it strange that even as an older girl she still played with dolls; others understood this as a substitute for the life in the theater she could never have. This was the mother Ibsen knew as a child, until he was about seven.

To understand Ibsen better it's impor-tant to know something about the world in which he spent his childhood and young adult years. In the early 1800s, there were just over a million people in all of Norway. It was still a primitive country, and rural people lived much as they had in the Middle Ages. Farmhouses deep in the country were still windowless. Instead of a chimney there was a hole in the roof to let out the smoke of an open fire. While fisher-men elsewhere were using nets, here they were still catching a few fish at a time on a line. The towns were little villages. Skien, where Ibsen was born, was a town of two thousand to three thousand people and considered large at that time. The people of Skien earned their living as craftsmen, fishermen and seamen, innkeepers, chandlers, ships' provisioners, shopkeepers, and mer-chants. There were a few wealthy people, but there were also many poor.

Norway was not an independent country, and Ibsen grew up against a background of political struggles for independence and national identity. A few years before Ibsen was born, Norway had belonged to Denmark. After a brief period of independence, when the Norwegians set up a govern-ment of their own inspired by the United States Constitution, the country was forced to accept the rule of the king of Sweden, although it was allowed to remain an independent kingdom and retain its democratic constitution. Ibsen wrote in his *Childhood Memories* of 1881:

I was born in a house on the main square, Stockmannsgaarden, as it was then called. This house stood directly opposite the front of the church, with its steep steps and lofty tower. To the right of the church stood the town pillory, and to the left the town hall, with its cells for delinquents and "lunatic-box." The fourth side of the square was occupied by the Grammar School and Lower School. The church stands isolated in the center.

Ibsen also remembered the fun.

Skien was, in the years of my childhood, an unusually gay and sociable town, very much the opposite of what it was later to become. Many highly cultivated, esteemed and prosperous families lived there then . . . and balls, dinner parties and musical gatherings followed each other in rapid succession, winter and summer.

Ibsen's happy childhood ended abruptly when the family fortunes changed. Knud went bankrupt, which, in those days, in a town of merchants and small businessmen, brought a heavy social penalty and the worst dishonor of any failure. The family was socially disgraced. Knud's friends abandoned him. Known for his generosity and hospitality, he became in his isolation more and more embittered.

The bitterness and anger at home turned Ibsen's mother into a cowed, melancholy woman. The beautiful, sensitive Mariechen of earlier years disappeared. She is remembered in later times as withdrawn, unable to open herself to others, possessing what Ibsen later called "the shyness of the soul." Ibsen's memories of her during this dark period might do for any woman of the day, including Nora: "She was a quiet, lovable woman, the soul of the household, and everything to her husband and children. It was not in her to be bitter or reproachful."

How painful it must have been for so small a child to watch the sparkle leave his mother's eyes and her life. He would never forget this time, and found it painful to think back on his childhood. When he was very old, his niece Anna recalled that he talked of returning to Skien and the place of his birth, but he couldn't bring himself to make the journey. He would just shake his head slowly as though looking back through all the years and say, "It is not easy to go to Skien."

The funny stories and happiness were suddenly and finally gone from Ibsen's life. He is remembered after this as a lonely boy who kept to himself. His sister recalls how "he loved to sit alone and play in a small room next to the kitchen, and there he sat drawing, painting and reading or playing with his toy theatre. This little room was everything to him and he was terrified lest anyone should come in and touch his things." His brothers and sisters would tease him, trying to get him to come out of his room and play with them. They would throw snowballs or stones against his door until he would charge out and chase them away.

At fifteen Ibsen reached the age when it was customary for children to leave home and find work. He had had no schooling to speak of and certainly no preparation for work. The "Danish school" he had been attending was a church school teaching only the barest essentials of, as one biographer put it, "reading, writing, arithmetic and the fear of God."

This was a time when many people were leaving for America and the promise of a farm in Wisconsin, Minnesota, or the Dakotas. From the upper floor of his house Ibsen could look out on the harbor and the bustle of immigrants on their way to freedom and opportunity, and surely he must have felt an urge to go with them, as he later wrote in his play *The Pretenders*, "towards the new, towards the unknown, towards the strange shore and the saga that is to come."

That didn't happen. Instead—in 1844, just two months short of his sixteenth birthday—Ibsen was sent off to the small town of Grimstad to become an apothecary's apprentice. The arrival of the apprentice at the apothecary's gave the owner the excuse he needed not to work, and so young Ibsen was left to do most of the work. He had little free time, the salary was miserable, and there was little to eat, but Ibsen kept his mind active. He painted, wrote his first poetry, and read every moment he could. He had brought a box of books with him from Skien and the apothecary, Reimann, allowed Ibsen to borrow his books. He devoured the works of his favorite authors—Charles Dickens, Sir Walter Scott, Voltaire, and contemporary Swedish and Danish novelists. It was during this period in Grimstad that Ibsen published his first poem. Actually it was a friend, Christopher Due, who sent the poem "In Autumn" to a newspaper in Christiana (now Oslo) without telling Ibsen.

The publication of "In Autumn" was a turning point in Ibsen's life, perhaps his first inkling that he might become a writer. Delighted by the possibilities of his own writing, Ibsen wrote many poems and sonnets during this period, poems reflecting his liberal sympathies with the revolutions and uprisings raging all over Europe.

These were also the years when Ibsen began to think about writing drama. An elderly Scottish woman, Miss Crawfurd, lent him copies of plays by the eminent Danish poet Adam Ochlenschläger. These were not the kind of plays Ibsen would eventually write. They were heavy melodramas typical of the time, but they were Ibsen's very first glimpse of theatrical tragedy. He set about writing his own play, a political drama set in ancient Rome, titled *Catalina*. It was politely but firmly rejected by theater managers and was published later only when a close friend paid to have it printed.

Modern critics recognize Shakespearean overtones in *Catalina* and similarities to scenes in *Julius Caesar*, yet, except for a play or two by Danish playwrights, Ibsen knew nothing about theater outside of Scandinavia. He knew Shakespeare only by name. Since he could not read English, French, or German, there was no way for him to read any of the important dramatists up to that time. What's more, it would be another few years before he would actually see tragedy performed on the stage.

Ibsen was beginning to find a voice. In 1850, he went off to Christiana to try to enter the university and, as it turned out, to write more lyric poetry and political satire, as well as a one-act play—*The Norsemen*. But this was not to turn out like *Catalina*. He submitted his play to the Christiana Theatre. It was accepted and then performed on September 26, 1850, with the new title *The Warrior's Barrow*. Although written in the older style of Ochlenschläger, it showed the young playwright's mastery of verse lines and dramatic conventions of the day. He would have to master the older, established forms before going on to develop his own style. *The Warrior's Barrow* won praise from the *Christiana Post* and, through the efforts of another friend, Ole Schulerud, a contract to publish an edition of four thousand to five thousand copies of the play. Ibsen was just twenty-two.

The Warrior's Barrow, all but unknown today, made Ibsen known throughout Scandinavia. In those days, theater in Norway was always Danish theater, performed in Danish. The nationalist movement in Norway, however, called for a return of the Norse language in literature and on the stage. When Norway's most famous son, violinist Ole Bull, returned from a world tour and standing ovations all over Europe and America, he decided to give his hometown of Bergen a gift. He would revive the long dormant Dramatic Society he recalled so fondly from his childhood and create a theater. In the summer of 1849, he rented a vacant theater, placed advertisements in the newspaper for musicians, dancers, actors—anyone who would like to perform—and announced the opening of the Norwegian Theatre in Bergen. The theater was a success from the first performance. But because Bull would soon be off on another world tour, he needed someone to direct the theater. He had heard of a student in Christiana who

Henrik Ibsen photographed in his later years.
UPI/BETTMANN.

had already written two plays, and so he invited Henrik Ibsen to be the Norwegian Theatre's first resident dramatist.

This appointment was to become Ibsen's first opportunity to "study" theater. He was not only to write plays but to be the stage manager and the producer. Included in his salary was money for traveling abroad to Copenhagen, Berlin, Dresden, and Hamburg, to the great theaters of Europe. It was a young dramatist's fantasy come true. In Copenhagen, Ibsen was given free tickets to the Royal Theatre, one of the most brilliant theaters in the world. He met and received expert advice on technical and theatrical techniques from the theater's stage manager, who, like Ibsen, was also the resident writer. And he met the greatest Dane of all, Hans Christian Andersen, who advised him to add Vienna to his theater itinerary. When Ibsen returned to Bergen, he embarked on a busy schedule. The new director staged fifty-four different plays in eighteen months.

The next years in Ibsen's life were years of exploring, experimenting, learning, growth, and maturity. He wrote dozens of plays, was appointed director of theaters in Christiana and Mollergaten, fell in love with, and married, Suzannah Daae Thoresen, and traveled with his new wife to Rome, Dresden, Munich, and again to Rome. These were not always idyllic times. The Ibsens were poor, and often Ibsen's new plays and theater productions were drubbed by the critics. But Norwegian audiences loved their first dramatist, and Ibsen's plays were appearing all over the world.

Always he experimented with new approaches. In *The Wild Duck* he used symbolism in a way not seen before on stage. Ibsen anticipated that the play would create a new kind of theater and new acting techniques. In a letter to his publisher accompanying the finished play, Ibsen tells how the characters themselves, despite all their defects and problems,

> have nevertheless become dear to me during my long daily association with them, but I have hopes they will also find well-disposed friends in the great reading public and not least among actors and actresses, for without exception they offer rewarding parts. But the study and rendering of these people will not be easy. . . . This new play has in some ways a place on its own in my dramatic production; the method diverges in several respects from my earlier work. . . . In this way I think that *The Wild Duck* might lure some of our younger dramatists into new ways, and that I consider desirable.

The Wild Duck along with *The Doll's House, Ghosts*, and other Ibsen plays, directly and indirectly influenced the next generation of playwrights, right up to the present day. Ibsen had begun to probe a new awareness of self and the individual. He began to explore, through his characters, the two aspects of our nature—our inner reality, the part of us that remains mostly hidden from others and even ourselves, and the part of us that is seen by others, the mask we show to the world. He also began to explore the depths of personality and character, the origins of our personality and nature.

The themes of Ibsen's plays—small people living their lives, suffering the pain of truth, and individuals in conflict with society—were universal themes in his day and remain so today. His plays survive, read and performed in almost every country in the world, because they make us face up to who we really are, a quest as immediate in our generation as it was in Ibsen's. Norwegian dramatist Helge Krog, in a memorial to Henrik Ibsen, explained it this way:

> We know that the light from space does not reach us until a certain time after it has left the stars. It is the same with the light from the works of great authors. The source is the same, and the light pours continuously, but it is always a new light. And so it is with Ibsen's great dramas. Fifty years, a hundred years after their creation there open from inside them new sources of light, which astonishingly illuminate our life and give us joy of first experience. And there is undoubtedly light *on the way* to us from Ibsen's writing.

Jean-Baptiste Poquelin (Molière)

1622–1673 French dramatist, actor, and master of comedy

He comes on the stage with his head in the air, his feet stuck out at right angles, and one shoulder thrust out in front of him; his wig, pointing all askew in the direction he is travelling, is adorned with more laurel-leaves than a York ham. Then he stands, his hands on his hips in a most unnatural posture, and with eyes staring wildly he begins his tirade, spacing out his words with heavy breathing, for all the world as if he had the hiccups.

W. D. Howarth, in his book *Molière: A Playwright and His Audience*, thus describes Molière as he must have appeared to his audience.

With a roar of laughter the Paris audience welcomes Molière, their favorite comedy player, in one of their favorite roles, the vain, pompous, stylish Marquis de Mascarille.

Before the play is over the audience will laugh until they hurt at silly men and women, hilarious horseplay, tripping and tumbling, ludicrous ballet, dazzling repartee, everything they expected to see when they came to see Molière, but were still surprised. The French love farce, and for over three hundred years they have loved Molière. When they laughed at the ridiculous characters he created, they were laughing at themselves. For the Marquis was not some fantastic being. He was one of them, a type—exaggerated, perhaps, but recognizable. That was Molière's genius. More than any other writer of comedies, he has given us funny but true glimpses into human nature, still valid and still able to make us laugh three centuries later.

Jean-Baptiste Poquelin—who later took the stage name Molière—was born in Paris in January 1622, the oldest of six children. The day is unknown. His father was Jean Poquelin and his mother, Marie Cressé. Little is known about Marie. She died very young, when Jean-Baptiste was nine. She knew how to read and write, which was an accomplishment in those days, especially for a woman, and she is remembered only as a pleasant person who busied herself with her household and the care of her family. We know nothing of Jean-Baptiste's stepmother, who married his father a year after his mother's death and died shortly afterward.

Master Poquelin was an upholsterer and a solid middle-class businessman. The family lived above the shop and workroom, which were frequently visited by the stylish women of Paris who came for elegant furnishings, all dressed in lace, velvets, and brocades. Among Jean-Baptiste's earliest memories was his father's shop, where perhaps a dozen weavers and their apprentices worked at the clattering looms making beautiful fabrics. France was ruled by Louis XIV, called the Sun King, and for the upper classes at least, it was an age of elegance and finery, beautiful palaces filled with exquisite furniture, much pomp, and military marching. It was one of those times in history when a gentle-man's costume was at least as showy and frilly as his lady's, maybe even more so. All of this would shape Molière's life and his art.

Theater was among the Sun King's pleasures, and so the Parisian theater was enjoying increasing importance and royal patronage. Young Poquelin's grandfather, Louis Cressé, a retired upholsterer, loved the theater and frequently took his grandson, who, though too young to understand the tragedies, enjoyed the gags, funny costumes, the clowning and swordplay of the farces, which followed the main piece. The visits with Grandfather to the Hôtel de Bourgogne, one of the great theaters of Paris, continued as Jean-Baptiste grew up, and it was these experiences that fostered the boy's early love for theater and especially for comedy.

Comedy was a national passion. The theaters were always crowded with laughing audiences who shouted out their approval and disapproval of the actors and each turn of events. Actors in ludicrous, multicolored costumes strutted and pranced about the creaking wooden stage in funny and scary masks. There were jugglers and acrobats who challenged the laws of gravity, and harlequins and buffoons, and funny ladies and all kinds of zanies singing and declaiming and making rude noises. There were fights and brawls and swashbuckling swordplay, all patterned after the Italian theater.

Monsieur Poquelin disapproved of his son's theatergoing. In his middle-class way he expected his son to follow in his work or even improve on his father's position by pursuing an honored profession. One day he turned on his father-in-law, angrily asking: "Do you want to make the boy an actor?" The old man answered with considerable excitement, "I wish to God he could turn out as good a comedian as Bellerose!"—referring to his favorite and one of the brightest stars of French theater.

A son in the theater was not a happy prospect for a middle-class businessman who, like Monsieur Poquelin, aspired to a position in Louis XIV's court. Actors were a class apart. They were subject to the grave ecclesiastical punishment of excommunication, which, in a Catholic country like France, meant the loss of all civil liberties, including a lawful marriage. (Actors who wanted to marry listed their occupation as "musician.") No person of quality, certainly no one considered a lady or a gentleman, would appear on the stage; these were boundaries that could never be crossed. Though an actor might be honored by the king, he was still a common player. Louis XIV attempted to change this when, in 1641, he issued a decree that protected stage folk from public social

discrimination and forbade their treatment as inferiors because of their profession. Still, the prejudice was ingrained in French attitudes. Even at the end of his distinguished life, the best loved of all of France's comedians, Molière's class was not forgotten. "The famous Molière died last night," a Paris newspaper reported. "Apart from his profession, he was very much a gentleman."

No, Monsieur Poquelin's son would not be a common player. Young Jean-Baptiste would enjoy advantages that he, a mere upholsterer, had missed. To begin with, the boy would have a broad academic education at the local parish school. Here, in addition to religious instruction and preparation for first Communion, he would study French and Latin, writing, arithmetic, ciphering, grammar, and plainsong. School hours were from eight to eleven in the morning and two to five o'clock in the afternoon. In addition, Jean-Baptiste served as an apprentice to his father, learning the upholstery trade. Despite his expectations for his son, Monsieur Poquelin was apparently not an unreasonable man, for he listened with understanding the day Jean-Baptiste confided in him of his loathing for the shop and the work and, worst of all, the prospect of becoming a valet in the king's court. Grandfather Louis applauded the boy's spunk and supported him in his request for further education. So it was that in 1636, at the age of fourteen, Jean-Baptiste was enrolled in the Collège de Clermont, one of the finest schools in all France.

At Collège de Clermont, young Poquelin would be taught by learned Jesuits whose objective was producing "the complete man." Here, for six years, he would study theology, mathematics, physics, chemistry, music, dancing, fencing (a gentleman was expected to be an expert swordsman), and theatricals. Along with his fellow students, he would perform tragedies and ballets in the school's properly equipped theater after demanding, painstaking rehearsals. Classes were conducted in Latin, and the young scholar would have the opportunity also to study as a private pupil with the celebrated scholar Abbé Pierre Gassendi, priest and philosopher, who was an equally distinguished chemist, physicist, astronomer, and musician.

We have no pictures of young Jean-Baptiste, but he is remembered as a "stocky, dark, wide-shouldered boy in the squaretoed buckled shoes, ample breeches, and linen-collared doublet of the period, his flowing untidy locks crowned by a wide-brimmed felt hat, with or without a feather and worn askew." He was a superior classical scholar.

It is likely, too, that the young scholar also enjoyed a young man's informal education, accompanying his friends on the town to cabarets and visits backstage at the theaters. He would see tragedies at the Théâtre du Marais and comedies at the Hôtel de Bourgogne and, at the Petit-Bourbon, Giuseppe Bianchi's Italian company. Here he would sit wide-eyed at the adventures of the famous character Scaramouche (and, perhaps, be thinking about characters for his own plays someday).

After leaving the college, it was expected of Jean-Baptiste that he find a profession. Though he was no doubt already dreaming about a life in the theater, what he told his father was that he would like to enter the law, and so began his studies at nineteen. It took only one term. The law diploma at the time was something of a joke, requiring only that one suffer a few routine questions and then cross the palms of the examiners with gold coins. This, more than the accuracy of the answers, assured graduation and a diploma.

But Jean-Baptiste would never appear in a court of law or draw up even one contract or will. One day, while carousing around Paris with his friends, he met Madeleine Béjart, an actress in a small touring company that sometimes performed for the king on his travels. Madeleine was one of ten children, at least five of whom acted on the stage. She was considered among the most talented in the world of itinerant actors, a commanding and powerful tragic actress who also wrote poetry. In addition to her acting talents, Madeleine was capable in money matters and, by the age of eighteen, had put aside a considerable amount of money and bought a little house with a garden. If Monsieur Poquelin had any hopes of tempting his son away from the bohemian life of the stage, beautiful, redheaded Madeleine ended them once and for all.

Jean-Baptiste confronted his father with his intentions. He did not want a career in law; he wanted nothing to do with upholstery. Not only did he intend a life on the stage, but he and some young friends, including Madeleine, planned to start their own theater company. What's more, he wanted his share of his mother's estate, the money to be used to finance the new theater. We can imagine Monsieur Poquelin trying to stop his son from committing what he saw as social and financial suicide. There were, no doubt, some harsh words and some abuse heaped on Grandfather Cressé for leading the boy astray. But in the end Monsieur Poquelin gave in and, though Jean-Baptiste was not yet legally of age, he gave his son his inheritance and, presumably, his blessing.

On June 30, 1643, ten people met at the Béjart home and signed a legal document founding a new theatrical company to be called l'Illustre Théâtre, committed to performing plays without charging admission. Among those who signed with Jean-Baptiste were Madeleine, as codirector; her sister Geneviève; and her brother Joseph. Jean-Baptiste decided also to take a new name to accompany him into his new life on the stage—Molière.

The place chosen for the new theater was a tennis court, and the first play was produced within about six months. They faced stiff competition from the established theaters in Paris, and the little company worked hard to keep alive. Still, in a short time it came to an end. They had had too little money to start off and were forced into debt to mount their productions. The situation got even worse when they borrowed money from moneylenders to pay off their creditors. But it was not all their fault; it is possible that there simply were not enough customers in Paris to keep three theaters open. Whatever the reason, the l'Illustre Théâtre soon folded and Molière found himself sitting in debtors' prison.

Whether or not Molière had to endure his father's "I told you so" is not recorded, but Monsieur Poquelin came through again, this time paying off his son's debts and getting him released from prison. Although we know little of the relationship between the young actor/manager and his father, it seems clear that if not encouraging he was at least reasonable and accommodating. Later, when Molière became wealthy, he returned his father's favors by making him a substantial loan when he needed it. The l'Illustre Théâtre regrouped around its freed codirector and now business manager, and they took their show on the road, out into the provinces south of Paris. This was not exile or banishment. The royal decree protecting actors from discrimination relieved the theater from many prohibitions and crippling restrictions. The result was a spirited rebirth in French theater, bringing support and opportunities for new companies and, no doubt, encouragement for young actors.

Now, out in the countryside, far away from the powerful monopoly of the Hôtel de Bourgogne, the little company of players found patrons among the noblemen who were jealous, or at least disdainful, of the power and money in Paris. What was missing in the provinces were theaters in which to act, and this too was turned to advantage. Anywhere they could they found makeshift stages, often lit with nothing more than a few candles. In the absence of scenery and props, the actors were required to develop new techniques to convey the magic illusion of place

A copper engraving depicts Molière reading his new comedy to his chambermaid. THE BETTMANN ARCHIVE.

through speech and facial expressions, gestures, and movements. The people in the provinces were hungry for theater, and it did not matter that the little cobbled-together stages were not as well equipped or as grand as the theaters of Paris. Of course audiences still hissed and shouted at the actors, and some of the country folk preferred the puppet shows and mechanical music contrivances, but what mattered was that the actors were here, among the people.

Sadly, little has been written of these exciting times in the provinces where companies like l'Illustre Théâtre honed their skills and developed their repertories. One of Molière's biographers, D. B. Wyndham Lewis, translated from the French a contemporary description of a traveling troupe like Molière's in a novel published in 1651. We can imagine the little troop

> . . . trudging the highroad with their ox-cart, piled with a pyramid of baggage and properties and rolls of scenery, on which reclines enthroned the leading lady. Most of the men are armed with large guns or long swords, some are weighed down with bass-viols and drums; their costume, less impressive than their bearing and gestures, is mud-splashed and shabby.

All the nights and all the "theaters" were different, but when the troupe arrived in Lyon, they found a very special difference. Lyon is but a few kilometers from the border with Italy, and it was there, at this gateway between the two countries, that Molière discovered for the first time the old Italian theater tradition, *commedia dell'arte*. Italian theater in Lyon was, by the time of Molière's arrival, over a century old, going back to 1513, when the city welcomed the first Italian actors. Compared even to Paris, the actors of the *commedia dell'arte* were finished and cultivated artists portraying with mask, costume, and mimetic gesture characters endowed with personalities.

Commedia dell'arte is comedy in its highest form, and it is all improvisation, changing from cast to cast, stage to stage, coming together differently each time. Before, Molière had known only drama of written words in which each performance is almost exactly like any other, because the words drive the action. But not so in *commedia dell'arte*. The actors make the characters with their voices and actions, moving around and against each other rhythmically like dancers and acrobats. Molière saw and understood the difference at once. And from this experience he would create his own kind of theater, a blending of the Italian and French comedy styles, in his first new play inspired by what he had seen at Lyon—*L'Estourdy (The Scatterbrain)*.

As with anyone attempting something new, Molière encountered resistance to new techniques in the theater. People went to plays expecting to be entertained, not to be shown new possibilities or to be enlightened. Though they might grow to like an innovation on the stage, even to prefer it to what they had been used to, the initial reaction was almost always disappointment and dislike. Eventually audiences applauded

A scene from an American production of *Le Bourgeois gentilhomme*, which carried the English title *The Would-Be Gentleman*. Bobby Clark *(second from left)* played the title role. PHOTOFEST. PHOTOGRAPH BY ALFREDO VALENTI.

Molière's new work and took him to their hearts.

When the troupe returned to Paris it was given the title The King's Troupe. French audiences loved Molière's new comedy plays, which lampooned types well known to the audience like *Le Tartuffe* (about a religious hypocrite), *Le Misanthrope* (an antisocial man), *L'Avare* (the miser), *Le Bourgeois gentilhomme* (the newly rich), and *Le Malade imaginaire* (a hypochondriac). For Molière, the stage of the theater was a miniature of the larger stage which is society. His genius was that he was able to so sharply delineate his characters—

characters who were not recognizable as individuals but as recognizable types—often in very few words.

There is much wanting in the way of details from Molière's life. He lived in a time so distant from ours that much has been lost or perhaps was never set down. For certain it was a time when feelings were perhaps best spoken by actors on the stage, leaving the playwright free not to speak. Fortunately, Molière has spoken clearly on what he knows best, the enthralling characters and comedy he brought to life on the stage. "If the purpose of comedy," he wrote in the preface to *Tartuffe*,

> is to correct men's vices, I do not see why any group of men should have special privileges. . . . To expose vices to everyone's laughter is to deal them a mighty blow. People easily endure reproofs, but they cannot at all endure being made fun of. People have no objection to being considered wicked, but they are not willing to be considered ridiculous.

William Shakespeare

1564–1616 English player, poet, and playwright

It is almost impossible to imagine the theater without Shakespeare. Every major dramatist has acknowledged learning more from him than from any other about the craft of writing plays. There has probably never been an actor—including those in film and television today—who has not dreamed of performing the role of Hamlet, Lady Macbeth, Othello, Desdemona, Ophelia, Lear, Richard III, or Juliet. The importance of the man lies not only in his art and the poetry and drama of his stories, but in the ageless truth of his themes and characters, which still, four centuries later, draws us to his plays.

Born on April 26, 1564, he was the oldest son of John Shakespeare and Mary Arden. William had an older sister, Margaret (1562), a younger brother, Gilbert (1566), a younger sister, Joan (1569), and another brother, Edmond (1580), who, like his older brother, became a player. There were three other children who died very young. The family lived in Stratford-upon-Avon, a beautiful country town of neat, half-timbered houses, each with a garden. The streets were lined with shops and churches and shaded by thousands of elms amidst pastures dotted with orchards. The town remains today much as it has always been, and it was here that young Will grew up. In those days, Stratford-upon-Avon was a prosperous market town with a population of about two thousand. Among the Shakespeares' neighbors were tailors, a brewer, an apothecary, maltsters, bakers, tanners, glovers, masons and carpenters, weavers, a draper, and several smiths. Later, in his plays, Shakespeare recalled many of these tradesmen as characters:

> I saw a smith stand with his hammer
>   thus,
> The whilst his iron did on the anvil
>   cool,
> With open mouth swallowing a tailor's
>   news;
> Who, with his shears and measure in
>   his hand,
> Standing on slippers, which his nimble
>   haste
> Had falsely thrust upon contrary
>   feet. . . .
>
> —*King John*

John Shakespeare was a wool dealer and a glover. Unlike the tanner, who worked with the hides of cattle and swine, John dressed the skins of deer, goats, and sheep. He was also a man of means. He had inherited money and property from his father, Richard, and an uncle, and at his marriage he had been given some farms by his father-in-law. John bought several houses in Stratford-upon-Avon, including the one on Henley Street where Will was born, which stands to this day. John was a man of importance in the community, serving as constable, inspector of bread and malt, assessor, alderman, treasurer, bailiff—a kind of justice of the peace—and eventually, mayor. Since these were elected offices, we can guess that John Shakespeare was a much-respected and upstanding member of the community. He was also, apparently, a good-natured man enjoying a close relationship with his sons, especially his oldest. Later, "as a merry-cheeked old man," John recalled: "Will was a good honest fellow," with whom he often joked.

It is important to understand the circumstances of Will's family because much has been made of the poet's "humble" beginnings. True, his father was a craftsman, but that meant a lot in sixteenth-century England. It's not known if Will's mother and grandfather could write; Richard Arden "made his mark" rather than signing his name, but that was a common practice even among men who could read and write. If Mary Arden Shakespeare could write, she would have been unusual because girls in those days were not sent to school as boys were, and most women could not write. Nevertheless, Mary's father was a wealthy landowner who provided a cultured home for his family; Will later recalled the eleven paintings hanging in the various rooms in his mother's home. John Shakespeare, judging from the high offices he held in Stratford and from his title, "Master," must have had some education. He certainly had money and, as one aspiring to the rank of gentleman, would have sent his sons to school.

> O, it is a verse in Horace; I know it well:
> I read it in grammar school long ago.
> —*Titus Andronicus*

As a youngster, Will attended elementary school, where he would learn his numbers and to read and write. At about age seven he would have been eligible to enter the King's New School of Stratford-upon-Avon. All education at that time was in private schools, and schools remained open through the summers when longer days meant more daylight hours for reading. Shakespeare left his bed just after sunrise

> The whining schoolboy with his satchel
> And shining morning face, creeping
>   like a snail
> Unwillingly to school.
> —*As You Like It*

He was to be in his place at his desk as the chapel bell rang (six o'clock in the summer, seven in the winter) where, with but a break or two, he worked at his lessons for eight or nine hours—six days a week, almost every week of the year.

The school day began and ended with readings from the Bible and prayers. Pupils learned the grace to be said before and after meals and to sing the psalms

in meter. Will was steeped in proper Elizabethan grammar and Latin, and piled on his desk would be an *ABC Book*,

> to sigh like a schoolboy that had lost
>   his ABC
> —*The Two Gentlemen of Verona*

a catechism in English and Latin, a Latin grammar, and easy translations of Seneca, Cicero, Virgil, and Ovid (young Will's favorite)—writers familiar to students studying Latin today. The difference is that the boys in young Shakespeare's class were expected to converse in Latin. The teacher would put questions to the pupil and the pupil would answer. Elizabethan education relied on rote learning, requiring of every schoolboy what students today would consider astounding feats of memory. Shakespeare had an amazing memory even as a student, a memory that allowed him to include later in his plays facts from history, entire orations, and passages from the Bible.

When he wasn't in school, Will helped his father and found time for sports. He must have loved bowling (lawn bowling), for references to the game show up often in his work:

> Sometimes,
> Like to a bowl upon a subtle ground
> I have tumbled past the throw.
> —*Coriolanus*

There are many references to falconry and hawking that show young Shakespeare's familiarity with the sport:

> We'll go a-birding together: I have a fine
> hawk for the bush.
> —*The Merry Wives of Windsor*

> Dost thou love hawking? thou hast
> hawks will soar
> Above the morning lark.
> —*The Taming of the Shrew*

Shakespeare lived in the time now called the Renaissance, a time when there was much interest in learning and educating the young, especially about classical Greece and Rome. William Shakespeare was not an untutored genius but an educated, cultured man. He did not create his plays from just what he saw on the streets of Stratford-upon-Avon and London— though there was plenty of that. His ideas, his plots, and the subjects of his plays, his language, the attitudes of his characters, everything he created is consistent with those of a man born and educated in the Renaissance.

Will, with his Latin learning, his way with words, intellectual talents, and wealthy parents, would have gone on to the university. But his education was cut short, ended when he was fourteen, the year his father fell into debt, lost his farms, and could no longer afford to send his sons to school.

The years that followed are familiar to many young people, years of thwarted ambitions, uncertainty, the lack of any sense of direction—what one biographer has called "the lost years." He lived at home and helped his father as best he could. Records show that he was punished by the local magistrate—"who had him oft whipped and sometimes imprisoned"—for poaching deer and rabbits on private lands. "He had, by a misfortune common enough to young fellows," as Shakespeare's earliest biographer suggested, "fallen into ill company."

At nineteen Shakespeare married Anne Hathaway and moved into the now impoverished family home where their first child, Susanna, was born. Two years later the couple had twins, Judith and Hamnet (an alternate spelling of Hamlet), named for friends, the local baker and his wife.

Bright students unable to attend the university furthered their education in other ways, one being teaching in grammar school. During the "dark years" Shakespeare apparently served as schoolmaster in the country. He shows a fondness for the schoolmaster in several of his plays, especially in *Love's Labours Lost* and *The Comedy of Errors*, where he appears in comic roles. The fruitful years that follow this dismal time in his life suggest that Shakespeare was reading and beginning to store up ideas for poems and plays, and being a schoolmaster would provide an ideal opportunity to do this. But this is a cloudy part of Shakespeare's life and little more is known.

These were horrible times in England, among the worst in all history. Bubonic plague was epidemic, killing a thousand people a week in London. The populations of Stratford-upon-Avon and many other towns were decimated. Meanwhile, scores of comedians and actors—vagabonds, as they were sometimes referred to—and no fewer than five royal companies of players fled London in 1587 for the countryside, performing as they went in towns and villages, including Stratford (bringing the plague with them and spreading it all over England!).

Theater flourished. For the first time, many small towns and villages that had never been visited by troupes of players were now enjoying mummers performing masked fantasies, religious pageants, and disguisings. The profession of actor was also taking shape, though it would not be until years later—due in large part to Shakespeare—that it would become an established career.

In these days, troupes were formed and supported by noblemen, the first patrons of the theater. And they were usually named for their patrons. So the records show that there came to Stratford in Shakespeare's youth the Earl of Worcester's Men (six times between 1569 and 1587), the Earl of Warwick's Men, and other troupes—Lord Berkeley's, Lord Derby's, the Countess of Essex's, and so on. Two or three troupes visited each year, and in 1587, five. Among them were the Queen's Players, the preeminent troupe in all the land. By the end of their stay in Stratford-upon-Avon they were short one actor. It seems he had drawn his sword and assaulted another player, this time in earnest, not in play, and was himself killed, stabbed through the neck. Before leaving they asked one William Shakespeare, age twenty-three, to join them.

Whether it was because of his "misfortune" in the forest and the punishments, his hasty marriage, the house full of children, his father's financial decline, or the crowded, depressing family home on Henley Street is not clear, but one thing is certain: Shakespeare had much reason to escape to London. And it turned out to be the perfect time. As the plague subsided, people returned to the theaters. New companies and permanent theaters sprang up, actors and stagehands were in demand, and writers responded with new plays.

An engraving of Shakespeare by E. Scriven, published in 1825. HULTON DEUTSCH COLLECTION LIMITED.

Audiences were excited by the language of the new theater, for the English language itself was expanding. As if long asleep, English suddenly began to flower, to take on new subtleties and nuances, due mainly to the new writing for the stage. "It is a world to see," a dramatist wrote then, "how Englishmen desire to hear finer speech than the language will allow." Playwrights experimented with new possibilities for poetry and dialogue, creating whole new kinds of performances. Among them were two that became immediate favorites of London audiences, Christopher Marlowe's *Tamburlaine* and Thomas Kyd's *The Spanish Tragedy*. The popularity of the new plays catapulted actors into stardom, capturing the hearts of young men and drawing them into the world of the theater.

Arriving as he did on this scene, the young Shakespeare easily found work in the theater. He probably started as a prompter's assistant or callboy, the one responsible for seeing to it that actors arrived in the wings on time to enter onto the stage at their cue. As was customary, Shakespeare was probably given some small roles. And he had the opportunity to read all the new and exciting plays being written, to analyze them, take them apart, and see how they worked. He was a Johannes Factotum, jack-of-all-trades about the theater: stagehand, actor, playwright, poet. But unlike the Jack of the old saying, he became master of them all. It's unclear just what happened during these years of apprenticeship, but there soon appear references to him as an actor of quality and excellence. One John Aubrey described the young actor as "a handsome, well-shaped man, very good company, and of very ready and pleasant smooth wit." Shakespeare's early portraits show him to have been an impressive figure with large, luminous eyes and high forehead, well suited for the stage, especially "kingly" parts.

Among the world's greatest dramatists, only two—Shakespeare and Molière—were also talented actors. This fact, to many, accounts for the success of Shakespeare as a playwright and for the great appeal of his roles. Again, among the lines of his plays, we find evidence of new acting techniques, clues from Shakespeare the director. He scolds the "dull actor" who forgets his part and has to leave the stage in disgrace, and the one who thinks acting is merely stomping about the stage, the

> strutting player, whose conceit
> Lies in his hamstring, and doth think it rich
> To hear the wooden dialogue and sound
> Twixt his stretched footing and the scaffoldage.
> —*Troilus and Cressida*

An artist's view of the staging of Shakespeare's plays during Shakespeare's own time. PHOTOSEARCH, INC.

He comments on the actor who tries to cover up his stage fright with bravado:

> an unperfect actor on the stage
> Who with his fear is put beside his
> part,
> Or some fierce thing replete with too
> much rage
> Whose strength's abundance weakens
> his own heart.
>
> —*Sonnet 23*

There are also specific instructions revealing to us the kind of acting Shakespeare admired—clear, truthful acting with natural gestures:

Speak the speech, I pray you, as I pronounced it to you—trippingly on the tongue. But if you mouth it, as many of your players do, I had as lief [willingly let] the town crier spake my lines. . . .

Nor do not saw the air too much with your hand—thus. But use all gently, for in the very torrent, tempest and, as I may say, whirlwind of your passion, you must acquire and beget a temperance, that may give it smoothness.

—*Hamlet*

And he encouraged actors, above all, to observe human nature, especially the personality and character of the person whose role is being played:

> The fellow is wise enough to play the
> Fool,
> And to do that well craves a kind of
> wit.
> He must observe their mood on whom
> he jests,
> The quality of persons, and the time,
> And, like the haggard [hawk], check at
> every feather
> That comes before his eye. This is a
> practice
> As full of labour as a wise man's art.
>
> —*Twelfth Night*

Throughout his years of acting, Shakespeare read avidly, more than making up for the university years he missed. Among the many books he devoured was one that, more than any other, shaped his love of history—Raphael Holinshed's *Chronicles of England, Scotland, and Ireland*—and another his poetry—Edmund Spenser's *Faerie Queen*. But he was doing more than acting, as fine as it was. By 1594, when our actor/poet appears again in the light of history, he is with the Lord Chamberlain's Company and, at thirty, has already written eleven plays—among them, comedies: *Love's Labours Lost*, *The Comedy of Errors*, *The Two Gentlemen of Verona*, *The Taming of the Shrew*, and *A Midsummer Night's Dream*; histories: *Henry VI* and *Richard III*; and tragedies: *Titus Andronicus* and *Romeo and Juliet*.

So it was that the young William Shakespeare quite suddenly appeared as poet, actor, and playwright to the excitement of all England. As much as his plays are performed and talked about today—and they are much performed—Shakespeare is not readily accessible to modern audiences. His purpose as a writer was very simple: to tell a good story on the stage, one that would entertain but also enlighten. But it's not that easy for us today. The stories he told, the characters, and the plots were all familiar to Elizabethan audiences. Even uneducated people could enjoy them and identify with the characters. The language of the stage was their

Mr. WILLIAM
SHAKESPEARES
COMEDIES,
HISTORIES, &
TRAGEDIES.

Published according to the True Originall Copies.

LONDON
Printed by Isaac Iaggard, and Ed. Blount. 1623.

The title page of an early edition of Shakespeare's plays. MARY EVANS PICTURE LIBRARY.

language, English of the 1600s, written in blank verse, poetic, but easily understandable.

We cannot just show up at a performance today and expect to understand Shakespeare as his contemporaries understood him. We need to know something of the customs and traditions of those distant years in order to understand much of the humor, satire, and wordplay. We need to listen carefully to the beautiful poetry. We need to learn about the history and the social and political issues of the day—the context of Shakespeare's England. And we have to get accustomed to the artistic conventions peculiar to the Elizabethan stage. All that takes some doing and it's well worth the effort. "The great significance of Shakespeare," one scholar has written, "is that in spite of the many differences between his age and ours, some perhaps trivial and some of far-reaching importance, he gives us in his plays life patterns that are continuous in the history of the human race."

PART II

Actors of the Eighteenth and Nineteenth Centuries

Sarah Bernhardt

1844–1923 French actress

On a misty morning late in September of 1858, a girl leaned out of her window and breathed in the air of Paris. She had just awakened from a beautiful dream and had rushed to the window without really knowing why, only that she was filled with a sense of excitement and anxious expectancy. Something important would happen today! Almost fifteen years old, Sarah Bernhardt had grown used to her strong emotions and sensitive nature. Had she not been a constant terror in the convent she had recently left? There, the other girls and the nuns who taught them were in awe of her wild temper tantrums, amused and exasperated by her crazy antics, and mystified by her excessive religious devotion. Many of the nuns at Grandchamps Convent were not sure that young Sarah was meant for the religious life, although she had persistently declared her intention of becoming a nun.

Certainly the idea of her daughter entering a convent had never occurred to Sarah's mother, Julie Bernhardt. Julie, or Youle, as she was called, was a lovely young Jewish woman who had moved to Paris from her native Holland. Unmarried, with three daughters from as many fathers, Youle, along with her sister Rosine, belonged to a world of elegant and beautiful women-for-hire who were kept in luxury by the wealthy and influential men of the day. Youle and Aunt Rosine had assumed that Sarah, when she was old enough, would follow in their footsteps and find herself a rich husband or "protector" to support her. But Sarah herself had no such plans.

As a baby Sarah had been virtually abandoned by her mother. Youle had found her child burdensome and had sent Sarah as an infant to the countryside. Her first four years were spent in Brittany, where she was cared for by a nurse. In her memoirs, Sarah admits that her mother, whom she adored, was a self-centered, unloving, and insensitive woman who sadly neglected her first-born daughter. She would send money, clothes, and cakes to Sarah and her nurse, but never came to visit. Her exciting life of travel and luxury came first.

One day in her fourth year, little Sarah fell into the fireplace and was badly burned. Her relatives were sent for at once. Sarah's mother arrived from Brussels, along with several doctor friends. Her aunts descended from all parts of the world. She remembers with love and bitterness her mother's sudden concern:

> She distributed money on all sides. She would have given her golden hair, her slender white fingers, her tiny feet, her life itself, in order to save her child. And she was as sincere in her despair and her love as [she had been before] in her unconscious forgetfulness.

Within a few weeks little Sarah was out of danger. After many kisses and false promises, her mother once more departed from her life.

Within a year, the nurse's elderly husband died. She soon remarried and relocated with Sarah to Neuilly, a suburb of Paris. At first Sarah was excited about the change; a long carriage ride was an adventure for her. But once in the city, she missed the open countryside, the flowers and woods and streams of Brittany. Worst of all, neither her mother nor her aunts ever came to see her. The truth was that Sarah's nurse had lost touch with Youle; no money had been sent for the child's upkeep for some time, and no one knew exactly where in Europe Youle was living.

And then one day an incredible coincidence occurred. Sarah was playing in the muddy street with a neighbor's child when she heard a familiar voice. She looked up and saw an unusually elegant woman visiting the house next door. It was Aunt Rosine! Sarah screamed with joy and dashed into her aunt's arms. She was sure that Rosine was going to take her away with her; surely she would be reunited with her mother! Rosine, shocked at finding her niece in the Paris area, had a hurried discussion with the nurse, paid her, and tried to slip away before Sarah could notice. But Sarah, having quickly packed her few possessions into her little suitcase, looked out of her window just in time to see her aunt about to step into her carriage and drive away. No! This could not be! Sarah was determined not to be left behind again. And without thinking about her actions, she stepped out onto the window ledge and threw herself off, falling more than ten feet to the pavement below.

Miraculously, she suffered only a broken arm and a shattered kneecap; for the rest of her life her knee would give her trouble. But the fall brought about the desired results; Sarah was taken to stay with Youle. The next year, bedridden and sickly, she would spend under her mother's roof.

By the time she had recovered from her fall, Sarah was old enough to attend school. She loved her mother dearly and could not understand why her mother was constantly irritated with her. It was true that she was not a docile, sweet, pretty child like her sister Jeanne, who was her mother's favorite. Sarah was high-strung and temperamental, with wild, unruly hair and eyes that were usually flashing with rage or swollen with tears. Her mother's friends and guests called her ugly in her hearing, and expressed their sympathy to Youle that she should be burdened with a child so troublesome.

Then, before she knew quite what was happening, Sarah was packed off once again, this time to attend boarding school. She stayed at the boarding school, Madame Fressard's, for two years, where she learned "reading, writing and reckoning."

Then one day Aunt Rosine came to the school with the surprising news that Sarah's father had contacted the family. Sarah had seen her father just twice before and only knew that he was tall and handsome. Like her mother, he was irresponsible, fond of luxury, and loved travel. He did provide well for Sarah and her mother, and had settled a dowry on Sarah of a hundred thousand francs, which she was to receive when she married. Now a sudden attack of guilt had seized him, and for once, he was looking into his daughter's welfare. He had decided that Mme. Fressard's school was not good enough; Sarah had learned little there, had been taught no social graces, and had received no religious instruction. He wanted her sent at once to the Catholic Convent of Grandchamps at Versailles, which had a high reputation for scholarship.

At Grandchamps Sarah met the person who was to help her heal her many emotional wounds. "I . . . saw the sweetest and merriest face imaginable, with large child-like blue eyes, a turn-up nose, a laughing mouth with full lips and beautiful, strong, white teeth. She looked so kind, so energetic, and so happy that I flung myself at once into her arms." It was Mother Saint Sophie, the Superior of the Grandchamps

Convent. From that moment Sarah loved her, and her fears of being in a "prison" dissolved.

The convent no longer seemed like a prison, but like paradise. Sarah remained at the convent for eight years. She was treated with kindness and encouragement, and her love and admiration for Mother Saint Sophie grew. She threw herself into her studies with enormous energy, and she often excelled—mostly due to her intense desire to please. She was a natural leader with many friends, and often her fellow schoolmates would do her work for her. A fearless girl who loved nature, Sarah played with animals whenever she could. She kept lizards and snakes in her pockets and boxes of crickets, beetles, and spiders hidden in her room. How the other girls would shudder when she would trap flies and feed them to her spiders!

When she was ten, Sarah heroically threw herself into a deep, muddy pool and saved the life of a younger girl who was drowning there. Later Sarah overheard Mother Saint Sophie telling the doctor that Sarah was one of the best girls at the convent and would be perfect once she had been baptized. This praise made a deep impression on Sarah. From that day forward she began to feel a deep religious devotion. She would do more than just be a good student and impress the sisters. She would pattern her life after her adored Mother Superior. She would become a nun.

It was at the convent that Sarah made her theatrical debut. An important occasion—a visit by the Archbishop of Paris—had turned the peaceful school into a hive of excitement. A special program was planned, including a short play, *Tobias Recovering His Eyesight*, based on an Old Testament story. Sarah was sure she would be cast in the production, and listened nervously as the parts were assigned. To her amazement, she received no role. Her best friend, Louise Buguet, was to play the angel Raphael. Sarah looked over the script longingly, and like a hungry dog, she went to each of the chosen players, examining their lines. She attended every rehearsal and learned every line from every part. It soon became evident that her friend Louise was having trouble with her role. Angelic she may have looked, but she was shy and terrified at rehearsals. At the dress rehearsal Louise threw herself down, sobbing, and declared that she could not perform. It was Sarah's chance at last. The rehearsal went on, with Sarah performing her role perfectly, and it was agreed that she should play Raphael for the Archbishop.

The play was a triumph. Sarah outdid herself as Raphael. The cast was assembled before the Archbishop, who gave each of them a medal and complimented them all.

Sarah was now over thirteen, and her mother wanted her to leave the convent. Although Sarah begged to be allowed to become a nun, it was decided that she would live with her mother, studying with a governess for two years. If at the end of that period she still hoped to become a nun—well, they would see.

And so, on a foggy September morning two years later, Sarah stood at her window, shivering not with cold, but with apprehension. Today, there would be a family meeting, and her fate would be decided. She knew that her mother, as well as her aunts, were aghast at the idea of her entering a convent. They wanted her to marry—even if it was to a much older man. At least one of her mother's male friends had expressed interest in the girl, young as she was. Sarah loathed the very idea of marrying without love. And if she did not marry, or become a nun, then what? Become a courtesan, like her mother or Aunt Rosine? Never!

The special luncheon for friends and family had ended. Sarah sat in her chair in the drawing room, the others circling her. She felt like an object, not a person. The talk swirled around her. "It's a shame she doesn't resemble you more, Youle. Then she might receive more offers of marriage." "No, no, we shall

have to think of something else." "But why not let the girl enter the convent?" "Utterly unsuitable! She is not the type." Suddenly her mother's friend, the Duc de Morny, burst into laughter. "Look at Sarah! She's trying to show us what a good nun she would make!" It was true. Sarah was trying desperately to convince everyone of her religious calling. She sat meekly, her hands folded in an attitude of prayer, her face and shoulders a study in piety. A sudden idea struck the duke. "Why not send her to the Conservatoire?"

The room erupted with talk. "She's much too thin to be an actress." "Impossible! There are hundreds of young people who strive each year to enter, and they only accept thirty-five!" "It's just possible . . . " "No, monsieur, you cannot be serious." Meanwhile, Sarah sat in a whirlwind of confusion. An actress? The Conservatoire? What was that? She did not know anything about this famous academy where young women and men were trained for the French stage. The truth was that Sarah didn't really want to be a nun. She just wanted to live somewhere where she felt loved and happy. The Conservatoire was a mystery to her, but it was exciting to think that something other than marriage was being considered for her.

That evening, Sarah was taken to see a play at the Comédie Française. When the curtain slowly rose and Sarah caught her first glimpse of real theater, she felt as if she would faint. In her memoirs, she vividly recalls, "It was as though the curtain of my future life were being raised. These columns were to be my palaces, the borders above were to be my skies, and these boards were to bend under my frail weight." She spent the evening in tears. The last piece performed that evening, *Amphytrion*, featured a tragic heroine who moved Sarah to loud sobs, which amused the entire audience and humiliated her mother and godfather. They left the theater early. Worn and exhausted by her emotions, Sarah was put to bed. Her godfather fumed. "She ought to be shut up in the convent and left there. Good heavens, what a little idiot the child is!" Her mother's friend, the famous writer Alexandre Dumas, was more gentle. He gave Sarah a kiss and whispered, "Good night, little star."

From that day forward, Sarah poured all the wild, untamed energy of her being into preparing for an audition at the Conservatoire. Everyone in the family helped. Books of plays were sent to her by all of her relatives, but she found most of them too serious and boring. She would look them over and go back to her favorite book, the fables of la Fontaine. These she knew by heart, and even played a game of reciting them backward, from the ending to the beginning.

A piece from a classic play was selected for Sarah to recite at her audition. She learned her part well, but still didn't enjoy saying it as she did her beloved fables. Finally the dreaded examination day arrived. At the auditions, she saw more than a dozen young people her age, all in various stages of tension and nervous excitement. They all sat in a little waiting room, eyeing each other, and watching closely as each was called in turn to go in to the audition. When Sarah was called, she was asked about her role. And then came the question, "And who will be giving you your cues?"

Cues? Suddenly she realized that her speech would sound ridiculous without the other character's lines coming at their proper time. She should have found someone to act with her, feeding her the cue lines. Now what could she do? Swiftly, Sarah made up her mind. She would turn to the recitations she knew and loved the best. "I will recite a fable," she replied. The man addressing her burst out laughing and wrote down her name and the title "The Two Pigeons," which she had given him.

Sarah went alone into the audition hall. She had never been alone for an hour in her life. Now she was in a strange-looking room, with a group of several men and one woman staring at her as she mounted the platform at one end. As she began her childish tale, the judges criticized her choice, one rudely saying that at least it wouldn't be as long as a whole scene, making the others laugh. Many growled for her to speak up, others spoke more kindly. No one was being very polite to her.

All of the interruptions, laughter, and criticism brought to life Sarah's fire and determination. She would show these people! She began her tale again, her voice resonant and full of emotion. When she finished her speech, Sarah stepped off the stage, thoroughly exhausted. The hall was silent. One or two of the judges were furtively drying their eyes; the rest were visibly moved.

"Well, little girl," said the director of the Conservatoire, who was, of course, one of the judges, "that was very good indeed. Both of the instructors want you in their classes." Wild with joy, Sarah exclaimed, "Then I have passed?"

"Yes, you have passed, and there is only one thing I regret, and that is that such a pretty voice should not be for music."

Sarah stayed at the Conservatoire for two years, studying every aspect of acting: diction, elocution, how to walk, how to sit, how to fall. She even took up fencing. After an uncertain beginning, Sarah poured all her fiery energy into her studies. And at the end of those two years, she became a *pensionnaire*, a probationary actress, at the Théâtre Française, as the Comédie was often called. After a short, unhappy internship there, she left to join a small, independent theater called the Odéon. It was there that she began to acquire a loyal following of young students who adored her acting.

The Odéon produced a new play just for her entitled *Le Passant*. Sarah was very successful in her performance as Zanetto, a young strolling minstrel. (She was to play many male roles, including Hamlet.) This was followed by several other plays, some good, some mediocre. She was consistently good, no matter what her role was.

Then came a turn in Sarah's destiny that was to lead her even closer to stardom. In 1871, the managers of the Odéon told Sarah that they were about to revive the play *Ruy Blas*, by Victor Hugo, who had long been exiled by the French court for his antigovernment ideas. To the people of France, he was a hero and poet like none other. Now he was back from exile, and the public longed to see his works performed once more. Sarah was given the leading role of Doña Maria, a Spanish queen. From the first, she was a triumph. The directors of the Comédie Française begged her to return to them. They could offer her three times the salary she was receiving at the Odéon.

Sarah Bernhardt as Hamlet in 1899. THEATRE MUSEUM/VICTORIA AND ALBERT MUSEUM/
LONDON.

When she told this to her manager, and suggested that the pittance she was receiving should be increased—after all, was she not doing wonders for the box office?—the Odéon's reply was that she was making up a story. The Comédie would never ask her to return. Furious, she resigned, and returned to the Théâtre Française.

By now Sarah had acquired a huge following of loyal fans. Many were calling her the finest actress at the Comédie, or in all of France. That argument was put to rest when Sarah took to the stage in the title role of Racine's tragedy *Phèdre*. As the audience watched spellbound, they realized that they were seeing dramatic history in the making. No one could doubt her greatness. That night, as the curtain fell in the House of Molière, the cast stood and waited for the applause. There was an unearthly silence. And then a roar shook the rafters of the theater as the audience, yelling, weeping, stamping, rose to its feet, shouting, "Sarah! Sarah! Sarah!"

She had been applauded before. She had received many bouquets, many notes and letters. In her Odéon days, she had had the horses of her carriage unhitched, and the young students had themselves pulled her through the streets. But this triumph was like no other. Ten curtain calls, twenty curtain calls. Over and over she was called

Sarah Bernhardt as Lady Macbeth in 1884.
PHOTOGRAPH BY NADAR. THE BETTMANN ARCHIVE.

back to the stage, while the audience screamed her name.

From that moment on, Sarah's life was changed forever. One success followed another, and with her fame grew the many legends and stories about her—stories that were sometimes false, sometimes exaggerations, and sometimes true. She was an extraordinary actress, partly because she was an extraordinary person. Her motto, "Quand même" (in spite of everything, nevertheless), was

Sarah Bernhardt with her granddaughter.
HULTON DEUTSCH COLLECTION LIMITED.

inspired by the deadly stage fright that would plague her always, even at the height of her fame. Sarah became a theater legend such as the world had never known. She traveled the globe, and everywhere she went, thousands of people lined the streets outside of the hotels she stayed in just to get a glimpse of her. Her performances were invariably sellouts.

Throughout her long and adventurous life, it was Sarah's incredible vitality, energy, and sheer love for her craft that kept her at the top of her profession. Even when she was older, ill, and had been forced to have her leg amputated, she continued to act. When Sarah died on March 26, 1923, she was in the midst of rehearsals for a play and a silent film. Seldom had the city of Paris seen a funeral like hers. Businesses and stores were closed, schoolchildren were dismissed from school, housewives left their chores. Representatives from many nations and their governments were in attendance. The rich and the poor, the world-renowned and the unknown—all turned out to bid The Great Sarah farewell. Perhaps one million people in all followed her coffin to Père-Lachaise Cemetery. But the French critic Francisque Sarcey said of Sarah, simply, "She is unique and no one will ever take her place."

Edwin Booth

1833–1893 The first great American tragedian

"Edwin Booth made two recordings in 1890, but for some time I was half afraid to hear them—afraid that Booth's voice and style might not measure up to the enthusiastic descriptions I had at second hand." So Eleanor Ruggles begins her biography of Edwin Booth. Like many people interested in the theater, she wondered whether the "greatness" ascribed to actors in the past would stand up to modern standards.

She knew that many reputations are safe because voices in the distant past could not be recorded. What did Edmund Kean or David Garrick or Sarah Siddons really sound like? We'll never know. Tastes in acting, like tastes in anything else, change from year to year, and if actors of a century ago could return to the stage today, the results would no doubt be embarrassing and confusing to both the poor actor, returned out of his time, and the audience. But Edwin Booth had been recorded on one of the first cylinders, and how would he sound a hundred years later?

"I had expected rant," wrote Ms. Ruggles,

but these were quiet tones. The diction was exquisite, the delivery formal and grand but stirring and unstilted. . . . The voice itself, though, was the most beautiful speaking voice I had ever heard, with great poetry and feeling, yet with no straining for effect, and I suddenly understood the ecstatic, nostalgic praises of the men and women, my own grandparents, for example, who had heard Booth in life.

Edwin Booth was born in a log cabin deep in the woods north of Baltimore, Maryland, on November 13, 1833. It is reported that a spectacular shower of meteors lit the sky like fireworks that night. The theater was his birthright, for Farmer Booth, as the neighbors referred to Edwin's father, was actually Junius Brutus Booth, one of the last century's most imposing and polished actors. He had bought the cabin in the country for its solitude, a quiet place away from the hubbub and stress of a busy acting schedule that took him from New York and Boston to Charleston; west to Pittsburgh, Nashville, and Louisville; by coach, sometimes on foot and on horseback, south to Natchez, Mississippi, and New Orleans and, eventually, out to California. Once, when he missed his coach, Booth walked twenty-five miles under the flaming July sun from Richmond to Petersburg, Virginia, here he was to perform. He was known for his interpretations of Shakespeare, especially Richard III, King Lear, and Iago in *Othello*.

Junius Brutus Booth was born in London in 1796, and was regarded as something of a genius. He was a talented painter and knew the printer's art. He served for a time in the British navy, wrote stories and poetry, and became a sculptor. All this before the age of seventeen, when he first appeared on the stage. Like the Kembles and Edmund Kean and many of the great actors before him, Booth joined a troupe of strolling players, playing a clown one night and a king the next. His audience taught him how to act. "Speak louder!" they screamed at him. "Don't fall asleep!" they roared with laughter. And finally, when they had lost patience with him, they called out in a chorus, "Get off the stage! Get off the stage!" The fruits and vegetables with which the audience pelted him went into the pot that night for his only meal. Booth accompanied his troupe when they crossed the English Channel to Holland and Belgium.

Two years later he made his first appearance in London as Sylvius in Shakespeare's *As You Like It*. In 1817, now twenty-one years old, Junius Brutus played Richard III at Covent Garden, a coveted role in one of London's oldest theaters, dreamed of but beyond the hopes of all but the most talented actors. So highly regarded was the young actor that the reigning giant of the English stage, Edmund Kean, invited him to be a guest actor at his own theater in Drury Lane. Kean considered the role of Richard III his own, and when the upstart actor debuted at the competing theater in the same role, Kean took it as a challenge, requiring a "stage duel." It was a battle of giants and the theater was filled to the roof. Kean played Othello to Booth's Iago, and the crowd got every penny's worth. By all accounts Kean showed up young Booth stunningly, but also revealed his true motives. Rather than welcoming the guest player as he pretended, Kean in his ruthless way attempted to destroy Booth's reputation and drive him off as a competitor. Though Kean would remain without equal for several more years, it was clear that if he was still king of the stage then young Booth was the most likely heir apparent.

Booth passed often through the Bow Street market on his way to Covent Garden and one day noticed a young woman at her flower stall. Mary Ann Holmes was devoted to the theater and had seen Booth perform Lear, but now, meeting him offstage, she could not believe her eyes: "Are you really that poor little old man?" she asked him. To his delight he discovered that she could also read and so gave her as a gift a tiny set of Lord Byron's poems beautifully bound in leather. Booth was smitten and, booking passage on a sailing ship, took her with him to America. He played Richard III brilliantly in Richmond, Virginia, his first engagement in the New World, and instantly became a favorite.

In some ways Junius Brutus was not suited to theater life. Once he wrote his father: "I'm sick of acting—much rather would I be home." He was a country person at heart and longed for quiet solitude far, far away from demanding audiences and prodding managers. So he bought his place in the country and here he would return to dig barefoot in his garden and enjoy his family.

He and Mary Ann had ten children. He was devoted to her as she was to him, and he could barely endure their times apart. "The Time seems long while away from you," he wrote while off on tour. "Let me hear from you by return and believe me ever and affectionately to be Your husband and worshipper, Junius."

There was another reason he preferred the farm. More and more now, on the road, he was missing theater engagements and performing badly because of his drinking. Once he was jailed for disorderly conduct; another time he broke up the furniture in a tavern and several times started drunken brawls. Junius became known as "crazy Booth the mad tragedian." But he didn't feel the need to drink at home.

The house Edwin and his brothers and sisters grew up in was not rustic. In Farmer Booth's living room was a magnificent library of books exquisitely calfskin bound, many in foreign languages. On the shelves along with the works of the poets, writers, and philosophers of classical Greece and Rome and Enlightenment England and Europe, were the holy books of many peoples—the Koran, the Bible, and the Talmud. Junius Brutus visited synagogues on his travels and discussed Jewish law and thought with the rabbis—in Hebrew. He meditated in Catholic cathedrals. He read Pythagoras and became convinced, as he was, that men's souls are born again in animals. He loved animals—he nursed back to health a poisonous copperhead he had accidentally injured with his plow—and forbade hunting and the eating of meat.

The year Edwin was born his father was thirty-seven and had been an actor seventeen of those years. He was the seventh child, named by his father for Edwin Forrest, the American tragedian. He is remembered as a quiet, melancholy boy who didn't shine like some of his brothers and sisters. There was already something of his father's fiery power in his quick, graceful movements, an occasional gesture and intense eyes, which grew enormous when he laughed. Edwin wasn't, right off, his father's favorite. That was Henry, who died at eleven of smallpox when the family was visiting England. He was buried there, and on his stone his father had carved the words of a poem he loved:

Oh, even in spite of death, yet still my
    choice,
Oft with the inward, all-beholding eye
I think I see thee, and hear thy voice.

After Henry his father loved John Wilkes best. He was sensitive like all the Booth children and shared the family's love of animals. Johnny was the brave, romantic hero of the family, storming through the woods on his horse or sitting quietly in the evening listening to the sad songs and Jew's harp tunes and the ghosts of the Negroes. Edwin's younger sister, Asia, played the guitar, and together the children often sat in the branches of their favorite tree on hot summer days and loudly recited Shakespeare. Booth didn't want any of his children on the stage. He encouraged them to work with their hands and become craftsmen. He urged young Junius to become a surgeon and Edwin to become a cabinetmaker.

Edwin was the only one of the Booth children who didn't get any consistent schooling. He learned his three R's in a class in Baltimore and was supposedly being tutored by a retired French naval officer, but they spent most of their time fencing. (Edwin had already learned the rudiments of swordsmanship from his brother Junius.) Edwin also began playing the violin with an Italian teacher and from a black farmhand he learned to sing the traditional songs of the slaves and to strum the banjo.

That was Edwin's life until he was thirteen. His father's drinking had gotten bad again, and he had broken his nose in a drunken free-for-all. Once, when he arrived from a tavern late for his performance and heard the audience yelling and stomping its feet impatiently, he burst from between the curtains and out to the footlights, waved his fist at the crowd and screamed at them, "Shut up, shut up! Keep quiet! You just keep still and in ten minutes I'll give you the goddamnedest Lear you ever saw in your lives." And he did, too. Edwin was chosen to accompany his father on his tours, to look after the wild genius and see that he stayed sober.

Edwin and his father became quite close. Junius needed and had come to depend on the boy's close companionship, and the two became inseparable. They walked to and from the theater together, Edwin with his long black hair and wearing a cape. Father and son ate together at the long tables of theatrical boardinghouses, joking and gossiping with other players whom Edwin came to know and like. Back in their simple room they shared a bed, and while his father prowled the room speaking his parts, working out a gesture or a movement, Edwin sat on the edge of the bed and quietly picked his banjo and sang to himself one of the old ballads— like "Barbara Allen," "Cotton-Eyed Joe," or "Old Zip Coon"—that his brother Johnny had taught him.

Edwin's banjo went with him everywhere, and once, when he was playing in his father's dressing room, the door

In this 1864 daguerreotype by Mathew Brady, the three Booth brothers are shown in a performance of *Julius Caesar:* John Wilkes at left, Edwin in the center, and Junius Brutus Booth, Jr., on the right. THE LIBRARY OF CONGRESS.

banged open and in came none other than Edwin Forrest, his namesake. Edwin stopped, thinking he had disturbed the venerable old actor, and tried to hide the banjo, but Forrest protested. "No, no, my boy, I like music. Give us some more." So Edwin played and Forrest, all dressed up in his top hat, began to dance about. Edwin was strumming and picking his heart out.

Wondering what the din was, Booth looked in and, dressed as Richard III, joined in doing turns and twists, jigs, and all the fancy heel-and-toe touches that came back to them now from childhoods long ago.

The two older men collapsed into chairs panting, when Forrest, breathless, gasped, "Well, this is fun, isn't it? It don't remind me of Shakespeare but it does of the Bible. 'Whatsoever thy hand findeth to do, do it with thy might.'"

What Edwin missed in school he picked up in the school of life and became, along the way, perceptive and observant of all the wonders around him. Not many boys his age at that time in America had the opportunity to travel all over to the major cities of the country, and Edwin took it all in. He got to be with his father backstage, explore all the mysteries of props and scenery in the wings, hear all the theater talk, walk onto the vast stages right up to the footlights and look out into the empty rows of seats of America's most beautiful playhouses, and watch endless hours of rehearsal. Perhaps most exciting of all was to watch his father playing Richard III or Lear or Othello from the wings and thrill to his curtain calls and the wild cheering applause of the audience; and, finally, as his father returned backstage, tired and smiling with the crowd's adulation, drenched with sweat, he would grab Edwin in a big hug, saying, "How they love me, m'boy, how they love me!"

It was inevitable that, having inherited his father's temperament and having spent so much time around theaters and actors, young Edwin himself would become a player. It happened, as it often does, by accident. His father was playing Richard III, and the prompter, who had been given the small part of Tressel—one of the boys attending Lady Anne—persuaded Edwin, then sixteen, to take the part. When his father found out about it he protested strongly against his son being on the stage. But Edwin persisted and his father finally gave in. Exiting the stage after his appearance, Edwin rushed back to the dressing room and his waiting father.

"Have you done well?" Booth asked, readying himself for his entrance.

"I think so."

For the rest of his life Booth always suspected that his seemingly unsentimental father had gone out into the wings to watch his son's first performance and then quickly returned to the dressing room.

It was a small part, to be sure, just a couple of lines, but it was the beginning of young Booth's life as an actor. Two weeks later Edwin played Cassio to his father's Iago in *Othello*. Audiences loved father and son acting together, though it was probably for the novelty of it rather than Edwin's acting ability. Edwin's voice was weak and his acting unremarkable, but he learned fast and soon began emulating his father's voice and style.

Junius still insisted he didn't want any of his children on the stage and suggested that Edwin might become a lawyer like his grandfather. Another son, John Wilkes, Edwin's younger brother, was also becoming infatuated with the theater. But the man who acted so well on the stage was not convincing in this matter. Once, Edwin recalled, when they were walking down Broadway, his father stopped to greet an old actor who asked Booth: "Upon which of your sons do you intend to confer your mantle?" Without hesitation, without a word, he reached up—for the boy was now taller than he—and placed his hand on Edwin's head.

Junius finally became reconciled to the undeniable fact that his son was hopelessly enchanted by the theater, and he never again raised an objection to the boy's acting. Soon the playbills were noting that Mr. Booth will be "supported by his son Edwin Booth." Edwin acted Laertes to his father's Hamlet, Macduff to his Macbeth, and Gratiano in *The Merchant of Venice*, growing into a more mature actor with each role. Then, the day Booth was to perform Richard at the National Theatre in New York, he awoke from his nap and told Edwin that he was ill and "didn't feel like acting."

"What will they do without you, Father?" Edwin cried.

"Go act it yourself." Stunned, Edwin left for the theater. As he put on his father's costume and carefully applied his makeup as he had seen his father do so many times, he practiced Richard's first soliloquy as a member of the company prompted him from the playbook. No announcement of the change was made to the audience. Recalling his father's performances, Edwin appeared, limping, his face twisted in the malignant hate and bitterness of the hunchbacked king.

Critic William Winter recalled:

Not until Edwin stood on the stage, and the applause for his father had abruptly lapsed into silence, did the gravity of the situation appear. The audience received the new Gloucester with surprise and coldness. An eager throng had gathered to see a famous tragedian in his most characteristic role. It might well have been astonished at sight of the stripling in place of the giant. Its behaviour, however, was considerate and generous. As the performance proceeded the identity of the actor became clear, and so did his unexpected power. Pleasure soon succeeded to surprise, and hearty approval finally rewarded a courageous effort.

The audience was more than pleased and their applause overwhelmed the young Booth; it would roar in his ears the rest of his life. Yes, he was an actor.

Later, when Edwin returned to his father's room he found him still in bed as he had left him. "Well, how did it go?" Booth demanded sternly, seemingly untouched by the boy's accomplishment that night. But Edwin caught a twinkle in his father's eyes that convinced him his father was not ill at all and—though he never let on—had probably hurried back to his bed after watching his son's debut from somewhere in the audience. In his own way Junius, never offering his son any advice or criticism, was showing that he had complete faith in the young actor's instincts.

Edwin's brother, the younger Junius, was in the meantime also making a name for himself—not as an actor but as a manager. He had been hired to run the Jenny Lind Theater in San Francisco, and now he returned to coax his father and brother to join him. Junius Brutus Booth was now fifty-six years old, accustomed to fame and looking forward to one more adventure. So it was that Edwin joined his brother and father on the deck of the *Illinois* for the long journey—the Panama Canal had not yet been built—that took them from New York, down the east coast of South America, around Cape Horn, up the west coast to Mexico, and into San Francisco Harbor. He was eighteen.

The three Booths played to packed houses in San Francisco, then went on to Sacramento and the gold-mining towns of the Sierras, Marysville, Nevada City, Grass Valley, and Rough and Ready. The rugged, surly miners who sat through performances with guns cradled in their laps loved theater, and many towns that had little else had real playhouses. In a tour reminiscent of Junius's early days in England, the Booths also played in saloons, barns, and even warehouses. Junius Brutus finally had enough of the prospector's life and, perhaps sensing that this was a young man's realm, returned to San Francisco for the voyage home. Edwin never saw his father again. The beloved tragedian died on a Mississippi steamboat between New Orleans and Cincinnati. Upon hearing the news, an old friend, Senator Rufus Choate, exclaimed in tears, "What, Booth dead? Then there are no more actors!"

From Sacramento and San Francisco the younger Booths voyaged on to Australia—it took seventy-two days, twelve of which were spent becalmed on the summer ocean—and performances in Sydney and Melbourne. Edwin turned twenty-one on this tour, and it was in Sydney that he made his first appearance as Shylock in *The Merchant of Venice*.

The theater business was so terrible in Melbourne that they boarded ship again and headed back to San Francisco. When they arrived at Honolulu Harbor, Edwin noticed a sign on an old building— THEATER. They got off the boat and with their last fifty dollars rented the theater for a month. Now Edwin would become, for the first time, a manager as well as an actor. Edwin would play Richard, by now his audiences' favorite, but who would play Lady Anne? He had had a quarrel with his lead actress, Laura Keene, who was now on her way back to England. The only choice was an American stagehand who, bowlegged, cross-eyed, with two front teeth missing, and speaking in a Dutch accent, tripped out onto the stage and, with the actors' muffled laughter behind him in the wings, was greeted by Richard's line—"Divine perfection of a woman." Watching the play from the wings was the king of Hawaii, Kamehameha IV, who after the performance complimented Edwin and told him how, as a boy traveling with an American missionary, he had gone to New York and there seen Edwin's father play Richard III magnificently.

Though he was an accomplished actor, loved by audiences, Edwin was still young and in need of discipline. After his success in San Francisco, brother Junius had wisely cautioned him, "You have had a wonderful success for a young man, but you have much to learn." He was on his own now, no longer protected by the reputation of his father. The critics, too, liked the younger player, noting his growing strength and maturity and encouraging him. "If he would apply himself," they said almost with one voice, "if he will but apply himself industriously, unceasingly and perseveringly in his profession, he will ere long rank among the foremost of living actors." Edwin was already in complete control of his techniques and was capable of reducing an entire audience, men as well as women, to uncontrolled sobbing. Even the hardest bitten actors were sometimes seen standing in the wings crying into their handkerchiefs.

Booth, now twenty-three, left San Francisco and sailed back to Maryland and home. He returned to the farm to find some changes. The old place was run down, the animals he remembered so fondly from childhood gone. His mother was somehow older than he expected, but she had kept the little farmstead together. All his brothers and sisters were grown. Most surprising was his youngest brother, John Wilkes. With everyone off around the world, it was Johnny who had taken care of their mother and helped with the farm. Now, at eighteen, he towered over his older brother. Deep set in his handsome face were those Booth eyes, and he had the Booth passion for the stage. Continuing what was becoming a family tradition, John Wilkes had already debuted as Richmond in *Richard III*.

Edwin, mindful of his brother's and the critics' advice, honed his acting skills to perfection. He played to packed houses in New York, but still he kept his humility and good nature. A young actor, Lawrence Barrett, finding himself in New York in Booth's company after many years in the countryside, arrived fiercely jealous of Booth and prepared to dislike him. Like many actors, he felt that Booth was getting a free ride to fame on his father's coattails. Barrett remembers awaiting Booth that first day of rehearsals. Instead of the arrogant upstart everyone expected, young Barrett found instead a "slight, pale youth with black flowing hair and soft brown eyes. He took his place with no air of conquest or self-assertion, and gave his directions with grace and courtesy which have never left him."

It was at the Boston Theater, playing in *Romeo and Juliet*, that Edwin met his Juliet. She was the young actress Mary Devlin, who called Edwin "my Hamlet." She was devoted to him and he so in love that he shared with her all the hidden secrets of his childhood and difficult years with his father. When they married, Mary left acting; Booth insisted on it. She wrote him during one of their many times apart:

You can, if you will, change the perverted taste of the public by your truth and sublimity, and you must study for this. Dear Edwin, I will never allow you to droop for a single moment; for I know the power that dwells within your eye, and my ambition is to see you surrounded by greatness. . . . If my love is selfish you will never be great: part of you belongs to the world. I must remember this.

Once when Edwin and Mary were on their way to Baltimore, they stopped to visit the grave of Edwin's father. On the stone Edwin himself had bought with some of the first money he earned, was the epitaph:

Behold the spot where genius lies,
O drop a tear when talent dies!
Of tragedy the mighty chief
His power to please surpassed belief.
Hic jacet [here lies] matchless Booth.

Edwin Booth was on his own as an actor. Though playbills sometimes advertised "The Three Sons of the Great Booth—Junius Brutus, Edwin, and John Wilkes," Edwin was acting a magic of his own.

It was now the 1860s, the dark days of the American Civil War, and a rift was splitting apart the Booth family. When Edwin had told John Wilkes in the midst of a political argument that he had voted for Lincoln, the younger brother became furious. Their sister Asia insisted they were Northerners, which only infuriated

Edwin Booth as Hamlet. UPI/BETTMANN.

Edwin Booth four years before his death.
THE BETTMANN ARCHIVE.

John more. "Not I, not I," he screamed at his shocked brother and sister. "So help me holy God! My soul, life and possessions are for the South!" John hated the president for wanting what he called "Nigger citizenship." Later, Asia discovered her brother was a spy for the Confederacy and that he had been smuggling medical supplies in horse collars to Confederate agents. What she and Edwin did not know was that their brother, along with two other men, was plotting the kidnapping of the president.

The story of the assassination of President Abraham Lincoln during the performance of *Our American Cousin* at Ford's Theater the night of April 14, 1865, by John Wilkes Booth is his own story, but it could not help affect the lives of his brothers. Those who hated the Booths for their success or for whatever reason had more cause now. When one actor heard of Lincoln's shooting, he snarled, "All those goddamned Booths are crazy." In Cincinnati, where Junius Booth was playing, a mob of hundreds roamed the city ripping down his playbills, bent on lynching the actor. In Boston, Edwin received a note at his hotel from the manager of the theater where he was playing Hamlet: "The President of the United States has fallen at the hands of an assassin. . . . Suspicion points to one nearly related to you as the perpetrator of this horrid deed. . . . With this knowledge, I have concluded to close the Boston Theater."

Booth replied immediately: "While mourning, in common with all other loyal hearts, the death of the President, I am oppressed by a private woe not to be expressed in words."

It was a terrible day for the Booths but, in a strange throwback to earlier attitudes toward theaters, it was a terrible time for all actors. Ugly crowds attacked theaters calling, "Arrest all actors!" At one point the Secret Service was convinced that all the actors at Ford's Theater were accomplices.

The Booths received hundreds of

threatening letters: "We hate the name of Booth leave quick or remember. . . . Bullets are marked for you. . . . Your House will be burnt. . . . Revolvers are loaded with which to shoot you down." Edwin left the stage, left life, and disappeared into his grief and shame. He swore to friends he would never act again.

But this was not the end of Edwin Booth. In January 1866, he returned to the stage of the Winter Garden in New York as Hamlet. The newspapers were brutal. "Is the Assassination of Caesar to be Performed?" the *New York Herald* asked with brutal sarcasm when Booth's return to the stage was announced. "Will Booth appear as the assassin of Caesar? That would be, perhaps the most suitable character."

It was not an audience but an angry, curious mob that packed the theater opening night. What would they do to Booth? The curtain rose and there sat the actor amidst the court of his fellow players. There was a moment of confused silence. And then William Winter, Booth's critic, friend, and biographer, describes what happened:

> Nine cheers hailed him upon his first appearance. The spectators rose. Flowers were showered upon the stage. Affectionate good-will beamed in every face and gave assurance, deep and strong, that the generous public had no intention of casting upon an innocent man the burden and blight of a brother's guilt.

Booth sat trembling in his carved chair, his head resting on his breast, tears streaming down his face, wetting his cloak. Then he stood, and the crowd broke into pandemonium, waving handkerchiefs, cheering, clapping thunderously. Slowly, Edwin Booth, dressed as the Danish prince, bowed deeply to his audience.

William Winter grew up watching the Booths perform. At the time of Edwin Booth's death in 1893 he wrote:

> Booth did great things in his day, and always good and never harm. He did not always reach the highest heights in Shakespeare: what actor does? or, what actor ever did?. . . It will be long, now that Booth has gone, before our stage again presents an actor whose range extends— not on three-sheet posters, but in mind, spirit, and faculty—from Hamlet to Overreach, from Richelieu to Don Caesar, from Bertuccio to Brutus. . . . He was a poetical actor, and his delicate and exquisite genius tended more to beauty and symmetry than to wild and whirling emotion. . . . Booth was a broader actor, in temperament and adaptability, than most of his predecessors in the illustrious line of English-speaking tragedians; and his excellence in several directions of artistic effort was without a precedent in recent stage history, and almost without parallel in the theatre of his time.

Eleonora Duse

1859–1924 Italian actress

She was one of the most loved actresses of her day, often compared to Mrs. Patrick Campbell in England and Sarah Bernhardt in France, but her life seems to have begun like any other. "It was not extraordinary from the beginning," her biographer, William Weaver, wrote.

She was no Mozart, stretching his fingers for the keyboard before his eyes could look down on it. Like dozens of other Italian actors of her time, she was born poor and born to act, since it was the family trade. She could have remained poor and obscure until her death, playing tear-jerkers and scary melodramas in cold, cramped theatres in provincial towns.

Instead she brought a new, more natural style of acting to all her roles, from Shakespeare to Ibsen. "Duse was not simply a mirror, reflecting the ideas of others; she was a contributor, a critic. And these were not roles; these were all genuine Duses, who, together, made up the extraordinary woman and her extraordinary life."

Eleonora Giulia Amalia Duse was born—as she was to die—in a hotel room, in Vigevano, Italy, on October 3, 1859. Inns, barns, and stables were "home" to her parents. Vincenzo Alessandro Duse described himself on the baptismal register as a "dramatic artist." His brother, Enrico, the infant's godfather, was an actor in the same company. Eleonora's mother, Angelica Cappelletto, appeared occasionally on the stage with her husband, but only out of necessity, to keep food on the table.

They were poor, outcast players wandering the countryside, sharing the rude stages at fairs with jugglers, tightrope walkers, and buffoons. One story has it that Eleonora was born on a train, but that was just one of the myths of a celebrated life. Her parents were too poor to travel any way other than on foot or by cart. Actors in Italy in those days were treated little better than animals—mocked, humiliated, often beaten up. Since their children were not allowed to go to school, many grew up illiterate.

Eleonora's grandfather, Luigi Duse, was the first actor in the family and the first male in living memory not to go to sea. His father's intention was that Luigi become a respectable merchant or civil servant, and so he was sent to school. But he had always been a restless boy. After all, how could a youngster, all of whose ancestors had been sailors, be expected to spend his days sitting at a desk? From earliest memory, Luigi was drawn irresistibly to the stage and the wandering life of a player. He was steeped in the long tradition of the *commedia dell'arte*, the comedy of masked actors so loved by Italian audiences. So he gave up all hope for comfort and respectability to become an actor.

The theater held a special importance in the lives of Italians in the 1800s. Italy was not yet a country, but a group of small states ruled by Austria. Revolution and independence seethed in every Italian, but as urgently as the heart cried out, the feelings could not be voiced, not on the streets or on the pages of newspapers or books. The theater was the one place where people of all classes could gather and talk politics. Up on the stage, forbidden ideas, veiled in comedy and parody, were spoken by actors who seemed to be talking about something else. Actors began using local dialects on the stage, which made it easier to hide serious, dangerous ideas in comedy acts.

Luigi became a favorite of Venetian audiences. Although he had begun playing the usual mediocre tragedies and melodramas of the time, he eventually found the roles, the plays, and the style of acting that best suited him. His skills grew until he was able to attract enthusiastic audiences and gather together a company of his own in Venice and Padua, the Compagnia Duse. In one of his most famous roles, Giacometto, he appeared in a black wig with a pigtail, two black spots over eyebrows constantly in motion, a white neckerchief, a long pale blue coat and flowered vest, red knee britches, white stockings, black shoes with big gold buckles, and, always, a three-cornered hat, which he swung about him. He became one of the most popular actors of his time. And one day, to his great joy, his five-year-old granddaughter, Eleonora, would appear on the stage with him.

Vincenzo did not at first share his father's love of the theater. He wanted to be an artist. But the enthusiasm and power of the actor-father overwhelmed him, and eventually he too succumbed to the lure of the stage. Though he had inherited his father's profession, he seemed not to have inherited his talent. Instead of the major theaters in Venice, Padua, or Milan, the brothers Vincenzo and Enrico had to be content with small-town audiences of rural Lombardy and Tuscany.

It was in one of the tiny, poor villages that Vincenzo met Angelica Cappelletto, who would become his wife and Eleonora's mother. Vincenzo described their meeting in his diary, which disappeared, but had been read and remembered by his daughter. According to Eleonora's biographer, William Weaver,

> As he was walking along the road one day, some earth, rubbish, and geranium leaves fell on him. He raised his eyes and saw that a girl was tending her flower box, where she grew geraniums and carnations. They gazed at each other, and he took to walking along the same road every day, passing under that same window. And one day he decided to climb the many stairs and speak to her. Angelica was the twenty-first child of the Cappelletti [*sic*] family, and when a young man came to ask for her hand, the father consented, although he may not have been pleased that she wanted to marry a poor actor.

Angelica traded the impoverished life of her family for the equally impoverished life of her new husband, but she is remembered as uncomplaining about her new roving life and devoted to her family. Again, her husband's diary reveals all we really know about her:

> She was extremely clever with her pretty hands and was an unsurpassed mender, a great asset in such a poor family. She taught her daughter that being poor and wearing old clothes did not matter, and that neatness and cleanliness were what was absolutely necessary, that all tears could be mended, that she was, however, never to spot her things (with grease or candle wax, etc.).

A photograph of mother and daughter comes down to us, showing Angelica confident and, with a presence unusual for the times, smiling into the camera. Eleonora, at three or four, has already a fierce independence gleaming in her dark eyes.

Angelica and her daughter had a life very different from most families. Instead of being together in a home, doing chores, cooking, they were mostly apart. From a very early age Eleonora was left alone and, as children do when they are without siblings or friends, made imaginary companions of the things around her. Years later she wrote to a friend about how her way of

The young Eleonora Duse. THE BETTMANN ARCHIVE.

speaking and imagining grew out of these times without her mother: "She was delighted when she saw how self-sufficient I was as a child, and how I used to talk to the chair, or to other objects close at hand, which for me, in their silence, contained a great enchantment—and they seem to listen patiently to me, who demanded no answer."

Even when the parents had to be away, there was in this home much love and caring. Angelica, who was probably illiterate as most peasants were then, saw to it that her daughter learned things she hadn't. Eleonora's own daughter, Enrichetta, later recalled to William Weaver what her mother remembered about these early years.

> Her childhood was hard indeed, and when she talked to me about it, she used to say that she wished no child to suffer as she had but that it had been a wonderful school. She never went to any school, her father taught her to read and write, her mother loved her and taught her other things, and as soon as she could read well, she bought as many books as she could afford, a thing she kept up until she died.

The family stayed together whenever possible even though they moved constantly from place to place, from theater to theater, from one fair to another, all over Italy. At first, there was the joy of meeting new people, but always it was followed by the pain of leave-taking, and eventually there would be no joy in the new acquaintances. There's a story a friend of Eleonora's tells:

> They were staying with kind people; outside it was a rainy day; but indoors there were warmth and kindness, and the child had for the first time a sweet and painful sense of home. The good-hearted landlady had given her her first doll, a lovely doll, worthy of all the love of a child. Eleonora never let it out of her arms, slept with it, and was still holding it to her heart when the new leave-taking came. She wept bitterly at first, then she became quiet, grasping the fact that there was no escape from this moving on. The cherished doll was clasped to her breast under her cloak. But after a few steps she tore herself away, ran back to the empty room, laid the doll in the bed where she had slept, and covered it up tenderly. Later she said: "I left it there, so that *it* at least might be warm."

Like her mother, Eleonora at first took to the stage more out of the need to help support her family than any real love of acting. Her father's earnings were not enough to keep them from hunger—once she sneaked into an unattended kitchen and ate all the food she could—and, often, they had a place to stay the night only because of the kindness of strangers. So Eleonora first appeared on the stage at age four, as Cosette in Victor Hugo's *Les Misérables*. What she remembered most her whole life about this performance was how someone whipped her legs with a switch, so that she would be crying when she was shoved out onto the stage.

By the time she was twelve, Eleonora was appearing regularly with her mother, father, and uncle. She went to school only now and then, when the little company stayed in one town long enough and when the teacher would agree to take her. School was never a friendly place. She was always the outsider, cruelly humiliated and insulted by the other children. "*Figlia di commedianti* (comedians' daughter)," they shouted after her.

Then, when she was still very young, she realized something terrible was happening. Eleonora sensed that her mother was changed, had become suddenly distant and indifferent, her beautiful face often twisted in pain, the bright lights in her eyes dimmed. And there was the coughing, the terrible coughing that racked her body.

There were new lessons to be learned in life now, about illness. Eleonora took care of her mother as best she could when she wasn't in school or learning new roles. Though she was always hungry herself, she would give her small portion to her mother, to keep up her strength. Angelica's illness meant the family could not stay together, and so they went off without her, Eleonora leaving behind the only real companion she had ever had.

The acting that Eleonora saw on the stage and learned from her father would surely make us laugh today. The lines were delivered in a stiff, declamatory style, as though the actor were giving a speech to the audience. Acting was explained in books that showed standardized postures, the positions of the feet, arms, and hands, which signaled the audience what emotion or attitude was being expressed. Becoming an actor required only that you mastered the poses shown in the book.

Somehow, acting was different for Eleonora, not just a set of practiced postures and gestures. She was feeling the intensity and emotions of the part and so tried to express them in a natural way, more like people would in real life. And she was beginning to feel acting not as work, but as a passion.

It began with her performance of Juliet in Shakespeare's *Romeo and Juliet*. Perhaps, in her youth and innocence, she did not realize that this was a role only older, more experienced actors would attempt. Nor was she daunted by the fact that Shakespeare was not popular with Italian audiences and seldom performed. The performance was in Verona, Juliet's own city, and it was this place and this role Duse always reminisced about in later life.

It was on a May evening that we went through the Palio Gate of Verona. I was choking with anxiety. I pressed to my heart the sheets on which I had copied the rôle of Juliet with my own hand. And I kept repeating endlessly her words when he enters:

> How now! Who calls? I am here.
> What is your will?

My imagination was excited by a strange coincidence; I was exactly fourteen, like Juliet . . . and gradually my own fate melted into that of the Veronese girl. At every street corner I thought I must be certain to meet a funeral procession bearing a coffin strewn with white roses. When I came in sight of the Scaliger Arch with its closed iron grating I cried, "That is Juliet's grave!" Suddenly I broke into sobbing and felt a confused longing for love and death.

Then one Sunday in the gigantic arena of the ancient amphitheatre under the open sky, before a people who had drunk in the legend of love and death with their very breath, I was Juliet. . . . At the instant when I heard Romeo saying: "O, she doth teach the torches to burn bright!" I was set on fire, I became a flame.

That such a young girl should break with the long-standing acting traditions—the only techniques she had ever seen—and follow her heart instead is astounding. But even more so is the way that Duse was beginning to envision every little detail of her performance beforehand. Her biographer E. A. Reinhardt quotes her:

> With my spare pence I had bought a great armful of roses in the flower market under the fountain of the Madonna. The roses were my only ornament. I made them eke out my words, my glances, my gestures. One of them I let fall at Romeo's feet when we met. I scattered the petals of another over him from the balcony, and with them all I covered his body in the tomb. The perfume of the roses, the air, the light, transported me. The words flowed from my mouth with marvellous ease, without any sense of effort, as in the delirium of fever, and came to me accompanied by the throbbing of my blood.

There is no other record of this performance. Italian newspapers at the time did not usually have drama critics and, even if they did, they would not have bothered with so young and unknown an actor. But there's no doubt that the audience was treated to one of the most natural and moving performances of their lives. This young actress had created before their eyes not merely a role but a young girl's love and tragedy. Duse had begun taking on the life she portrayed on the stage, acting it—not from without with the required gestures—but from within, with the heart. For the rest of her life, on the stage and in her home, Duse surrounded herself with flowers, and always with her favorite—roses.

The mystery of these real emotions both confused and excited her. We can feel with Eleonora the excitement of an adolescent girl discovering the romance of love and death, heady with the scent of roses and the mystery of the theater. But we must also understand that this was a time and a culture in which young women were not allowed the freedom to express such intimate feelings privately, much less in public. Only on the stage was the expression and the acting out of such passionate feelings permissible, and then only if they were acted out in an acceptable, stylized way. (But there were limits even on the stage; an actress whose kiss was deemed too realistic was fined for immorality.) Acting, then, became Eleonora's secret; here was a way for a solitary, withdrawn woman to let out, to live, the feelings in her heart, a privilege all the more exciting because it was forbidden to everyone else.

There was something else even more intoxicating about acting, Duse discov-

ered. When she left the stage she didn't just become herself again, but continued living her part. It was as though she had found a magic potion that somehow transported her from the poverty and constant hunger, the terrible loneliness and sadness of her real life.

In the audience, watching her not performing, but *being* Juliet, was someone who would become one of Duse's closest friends, and he tells us what happened.

> The footlights were extinguished and the people had scattered, when Juliet arose still trembling out of her coffin . . . she was too excited to go home, and she wandered for a long time through the streets; her father followed her, he respected her silence and did not talk. She wandered about for hours. Midnight struck from all the clock-towers of Verona. "Come to supper, my girl," the father insisted. She let herself be led home and sank on to her bed. Her impressions had been too violent, they almost suffocated her. The garret, the squalor around her, all were gone . . . she had been Juliet.

The young actress took on more and more demanding roles, but it was different for her now. Acting was no longer just the family trade; it was her whole life. In the next few years, she would need her magic potion even more. When she was seventeen, her mother died, alone in a distant hotel room, without even a friend at her side. Duse could not afford to go to her or even buy proper mourning clothes, only a little scrap of black cloth which she pinned to her dress. Her father's company fell on hard times, and the brothers went their separate ways. Now she was alone and on her own.

Duse went from company to company, not finding a stage home or many audiences that appreciated her acting. Then, as is often the story, fate gave her the first step up. She had joined yet another small company, this time in Naples as understudy to the lead actress, Giulia Gritti. One night the star was too ill to appear and so Duse stepped into her role. The audience was entranced with the twenty-year-old actress who had unexpectedly appeared that night.

It so happened that in the audience was one of Italy's most renowned actors, Giovanni Emanuel. Seeing Duse's performance inspired him to start his own company with his new discovery and Giacinta Pezzana, a young favorite of Italian audiences. Now "la Duse," as she was becoming to her audiences, would get to play important roles such as Shakespeare's heroines Ophelia and Desdemona.

Now came critics from the newspapers, including one who wrote: "Eleonora Duse was as ideal as a vision, courtly as a princess, sweet as a maiden,

beautiful as Ophelia. She was Ophelia!" At the end of the performance the audience called her out to the footlights five times. This was more than just an appreciative public, as another critic explained: "Signorina Duse was applauded. To win applause, to win attention, with la Pezzana, Emanuel Maieroni, veteran and strong artists, cannot have been easy. But she succeeded, thanks to the great love she brings to her art, her intelligence, her spontaneous, candid but effective feeling." In her mail, Duse found a letter of appreciation from the great French writer Emile Zola.

In 1880—she was now twenty-one—Duse moved from Naples to Turin. Her performances there were not well received, but that didn't seem to matter. Duse saw acting like she had never seen before, so extraordinary it would change her life forever. To the Teatro Carignano, where she had been acting, came the international star Sarah Bernhardt. Duse had no money to go to London or Paris or any of the other theater cities, and famous personalities never came to the provincial towns she played in. This was the first time she had ever seen a really famous actress who had performed all over the world.

"I went every evening and cried." Duse watched the French actress closely, every movement, listening intent on every word, living Bernhardt's acting as if she were there on the stage. "Here is a woman," she wrote, "who uplifts our work, who makes the audience respect what is beautiful, and bow before her art." Bernhardt affirmed Duse's intuition about acting; now she was even more sure of her direction:

> To me it was as if with her approach all the old, ghostly shadows of tradition and of an enslaved art faded away to nothing. It was like an emancipation. She was there, she played, she triumphed, she took possession of us all, she went away . . . but like a great ship she left a wake behind her, and for a long time the atmosphere she had brought with her remained in the old theatre. *A woman had achieved all that!* And in an indirect way I, too, felt myself released; I, too, felt that I had the right to do what seemed right to me, and something quite different from what I had previously been compelled to do. And actually they did not interfere with me after that.

Duse gained new confidence. She confronted the director, Cesare Rossi, on the hackneyed old plays he wanted to continue even after Bernhardt's performances. "If I'm to act tomorrow," she insisted, "it will be in *The Princess of Baghdad*, and in nothing else." Rossi refused to change the schedule.

That play, he argued, had been hissed off the stage in Paris. Duse threatened to leave the company. She played *The Princess of Baghdad*. The play was a hit and, night after night, audiences applauded and cheered loudly. "One must let her have her own way," Rossi conceded.

A few days later a letter arrived from none other than the dramatist himself, the most celebrated of his time, Alexandre Dumas. A friend who had attended Duse's performance had written the French playwright telling him of the success of his play and that it was Duse who deserved his thanks.

Duse's success in Turin was repeated in Venice, Milan, Florence, and Rome. Rome was especially important because it represented the highest achievement for an Italian actor. She was on the verge of becoming an international celebrity, but still she worked at her craft, creating a style that, though controversial, would eventually set the standard for acting. "A part of the public does not yet accept me as I wish to be accepted," she told an interviewer when she was twenty-four, "because I do things in my own way: I mean, in the way I feel them."

Although her approach to each of her roles was intuitive and from the heart, Duse nevertheless worked very hard on every detail. The care with which she

An engraving of Eleonora Duse is surrounded by vignettes of her in her famous roles. MARY EVANS PICTURE LIBRARY.

prepared for each performance shows in the many notes she penciled on her script. One scene, she felt, turned on a single word, or a sound, really: "puah," an expression of disgust. In the margin Duse directs herself to: "stand erect, summon to the spirit all the words spoken, feel again all the torments of the love that is dead, reflect, realize that *he* never loved her in return: sum up all this in a single exclamation: puah!"

Early in her career, Duse refused to perform outside Italy, protesting that no one would sit through a play performed in a language they didn't understand. Still the requests for appearances continued and, eventually, Duse went out into the world—to South America (1885), Egypt (1889), Moscow (1891), and then Paris (1894)—to discover that she had been quite wrong. She was warmly received all over the world by audiences who, though they may not have understood a single word, thrilled to her acting. After the Russian writer and dramatist Anton Chekhov attended her performances in *Antony and Cleopatra* in St. Petersburg, he wrote his sister:

> I have just seen the Italian actress Duse in Shakespeare's Cleopatra. I don't know any Italian, but she acted so well that I felt I understood every word. What a superb actress! I've never seen anything like her. I looked at her and felt sad to think we have to educate our temperaments and tastes with . . . wooden actresses whom we think great because we have seen none better. While I was watching Duse I realized why one is bored at the theatre in Russia.

Now Duse was sought by the world's most famous dramatists. It was Duse who first acted Nora in Ibsen's *A Doll's House* in Germany and Austria. She performed in a play by the German writer Goethe in Berlin, her lines in an Italian translation while the other actors spoke German. She acted in Ibsen's *Hedda Gabler* and in Maxim Gorky's *Lower Depths*. Throughout her career she enjoyed performing new works that brought new challenges, but it was to the plays of Ibsen that she attributed her greatest growth as an actress. Duse was perfectly suited to the natural acting Ibsen demanded. She chose his play *Lady from the Sea* for one of her last performances. The impressions of one who was in the audience speaks so well to Eleonora Duse's life and her art:

> From act to act we saw her rising to greater heights, yet the greatness of her presentation was veiled by the spark of simplicity of her speech. She seemed to speak in an ordinary, everyday voice, without any emphasis or striving for effect, but gradually we were carried away by a spirit and a music which forced the tears into our eyes. There was not a word which did not seem to flow past as lightly and clearly as running water, yet every word revealed a mystery to us.

David Garrick

1717–1779 English actor, playwright, and theater manager

He was so revered as an actor and so changed the techniques of acting that his long tenure on the stage is remembered as the Age of Garrick. Within two years after his first appearance on the stage, David Garrick was greeted every evening with packed houses. He had set new standards for acting Shakespearean roles and restored many of the plays to their original brilliance. He made the English theater the most admired of world theaters or, as one foreign visitor put it:

> The English theatre is said to have attained its greatest degree of perfection during the last years of Garrick's life; and, without doubt, this is its most brilliant period. The principal works of the immortal Shakespeare, and other celebrated dramatic poets, were then represented with a justice, a dignity, and a magnificence before unknown.

David Garrick was born at the Angel Inn, in Hereford, England, on February 28, 1717—one hundred and one years after the death of William Shakespeare. For all of his life, though, Garrick claimed nearby Lichfield as his "own native place." David was named for his grandfather, who was born in France. The family's name was de la Garrigue (from the region of Garrigue). When they fled to England to escape religious persecution and this first David became a British citizen, he adopted the spelling *Garrick*.

Peter, the actor's father, was a lieutenant in the army who traveled constantly. It was during his travels that he met his wife, Arabella Clough, while being quartered at Lichfield. Their first child was also named Peter. Then came a daughter, Magdelene, and the third child, David, who was born while his father was assigned in Hereford. Four more children would follow: Jane, William, George, and Merrial. Lieutenant Garrick's army pay was now insufficient to support his growing family, and so he was forced to take a higher-paying captaincy, which also meant he would be separated from his family for five years, far away in Gibraltar. Since the oldest brother, Peter, was sailing as a midshipman in the West Indies, David became, at fourteen, the acting head of the family.

One of the few advantages of the absence of Garrick's father—for us—is that young Garrick became a writer of letters at an early age, endeavoring to cheer up his father on his lonely watch with news of the family. Even with their father now on captain's pay, life remained difficult for the Garrick children. The family found it hard to pay its debts, and Mrs. Garrick was now ill much of the time. Still, David managed to be cheery in his letters.

It is not to be expressed the joy that the family was in at the receipt of dear papa's letter, which we received the 7th of this month [he wrote to his father].

My poor mamma was in very good spirits two or three days after she received your letter, but now begins to grow maloncolly [*sic*] again, and has little ugly fainting fits. She is in great hopes of the transports going for you every day, for we please ourselves with the hopes of your spending this summer with the family.

In many of his letters, David has to ask for money for himself and his family, but he always does so with good humor:

I must tell my dear papa that I am quite turned philosopher. You perhaps may think me vain, but to show you I am not, I would gladly get shut of my characteristic of a philosopher, viz. a ragged pair of breeches. Now the only way you have to cure your son of his philosophic qualification is to send some hansome [*sic*] thing for a waistcoat and pair of breeches to hide his nakedness; they tell me velvet is very cheap at Gibraltar. Amen, so be it.

Other than young Garrick's references to her illness, we know little of Mrs. Garrick. In the words of Samuel Johnson, a school friend of David's who later became a well-known author, "Mrs. Garrick, though not beautiful in her person, was very attractive in her manner; her address was polite, and her conversation sprightly, and engaging; she had the peculiar happiness, wherever she went, to please and to entertain." She worked hard to pay the family's debts and keep her children clothed.

Of David's father we have only the sketchiest impressions. "He is pretty jolly," David wrote to a friend, "and I believe not very tall." The truth is the only things the Garrick children knew of their father were his occasional letters—many of which, apparently, were lost between Spain and England—and a portrait in military dress he sent them. When Captain Garrick did return, he died within the year, sadly, never having had a chance to form a relationship with his children.

We know less about Garrick's younger years than of other actors and playwrights in this book. Part of it is the times; people wrote less intimately of themselves and others in those days. But for lots of reasons the picture of young Garrick is sketchy. Though he had not a father except for the distant man with whom he corresponded, Garrick did have other adults in his life who cared about him and shaped his life.

One, already mentioned, was Samuel Johnson, whose father kept a bookshop in Lichfield. Johnson was eight years older than Garrick, and though they attended the same grammar school, they were not there together. Later Johnson started his own school, Edial, which

David and his brother George attended, studying Italian and French. Once, when Mrs. Garrick inquired how little David was getting on at school, Johnson predicted that he would probably come to be hanged or come to be a great man.

It was at Edial that Garrick became interested in theater. His "thoughts were constantly employed on the stage," Johnson later told one of the actor's biographers, "for even at that time he was very busy in composing plays [and] he showed [me] several scenes of a new comedy, which had engrossed his time; and these were the produce of his third attempt in dramatic poetry." Garrick produced at least two plays during the brief time he was at Edial, along with his sisters, and assisted and inspired Johnson in writing his own tragedy *Irene*. After a time, Edial closed, and Garrick and Johnson set out for London together in search of education and careers. They remained close friends for the rest of their lives.

During his twenty years growing up in Lichfield, Garrick had found a second father in Gilbert Walmesley, a wellborn Oxford University graduate who introduced Garrick to literature by opening his home and his immense personal library to him. Walmesley had also been the one who encouraged Johnson to start up his school. Before Garrick left for London, Walmesley wrote a letter of recommendation for him to the headmaster of the Rochester School, suggesting that, although Garrick could not afford a university education, he would benefit from the headmaster's tutoring. In his letter, Walmesley gives one of the few glimpses of young Garrick. "Davy was in and out every day," he wrote. "This young gentleman, you must know, has bin much wth me, ever since he was a child, almost every day; & I have taken Pleasure often in Instructing him & have great affection & Esteem for him."

It was when Garrick was studying with the headmaster that his father died. As was usual in those days, the death of a father and provider meant the end of education. Garrick was now on his own and would have to start earning a livelihood. He joined his brother Peter, and for the next few years, from the time David was twenty-one until he was about twenty-five, he worked in the wine trade. Still, his heart was in the theater. Almost from the first day he had arrived in London, Garrick went to plays and made friends with the actors. Among them was Henry Giffard, who was trying to establish his own theater at Goodman's Fields.

Garrick wrote and produced his first play, *Lethe*, at the Drury Lane theater. The play was a success and drew large audiences. A year later, his next play,

The Lying Valet, was produced at Goodman's Fields. This second play was also a success, and audiences had become devoted to the new actor. To his brother's irritation, Garrick was spending more and more time at the theater and less and less selling wine, until finally it was time to give up the wine trade. Peter wrote to his younger brother, admonishing him for taking such an impractical and unsuitable direction in his life. David answered that his aspirations for success in the theater were not just idle dreams. For many years the brothers could not see eye to eye, but all ended well between them.

Garrick took on the lead role in Shakespeare's *Richard III* at Goodman's Fields, portraying the royal villain with such power that he chilled every heart. Billed as "a Gentleman who never appear'd before," Garrick astonished the audience that first night. "[His] reception was the most extraordinary and great that was ever known upon such an Occasion," a journalist wrote the next day. Garrick's acting and interpretation of his role were unlike anything ever seen on the stage before and audiences were enthralled. The English poet Alexander Pope remarked on this first performance, "that young man never had his equal, and he never will have a rival." Pope returned again twice

David Garrick in the role of Richard III. THE BETTMANN ARCHIVE.

to see Garrick's Richard. Within a week of that first night, the theaters of London emptied, and lines of carriages could be seen making their way out to the little theater in Goodman's Fields.

To understand what all the excitement was about you must know about acting before David Garrick. Following the older, conventional style, actors used one voice and one approach to all their characters, which were distinguished one from the other only, as one writer put it, "by costume and outbursts of fury." There was little variety in the voice and movements, resulting in characters that, rather than displaying individual personalities, all came off pretty much the same. Actors used a limited vocabulary of gestures that were more symbolic than real.

In skillful playwriting, such as Shakespeare's, for instance, the characters undergo changes as the story—and their lives—progress. The formal old style would not allow these changes to emerge. Regardless of who the character was, the voice was still heavy and melodramatic, the movements stiff. What you came away with was a strong impression of the actor and his style, but knowing nothing of the feelings, moods, voice, and personality of the character being portrayed. In other words, the actor positioned himself between the playwright and his characters—Richard III, Hamlet, or Macbeth—and the audience.

The new Garrick style was something else. His was the first acting that, while not exactly realistic, was more sensitive to human nature. The difference was even more striking because Garrick played with actors who were still acting in the traditional way. Audiences recognized the difference instantly. As one member of the audience expressed it: "When, after long and eager expectation, I beheld little Garrick, young and light, and alive in every muscle and feature, come bounding on the stage—Heavens, what a transition! It seemed as if a whole century had been stepped over in the transition of a single scene." Still, the theater was not transformed overnight. For decades to come, players and critics would disagree, and the change in acting would be slow and gradual.

Garrick would also demonstrate to audiences his incredible versatility, that he was not just a one-role actor. In the month that followed his performance of Richard, he played with equal skill comedy, tragedy, and farce. He played the roles of young, middle-aged, and old men. What's more, they were not all recognizable as "Garrick"; each was in its own way special, as the role demanded. He had the power to convince and to control.

A life in the theater would mean some changes in Garrick's life, for at this time the theater was not considered a proper activity for a gentleman. Players were considered among the lowest, but he was hooked on the acting life and there was no turning back now. His performances were attracting bigger crowds than had ever come before to the Drury Lane and London's Covent Garden. Nor would he have to wear a "ragged pair of breeches" ever again. So great was his success at Drury Lane that he was given the highest salary ever given any actor. With his talent Garrick had transformed the theater; by the example of his character he would eventually change the public's attitude toward players.

What was it about Garrick's playing that was so remarkable? Consider the problem of trying to describe an actor's art two hundred years ago, or ten years ago—or yesterday, for that matter.

Garrick was often criticized, for instance, for pausing in the middle of a line, which some saw as distracting and disruptive of the rhythm of the verse. Others gasped at the poignancy of the moment—"He paused a little before that line, but at the close 'to love,' no language could describe his manner, or the effect produced." So, how are we to know?

Unlike the work of painters and writers, the voice and gestures of the actor, like the sounds of a musician, are gone in an instant. What's left after the last echo has died are our impressions and the emotions the words and actions have left in our minds and hearts.

Garrick was noted for his "lively and piercing eyes" and for the power he conveyed even in a whisper. He was able to convey subtle motions and expressions even to a large audience. Garrick brought bigger crowds to the theater and theaters were getting bigger. Drury Lane at that time held twelve hundred people and more, since the theater was always oversold. Covent Garden could hold about thirteen hundred and, as we'll see later, the audience was not the quiet, respectful audience of today.

Garrick drew people into the theater who had never gone before. For the first time, English theater audiences were composed of people from almost every level of society or, as it was put in those days, "all Degrees of People go to Plays." It's been estimated that during the Age of Garrick theater audiences increased twenty times.

Performances began between six o'clock and six-thirty, but the audience arrived much earlier. When James Boswell, Samuel Johnson's friend and biographer, wanted to see Garrick in Shakespeare's *King Lear*, he found the pit full by four o'clock. The pit in front of the stage is where the "professional classes" sat, for every class had its place in the theater as well as in life. Servants and sailors sat high in the upper gallery; tradespeople sat in the lower or "best" gallery, and the very wealthy and the aristocracy sat in the boxes above and to the sides of the stage.

Actors usually played to the gallery for it was from the upper gallery that the most passionate expression of appreciation or dislike of the actors came. Here, well-acted comedy met with raucous guffaws, but woe betide any actor who offended. Apple cores, orange peels, walnut shells, even bottles and once an empty beer keg (which had, however, arrived in the theater full) rained onto the stage and pit. One evening's performance so angered the aristocrats in the boxes that they began to protest, which infuriated the rest of the house.

As the *Chester Chronicle* reported:

An universal uproar ensued, and those who attacked the piece were saluted with volleys of oranges and apples, and even halfpence; numbers of the audience at length got upon the stage; several persons were knocked down, and many turned out of the house. A man was thrown from the gallery, but saved himself from hurt by hanging on the chandelier; and a lady of high rank was struck in the face with an orange.

Garrick came out to plead with the audience for order, but to no avail. They were satisfied only when he announced that the author, with all copies of the play in his possession, had left—fled, would be a better word—the theater.

The theater was certainly more exciting in those days. Members of the audience were considered fair game, but managers called the police and often cleared the upper gallery if any player was hit. Those in the boxes and pit came just to be seen, to be ogled and admired by others, and they talked through the entire performance.

Toward the end of his career Garrick, with a partner, took over the famous Drury Lane theater, and thus he became manager as well. Garrick brought with him the strong discipline he had learned over a lifetime of acting, as well as new levels of excellence in stagecraft and set

Garrick with his wife. MARY EVANS PICTURE LIBRARY.

design, makeup, and costume. He taught a new generation of young actors how to study the mind, motives, and manners of characters they were playing, how to understand human nature and interpret it on the stage. He demanded they steep themselves in their roles: "But above all, never let your Shakespeare be out of your hands or your pocket. Keep him about you as a charm. The more you read him the more you'll like him, and the better you'll act him."

David Garrick was a joy to watch, his every movement chosen to reveal the character, but performed so naturally that audiences were moved to feeling. His every performance demonstrated his belief that a great actor must interpret the verse, give it meaning and life, not just recite the lines. He was guilty of sensationalism as when he actually had a bonfire set on the stage of Drury Lane (and panicked the audience). But in bringing people in off the street to act as townspeople for a crowd scene at Stratford-upon-Avon, he showed his flare for innovation.

Oliver Goldsmith asked of him, "The man had his failings—but is that a crime?" As one of his biographers sums up his artistic life, "Garrick cared for his people and for the elegance of his theatre as one of England's great cultural institutions." In the Age of Garrick, the English theater became the envy of the world.

Henry Irving 1838–1905
and Ellen Terry 1847–1928

Reigning stars of the British theater during the Victorian age

At the end of the nineteenth century, two British actors stood above all others, perhaps in all the world. Although their names are usually linked, Ellen Terry and Henry Irving deserve and have achieved their separate fames.

Irving was not simply the best actor in Victorian theater, he was considered by many to *be* the Victorian theater. Although drawings and photographs show what seems to us today a very mannered, melodramatic old-time actor, Irving was regarded in his day as an innovator, staging Shakespeare in a splendid way never seen before. He was the first actor to ever receive a knighthood, the highest honor that can be given a British subject.

Terry too was so honored, being named a Dame of the British Empire, and there are those who say that her playing of some roles has never been surpassed to this day. She was the most highly paid woman in England and, because of her stature, raised actresses out of a sordid class of "public women."

When these two actors joined forces at London's Lyceum Theatre—what Winston Churchill called "the happy conjunction of [Ellen Terry's] gay and charming genius with the mysterious and sinister grace of Henry Irving"—the effect was electrifying.

John Henry Brodribb—he later took the name Henry Irving—was born in 1838 in the Somerset village of Keinton Mandeville, a gray, dour collection of houses that seems today incapable of raising up so colorful and imaginative a person. His father, Samuel Brodribb, was a traveling salesman representing ten tailors in the town's more prosperous days. It was a good job for an adventurous young man, giving him the opportunity to visit towns great and small and to meet people other than those he saw in the village everyday. One of them was Mary Behenna, who Samuel married and brought back to Keinton Mandeville. John, their only child, grew up breathing the cool fog and the scent of the sea that rolled in from Bristol Channel. It was a wonderful playground, and John spent his days outdoors exploring the nearby woods, pastures, and farmyards.

But this was not to be. The manufacture of cloth in factories made small tailor shops and hand-woven cloth unprofitable and, since this was the work of Keinton Mandeville, the town began to decline. There was no longer a need for a traveling salesman, and so Samuel and Mary thought about moving to the city of Bristol. A new railway to London had just been completed and the growing city offered better opportunities for work. Samuel knew all too well from his visits the poor sanitation and poor living of the big industrial city and so decided to send Johnnie off to live with his aunt and uncle and three cousins. Later, when Johnnie was about ten years old, his uncle died and the boy returned to live with his parents, now in London.

There are those who say young Johnnie learned about holding an audience spellbound at church, roused by the histrionics of the Methodist preacher every Sunday. And then there was Dr. Pinches, headmaster of the City Commercial School where Johnnie was sent when he arrived in London. The headmaster loved acting and recitation, and taught his students elocution, correct and proper public speaking. At the end of the term, Pinches would show off his most promising students at a public recital of Latin verse and more modern writings. Johnnie had had a stammer, but the elocution lessons brought him clear, precise speech and he loved to show off his new vocal skill in front of an audience.

William Creswick, a well-known actor who was at that very time playing Hamlet at the Surrey Theatre and a friend of Dr. Pinches, came to one of the recitals and later recalled hearing Irving:

> The room was filled from wall to wall with the parents and friends of the pupils. I was not much entertained by the first part. But suddenly there came out a lad who struck me as being a little uncommon, and he riveted my attention. The performance was a scene from *Ion* in which he played Adrastus. I well saw that he left his schoolfellows a long way behind. Seeing that he had

dramatic aptitude I gave him a word of encouragement—perhaps the first he had ever received.

After his recitation, Johnnie, his mother and father watching with pride, was introduced to Creswick, who spoke to the boy with such friendship. This was especially important. Mary Brodribb was a sternly devout religious woman who considered acting and the theater the very depths of sin and iniquity. But so impressed was she with Dr. Pinches's dignity and the great actor who appreciated her son that she gave her reluctant consent for Johnnie to continue acting. She even agreed to let Johnnie go to the theater, but on one condition—he was allowed to attend only the works of Shakespeare. She would not go herself— nothing could induce her to sin so—but the boy and his father could go.

So, when he was twelve, Johnnie was taken by his father to see Samuel Phelps play Hamlet at Sadler's Wells. What a fortunate first experience it must have been. Phelps, who sometimes acted with Creswick, was noted for having produced thirty-four of Shakespeare's plays. Johnnie was spellbound. Tall and lean, Phelps was a commanding figure, and his Hamlet was considered the best of the day. The boy watched entranced at the expressions on the actor's face. Phelps played Hamlet more realistically

than was customary for the day, revealing the actor's understanding of human nature. And the lovely words were spoken like music. At one moment Johnnie's eyes filled with tears, and at another he broke into uncontrollable laughter at Hamlet's antics with Polonius. He thrilled to the swordplay and gasped aloud when a ghost magically vanished. For the rest of his life Johnnie Brodribb remembered that night.

Johnnie's schooling came to an end when he was thirteen. He could read and write, but without further education, his choices would be limited. He was sent to work as an office boy in a law firm, replenishing the blotting paper, sharpening quill pens, filling inkpots—boring work for a boy captivated by the enchanting world of the theater. Still, there was time while on his errands to hang around bookstalls, to browse and buy penny editions of old plays. He would learn them by heart and then, when he had saved enough money from his small salary, he would go to Sadler's Wells in the evening.

By this time there was no doubt in Johnnie's mind that he would act. There was still the disapproval of his mother, but as he was getting older and more independent that concerned him less and less. She had even enlisted one of his friends to try to talk him out of his passion for the stage, pointing out that it was a difficult life, ill-paid and full of disappointment.

But Johnnie had decided on his path. He attended the City Elocution Class in the evenings, where aspiring young actors received coaching. There were no drama schools in those days, but the Elocution Class had good teachers. Fortunately for Johnnie, they rejected the old-fashioned declamatory style of acting and taught more modern, natural-istic techniques. The students taught one another by listening and then point-ing out mistakes like bad pronunciation, wrong accents, and dropped *h*'s—the mark of the English working class. They watched each other's hands and feet for awkwardness and criticized each other's posture. Johnnie also found time to do some amateur acting—his first Shakespearean role, Romeo.

If all this emphasis on elocution, proper speech, intonation, and deport-ment seems strange in this day of such naturalistic theater and film acting, it's because Victorians didn't want realism. What they expected to see on the stage was an idealistic view of real life, bet-ter and more refined than real life could ever be. Audiences expected to see ladies and gentlemen portrayed in such a way that they, and especially their children, would have proper models of behavior from which to learn. Lower-class characters speaking

and acting in a "vulgar" way were to be laughed at and despised as the worst of society (and reminders to many of the life they had left behind in their rise to the middle class).

For Johnnie, amateur performances brought no satisfaction. While he had been hanging around Sadler's Wells, he had met William Hoskins, a friend of Phelps and an Oxford graduate. Hoskins was impressed with the boy's devotion to the theater and offered to coach him early in the morning, before Johnnie had to be at the office. Hoskins was soon off to Australia to find work as an actor, but before he left he tried to convince Mrs. Brodribb that her son should accom-pany him. She refused, but Hoskins gave the boy a letter, a magic letter like some-thing in a fairy tale. It was written to E. D. Davis, manager of a new theater. "You *will* go on the stage," Hoskins reassured Johnnie. "When you want an engagement, present that letter, and you will find one."

At eighteen, Johnnie was on his way to the New Royal Lyceum Theatre, Sunderland. Before setting off from London, he had bought wigs, tights, gloves, shoes, a hat with an immense feather, and three swords—"My court sword," he explained to a fellow clerk, "my fencing sword, and my sword for battle." He would also take with him a new name. Brodribb would not look good on playbills, and besides it would be an embarrassment to his mother if she happened upon his name on a theater. He would take Henry, his own middle name, and Irving from the American writer Washington Irving, who he admired. He had a new name and soon a new career.

There was nothing in those first performances at the Lyceum that suggested any greatness in Henry Irving—he was a disaster. He forgot his lines. He suffered stage fright and froze, unable to speak or move. Once, forgetting his lines, he could do nothing but walk off the stage to a chorus of hisses. A local drama critic suggested that he give up acting and take the first steamship back to London.

But Irving refused to give up. Davis did not ask him to leave, but instead stood by him, recognizing his hard work and commitment if not talent. He and the other actors coached and encouraged young Irving until his self-confidence returned. He was able to work with some of the best actors of the day, who gave him practical advice and suggestions on technique. Irving pulled himself up, won the respect of his fellow actors, and, after the first month, was even given a salary. He received an offer to join the Theatre Royal in Edinburgh, Scotland, and accepted it.

Irving continued his apprenticeship

for two and a half years in Edinburgh. He played in that time somewhere between 350 and 400 parts, never playing in fewer than three pieces a night. On several nights he was called on to play four diverse parts. Curtains rose at 6:30 P.M. and the entertainments went on for more than four hours. Here, too, he got to act with and learn from the greatest actors on the stage, like the Irish tragedian Barry Sullivan and Helena Faucit with whom he won his first applause from the house. Sadly, much criticism of Irving focused on his appearance. Audiences of the day preferred "noble-looking" heroes, and Irving did not look the way audiences thought an actor should.

Still he was winning praise and encouragement. A critic wrote: "Mr. Irving is a young actor of greater promise and intelligence than any who have appeared in the ranks of the Edinburgh company for a long time."

Though the Scots had grown to love Irving and considered him their own, and though another actor might have been tempted to stay and make it his theater home, Irving had only one thought in mind now at twenty-one: acting in London. At his going-away benefit he said good-bye to old friends and thanked his devoted audience. His closing remark, offered without any kind of bitterness but in a spirit of reflection, reveals his wisdom at so young an age: "I was sometimes hissed in this theatre, and I can assure you that thousands of plaudits do not give half so much pleasure as one hiss gives pain—especially to a young actor."

Irving found no work in London, nor did he get much satisfaction from performances in Glasgow and Dublin, where he was offered only small parts. It was as though his career had taken a step backward. In Manchester—he was now twenty-six—Irving was given his first chance to play the part he had dreamed of, Hamlet the Dane. To the critics it was presumptuous of such a young actor to even attempt such a role. Irving's voice was not up to the demands of the part, they said, which also called for a more robust body and personality. Eventually, however, audiences warmed to him and, later, when more mature, Irving looked back with wonder that he had even attempted such a role. But he had. And that's what leads to greatness.

He was given other Shakespearean roles: Claudio in *Much Ado about Nothing* and Edmund in *King Lear*. His apprenticeship continued for the next ten years, touring and playing night after night, sometimes to applause, but often to indifference. In all, he played 588 parts. One of his parts was described by a critic as "the finest piece of undemonstrative acting that I have witnessed." And he was still only twenty-eight years old.

Fame often comes to an actor with one part, a part which touches him especially and into which he pours all of his heart and soul. For Henry Irving that part came at the age of thirty-three, in the play *The Bells*. It was not a great play, all but unknown to audiences of today, but Irving took on one of the roles and made it his own. The audience was totally in his grasp. The complexity of his interpretation and its effect on the audience was described by a critic in the *Times* of London:

> Mr. H. Irving has thrown the whole force of his mind into the character and works out, bit by bit, the concluding hours of a life passed in a constant effort to preserve a cheerful exterior, with a conscience tortured 'til it has become monomania. He is at once in two worlds between which there is no link—an outer world which is ever smiling, an inner world which is purgatory.

The tide had turned. Not only the critics but Irving's colleagues in the theater began acknowledging his talent. How sweet it must have been for him to receive a letter from Helena Faucit, the actress with whom he had worked years before when he was a teenager, telling him how much she enjoyed his acting in *Charles I*: "It is a fine play finely acted. . . . I feel that your conception of the character has grown and deepened. You have lived into it and so get within the soul of it. This must be the case in all fine art and thus no first efforts can ever be the best!"

Finally, Irving's dream of doing Shakespeare was within his grasp. Based on his success in *The Bells*, he was given a budget to do his own production of *Hamlet*. A huge crowd filled the Lyceum Theatre on the first night. Despite the shabby scenery and uneven performances of the supporting players, Irving's Hamlet was a success. The play ended in a tumult of cheers and Irving was called back again and again by the audience, on its feet and applauding wildly, waving hats and handkerchiefs. He had given them the most human Hamlet they had ever seen and they could not thank him enough. "He has," one critic wrote, "made Hamlet much more than a type of feeble doubt, of tragic struggle, or even of fine philosophy. The immortality of his Hamlet is immortal youth, immortal enthusiasm, immortal tenderness, immortal nature." The play ran for two hundred nights. Irving went on to do *Macbeth*, *Othello*, and *Richard III*.

Henry Irving was almost forty, still young but now certain of his accomplishment. After Shakespeare there was yet another dream: a theater and a company of his own, "where," as he said, "I shall be sole master." Irving arranged to lease the Lyceum Theatre, a beautiful old place full of history and so much a part of his life. It was built in 1834, decorated outside with six stately Corinthian columns and inside in gold and crimson, everywhere flowers and frolicking cupids. It had been the first theater in London to have gas lighting. Irving would keep the gas lighting and install softer upholstered seats. He respected and loved the history of the old Lyceum and restored rather than changed the interior.

For his new theater Irving would need a new leading lady and turned to a longtime friend. Lady Juliet Pollock, whose knowledge of the theater Irving greatly respected, suggested a young actress named Ellen Terry. A meeting was set. "I look forward to the pleasure of calling upon you on Tuesday next at two o'clock," Irving wrote. And so began one of the great acting partnerships of all time.

When Henry Irving and Ellen Terry met in 1878, it was not for the first time. Terry was returning after several years of absence from the theater. They had acted together years before. What's more, she was a much loved, successful actor who, like Irving, had enthralled audiences and recreated roles in her own personal vision. Two years before their meeting, Terry had enjoyed a major

Henry Irving at the height of his career.
HULTON DEUTSCH COLLECTION LIMITED.

of the day: "No wonder this fascinating Olivia became the rage of the day. Her photographs went like wildfire; the milliners' windows were full of Olivia hats, caps, 'kerchiefs and other items of feminine adornment; everywhere such dainty trifles were in evidence; and how many little 'Olivias' were christened in 1878 would be hard to say." Critics debated her greatness, but for certain she was loved by her audiences. Sarah Bernhardt put it this way: "She is not a great actress, but she is more a woman than all the women in the world."

Her father, Ben Terry, was born into an Irish family and at eighteen joined the orchestra of a local theater. At nineteen he married twenty-year-old Sarah Ballard, whose parents were Scottish. Together they started off on a new life as strolling players. All but two of their children would find homes in the theater. Ben, the first-born (1839), was a traveler drifting in and out of jobs around the world. Kate (1844) was about to become a leading actress when she chose marriage instead. Younger than Ellen were George (1850), who began as a cabinetmaker and joined the Lyceum Theatre as a master carpenter, eventually managing theaters of his own, and Marion (1853), who was an actor, as were Florence (1855) and Fred (1864). Charles (1857) became a theater manager, and

success in a contemporary play, *New Men for Old Acres*. In 1877, she had played Lady Teale in Sheridan's comedy of manners *The School for Scandal*, written a century earlier. Then she was chosen for the title role of *Olivia*, an adaptation of Oliver Goldsmith's novel *The Vicar of Wakefield*. Terry became a "star" like the movie stars of Hollywood in the 1930s. London went wild over her. One of her biographers, David F. Cheshire, describes the "Olivia" madness

Tom (1860) went to sea vowing never to set foot in a theater.

Ben coached all his children in acting and stagecraft. It must have been a joy for him to see his children, often together, on the stage. "I can't even tell you when it was first decided that I was to go on the stage," Terry wrote in her memoirs, "but I suspect it was when I was born, for in those days theatrical folks did not imagine that their children *could* do anything but follow their parents' professions."

At the age of eight Kate was invited to act at Charles Kean's Princess's Theatre, and so she and her brother Ben went off with their mother to London. Meanwhile, Ellen accompanied her father to Liverpool, where he had an engagement. "He never ceased teaching me to be useful, alert and quick," she recalled. "He always corrected me if I pronounced any word in a slipshod fashion. He himself was a beautiful elocutionist, and if I now speak my language well it is in no small degree due to my early training."

While touring together Ben taught his children reading and writing—Ellen wrote in a beautiful, flowing script— and their numbers. Middle-class children would have seen Ellen as a social outcast, a strange and undisciplined child—actors were considered disreputable—yet the education she received from her father and mother was in many ways better than what most little girls got in England in those days, and Ellen, Kate, and Ben were happier than most.

Ben also joined Kean's company and Ellen, now ten years old, was given the role of the duke of York, a young prince, in *Richard III*. Two years later Ellen auditioned for another part in *The Winter's Tale*, and acted performance after performance for 102 consecutive nights. Queen Victoria and Prince Albert were in the audience Ellen's first night. But that first night was an embarrassment she never forgot. She had as a prop a little toy replica of a cart, a picture of which had been found on a Greek vase in the British Museum. "It was my duty to drag this little cart about the stage," she recalled, "and on the first night, when Mr. Kean as Leontes told me to 'go play,' I obeyed his instructions with such vigour that I tripped over the handle and came down on my back! A titter ran through the house, and I felt that my career as an actress was ruined forever. Even now I remember how bitterly I wept, and how deeply humiliated I felt."

But she was wrong. Lewis Carroll, the author of *Alice's Adventures in Wonderland*, saw her a few nights later and remarked that he "especially admired the acting of the little Mamillius, Ellen Terry, a beautiful creature who played with remarkable ease and spirit."

When next she appeared on the stage

it was in *A Midsummer Night's Dream*, and a London reviewer wrote: "A little girl . . . played Puck better than I have ever yet seen the trying part filled; there was a clearness of voice, a gracefulness of pose, and a hearty appreciation of the mischief she was causing." Carroll went back to see her again and said she was "the most perfectly graceful little fairy I ever saw." Ellen played Puck for 250 consecutive nights.

While at the Princess's Theatre, Ellen found a mentor and stage "mother" in the lead actress, Ellen Kean. At first she frightened young Ellen, but Kean's sternness was tempered by kindness and tenderness toward the little actress. Ellen remembers how in one scene she was supposed to be in terror but instead stood paralyzed, unable to act.

> Mrs. Kean stormed at me, slapped me. I broke down and cried, and then, with all the mortification and grief in my voice, managed to express what Mrs. Kean wanted and what she could not teach me herself.
>
> "That's right, that's right!" she cried excitedly. "You've got it! Now remember what you did with your voice, reproduce it, remember everything, and do it!"
>
> When the rehearsal was over, she gave me a vigorous kiss. "You've done very well," she said. "That's what I want. You're a tired little girl. Now run home to bed."

During the next few years Ellen and her sister Kate took on a variety of more adult roles. They were making friends outside the theater, too, among artists and writers. One especially who would play an important role in Ellen's life was George Frederick Watts, who painted a double portrait of Kate and Ellen while they visited him at his studio.

Perhaps Ellen was tired of the endless demands of the stage and her audiences. Maybe she feared not being able to grow into the roles of the great actress everyone was predicting she would be. Perhaps, as her mother had hoped, Ellen began to aspire to a more proper middle-class life. More likely it was that after a life of moving from lodging to lodging, living out of a trunk, moving from town to town, theater to theater, she saw the possibilities of a more settled life and, at last, a home.

She found herself, she recalled later, "dreaming of and aspiring after another world, a world full of pictures and music and gentle, artistic people with quiet voices and elegant manners." She had fallen in love with Watts's studio and his life at Little Holland House but not, seemingly, with the artist himself. Watts's interest in Ellen was not so much love as a paternalistic interest. "I have determined," he wrote to a friend after meeting Kate and Ellen, "to remove the youngest from the temptations and abominations of the Stage, give her an education . . . taking the poor child out of her present life and fitting her for a better."

Though it appeared to have happened for all the wrong reasons, George Frederick Watts, age forty-seven, and Ellen Terry, not yet seventeen, were married.

The dream soon vanished; the marriage lasted less than a year. Watts expected Ellen to grow into a quiet, timid, oppressed Victorian woman and give up the exuberant and vivacious girl she had been on the stage. The very qualities that made her such a loved actress were now to be somehow repressed, put aside. She resented being scolded like a naughty, willful adolescent. The "gentle, artistic people" ignored her, treated her like a child. She was lonely.

Ellen returned to live with her parents and immediately returned to the stage. She took on roles in five productions, ending the year playing in David Garrick's adaptation of Shakespeare's *The Taming of the Shrew*, called *Katherine and Petruchio*. To her Katherine, a young actor named Henry Irving played Petruchio. Ellen hated the play because it lacked Shakespeare's sensitivity, especially to his heroine. Shakespeare's Kate eventually submits to dependence, but she grows and attains an inner freedom. Garrick's

Ellen Terry as a young woman. HULTON DEUTSCH COLLECTION LIMITED.

Katherine merely gives in and becomes the ideal of the submissive Victorian woman. Neither did Ellen care much for Irving, who she found "stiff with self-consciousness." Irving found her a boisterous, ill-bred tomboy. Ellen was nine years younger than Irving, but the differences in their salaries for this engagement is interesting. Irving received just over two pounds for his part; Ellen was paid five pounds.

Early the next year Ellen retired from the theater again, this time to live with Edward William Godwin, a bright, young architect and designer of interiors and furniture. Ellen was enchanted once again with an artist's life, a country idyll, one that promised the home, the solitude, and quiet she never had. The lovers lived in a beautiful little country house Godwin designed, Fallows Green, and it was here that their two children grew up. Ellen gave Teddy and Edy an upbringing she had never enjoyed, filled with walks in the country, Walter Crane picture books, and wooden toys. This was a time when European artists and architects had "discovered" Japan, and so the children's nursery was exquisitely Japanese, the walls covered with woodblock prints and fans.

Though Ellen was much more grown up in this life with Godwin than she had been in her child-bride marriage to Watts, there was something about this that could not go on. The privacy, the children, her role as artist's wife, Godwin's artistic and aesthetic life, the trees and animals of the woods surrounding Fallows Green all changed Ellen forever. "I have been having a very happy time," she told a friend. But like so many magical times, the beautiful bubble of Ellen's dream world was fragile. When real life suddenly intruded—Godwin's dwindling commissions and legal problems arising out of a failed partnership led to financial difficulties, more debts than they could pay, and the need to mortgage Fallows Green—the bubble burst and the dream faded.

The family moved to London and remained together another year, but somehow Godwin drifted out of Ellen's life and it was over. For the rest of her life Ellen would look back with nostalgia on those six years of a peaceful, contented life in the country, watching her children grow up in that perfect childhood setting. Whenever she could, she would try to return to a small country cottage somewhere.

In February 1874, Ellen Terry returned to the stage once again. She played in London and toured throughout the countryside in productions by her friend Charles Reade. She ended the year playing Kate Hardcastle in Oliver Goldsmith's *She Stoops to Conquer* and began the next with what would be one of her most famous roles, Portia in Shakespeare's *The Merchant of Venice.*

The greatness of actors like Ellen Terry is their skill in taking words printed in ink on a page and finding in them emotions and intentions. Well-written characters in a play, like real people, don't or often can't express their true feelings in what they say. There are times when we deliberately try to hide our true feelings, covering pain and anguish in our hearts with a smile on our faces. Intimate friends and good actors can see through the words, deep into the heart and mind of a friend or a character. They can identify with the character because they too have felt what he or she has felt.

So it was with Ellen Terry and Portia. Usually, Portia was played either as a tragic character or as a coquettish meddler. But Terry saw something deeper in Portia, perhaps what Shakespeare intended: "Portia is the fruit of the Renaissance," Terry wrote, "the child of a period of beautiful clothes, beautiful cities, beautiful houses, beautiful ideas. She speaks the beautiful language of inspired poetry. Wreck that beauty, and the part goes to pieces." Theater audiences, often disappointed when their "old favorite" is not there, didn't like Terry's Portia. But at least one critic saw what Terry was trying to do. "They will say it was not Portia because it was perhaps like no other Portia ever seen by Shakespeare students, so fresh and charming is the presentation . . . no renewal of old business."

The year was 1878. Terry was an established actress, by most accounts the most loved in all of England, and she was but thirty years old. Accepting Henry Irving's offer to join him at the Lyceum Theatre, Terry would play Ophelia to Irving's Hamlet. Irving had played in *Hamlet* many times before with Charles Fechter, the leading British Hamlet, and Edwin Booth, America's best-known Hamlet of the 1860s. But now he would have a chance to play the role as he wished. This would be Terry's first time in the role of Ophelia, and she put in much work on the part. She was dismayed that Irving seemed to be ignoring her, until finally, ten days before the first night, unable to stand it any longer, she told him, "I am very nervous about my first performance with you. Couldn't we rehearse *our* scenes?"

"We shall be all right!" he replied.

Clearly Irving understood Terry's genius. She was an equal, as men and women were more often as actors and actresses than in real life. She was a professional, a star, but more interesting to students of the theater, she was also creating new techniques that were quite unheard of. Concerned about how to play a madwoman, Terry visited what was called a madhouse in those days, to actually see insanity. She looked about her for something, and then she saw what she wanted, a young girl just gazing at a blank wall. "I went between her and the wall," Terry remembers, "to see her face. Suddenly she threw up her hands and sped across the room like a swallow." In the pathetic flutterings of the insane girl, she found a model that she could transform into Ophelia.

On opening night the Lyceum was packed. Irving was a favorite of all the British, admired by the rich and the poor. "For such a spectacle as the house presented," a member of the audience that opening night wrote, "we have no precedent in England. The great players of the past could rely for ardent support upon only one section of their audience. Mr. Irving seems popular with all classes."

The shock of the evening was that Terry did not appear for her curtain calls. Convinced she had failed, she had run off into the night toward the river, intent on drowning herself. She was returned home by an old friend, to discover, in a less emotional moment, that the play was liked. "The representation of Hamlet supplied on Monday night," a critic wrote, "is the best the stage during the last quarter of a century has seen, and the best to be seen for some time to come." Lewis Carroll proclaimed: "Ellen Terry as Ophelia was simply perfect." The play ran 108 nights and for the first time in memory, Shakespeare made money for a theater.

From the beginning Terry and Irving forged a true stage partnership with all the give-and-take necessary for the success of such a team. When she insisted that mourning black was a better choice for Ophelia's mad scene, Irving listened but did not argue. But when the costume adviser arrived the next morning, he explained that only Hamlet was allowed to wear black, and Terry agreed to the customary virginal white.

At another time, she noticed his terrible first-night nervousness. She suggested, always the practical one, that it was standing in the wings and watching the audience that was so terrifying. "I suggested a more swift entrance from the dressing room." Irving found that her suggestion worked for him too and adopted it. He also respected and took her advice about acting voice and makeup, recognizing Terry's sure professional touch.

As true a partnership as it was, it was not possible outside the theater. Until the turn of the century, Terry never received billing equal to Irving's; that would have been contrary to British custom. But in America, everything was different. There Terry received billing equal to Irving's and she was accepted that way socially as well.

To look at the old drawings and photographs of Irving you might not guess that he had a zany sense of humor. Terry, too, was one for playing pranks. Once, she started giggling in a play with Irving, and then continued to giggle and giggle, leaving him trying desperately to keep his solemnity and make it through

Henry Irving and Ellen Terry in *Olivia*, an adaptation of *The Vicar of Wakefield*.
THE BETTMANN ARCHIVE.

the scene. A friend relates this scene during a rehearsal:

> I have seen her in one of her irresponsible moods, catch hold of a bit of scenery that was being hoisted to the flies, hanging on with one hand until she was high above the stage. The terror-stricken carpenters hastened to lower their precious burden so soon as they perceived that they were hauling heavenward one of the mainstays of the Lyceum. The only answer she vouchsafed to the perplexed managers and anxious friends was an impromptu Irish jig, to show how much better she felt for her aerial flight.

Henry Irving and Ellen Terry acted together for almost thirty years. They played hundreds of parts, especially the great Shakespearean roles. Terry went on to do Lady Teazle in Sheridan's *The School for Scandal*, Lady Anne in *Richard III*, Beatrice in *Much Ado about Nothing*, Juliet, Viola in *Twelfth Night*, Cordelia to Irving's Lear, and Lady Macbeth. For *Henry VIII*, Terry and Irving were together for 203 performances; 156 for *The Merry Wives of Windsor*; *Cymbeline*, 72 performances. As Margaret in W. G. Willis's *Faust*, Terry was on stage for 388 performances.

Together and individually they toured throughout the United States and Canada, seven tours in all, to Philadelphia, Boston, Baltimore, Brooklyn, Chicago, St. Louis, Cincinnati, Indianapolis, Columbus, Detroit, Toronto, Pittsburgh, Portland, Seattle, Tacoma, San Francisco, Minneapolis, New York, and Montreal, to many places several times. They toured across Australia. It's hard to imagine the energy and the unbelievable work involved in performing, much less mastering so many roles.

The two went on together until February 1905. Irving had been ill but, as was his way, went on tour anyway with two strenuous plays, *The Bells* and *Becket*. The doctor advised that Irving rest, that he never play *The Bells* again, because he lived the part so deeply that at each performance he would almost die Mathias's death. But Terry knew better, that he would work as hard as ever. Once Terry asked Irving what he thought it was going to be like to get old and face death. "Where there's art, where there is genius, there is neither old age, nor loneliness, nor sickness, and death itself is robbed of half its terror."

"And the end," she asked, "how would you like that to come?"

He snapped his fingers and said, "Like that!"

On October 12, after playing *Becket*, taking his curtain calls and the audience's cheers, he stopped briefly to talk with his old friend Bram Stoker (creator of *Dracula*) and headed back to the hotel. There, in the main hall, it happened, like that.

Irving was buried in Westminster Abbey along with others of England's greats. Ellen walked in the funeral procession. In her memoirs she wrote:

> How terribly I missed that face at Henry's own funeral: I kept on expecting to see it, for indeed it seemed to me that he was directing the whole most moving ceremony. I could almost hear him saying "Get on! get on!" in the part of the service that dragged. When the sun—such a splendid, tawny sun—burst across the solemn misty grey Abbey, at the very moment when the coffin, under its superb pall of laurel leaves, was carried up the choir, I felt that it was an effect which he would have loved.

After Irving's death, Terry found new lives. She began acting in modern plays, beginning with her role as Cicely Waynflete in *Captain Brassbound's Conversion*, which George Bernard Shaw had written especially for her. In addition to this role, Terry would play three Shakespearean roles in 1906—Mistress Page in *The Merry Wives of Windsor*, Francesca in *Measure for Measure*, and Hermione in *The Winter's Tale*.

It was also her fiftieth year as an actress, and she was celebrated at a spectacular benefit performance at the Theatre Royal, Drury Lane. All the great actors and actresses of the day were there. The celebration actually began the night before, when people gathered for what the director guessed was "one of the first instances of an all-night theatre queue." The *London Times* reported that "from shortly after noon till six o'clock, they filled Drury Lane with a riot of enthusiasm, a torrent of emotion, till they were hoarse, laughed to the verge of hysteria, and sang 'Auld Lang Syne' in chorus, not without tears."

Terry promised her admirers that this was not the end of her career, far from it. "I will not say good-bye," she said, wrapped in the enveloping warmth and love of the overflow audience. "It is one of my chief joys that I *need* not say good-bye—*just yet*—but can still speak to you as one who is still among you on the active list—Still in your service—if you please."

They pleased. The next year she toured the United States with her new husband, the American Shakespearean actor James Carew. She would play in full, busy seasons with seemingly unflagging energy for another sixteen years. Her health was failing, though only those close to her had any idea of it. In 1912 she suffered what Terry herself called a "ditheration of the brain," more like a nervous breakdown.

She continued on her lecture tours, reciting passages from Shakespeare and commenting on them. Her performances were always fresh and held surprises still for audiences who had been seeing her for years. The actor A. E. Matthews never tired of observing her technique: "Each night she would give a different rendering of her part, handling it according to the inspiration she got from the particular audience. As audiences varied so did her performances."

Terry's last full season was in 1922, when she played eight roles, including a dramatization of Jane Austen's *Pride and Prejudice* and Shakespeare's *King John*. For the next two years she didn't appear. And then, in November 1925, she made her last appearance on stage, as the ghost of Miss Susan Wildersham in Walter de la Mare's *Crossings*.

Friends noticed her becoming frailer by the day, "drifting away," as a friend put it, "into a vague world where nothing is real and people bear no names." On July 21, 1928, Ellen Terry passed away quietly in her beloved farmhouse. Her daughter, Edy, was with her and recalls the last few moments when her mother held her hand and slipped away, softly repeating the word *happy, happy* over and over again.

Edmund Kean

1787?–1833 English actor

Samuel Taylor Coleridge, the eminent philosopher and poet, once said that to see Edmund Kean act was "like reading Shakespeare by flashes of lightning." Kean was a tragedian of such genius that there are those who still say, over a century and a half after his death, that he was the greatest actor of all time.

That was Edmund Kean the actor. Edmund Kean the man lived out a miserable tragedy, a life so successful but at the same time so destructive and bitter, that soon after his death those who knew him, while still acknowledging his greatness on the stage, preferred to forget him. William Macready, himself a great tragedian, who once admired Kean the actor, admitted to nothing but hatred and contempt for the man. "Kean," he said, "was the greatest dis-grace to the art of acting of all the disgraceful members that ever practised it."

Since his death, Kean has been seen differently by each new generation of actors, and today we judge him—if we judge him at all—with different sensibilities. Still, he remains the most phenomenal figure in the entire history of the theater.

From the very beginning, Edmund Kean's life was a mystery. His birthplace was most certainly London, but that's where all certainty ends. As the question mark in his birthdate suggests, not even the year of his birth can be agreed upon. Kean himself cannot be trusted on this matter, because he always made himself out to be younger than he really was, and, besides, he probably didn't know either. The dates most often given are

March 17, 1789, and November 4, 1787. His most careful biographers think the latter is more likely, though Kean himself gave the first date for his passport.

Kean surely did not know who his real parents were and, unlike most of us, he had the privilege of making that choice himself. It seems that he was the son of Edmund Kean and Ann Carey. Edmund was a surveyor and it was while his firm was building the Royalty Theatre that he met the actress who liked to be called "Nance." There was acting in their blood. Edmund was a tailor's son, but he is remembered as an accomplished orator and "distinguished speaker" at the debating clubs that were popular in those days. His brother, Moses, enjoyed some acclaim as a ventriloquist and mimic. Nance was the daughter of an entertainer, and had run away from home at fifteen to join a company of strolling players. She was, by all accounts, not a very good actress, and her real stage seems to have been the streets of London.

Kean wanted to believe that his real parents were his aunt, the actress Charlotte Tidswell, and Charles Howard, the Duke of Norfolk. Charlotte was not really his aunt and the duke was not his father, but that's a long, complicated story. The facts are that soon after the boy's birth, he was given over to some unknown nurse so that Nance could return to her roving life. Edmund was no help to his infant son because he was always drunk. The boy was so badly neglected that finally his uncle Moses could take it no more and put the half-starved, sickly two-year-old in Charlotte's care. Charlotte and Moses were not married—she pretended in public to be his wife, though they actually lived apart—but she took to the little boy, loved him dearly, and raised him as though he were her own. Her devotion to the boy suggests to some biographers that she and Moses were actually his parents. It was Charlotte who gave the lad his name, Edmund, after his father.

Aunt Tid, as Edmund called her, had an even greater gift for him, an introduction to the world of the theater. Charlotte had been for many years a supporting actress at Theatre Royal in Drury Lane, London, and the stage was the only life she knew. Something in the boy suggested promise to her, that perhaps he could become not just an illiterate, common player, but a tragedian, like the renowned David Garrick. She lived just a few minutes' walk from Drury Lane and little Edmund would always accompany her, playing backstage while she rehearsed. Soon the theater became his life as well, his playground and his school.

When he was six or seven Charlotte

arranged to have him taught dancing at odd hours by Drury Lane's dancing master and singing by the music master. He learned pantomime and tumbling, and the fencing master taught him to handle the sword that would someday, when he was grown up, give power and majesty to his Shakespearean roles. Charlotte introduced the boy to Shakespeare, sharing with him the techniques she had learned during her ten years in the theater, which included supporting roles with many of the most illustrious actors of the day. As Edmund repeated the lines after her, she encouraged him to feel the meaning as well as the poetry of the words. Then she would place him in front of a mirror, where for hours on end he would rehearse his speeches.

Of formal schooling and the three *R*'s, Edmund knew little. Apparently he did attend day schools from time to time, but only when he had to. He was a restless, independent child—"active, forward, prone to mischief and neither to be led nor driven," as Charlotte described him. He didn't fit in with the other children in school who, after his experiences in the theater, must have seemed goody-goody and uninteresting. Charlotte tried to discipline him—she hoped he would become a gentleman—but to no avail. She beat him and locked him in his room, even tied him to his

bedpost. Still the boy defied her, running away every chance he got to roam the streets of London, a wild guttersnipe.

Sometimes he disappeared for days, spending nights under shrubs or in trees, walking the streets aimlessly, cold, lonely, hungry. Once Charlotte found him in a tavern singing and reciting to the customers in exchange for a little food and a warm place to stay. In desperation Charlotte put a large dog collar on him inscribed with the instructions, "Bring this boy to Miss Tidswell, 12 Tavistock Row."

The only thing that held the youngster's attention, the only place he called home, was the theater. His acting was well beyond his years. An actress remembers hearing a noise in the theater after the company had left for the evening, and being told: "It is only young Kean reciting Richard III in the green-room; he's acting after the manner of Garrick. Will you go see him? He is really very clever."

By the time he was eight, Kean had already appeared on the Drury Lane stage in small parts. Aunt Tid saw to it that he was considered whenever there was a child part in a play. The slim, handsome, dark-eyed boy, small for his age, with his wild head of black curly hair, was fussed over, cuddled, and hugged by the actresses. Often he would be found in the middle of a circle of actors who were listening, fascinated, as he recited the speeches from Shakespeare he had learned with Aunt Tid. England's leading tragedian, John Philip Kemble, was the stage manager then, and Kean would amuse the stagehands by mimicking the great actor's mannerisms. Once Kemble caught him at it and was not amused.

Nor was the boy any more serious about his acting. One of his first appearances was at the opening performance for the new Drury Lane after the old theater had burned down. He was seven and was cast as one of the infant goblins that suddenly scurried onto the stage in *Macbeth*, made up like winged beetles. When he had become a famous actor, he loved to tell the story of how he deliberately tripped up the other kids, causing the whole swarm of beetles to tumble about the stage "like a pack of cards." Once again, Black Jack Kemble, as Kean remembered him, was not amused. The first time Kean's name actually appeared on the playbill was when he was nine, playing Robin in Shakespeare's *The Merry Wives of Windsor*.

It's not clear how many roles he had after this, but soon life in the theater and with Aunt Tid took a sudden, dramatic turn. When he was eight or nine years old, Edmund's mother appeared. Ann Carey had come to visit him occasionally in the past, but this

time she returned to reclaim her son. Charlotte agreed, but not because she didn't love Edmund. It was, no doubt, as clear to her as to everyone else that Nance had returned not out of love for her child, but because he was of use to her. Perhaps Charlotte felt a failure for not being able to make the boy the gentleman she so much wanted him to be. Edmund was becoming more and more rebellious as she became more strict and controlling. She must have sensed that he wanted to leave, that he was happy to go with his mother, for there was apparently no scene, no defiance from Charlotte. And so Kean re-entered Nance's life, more out of spite of Charlotte than any love for his mother.

It was not a life, really—not the kind of life Aunt Tid had tried to give him. Nance Carey still lived on the streets hawking perfume or whatever, and she had really nothing to offer her son, no security or stability, not even a permanent address. But even after all of Aunt Tid's efforts, Kean still had no longing for or sense of home. The streets had always been home, the one place where there was no discipline, no punishment, no expectations that he would behave or act like a gentleman.

Nance Carey instead encouraged her son's vagabond life, sending him here and there to run errands, to carry messages, making him perform on the streets, exploiting his talent and then taking whatever money he earned. She beat him and then left him with strangers when she couldn't deal with him anymore or it suited her own roving life. With Nance there was none of the love, kindness, the careful instruction and tutoring, and the encouragement that he had had with Aunt Tid.

Edmund, his half-brother, half-sister, and his mother joined up with troupes of itinerant actors whose "theaters" were barns and stables. They performed melodramas and pantomimes, sharing the stage with dwarfs, mermaids, and educated dogs and pigs, at markets and fairs all around London. Kean rode on the back of a galloping horse, tumbled with the acrobats, and played the clown, the tricks of a strolling player.

Nance was well aware, too, of the public curiosity about prodigies; young geniuses were all the rage, and they were invited into private homes and small halls to entertain. Beginning when he was about eleven years old, Kean was dragged by his mother from home to home to recite scenes from famous plays for the hosts and their guests. His reputation grew, and he was frequently called on to give his most extraordinary performance, a recitation of the whole of Shakespeare's *The Merchant of Venice*. A London playbill announced:

The celebrated Theatrical Child, Edmund Carey, not eleven years old, will for one night only, for the benefit of his mother at the Great Room, No. 8, Store Street, Bedford Square, give his inimitable performances which have been received by the Nobility and the Gentry, with uncommon approbation. Talents so rare in so juvenile a frame was scarcely seen before. Part I. To open with an Address, Pizarro, and Blue Beard. Part II. King Richard III.

Young Kean's credits were no exaggeration; he had performed for and been applauded by royalty. It is to Nance's credit that she sought the best situations for her son, though her motive was clearly to make more money for herself. (Notice for whose "benefit" the performance was being given.) Edmund performed *Hamlet* for Lord Nelson, England's naval hero, and Lady Hamilton. Nance placed him in Richardson's traveling company, with whom he performed at Eton school and gave a command performance for King George III, a patron of the theater. And he was invited to Covent Garden, where he was presented as "the celebrated Master Carey."

Nance acted as his manager, and took all the proceeds as well. The boy was a favorite in London, charming aristocratic ladies and gentlemen with his beautiful recitations and his presence.

Even at this early age Kean was striking in his appearance, causing one member of his audience to comment that he had the blackest and most penetrating eyes he had ever beheld in a human head.

It's hard to imagine what all this tramping about, the starving, and uncertaintly must have done to young Edmund. In those days, the feelings of children were not much thought or cared about, and while we might not find it in our hearts to praise Nance, it was not the worst of childhoods she was giving her son. These were purposeful years of intense work and preparation in the school of hard knocks. Though he had no coherent training, as one might have in an acting school, he came into contact with many unrecognized but talented players. These were years of apprenticeship, tumbling, singing, riding horseback, dancing, playing the mimic, reciting, performing pantomime. One day he was the harlequin, the next Othello; the next day he played in a farce, and the next portrayed Richard III or Hamlet, learning thousands of lines by heart, mastering his craft. It was the life of an actor.

Carey was a cold, hard woman, but she did manage to give her son a chance at a life better than hers. Kean began to resent her. He was old enough now to understand that she did not love him, but only wanted to use him. He missed Aunt Tid, realizing that she was the one who really cared about him, who loved him. He returned now and then to 12 Tavistock Row to visit her, and it was at this time in his life that he began conjuring up the fantasy that she, rather than Nance, was his real mother. When he discovered that she had once had a relationship with the duke of Norfolk, the fantasy could be completed. The duke was really his father, not the insane drunkard who had just killed himself, jumping off the roof of his house in grief over the death of his brother, Moses.

Much was beginning to dawn on the adolescent actor; he was sorting out who the caring adults were in his life. He was realizing, too, that he was getting too old to be a prodigy, that the dark-eyed child who had charmed the beautiful ladies was becoming a gangling adolescent. He had been spoiled by all the adulation, but now he was insignificant.

And he was learning how important it is to be able to take care of yourself, to survive in a life which seemed to him to offer only more of the empty wandering and wretchedness he had always known. There was no turning back now. He loved the applause from the audience. He dreamed of recognition and fame, of being a great actor like Garrick. But that remained only a dream. The prodigy's fame is short-lived and no guarantee of greatness as an adult actor. The loneliest and cruelest part of his apprenticeship was yet to come.

There would be no shortcuts to fame. Going out into the country, enduring seemingly endless years of wandering from town to town with troupes of strolling players, suffering, starving, hoping—that was the school of dramatic art. At this time there were only two theaters in London—Covent Garden and Theatre Royal of Drury Lane—licensed to stage drama of the spoken word. These were the only "legitimate" theaters. All the other theaters were required by the law to limit their performances to melodrama, comedy, farce, burlesque, ballet, and pantomime. Since Kean was not employed by either of these legitimate theaters, his only chance to play the tragic roles of Shakespeare or any of the other important dramatists was to leave London, to play in the provinces. Kean was up to it. He didn't mind hard work; he loved to act, to show off his talents, to learn new roles, hundreds and hundreds of lines, seemingly without effort. And survival? He was good at surviving, living on a few shillings.

What followed were years of disappointment, horrible poverty, and failure. Kean, his wife, Mary, and their two children, Howard and Charley, traveled from town to town on foot pushing a handcart that held everything they owned. Arriving at a town, Kean would get them a room at an inn and they would perform for the few coins listeners would give them. Mary later recalled:

> My Husband took a Room and the principal Inn & gave recitations singing & and a gentleman who kept a large establishment for the Education of Young gentlemen was very kind & the gentlemen called next day with their pocket money & left it with the Land-lady addressed to Mr. Kean the sum amounting I think to eleven shillings & sixpence. There is something in the generosity of youth.

Exhausted with worry, struggling desperately with his failure, Kean took to heavy drinking. Mary wrote in a letter to a friend: "I was so ill no one expected I should ever get better—the two boys dying in measles and whooping cough, Edmund entirely ruining his health with Drink. I saw nothing but misery before me."

Occasionally Kean found work at a theater. Although he might even play Shakespeare, he was usually given only second and third parts, never the lead tragic role. It may have had less to do with his acting than his appearance. "Mr. Long [the stage manager]," Kean wrote in a letter, "kept me in the background as much as possible and frequently gave those characters which undoubtedly

Edmund Kean as a young actor in costume. HULTON DEUTSCH COLLECTION LIMITED.

were mine to fellows who certainly would have adorned the handles of a plough but were never intended for the stage; but these met with Mr. Long's approbation because they were taller than me." There is certainly some of Kean's arrogance here, and he was given to neurotic fears of plots against him, but in truth the public demanded tall tragedians—he was five foot six and three-quarters inches tall—and managers complied.

There was incredible strength in this man. He struggled to find a place on the stage wherever he could, no part being too small or too demeaning. When he could, he returned to London and showed up at Drury Lane hoping they would give him a role. Actors he had worked with in the past snubbed him and walked right past him. The small figure in his shabby, oversized coat had become a joke.

When his son Howard died, it seemed the end of him. "I with many other forlorn ones, shed the tears of Misery," Mary wrote her sister, "*no hope now— no, no resource*—cold, cold in the Earth is that jewel that was my only consolation . . . we are now at the very Climax of Misery . . . I have no one to speak of him, his father can't name him." How much more could this man endure?

After all the times he stood out in front of Drury Lane hoping for a chance to prove himself—"Let me but once set my foot before the floats and I'll let them see what I am," he had once said— those doors finally opened for him. Drury Lane was losing in its competition with Covent Garden and was facing bankruptcy. Many of the actors, including the renowned John Philip Kemble, had not been paid. Finally, after fifteen years, Kemble and his sister Fanny, one of the most brilliant actresses of the day, left Drury Lane for Covent Garden. It was the final blow. Actor after actor was brought in, but each one failed and the illustrious old theater faced having to close its doors. The owners decided to give Kean a chance. They were desperate—and, after all, what had they to lose? It was announced that Edmund Kean would appear at Drury Lane on Wednesday, January 26, as Shylock in Shakespeare's *The Merchant of Venice*. He was twenty-seven years old.

The small crowd that appeared that cold, bleak evening was curious about this Kean fellow but expecting what they were used to: the cold, formal, declamatory style of Kemble and the other renowned actors of the day. The audience and the critics had become bored with the Shakespeare offered up in this style, and some, like Coleridge and the prominent critic William Hazlitt, said they preferred to read Shakespeare rather than see him on the stage. Still,

Hazlitt frequented the theater, hopeful, and he was one of only two critics at Kean's first performance.

Unable to afford a carriage, Kean set out for Drury Lane trudging through the deep slush, carrying a bundle containing his costume and makeup things. He arrived without any acknowledgment or greeting from his fellow actors, and headed below stage to put on his costume, stopping only to get a glimpse of the audience through a hole in the curtain. The boxes, where the wealthy patrons sat, were completely empty, the pit and the gallery barely half full— "There will be nothing till half price," one of the actors lamented. Everyone seemed dejected, resigned to yet another failure, and Kean went about his business dressing, carefully putting on his makeup alone, silent and doleful. "Last Music," came the whispered call from the prompter, and the callboy went off to summon Kean, finding him already standing in the wings, quiet, composed but without any sign of emotion on his dark, expressive face. The curtain rose and the play began.

When Edmund Kean stepped out on the stage, the effect of his presence was immediate, sending a ripple of excitement through the audience. Dr. Drury, tense and expectant, told Kean later: "I could scarcely draw my breath when you came upon the stage. But directly you took your position, and leaned upon your cane, I knew that all was right." A member of the audience would remember that evening years later: "There came on a small man, with an Italian face and fatal eyes, which struck all. 'Three thousand ducats: well—,' said the small man. The fatal eyes rested on Antonio: the Italian face was live with meaning."

His first lines drew applause; already the audience sensed that this was no ordinary player. Kean's biographer, Harold Newcomb Hillebrand, describes what was so extraordinary about the acting:

> The Shylock he unfolded was seen to be new, and therefore it was interesting; but what was far more important it was seen to be alive, alive with energy, in every muscle, glance, and intonation. The arms and hands were eloquent, the whole face spoke before the words were uttered, the eyes, the marvellous black eyes which were Kean's most precious instrument, darted intelligence. As the familiar lines fell from his lips they seemed to be rediscovered, as though for the first time was revealed their true meaning.

The audience was ecstatic at the end of the performance, standing on the benches, shouting and waving. Kean left the stage, walked past the actors offering their congratulations, and hurriedly got out of his costume and into his street clothes. He rushed to his lodgings, and bursting through the door into their little rooms, he cried, "Mary, Mary, you shall ride in your carriage, and Charley shall go to Eton." In the morning they grabbed up the two newspapers who had sent reviewers. The ever hopeful Hazlitt had come and found what he had dreamed of. "Mr. Kean's appearance was the first gleam of genius breaking athwart the gloom of the Stage." He was excited about being able to see Shakespeare on the stage again. "For voice, eye, action, and expression, no actor has come out for many years at all equal to him . . . his performance was distinguished by characteristics which at once fix him in the first rank of his profession." Kean had shown himself to be not only a powerful, sensitive actor but an original interpreter of Shakespeare's characters.

Edmund Kean's rise in the theater after this first performance was, as they say, meteoric. No longer did he play to a half-empty house. Drury Lane's future was secured. A month later he appeared as Richard III to a sold-out house, and the second night crowds stormed the doors of the theater demanding seats. What they liked most about him was the natural way he portrayed his characters. He had brought Richard to life before their eyes. Some felt as though they were seeing the real Shakespeare for the first time.

Edmund Kean in his famous role as Shylock in Shakespeare's *The Merchant of Venice*. THE THEATRE MUSEUM/VICTORIA AND ALBERT MUSEUM/LONDON.

When Kean played madness, it was said, the audience was shocked into silent awe, women fainted or became hysterical and had to be carried out of the theater, and the actors were struck dumb on the stage. Among the audience now were some of the most famous people of the day, including the beloved English poet Lord Byron. "By Jove," the poet exclaimed at the end of the performance, "he is a soul! Life—nature—truth without exaggeration or diminution. Kemble's Hamlet is perfect; but Hamlet is not nature. Richard is a man; and Kean is Richard."

Time has not been kind to Edmund Kean. Kean the actor is known and revered by players, theatergoers, and historians. But Kean the man has suffered greatly at the hands of the public. Throughout his later years it seems that his private life drew more attention from the press and public than his acting, which was often mediocre.

Today, the scandals that dominated Kean's life and eventually ruined him would probably not offend us. But in his day people expected that their stage idols and public figures would keep their private lives—no matter how sordid they might be—private. Besides, we're more likely to forgive

him because we understand the role of childhood in the fashioning of the adult.

Still, Kean is considered one of the greatest actors of all time, alternating places, depending on the age and who is speaking, with David Garrick. But, in the end, history is uncaring. "In a nature like his," wrote Hillebrand,

are depths which cannot be fathomed. What gave him his demonic energy, his powers of application, his knowledge of the road he had to walk, and his confidence in his own rightness? He flashed upon the world, on the twenty-sixth of January, 1814, completely formed and astonishingly new, like a bomb thrown out of the mortar of destiny. Even the most matter-of-fact historians must be struck by the fitness . . . of his eruption. And it almost seems as though destiny, having done what needed to be done with this lump of clay into which a divine spark had been infused, forthwith tossed her implement into the scrap heap, brushed her hands, and turned to other matters.

PART III

MODERN PLAYWRIGHTS/ SHOWMAKERS

Amiri Baraka (LeRoi Jones)

1934– African-American dramatist, poet, and writer

Amiri Baraka is a man of action as well as a man of letters. Since 1961, when his first work—*Preface to a Twenty Volume Suicide Note*—was published, he has written more than twenty plays, eleven collections of poetry, and nine volumes of fiction. He has encouraged countless young people to write and has collected the writings of African Americans in several anthologies. His *Blues People* is one of the most important studies of black music in America.

Not content to just write about the black experience, Baraka has also been an activist and a spokesman for the black nationalist cause since the very beginnings of the civil rights movement of the 1960s. He has stood shoulder to shoulder with Stokely Carmichael, H. Rap Brown, Eldridge Cleaver, and Huey Newton. He helped found the Black Arts Repertory Theatre/School in Harlem, and The Spirit House Movers and Players in Newark, New Jersey. Baraka edits literary magazines devoted to African-American writers. He has been called the Malcolm X of literature.

Amiri Baraka was born Everett LeRoi Jones on October 7, 1934, in Newark, New Jersey. "Growing up was a maze of light and darkness," Baraka says in his autobiography. "I have never fully understood the purpose of childhood." He does remember a few things from his earliest days. "I was not only short, little, a runt. But skinny too. Short & Skinny. But as a laughing contrast I got these big bulbous eyes. Big eyes. And that was no secret where they came from, my old man."

Baraka's father, Coyt LeRoy Jones, was a postal worker and even though he made a fair salary, it was not enough to pay the twenty-four dollars a month rent of their "luxury" project. The family moved to another, less expensive place; in all, they lived in three places before LeRoi was six. "And we were all there. Mamma Daddy Nana Granddaddy Uncle Elaine and me. On Dey Street. The niggers were so cynical they called it *die*." Baraka was five or six when they moved to the

> orange house with a porch you sit on or crawl under. . . . Living room, dining room, kitchen, left turn, bathroom. Back door and little yard, edged by cement and a two-car garage. Second floor: narrow bedroom (Uncle), middle bedroom with big oak bed with a back tall as a man and foot post taller than a six-year-old (Nana and Granddaddy). Front bedroom (Mama & Daddy and little kids, us). . . . It seemed normal to me but maybe it wasn't. In the end there was loudness and tension—it seemed bad feeling and we went our separate ways. But it seemed normal to me. What dry types call "the extended family" and what not.

By the time Baraka was in elementary school his father was driving a mail truck delivering packages. "He'd come home winter times," Baraka remembered years later, "and stand on the grating the hot air came through from the furnace, the 'register' we called it, and stand there trying to get warm. He was almost frozen stiff. (Before I got to high school he'd got inside the P.O., and by time of college he was a supervisor.) . . . So that's where we was coming from. The church of specific reality."

It was in Newark that Jones met his wife and Baraka's mother, Anna Lois Russ. Her family was from Alabama, where they made their living in a grocery store and two funeral parlors. After their funeral parlors were burned down— it was arson, they said, "jealous crackers"—the family moved to Newark by way of Pennsylvania. Anna Lois's family was considered rich by black standards. "But see, they had sent my mother to Tuskegee (when it was a high school) and then to Fisk. I used to look at both yearbooks full of brown and yellow folks."

Baraka was born during the Depression, and World War II would be the background of his childhood. His "maximum heroes" were the heavyweight boxing champion Joe Louis and President Franklin Delano Roosevelt. Before the war, Anna Lois Jones worked in various sweatshops crammed with sewing machines, mountains of cloth, and dress patterns. But the war would change that as it would the lives of many black people. For the first time government and factory jobs were opened to them. Anna Lois, who had been to college, now had a chance for a better job. She went to work as an administrator for the Office of Dependency Benefits, the agency responsible for getting GI paychecks to their families. Baraka was too young really to understand what the war was about, but he remembered that his life changed in one important way: With his mother and father working, he and his sister were now being raised by their grandmother.

Baraka attended Central Avenue school, which was just a vacant lot and another house away. Like most little kids he was not really sure what he was doing there, only that day after day, year after year his mother got him up every morning and sent him off to school. For him "school was classes and faces and teachers. And sometimes trouble."

Baraka grew up in a world that was "mysterious, wondrous, terrible, dangerous, sweet in so many ways." Cities were different then. He explored the streets, enjoying the feeling of running, running, running. Parents and kids didn't feel threatened and scared, the city streets being an endless playground. There were pitched battles between blacks and whites but that seemed like just another adventure and, besides, it involved older kids, not him and his friends.

There was the world "out there," and there was the world of "home," which made the world out there comfortable. No matter what went on in the outside world, Baraka later realized, "the Jones/Russ orangish-brown house was one *secure* reality and the scrambling moving changing colors and smells and sounds and emotions world at my eye and fingertips was something connected but something else. I knew that many of the kids I ran with did not have the same bulk of bodies and history and words and *articulation* to deal with what kept coming up every morning when I'd rise. There was a security to my home life. That's the only way I can describe it. A security that let me know that all, finally, was well. That I'd be all right."

His was a vibrant world, an immense African-American family, all bloods. It was a time when black athletes could not play on major league teams, and so the community supported its own black teams in the Negro National League. The crowd was as much fun as the game. Newark was like a small town then, and many black people knew one another. They lived in the same neighborhoods, worked together, went to church and school together, played sandlot baseball and basketball together.

It might surprise Amiri Baraka's audiences to know that he could be so sentimental, but he loved those events. "Coming into that stadium those Sunday

Amiri Baraka in a photograph taken in 1975. UPI/BETTMANN.

afternoons carried a sweetness with it. The hot dogs and root beers! (They have never tasted that good again.) A little big-eyed boy holding his father's hand."

And he knew there was this thing called "the future." Anna Lois believed in the future. Baraka, even as a boy, was learning that one grasped opportunity and that meant black people, too.

Baraka, looking back on those days in the streets with his friends, remembers the sounds, the voices of his people. "Even the poetic line of speech that comes from my heart is theirs, so purely, the cutting edge of life description was once simple dozens." The "dozens" was a verbal duel, a bawdy insult game anthropologists call "African recrimination songs," and these were some of the earliest sounds he recalls. From these games black children acquire a way with words, a rollicking, rhythmical street poetry. It's where rap comes from and the lyrics of African-American songs. It's there in every sentence, every play, every poem and story Baraka writes. To outsiders it seems cruel and unnecessarily vicious—"Your mother wear combat boots"—but the point is not so much what is said but the ritual, the tempo and cleverness, the surprise and the rhyme of the response.

Baraka played baseball and basketball in high school as he had in elementary school. "For us, athletics was art, a high expression of culture." And sometime during high school he began writing short fiction. He was a gifted student, and when he graduated, Baraka received several scholarships. From among them he chose Rutgers University. It was from Rutgers that a brilliant black poet and actor of an earlier generation had graduated with highest honors, Paul Robeson. Baraka, however, would not graduate from Rutgers—his freshman year was his last—but not because he wasn't good enough. For the first time in his life he was made conscious of his blackness and though he had grown up in mixed neighborhoods and schools, he never fit in at Rutgers, feeling always the outsider. In his sophomore year he entered Howard University in Washington, D.C., from which he graduated in 1954.

These college experiences shaped Baraka's social consciousness and the direction of his thought and art. Although welcomed to Rutgers as other blacks had been, Baraka felt that the intent of the education there was to make him a white man, to replace the black language and culture he loved, and in which he had grown up so secure, with white language and values. He later called it "the old blackbrownyellow-white phenomenon."

The cultural isolation at Rutgers had led to a hunger for black companions, for the old talk and friendship he knew in childhood. But when he got to Howard University, he was shocked to find that the emphasis of America's most respected African-American university was not much different. At Howard, too, the intent seemed to be to shape young blacks into middle-class white people with black skins. The school seemed to him nothing more than an employment agency preparing blacks for "super-domestic service." He called Howard "the university of false blackness."

But he read, read, read—literature and philosophy, mostly—and he learned about black music, especially the history of jazz. He was aware that most of the plays, poetry, and fiction he was reading had been written by Europeans and Anglo-Saxon Americans—what he calls "white people's words." Perhaps during these years he began to think of changing that, of adding his powerful, street-beautiful black voice to the world.

There were some bright moments, though, and he did meet black intellectuals he admired. At Howard, Baraka studied with professor E. Franklin Frazier and read his book *Black Bourgeoisie*. Now Baraka understood in intellectual terms his feelings of alienation, why he was distancing himself more and more from his own middle-class black beginnings. Frazier explained that middle-class blacks directed all their anger and hostility "inward toward themselves. This results in self-hatred, which may appear from their behavior to be directed toward the Negro masses but which in reality is directed against themselves. . . . They are insulted if they are identified with Africans."

Baraka continued to read, discovering Asian thought and Zen Buddhism while serving in the Air Force. At twenty-two, he was writing poetry to fill the long hours and days of boredom. "I got rejection slips from all the quality magazines," he recalls, "the *Saturday Review*, *The New Yorker*, *Harper's*, and *The Atlantic Monthly*. They all showed the good taste to turn me down flat and very quickly." When the Air Force discovered that he was reading literary magazines like the *Partisan Review* and that he had joined an organization called the Civil Rights Congress, he was charged with being a Communist and released with an undesirable discharge.

"The desperate years" is how Baraka remembers these days, feeling more and more dejected, feeling he was going nowhere in a nowhere life, alienated from the white world and from the blacks who were all trying to be white. When he was discharged from the Air Force he was unable to find a job and, besides, he didn't want any of the jobs black people were being offered.

Instead he moved to Greenwich Village in New York, where, like many young intellectuals of the day, he was attracted to the exciting intellectual climate, the liberalism, and the acceptance of him as a black man. "I'd begun to write now. Slowly, pitifully (to me), I began to put a few words down. I'd even written a few pages of a play, a musical. I'd begun to write it not knowing what the hell I was doing."

It was 1957, and Baraka became a founding member of the "beat generation," the circle of writers and artists alienated from the racism, cynicism, materialism, and cold-war hysteria of mainstream culture. He met other writers of his generation—Allen Ginsburg, Jack Kerouac, William Burroughs, Diane DiPrima—and jazz musicians like Thelonius Monk and Ornette Coleman. And he saw more possibilities than ever before in their lives—and in his. He started literary journals, helped found the American Theatre for Poets, and, returning to the sounds he had always loved, organized jazz workshops and concerts, and became a critic for important magazines like *Down Beat*.

Baraka spent seven years in Greenwich Village. In that short time an alienated, dejected Air Force sergeant became not just a writer, but a literary figure of note. He poured out his black

Robert Hooks and Jennifer West in a scene from the 1964 production of Amiri Baraka's *Dutchman* at the Cherry Lane Theater in New York. PHOTOFEST. PHOTOGRAPH BY ALIX JEFFRY.

heart and soul in poetry—*Preface to a Twenty Volume Suicide Note* (1961) and *The Dead Lecturer* (1964). He wrote his first plays, *The Toilet* (1963), *Dutchman*, and *The Slave* (both 1964). He wrote music criticism and history—*Blues People* (1963)—and a novel, *The System of Dante's Hell* (1965). He received literary awards and fellowships and, at the age of twenty-eight, invitations to lecture at the New School of Social Research and the University of Buffalo. He was just thirty when he received one of the highest honors, a Guggenheim Fellowship. Later he would be invited to lecture on black literature at San Francisco State College and Yale University.

A change in politics accompanied those Greenwich Village years. Baraka was becoming more the rebel and radical. He left behind his allegiance to the Civil Rights movement and answered the call of the black nationalist movement— Black Power! Baraka had been invited, along with other African-American writers, to Cuba in 1960, there to witness firsthand a social revolution in the making. "I carried so much back with me that I was never the same again. The dynamic of the revolution had touched me. . . . Seeing youth not just turning on and dropping out, not just hiply cynical or cynically hip, but using their strength and energy to *change* the real world—that was too much. When I returned I was shaken more deeply than even I realized. . . . It was not enough just to write, to feel, to think, one must act! One *could* act."

And act he did. The Cuban experience convinced Baraka that African Americans could never find spiritual and cultural freedom in America. He became a black separatist and discarded his "slave" name, taking instead a name from his new Muslim faith, Amiri Baraka, Blessed Prince. Baraka returned home to Newark and formed the Black Community Development and Defense Organization, which supported nonwhite political candidates for local offices. He helped organize the Congress of African People in Atlanta, Georgia, and wrote plays—sometimes two, sometimes three a year—*The Death of Malcolm X*, *Arm Yrself or Harm Yrself*, *Police*, and a score of others, all with a renewed revolutionary urgency.

The critics argue that Baraka's recent works, those with a strong political message, have not the poetry and the art of his earlier plays and poetry. He himself recognizes the conflict in his soul between being a writer/artist and a revolutionary. And he's made his choice. But looking over his poems and plays, he would remind us as he does in *Black Magic*:

> There are mostly portraits here.
>   Portraits of life. Of life
> being lived. Black people inspire us.
>   Send life into us . . .
> We wanted to conjure with Black life to
>   recreate it for ourselves. So that the
> connection with you would be a bigger
>   self. . . .
> The artist completing the cycle
>   recreating.

P. T. Barnum

1810–1891 Producer of the Greatest Show on Earth, the American Circus

The circus is coming! The circus is coming! To generations of American children these words brought shivers of excitement and anticipation of seeing wondrous things. The circus traveled by train all over the country bringing exciting pageantry and entertainment to cities and small towns long before there was anything like television, movies, or radio, at a time when many people in America lived on farms and never got to the big city or even the nearest town. The circus was announced by beautiful posters, as colorful as the circus itself; all spangles, and bunting and flags, funny clowns, bareback riders, daring trapeze artists, and the animals.

Oh, the animals! Imagine living on a farm or in a small town somewhere in Ohio, Arkansas, or Oregon a hundred years ago. Suddenly there appears down by the station house a gaily colored circus train. As you watch, and thrill to the biggest brass band you've ever heard, the trainers open the doors of the cars and lead out elephants and giraffes from Africa, tigers and pandas from China, pumas and prancing horses, ferocious, roaring lions and huge brown bears (who can ride bicycles), monkeys, and peacocks, and camels and zebras, yippy little dogs, and a hippopotamus. Animals from all over the world are here, right in your town, to be seen and heard and, yes, even touched.

The circus is not an American invention. Like much that we consider our own, the circus began back in England and in the Old World long before the certainty of history. For centuries there had been a tradition of traveling musicians, acrobats, magicians, jugglers, and clowns wandering from village to village in wagons.

In 1793 an equestrian show that featured the spectacular rider John Bill Ricketts came from England to Philadelphia. In the audience was President George Washington, and the show was so successful that Ricketts took his circus on the road to New York, Boston, Hartford, and Charleston. President Washington must have enjoyed the performance, because when the show returned to Philadelphia, he attended again.

Here were the very beginnings of the circus in America. It was a breathtaking show, to be sure, but in the years that followed it would become even greater, bigger, and more colorful—The Greatest Show on Earth—and mostly because of the dreams, energies, and skills of the showman P. T. Barnum.

Phineas Taylor Barnum was born in Bethel, Connecticut, on July 5, 1810. Barnum's grandfather was a captain in the American Revolution and his father a tailor, farmer, and sometime tavern keeper. Phineas's boyhood was like that of most children of his day. "I drove cows from the pasture," he wrote in his autobiography, *Struggles and Triumphs or Forty Years Recollections*, "shelled corn, weeded the garden; as I grew larger, I rode [a] horse for ploughing, turned and raked hay; in due time I handled the shovel and the hoe, and when I could do so I went to school."

Barnum began attending school when he was six years old, and learned discipline from the punishing blows of a ferule, or stick.

The ferule, in those days, was the assistant school-master; but in spite of it, I was a willing and, I think, a pretty apt scholar. . . . In arithmetic I was unusually ready and accurate, and I remember, at the age of twelve years, being called out of bed one night by my teacher who had wagered with a neighbor that I could calculate the correct number of feet in a load of wood in five minutes. The dimensions given, I figured out the result in less than two minutes, to the great delight of my teacher and to the equal astonishment of his neighbor.

From the time when he was five and saved up enough pennies to exchange for a silver dollar, Barnum was in business. He earned ten cents a day riding the horse that led the ploughing ox teams, and he sold molasses candy, gingerbread cookies, and cherry rum, which he made himself. When he was twelve, Barnum was given a job as a cowboy, helping drive a neighbor's cattle to New York. Though he had no inkling of it at the time, it was on this trip that Phineas Barnum's true calling began to emerge. In New York he found a toy shop where he purchased a pop gun that would shoot a little stick some distance. He returned to his inn, the Bull's Head, and while playing with his new toy, "shot" the barkeeper, who "forthwith came from behind the counter and shook me and soundly boxed my ears, telling me to put that gun out of the way or he would put it into the fire. I sneaked to my room, put my treasure under the pillow, and went out for another visit to the toy shop."

This time Barnum bought some torpedoes, little firecrackers that explode on impact. He intended to save them to impress and entertain his friends back in Bethel.

> I could not refrain, however, from experimenting upon the guests of the hotel, which I did when they were going in to dinner. I threw two of the torpedoes against the wall of the hall through which the guests were passing, and the immediate results were as follows: two loud reports—astonished guests,—irate landlord,—discovery of the culprit, and summary punishment—for the landlord immediately floored me with a single blow with his open hand and said: "There, you little greenhorn, see if that will teach you better than to explode your infernal fire crackers in my house again."

After this adventure, Barnum went to work in his father's general store. He remembers learning a lot about business, money, and bargaining in those days, a time when he was learning to be independent and self-supporting.

That would have been an important skill for Barnum or any child of his day. A century or two ago people didn't usually live as long as they do now, and children often lost members of their family quite young. When he was fifteen Barnum lost his maternal grandmother and his father. His mother was left with debts and five children, the youngest seven. Irena Barnum managed to keep her family together, run her husband's tavern, and earn enough to pay for their house. Young Phineas had not even a pair of shoes to wear to his father's funeral and convinced a local merchant to give him a pair, trusting him until he could somehow pay for them. "I literally began in the world with nothing," he recalled, "and was barefooted at that."

Over the next few years he worked as a clerk and proved himself a shrewd businessman. At eighteen he opened his own fruit and confectionery store in Bethel and, at nineteen, married his first wife, Charity Hallett, a tailor. Barnum was proud of this first business of his own, as you might expect a young man his age to be. He described it as "an eventful era in my life. My total capital was one hundred and twenty dollars, fifty of which I had expended in filling up the store, and the remaining seventy dollars purchased my stock in trade."

Now Barnum's life took a different turn. He had become concerned about political issues surrounding him. One in particular—the intrusion, as he saw it, of religious issues into political affairs—prompted him to write letters to the local newspaper. The newspaper refused to publish his opinions and so, at twenty-one, young Barnum bought a printing press, fonts of type, everything he needed to print his own newspaper. On October 13, 1831, the first issue of *The Herald of Freedom* appeared, and the vigor of his writing and ideas soon received national attention.

Looking back when he was much older, Barnum realized that he was at the time too young, lacking the restraint and carefulness required of a journalist. Three times in three years he was prosecuted for libel, and one trial ended with his being sentenced to a fine of one hundred dollars and sixty days in the Danbury jail. Barnum was made quite comfortable in jail. His cell was papered and carpeted, and he was constantly visited by friends. He continued to edit *The Herald* from jail as the subscription list grew.

The libel trial had attracted a lot of attention to Barnum and his causes, but it seems that he and his newspaper were genuinely loved if not respected. At any rate, his release from jail after serving his sentence was certainly one of the most colorful events in Connecticut history and may have been the earliest circus parade in all America. As he walked out of jail Barnum was met by a brass band and a coach drawn by six horses. His coach was preceded by forty horsemen and followed by sixty carriages of his friends and admirers, all assembled to escort the editor home to Bethel.

For all the satisfaction and experience business had brought him, Barnum knew that this was not what he wanted to be doing. At this young age he predicted that his real purpose in life was "to cater for that insatiate want of human nature—the love of amusement. . . . I should appear before the public in the character of a showman."

Barnum claims he never did seek such a position, but that it found him. And here, as Barnum recalls, is how it later happened. In 1835 he was shown an advertisement appearing in the *Pennsylvania Inquirer* for "one of the greatest natural curiosities ever witnessed." The curiosity was Joice Heth, a black woman said to be 161 years old, who had belonged to Augustine Washington, the father of the first president of the United States. What's more, she was said to have been George Washington's childhood nurse. On display also would be, for anyone who doubted the claim, the original bill of sale of Augustine Washington, in his own handwriting, dated February 5, 1727, conveying "one negro woman, named Joice Heth, aged fifty-four years, for and in consideration of the sum of thirty-three pounds lawful money of Virginia."

> I was anxious to become proprietor of this novel exhibition [Barnum wrote] which was offered to me at one thousand dollars, though the first price demanded was three thousand. I had five hundred dollars [a tidy sum in those days!], borrowed five hundred dollars more, sold out my interest in the grocery business to my partner and began life as a showman.

Joice Heth died only a few months later, and a postmortem examination determined that she was considerably younger than was claimed. In the meantime, Barnum had made a lot of money from what was probably a fake. "I had at last found my true vocation," he wrote.

Barnum had learned from his first experience as showman the power of advertising. He realized that success with this venture required stirring up curiosity, making people talk and become excited about seeing Washington's nurse. "Accordingly, posters, transparencies, advertisements, newspaper paragraphs—all calculated to extort attention—were employed, regardless of expense." He had learned how to attract attention to a spectacle, to exploit it, and to make a lot of money from it. He had learned too that Americans were a curious lot and hungry for drama and spectacle, the more bizarre the better.

The American circus was beginning to take shape in the mind of P. T. Barnum, and he began looking for another show, another "rare spectacle," to promote next.

What Barnum found next was "Signor Antonio," an Italian who performed remarkable feats of balancing. Antonio had been performing in several cities in England, Canada, and the United States, truly exciting acts including walking on high stilts, spinning plates, and balancing. Barnum took him on, gave him the stage name Signor Vivalla, and began promoting his act to theatrical managers in New York. Acts like this were quite common and managers were not interested, but Barnum got one manager to agree to engage Vivalla for one night for free.

Using the skills he had learned promoting Joice Heth, Barnum drummed up a huge audience and the house was crammed. The manager was so delighted with the turnout and the deafening applause that followed the act that he engaged Signor Vivalla for a week and then a second week. Barnum took Signor Vivalla to Boston and then to Washington, but audiences had grown tired of such acts. Barnum soon realized that something had to be done to stimulate the public.

> And now that instinct—I think it must be—which can arouse a community and make it patronize, provided the article offered is worthy of patronage— an instinct which served me strangely in later years, astonishing the public and surprising me, came to my relief, and the help, curiously enough, appeared in the shape of an emphatic hiss from the pit!

The hiss, it turned out, came from a circus performer, a balancer and juggler named Roberts who boasted to Barnum that he could do all that Vivalla was doing on the stage—and more! Barnum came up with the idea of a challenge from Roberts, which would lead to a trial of skill before the audience. Posters and announcements in the press stirred public excitement to a feverish heat, and sales of tickets had to be called off because all the seats were quickly sold out. The crowd got its money's worth, and word of the contest spread so that the competition went on for a month of packed houses.

The year was 1836 and Barnum for the first time joined the circus, as a ticket seller for Aaron Turner's traveling show. From this experience he learned quickly that he didn't want to work for anyone else but himself. He soon left the traveling show and traveled with a show of his own, only to discover that this was not what he wanted either.

Wanting both a permanent address and more respectability, Barnum found them in his next venture. In 1841, he purchased Scudder's American Museum in New York, and on New Year's day, 1842, reopened it as Barnum's American Museum. His intent was to present wholesome, family attractions for a price within reach of working-class America—twenty-five cents for adults and half price for children.

The museum began as a collection of curiosities, but it soon became more than that, a combination of theater and entertainment—in other words, a circus. It started with a few evenings a week, then afternoons as well and Saturdays. On holidays twelve performances were given to as many audiences—talking and counting dogs, trained fleas, jugglers, ventriloquists, giants, dwarfs, rope dancers, marionettes, instrumental music, singing and dancing, the first performance of the English Punch-and-Judy show in America, mechanical figures, glassblowing demonstrations, pantomime, knitting machines and other new inventions, biblical dioramas, panoramas, American Indian ceremonies, flower

The showman P. T. Barnum. HULTON DEUTSCH COLLECTION LIMITED.

shows, dog shows, and one of his brightest stars, soprano Jenny Lind, the "Swedish Nightingale." The Greatest Show on Earth was taking shape.

Though it would be considered un-thinkably cruel today, Barnum discov-ered that displaying humans with deformities brought the crowds into the museum. He exhibited giants, but his most popular exhibit by far was a midget named Charles S. Stratton. Even Barnum was astounded.

> He was not two feet high; he weighed less than sixteen pounds, and was the smallest child I ever saw that could walk alone; but he was a perfectly formed, bright-eyed little fellow, with light hair and ruddy cheeks and he enjoyed the best of health. . . . After see-ing him and talking to him, I at once was determined to secure his services from his parents and to exhibit him in public.

Coached and trained by Barnum, Stratton emerged a few weeks later as Tom Thumb and soon became the most famous midget in history. Tom Thumb instantly became a public favorite and performed not only at the museum but in cities all over the country. It is to Barnum's credit that though he made a fortune from his museum and traveling shows, he rewarded his stars. Although Stratton was hired at seven dollars a week plus all traveling and living expenses, within a year Barnum raised his pay to twenty-five and then to fifty dollars a week—a considerable sum in those days. Whenever Tom Thumb traveled, he was always accompanied by his parents and a tutor whose expenses were paid by Barnum.

Soon the midget who had become the talk of all New York, indeed the entire country, was on his way to Europe. Barnum took Tom Thumb to England, where he dined with the likes of Baroness Rothschild, wife of the richest banker in the world. Then, one night, a disappointed crowd milled around the dark theater. On the door a placard read: CLOSED THIS EVENING, GENERAL TOM THUMB BEING AT BUCKINGHAM PALACE BY COMMAND OF HER MAJESTY.

Barnum and Tom Thumb were com-manded to return to the palace twice more and then they went on to Paris. Here they met even more acclaim.

> Statuettes of "Tom Pouce" appeared in all the windows, in plaster, Parian [porcelain], sugar and chocolate; songs were written about him and his litho-graph was seen everywhere. A fine café on one of the boulevards took the name "Tom Pouce" and displayed over the door a life-size statue of the General.

They went on to Spain, where Tom Thumb attended a bullfight with Queen

Isabella, and then to Belgium as guests of King Leopold.

Stratton and Barnum became friends, and Barnum made him an equal partner to receive half the profits. Barnum educated the boy. "I took the greatest pains to engraft upon his native talent all the instruction he was capable of receiving," he recalled in his memoirs.

> He was an apt pupil, and I provided him the best teachers. Travel and attrition with so many people in so many lands did the rest. The General left America three years before, a diffident, uncultivated little boy; he came back an educated, accomplished little man. He had seen much, and had profited much. He went abroad poor, and he came home rich.

In July 1865, the American Museum chapter in Barnum's long, colorful life ended tragically. Two fires—the first set by Confederate arsonists intent on burning New York City, and the second begun accidentally in the engine room—set the museum ablaze. But even in this, the darkest moment of his life, Barnum provided entertainment. A heroic fireman appeared in a flaming doorway with the four-hundred-pound fat lady on his shoulders. Anna Swan, the seven-foot-eleven-inch giantess who could not fit through any of the doors, was hoisted from the third floor by a derrick and swung down to the street over the heads of a wildly cheering crowd.

A Bengal tiger and several poisonous snakes escaped onto Broadway, scattering the crowd, and invaded the offices of the *News* and the *New York World*. The crowd watched a large black bear bound out of the inferno into Ann Street, make his way down to Wall Street, and climb the stairs of the Custom House, causing quite a sensation. An orangutan made it into the *New York Herald* building and the office of publisher James Gordon Bennett. Firemen flung open the cages on the upper floors and hundreds of cockatoos, parrots, condors, vultures, and eagles flew out over the city. Fortunately, most of the animals and all the visitors and performers escaped. But the American Museum was no more. In all, six hundred thousand exhibits were destroyed.

The news reached Barnum in Hartford on the floor of the Connecticut legislature, where he was serving as an elected representative. Barnum was distraught. His losses in the fire totaled $400,000; he had only $40,000 worth of fire insurance. In an instant he had lost everything and now he was poor. When he arrived at the smoldering debris that had once been his American Museum he was overcome, and for the first time in his life he talked of quitting.

It was not P. T. Barnum's nature to consider quitting very long. The people of New York rallied to his support and his old friend Tom Thumb—now touring on his own—offered to do benefit performances to get him back on his feet again. But Barnum would do it on his own. Another friend, newspaperman Horace Greeley, predicted what would happen after the destruction of the museum. "We mourn its loss," he wrote in a *New York Tribune* editorial,

> but not as without consolation. Barnum's museum is gone, but Barnum himself, happily, did not share the fate of his rattlesnakes. There are fishes in the seas and beasts in the forests; birds still fly in the air and strange creatures roam in the deserts; giants and pigmies still wander up and down the earth; the oldest man, the fattest woman, and the smallest baby are still living; and Barnum will find them.

Barnum did not disappoint his old friend and the thousands upon thousands of Americans who expected to be "amused, instructed, and astonished" by the great showman. Determined once again to return to show business, Barnum accepted the offer from his miniature friend to work together again. Then he signed up the nine-year-old actress Cordelia Howard, who was making a hit as Little Eva in a stage production of Harriet Beecher Stowe's *Uncle Tom's Cabin*, and took the play to London. Barnum was his old self again and he was thriving. He signed up an albino family in Holland and took Tom Thumb on a tour of Scotland and Wales. Barnum lectured before a hundred audiences totaling an estimated 1.3 million people. In 1868, the veteran entertainer of millions returned to New York to open a new museum.

Now in his late fifties, P. T. Barnum embarked on another adventure. He had joined up with James C. Adams, known all over the West as "Grizzly" Adams. Adams had collected a menagerie of animals, most of which had never been seen in New York and the East. His collection was impressive even by Barnum's standards—twenty huge grizzly bears, six other species of bears, wolves, mountain lions, buffalo, elk, and a sea lion named Old Neptune. Many of the animals Adams had trapped himself in the Sierra Nevada and trained at considerable risk.

Barnum set up a huge canvas tent in a vacant lot on the corner of Broadway and Thirteenth Street. After his usual storm of publicity, he treated New Yorkers to what may have been the largest and, perhaps, the very first circus parade in America. It began with a blaring marching band stepping smartly down Broadway. Coming up behind the big bass drums, on a horse-drawn wagon, was the gnarled, weather-worn old hunter "Grizzly" Adams in his buckskin shirt and pants trimmed with animal tails, astride General Frémont, considered the most ferocious and unpredictable of all his bears. A long line of wagons followed, each with a cage and a roaring, pacing animal. As the parade made its way through the streets, it drew a huge, curious crowd, which was led right to the tent. Barnum was at it again.

Although he's thought of primarily as a circus man, Barnum did not actually produce his first circus until 1871. That was the year he joined Cameron Coup, a sideshow manager, and Dan Castello, a clown, to form the biggest outdoor circus of all time. Barnum's biographer, Irving Wallace, wrote that Barnum did not invent the circus; "he gave the circus its size, its most memorable attractions, and its widest popularity." Imagine the awe of those who attended the opening of the circus that day in Brooklyn. "At the outset the exhibition was truly a mammoth one . . . absolutely colossal, exhaustive, and bewilderingly various . . . requiring the services of 1,000 men and 300 horses."

The circus began with the most spectacular parade anyone in those days had ever seen. It was pure P. T. Barnum. Once again he had lived up to

An advertisement for Barnum's museum.
THE BETTMANN ARCHIVE.

his motto: "Get the best regardless of the expense."

"My canvas covered about three acres of ground," Barnum recalled, "and would hold nearly ten thousand people, yet from the start in Brooklyn, and throughout the entire summer tour, it was of daily occurrence that from one thousand to three thousand people were turned away." Factories had to close because too many of their workers had just taken the day off to go to the circus. "My aim was to combine in the several shows more startling and entirely novel wonders of creation than were ever before seen in one collection anywhere in the world."

And he had done that. Crowds thrilled to a daring aeronaut who ascended high into the sky above the big top, fire eaters, and sword swallowers. They sat tense on the edges of their seats, eyes fixed on the tightrope walkers and gymnasts defying death high above the sawdust ring. They gaped at the three-legged man, the bearded woman, Siamese twins (who hated each other), living skeletons, and four "Fiji cannibals." There was the only giraffe anywhere in America, forty camels, several elephants eating peanuts, a mermaid, seals and sea lions, some weighing a thousand pounds and brought all the way from San Francisco on the Union Pacific Railroad.

Barnum had found in Italy a goat taught to ride a horse bareback, leap through hoops and over banners and land on his feet on the back of the horse galloping full speed; a unicorn (which was actually a rhinoceros), a woolly horse, and the first hippopotamus ever seen on this continent. To this would be added perhaps the most famous and loved elephant of all times—Jumbo. He was thought to be the largest or, at least, the second largest pachyderm in the world, standing twelve feet tall at the shoulders and weighing six and a half tons. Every day Jumbo ate two hundred pounds of hay, fifteen loaves of bread, and various fruits and vegetables, and drank five pails of water and a quart of whiskey. But "the first living curiosity that one meets at the Rink," noted one reporter, "is Barnum himself—uncaged."

The name P. T. Barnum has become synonymous with circus. He gave us the Big Top, the colorful parades, the circus train, three rings, and what became known as The Greatest Show on Earth. But what made Barnum happiest was knowing that he had entertained us. "A popular Eastern poet," he wrote in the last pages of his autobiography, "has said the noblest art a human being can acquire is the power of giving happiness to others. I sincerely hope this is true, for my highest ambition during the last thirty years has been to make the public happy."

Bertolt Brecht

1898–1956 German expressionist playwright and poet

The plays of Bertolt Brecht are seldom performed in America, perhaps once or twice in a decade. You might go your entire lifetime without ever seeing a Brecht play. That would be unfortunate, for to see a performance of *Mother Courage*, or *The Caucasian Chalk Circle*, *Threepenny Opera*, or *Galileo* is a theater experience unlike any other you could imagine. Brecht might frustrate you or even make you angry, but he would force you to see the stage, the actors, and the characters in ways you'd never seen them before.

He insists not that you identify with the characters, to feel what they feel, but that you stand apart from them, to watch them and judge them. He asks that you not sit back and be entertained but that you think and work hard at understanding your attitudes, especially what you think about war, man's inhumanity, oppression, social injustice, and the evils of modern city life. These are not the usual concerns of theater. But then, Brecht is not your usual playwright.

Eugen Bertolt Friedrich Brecht was born in Augsburg, in the south of Germany, on February 10, 1898. Augsburg had once been one of the centers of European trade, but by the time Brecht was born it was a sleepy, provincial town set in the countryside, surrounded by small farms. "Past my father's house," Brecht remembered, "there ran an avenue of chestnut trees along the old city moat; on the other side there lay the city wall with the remnants of ancient fortifications. Swans swam in the water that was like a pond." Brecht loved autumn best, when "the chestnuts shed their yellow leaves" and covered the walkways and streets. He began writing poems very young, and many of them reveal his love of nature and life in the country, swimming, and hiking, like this one, "Of Climbing in Trees":

> The little stiff leaves of the undergrowth
> Are sure to graze your backs, which
>   you must squeeze
> Firmly between the branches; thus
>   you'll climb
> Groaning a little, higher in the trees.
> It is quite fine to rock upon the tree

We know less of the intimacies of Brecht's life than those of other dramatists, who left autobiographies and diaries. He hated anything sentimental and always had his eyes on the future rather than the past. He very deliberately left his middle-class childhood behind him, explaining in a poem:

> I grew up as the son
> Of well-to-do people. My parents
> Put a collar round my neck and taught
>   me
> The habit of being waited on
> And the art of giving orders. But
> When I had grown up and looked
>   around me
> I did not like the people of my own class
>
> .   .   .
>
> And I left my own class and joined
> The common people. . . .

Brecht grew up in a comfortable home with a father who was the director of a paper mill and a mother who was the daughter of a civil servant. There were two boys in the family, a younger brother who early on became interested in the paper business and later became a professor of paper manufacture at a technical university. The father was Catholic and the mother Protestant, an unusual marriage at a time when people tended to marry within their own religion. Brecht was raised Protestant and grew up with the language of Martin Luther's Bible. Some recognize the influence of Luther's German on Brecht's poetry and the language of his stories. Whether he was "Bertolt" or "Bert" depended on his changing moods; he signed his work Bertolt, but liked to be called and was known to his friends as Bert.

While it is not entirely accurate to look to a writer's poems, stories, and plays for clues to his life, some of Brecht's most personal feelings, those not spoken in public, reside in his writings. His revolt against his parents' life, for instance, is sometimes attributed to his father's mother. When she was seventy-two, his grandmother was widowed and suddenly began to discard the staid conventions and gentility of her long life, even attending the cinema, which no elderly woman would do then. She was obviously important to the young writer, because later Brecht wrote about her, "Mrs. B," in a short story, "The Unseemly Old Lady":

> She was a little thin woman with lively lizard's eyes, though slow of speech. . . . She frequented a cobbler's workshop in a poor and even slightly notorious alley where, especially in the afternoon, all manner of not particularly reputable characters hung about: out-of-work waitresses and itinerant craftsmen. The cobbler was a middle-aged man who knocked about the world without it leading to anything. It was also said he drank. In any case, he was no proper associate for my grandmother.

She began eating at the inn every other day and regularly hired an elegant horse-drawn carriage for outings, and even began to travel by train alone!

The young Brecht is recalled by friends as a sensitive, quiet child, rebellious in subtle ways. He found little to interest him in school: "Elementary school bored me for four years," he later wrote to an old school friend. "During my nine years at the Augsburg Realgymnasium [grammar school] I did not succeed in imparting any worthwhile education to my teachers. My sense of leisure and independence was tirelessly fostered by them." Already there are the beginnings of Brechtian humor and irony.

When Brecht was sixteen, Europe erupted in what became World War I. It turned into a horrible conflict, the first modern war, fought not with gallant officers charging, sabers held high, but machine guns, tanks, deadly artillery, submarines, and airplanes dropping bombs on soldiers dying by the millions in the trenches below. Brecht wrote essays for class opposing the war and was threatened with expulsion. One of his teachers saved him by convincing the school officials that the boy was so sensitive and artistic that the death and destruction of the war had driven him temporarily mad.

It was at this time, too, that Brecht began contributing poems and book reviews to a local newspaper. He was remembered by the newspaperman who helped him get started by publishing his work as "a shy, reserved young man, only able to speak after the clockwork inside him had been wound up."

At eighteen Brecht left the Gymnasium and moved to nearby Munich, where he enrolled in the university to study medicine and science. The war continued—it would not end until 1918—and Brecht was drafted into the army to serve as a medical orderly in a military hospital. The horror of the military hospital caused Brecht to write one of the first poems to use the coarse, vulgar style meant to shock the reader out of any sense that war was all about gallantry and bravery. "The Legend of the Dead Soldier" tells the story of a man killed in the war whose body is dug up so that he can fight for Germany still again. In another poem, "Legend of the Unknown Soldier Beneath the Triumphal Arch," he wrote:

1

We came from the mountains and from
    the seven seas
To kill him.
We caught him with snares, which
    reached
From Moscow to the city of Marseilles.
We placed cannon to reach him
At every point to which he might run
If he saw us.

2

We gathered together for four years
Abandoned our work and stood
In the collapsing cities, calling to each
    other
In many languages, from the mountains
    to the seven seas
Telling where he was.
Then in the fourth year we killed him.

If Brecht seems obsessed with death and war, killing and starvation, with only the dark side of life, we should ask, how could anyone experience the horrors he did and not be affected? To see human beings maimed and blasted to pieces, to actually do the gruesome work of amputation and battlefield surgery has to have

left lasting traces on his character and his work. No wonder, then, that Brecht became so fanatical a pacifist, so angry and outraged that he had to lash out against those who were responsible for the horror, pain, and misery.

Understanding the mind of Bertolt Brecht requires us to try to understand the time into which he was born and grew up, the time in which his personality and beliefs were being shaped, the time in which he was learning his craft as a writer and dramatist. Brecht's generation experienced one of the most chaotic times in all history. It was a period of widespread political, economic, and social upheaval. His life spanned two world wars and massive revolutions that brought an end to the old order in Austria, Germany, Russia, and much of Europe. He was caught up in a devastating worldwide economic depression, the emergence of mass Communist and Fascist movements, the rise of the Third Reich, and the death of millions gassed and burned in concentration camps. After World War II, Germany was divided into East and West. Africa, Asia, and the Middle East erupted in revolution and terrorism. It seemed that any day the planet would be destroyed in a storm of nuclear warheads.

Brecht's world was a world on fire. It was impossible for a man so sensitive to social injustice, so opposed to war and violence, to ignore it all somehow and write happy plays for entertainment.

Brecht had to speak out against the inhumanity that engulfed the world, against the sacrifices of human beings to the gods of war, against poverty and hunger that go ignored while the world's resources are squandered on weapons of mass destruction. Nor could he ignore the millions of workers who toiled long hours for low wages and lived in the slums of the world's great cities. If the theater were to have a role in making audiences aware of the suffering in the world, if there was any hope that through the theater the world might change, then Brecht would devise a revolutionary kind of theater.

After World War I, Brecht drifted back into the chaos that was Germany, back to Munich and his medical studies. But the world had changed and it was impossible to just pick up the pieces and put life back together as it had been. He was less interested in medicine now, and sometime during the last year of the war, he began writing plays. Disillusioned by the false idealism and sentimentality of prewar German writers, Brecht set out to make his own voice heard. He made a wager with a friend that he could write a play in four days. He did, *Baal*, which was probably his first. Then, realizing that this play would never be performed in the German theater as it was then, he wrote another, which he titled *Spartakus*, and later renamed *Drums in the Night*.

Brecht's writing was still unknown except to his friends, with whom he spent long evenings in smoke-filled taverns and cafés discussing literature, poetry, and theater. For money, Brecht would make up melodies for his poems and sing the "Ballad of Baal" and "The Legend of the Dead Soldier" in his high-pitched voice while accompanying himself on the guitar or banjo. Here he met other writers and friends, like Peter Suhrkamp, who would later become his publisher, and the novelist and playwright Lion Feuchtwanger. Feuchtwanger remembers the first time he encountered Brecht, singing his ballads in a rural tavern.

Of course, this fellow was always unshaven. But the way he made his hair grow over his forehead had a kind of naïve coquetishness. He smelt like soldiers on the march. . . . There was an unmistakable odour of revolution about him. Clearly it was his way of singing crude ballads that did it.

It was now 1919. Brecht was writing as the theater critic for an Augsburg newspaper and at the same time writing *Drums in the Night*. The manager of the Munich Kammerspiele theater was so impressed with Brecht's new work

Bertolt Brecht as a young playwright. THE BETTMANN ARCHIVE.

that he decided to produce it, and invited the author to become the theater's resident playwright and play adapter. In addition, Brecht would be the literary adviser to the manager and editor of the theater program.

More and more, Brecht was becoming recognized as a brilliant young dramatist and included in the Berlin literary scene. The German playwright Arnolt Bronnen recalls in his memoirs what happened one evening at a gathering of literary friends:

> From one of the rooms I could hear guitar music. . . . I went in. It was rather dark there; at first I could only hear a croaking voice. . . . Then I saw the singer: an emaciated young man of twenty-four with steel-rimmed glasses and untidy dark hair that fell over his forehead. I stared at him. I was as if under a spell. I experienced a sensation which perhaps is only given to very lonely human beings: to be suddenly confronted with man in all richness of his being. He sang, he spoke, he read aloud, there were four other young people in the room; I did not see them. I only stared at this one young man. Later Otto Zarek told me that his name was Bert Brecht.

The world premiere of *Drums in the Night* was a tremendous success. An influential critic for a Berlin newspaper was there and wrote enthusiastically about a play unlike any other German theater audiences had ever seen. "The twenty-four-year-old poet Bert Brecht," Herbert Ihering wrote, "has changed the literary physiognomy of Germany overnight. With Bert Brecht a new tone, a new melody, a new vision has entered our time."

Germany's renowned theater director Max Reinhardt was also in that first-night audience, but this was not the first time he had seen the play. So fascinated was he by Brecht's new vision of the theater that he had attended the rehearsals every day for three weeks.

What Brecht asked of his audience was that they look at the set, the characters, and the action with an entirely new perspective. Even the atmosphere of the theater itself was changed. To understand this difference, let's imagine what it is like to be in the audience of a conventional play. The lights in the auditorium dim, the footlights come up, and the curtains open to reveal a "real" place—a room in a house, a street corner, the battlement of a castle. In the stage room are tables and chairs, rugs, doors and windows, pictures on the walls, everything that we expect to find in a real room. The actors appear made up and costumed in the style of the period of the play. The actors move about, talk to each other, behaving naturally toward each other in a way—if skillfully acted—that lets us pretend that what is happening on the stage is real. Time passes, hours, days, weeks, and years go by, all compressed in a few hours, but convincingly. The spectators are drawn into the action. We are moved by the actors, amused, disgusted, angered, shocked, frightened, even brought to tears. All the time, the actors appear unaware that we are even there, and we feel as if we're peeping through an imaginary wall into someone's living room.

But the feeling is very different at a Brecht play. As we get comfortable in our seats, we notice that the curtains are open and everything—the side lighting, flats, platforms, down lights, scaffolding, props, flies, projectors, and screens, all the stage machinery—is in plain view behind the simplest suggestion of a set. As you await the beginning of the play, you notice the actors mingling with the audience, chatting with the musicians, sitting on the edge of the stage talking with one another or donning their costumes.

Suddenly, a loud, brassy band, which includes strange instruments such as automobile bumpers or coil springs played with hammers, will begin a jarring, discordant tune. All the actors converge on the stage from wherever they happen to be at the moment and sing the opening song. When the song ends, an actor announces the scene, and the others switch into acting the first episode of the play. Sometimes the actors talk with one another, but often an actor will turn to the audience and address us directly, demanding that we judge what is happening or make a decision. The way the actors talk is almost as though they are cartoon characters. The scenes do not necessarily flow one into another, but instead, are separate events, each complete in itself.

Brecht's intent was to do away with the old theater of illusion. Instead of being brought into the action, we are placed in front of it, we are distanced from it, watching, observing always apart from it. It's as though we are hearing an exciting, animated lecture rather than watching a play. Rather than feeling what the character feels, we are told what he feels. Rather than surprise us or fill us with suspense, the playwright tells us the outcome or the end of the story in advance. The effect is the exact opposite of what most playwrights wish to have happen.

In the years following his first successful productions, Brecht wrote poems, short stories, and plays with astounding energy. He was in his late twenties, a recognized playwright, and still he found time for self-education. Perhaps most important to him of anything he read during this period was Karl Marx's *Das Kapital*, from which Brecht was learning about Communism. Marx spoke to Brecht's disdain for the middle and upper classes and his commitment to the cause of the workers. He married the brilliant actress Helene Weigel, who played lead roles in many of his plays. And he began to work with the young composer Kurt Weill, who would provide musical scores for Brecht's plays, probably the most famous of which was *The Threepenny Opera*.

The plight of the workers became the main theme of Brecht's plays. The American Depression, which began in 1929, affected the economies of countries all over the world. By 1930, millions of Germans were unemployed and Brecht walked the long lines of hungry workers at the Salvation Army soup kitchens all over Berlin. He was reading the works of the American writers Upton Sinclair and Lincoln Steffens, who wrote about the terrible conditions of the poor and the working class. In one of his most famous plays, *Saint Joan of the Stock Yards*, set in Chicago, there is a chorus of workers who speak for workers all over the world demanding a living wage:

We are seventy thousand workers in
   Lennox's packing plant and we
Cannot live a day longer on such low
   wages.
Yesterday our pay was slashed again
And today the notice is up once more:
ANYONE NOT SATISFIED
WITH OUR WAGES CAN GO.

.   .   .

But now
By twelve hours' work a man can't
   even
Earn a stale loaf and
The cheapest pair of pants. Now
A man might just as well go off and
Die like a beast.

In 1933, Adolf Hitler came to power in Germany, and within a few days storm troopers were rounding up Communists and intellectuals. The books of many of Germany's greatest writers were burned in huge bonfires, and Brecht's plays were among them. He knew now it was no longer safe to remain in his homeland. The name "Bertolt Brecht" was number five on a Nazi list of people to be arrested—and liquidated.

Brecht, his Jewish wife, and his little son, Stefan, left Berlin for Vienna. So quickly did they have to depart, that there was not time to get their younger child, Barbara, who was visiting Brecht's father in Augsburg. Later, Barbara was smuggled out of Germany to her parents in Switzerland and then accompanied them to Denmark.

Now thirty-three, known as an innovator and experimenter in the German theater, Brecht was forced to go into exile, out into a world in which he was barely known. *The Threepenny Opera* had been performed in the larger cities

A scene from a German production of *Mother Courage*. PHOTOFEST.

of Europe and in an English translation in New York, but his language, the language of his poems and his plays, was German, and it seemed that there was no place for him now. They fled Denmark for Sweden and then on to Finland. But Finland, now a declared ally of Germany, was no longer safe, and the exiled family traveled east, across all of the Soviet Union to the port of Vladivostok, where they sailed, safe at last, to America, where he joined other anti-Nazi writers, artists, and musicians in exile in California. He wrote:

> The exile moves stiffly through cities of woe,
> Learns a language he never had wished to know.
> His rapid heartbeat
> Fills the foreign street.

In America, in the 1940s, Brecht was able to write and find theaters that would produce his plays, but he never felt welcome in his new land. In the anti-Communist frenzy of the postwar years, Brecht was called up before the House Un-American Activities Committee and accused of being a Communist. He survived the hearings, even triumphed. "When they accused me of wanting to steal the Empire State Building," he told a friend in Paris, "I thought it was high time for me to leave."

The year 1948 found Brecht back in Berlin, where he had been invited to produce *Mother Courage*. Eventually, he would settle in East Berlin, where he would become the artistic adviser of the Berliner Ensemble. Helene Weigel was appointed the theater's director. Brecht's dreams had come true, a theater of his own with a company of sixty actors and almost two hundred design-ers, producers, playwrights, musicians, lighting technicians, scene painters, set designers, and mechanics.

In these later years he became interested in Asian theater, the Japanese Noh play, kabuki, and Chinese drama. He read the works of Confucius and Buddha and finally found, his friends said, an inner peace.

"Bertolt Brecht," Eric Bentley has written, "was nothing if not the creator of a new theater." Were he alive today, he would enjoy the honor, and like the dying heroine of *Saint Joan*, simply say:

Make it not your goal
That in the hour of death,
You yourself be better.
Let it be your goal
That in the hour of death
You leave a bettered world.

Oscar Hammerstein II

1895–1960 American songwriter and creator of musical plays

"He *was* a giant," wrote lyricist Stephen Sondheim.

> He changed the texture of the American musical theater forever, first with [Jerome] Kern, then with [Richard] Rodgers. And to change that means not only to change musical theater all over the world, but to change all American theater as well, because musical theater has affected playwriting profoundly and permanently. . . . To be alive at the same time as Oscar Hammerstein II was an enormous privilege. He sang for all of us.

Any one of Hammerstein's musicals would have been an accomplishment, but he wrote so many—*Show Boat, Desert Song, Oklahoma, Carmen Jones, The King and I, The Sound of Music,* *South Pacific, Carousel,* to name just a few—and so many hit songs that it is hard to imagine American life without him.

Oscar Greeley Clendenning Hammerstein was born on July 12, 1895, in New York City. His mother, Alice Nimmo, was of Scotch descent, her father and mother having emigrated from Glasgow to New Orleans. Allie, as she was known, was an important figure in her sons' lives; Oscar had a younger brother, Reginald. Although she was in every way a proper Victorian lady, she was also very modern in other ways. Allie was active in women's movements of the day, including women's suffrage and family planning. She loved the theater and attended a matinee at least once a week. Though only one portrait of her—a painting—remains, it is clear that she was a beautiful woman. Young Oscar loved her. "I did not fear her," he recalled later, "but somehow I couldn't have borne the thought of displeasing her. I adored her with all my heart."

Oscar grew up in the same house with his grandparents. Grandma Nimmo took him out into the city for walks every day. His grandfather, James, loved to paint and sketch, and included his grandson in his daily routines. Oscar never forgot his snow-white, wavy hair and kind blue eyes. Every morning began with James mixing up a punch of milk, whiskey, and egg, which he shared with Oscar to start the day off right. Then they'd go off to a local park with drawing paper and pencils where James and Oscar would sketch together. On the way they'd stop at the neighborhood candy store so that Oscar could get a handful of sourballs to have for the day. Each evening, just before bedtime, James and Oscar would share a bottle of Guinness stout.

His other grandfather, Oscar Hammerstein I, was quite different. Actually, Oscar didn't like him very much. He was a distant, imposing figure, elegantly dressed in his dark coat with wide lapels, striped black-and-white trousers, and top hat. He sported a carefully trimmed and combed goatee and seemed never without a cigar. He was a fiercely independent man. From an early age he had been a serious music student, his childhood days spent at the conservatory and practicing violin and piano. One day, when he was fourteen, he stayed late ice skating, so late that he missed his afternoon Hebrew classes at the synagogue. When he returned home, his father, infuriated with his disobedience, tore a strap from the boy's skates and beat him brutally, leaving a deep gash in his forehead. That very night, when he was sure his parents were asleep, Oscar sneaked out of the house and took his violin to a local pawnbroker. He got thirty-five dollars for his fiddle. He spent thirty dollars for a ticket on a cattle boat that would take him to New York, and with only a few dollars and the clothes on his back, he was on his way to America.

Grandfather Hammerstein had become a famous man by the time Oscar knew him, beginning with his invention of a cigar-making machine that he patented and sold for a small fortune. This money allowed him to realize his dream of acquiring an opera house, and later he built several opera houses in New York City. But his grandson cared little for Hammerstein's fame and notoriety and would rather have had him be a simple, loving man like his grandfather James.

Oscar wrote in an introduction to a biography of his illustrious ancestor:

As a child I was not proud but ashamed of having so colorful a relative. It seemed that he was always getting into the papers. He would write insulting letters to prominent men and they would be printed in the papers. He would write love letters to women and they would be printed in the papers. What was the matter with him? Why couldn't he be like the grandfathers of my schoolmates—nice, quiet, respectable old men? I couldn't see why he wasn't a pain in the neck to everyone, as he was to me.

Perhaps it was because of this grandfather and his father's consuming involvement in the theater that Oscar never thought of following in their footsteps. Willie, Oscar's father, didn't love the theater. He hated going to the theater and disapproved of his wife's going. It was a job, the only way he knew how to make a living for his family. And it was his whole life. All Oscar really remembers of his father—he never punished or scolded him—was his good-bye kiss in the morning and his hello kiss in the evening. Willie Hammerstein understood his feelings toward his son, though he never talked to Oscar about them. He loved the boy. But growing up as he did with an impersonal, busy, absent father and a mother who had

died when he was four, he knew little of love and affection.

Oscar began his schooling at P.S. 9. He was a good boy and a good student, always getting excellent marks on his report card. Later, when he was a famous man, his friends noticed that he had hung up in his office some of his "A Good Boy" report cards in a frame. He liked to write and got good marks in spelling. Most of all, he loved to read and regularly read two books a day. His one worry seems to have been his height. He was short for his age and remembers how seriously he took Grandma Nimmo's warning that he must lie very straight in his bed every night so that he would grow tall.

Although he never thought of himself in the entertainment business, Oscar looked forward to the day when his mother might take him along to the theater. He was curious about the Victoria Theater, where his father worked, but Willie said no most emphatically whenever his son asked to be taken there. The theater, in those days, was still considered low life, not the proper profession for a middle-class child. Willie knew the theater and actors all too well, and because of that thought the less of it.

But one day, when Oscar was about seven, his father relented and the brothers were taken to a Saturday afternoon matinee to see a new comic opera, *The*

Fish Maiden. Oscar was enthralled by the lights, the gorgeous curtains and glittering interior, the music and dancing. Willie could no longer resist his sons' excitement, and so Oscar and Reginald became frequent patrons of Saturday performances at playhouses all over New York.

When he was eight, tragedy struck in young Oscar's peaceful life. Grandma Nimmo became ill. Oscar was terrified by his grandmother's sudden silence, what the adults referred to in whispered voices as a coma, and the coming and going of oxygen tanks in her darkened room. Once his mother took him and his brother by the hand and quietly led them to their grandma's bedside. Oscar was too young to understand why Grandma Nimmo couldn't talk to him, why she didn't take him out for walks anymore. Many nights, alone in the dark and in bed, he cried for her.

Grandma Nimmo's death would bring some changes to Oscar's life. The family would have to move—it was unthinkable to stay in an apartment where a member of the family had died. But the family as Oscar knew it would be broken up. He and his brother, their mother and father, would move to a new apartment in a nicer neighborhood. But Grandpa Nimmo and his sister, who the boys called Aunt Mousie, would move elsewhere.

The new apartment reflected the family's growing income. It was now possible for nine-year-old Oscar to begin piano lessons, which he loved, and he soon learned to read music and play for his own fun. He had also reached an age when his father, now resigned to his son's obsession with the theater, allowed Oscar to see evening performances. The boy thrilled to the singing and dancing, the minstrels, and other vaudeville acts.

Oscar at thirteen was no longer concerned about his shortness. He was now a lanky six feet one and a half inches; Grandma Nimmo's advice, it seems, had worked. Oscar found a new love, basketball, and played often with his friends from the new private school he was attending, the Hamilton Institute.

In his fifteenth year Oscar would learn yet another lesson about death. At thirty-five, Allie lay seriously ill from an infection, but surely, Oscar believed, she couldn't die and leave him. When she died he consciously steeled himself against the shock of death and the grieving of all those around him. Fifty years later, when he faced his own death from stomach cancer, he confided in a friend how he had decided that day, back in 1910, that there would be no more tears. He went out to the store, bought a scrapbook, and, returning to his room, busied himself pasting up pictures of famous athletes.

> Then I went for long walks and thought it all over, and began to adjust myself. All by myself. I never felt like going to anybody for help. And while I don't quite understand this, I know this is what happened. I also know it crystallized an attitude toward death I have had ever since. I never feel shaken by death. . . . I received the shock and took it, and sort of resisted, as an enemy, the grief that comes after death, rather than giving way to it. I get stubborn and say this is not going to lick me, because it didn't then.

Oscar entered Columbia University at seventeen, intending to become a lawyer. It was what he had promised his father. In a rare moment of intimacy between the two, Willie finally came out with what he had wanted to say for a long time: "Ockie, you must promise me you will never do anything so foolish as to consider making the theater your livelihood. Become a lawyer. You'd be great at it and it's also one of the more secure professions I know of." So Oscar was getting good grades as he had always done in school, played first base on the baseball team, and looked ahead to law school.

Two years later Willie Hammerstein died suddenly. Oscar was surprised by the *New York Times* headline the next day: HAMMERSTEIN, THE BARNUM OF VAUDEVILLE, DEAD AT FORTY. The theater world was stunned and, perhaps for the first time, Oscar realized how well loved and respected was his father. At nineteen Oscar had lost both his parents. Death was becoming an old friend.

It was happening without his realizing it. Oscar had joined the Columbia University Players Club after trying out and being given a comedy part, the poet Clarence Montegue, in the musical *On Your Way*. Although it was a student production, the near-professional quality of the productions and acting at Columbia attracted the attention of New York critics. The critic from the *Evening World* liked the young man's first attempts at acting:

> Oscar Hammerstein II, the consumptive looking poet, was fun without trying to be. Maybe he wasn't intended to be funny but he was light as a feather on his head and feet. He danced like Al Jolson and had some original steps and faces of his own. Oscar is a comedian, and as a fun-maker he was a la carte, meaning all to the mustard.

Oscar was still committed to law school, but more in honor of his father's memory than anything else. His heart was really with the Players. He was pleasantly surprised one day when his faculty adviser, the noted historian and writer Carl Van Doren, asked what he intended to do after graduation. Oscar replied, probably without much enthusiasm, that he was applying to law school. Van Doren looked disappointed. "Oh . . . well . . . I thought you were going to be a writer." It was as if Van Doren had been reading his deepest, most personal thoughts, and it was the very first time he had received any encouragement in this direction. "This is precisely what I was dying to hear somebody say. I left his office in Hamilton Hall and floated down Morningside Heights."

The autumn of his senior year found Hammerstein in law school. He even went to work for a law firm, hoping this would somehow spark his enthusiasm, but what he quickly discovered was that he had no interest or aptitude whatsoever for practicing law. What really mattered that fall was his part in the 1916 varsity show *The Peace Pirates*. Hammerstein wrote several routines and played the comedy roles. It was in this production, too, that he would first meet other students who would become lifelong friends. The musical was written by Herman J. Mankiewicz, who would someday be an Academy Award–winning screenwriter. Hammerstein played with Larry Hart, and one day, a fourteen-year-old admirer, Richard Rodgers, appeared backstage to meet the talented Oscar. Later in life,

Hammerstein would collaborate with both men on musicals, and *Rodgers and Hammerstein* would be spoken in American households as if one word. Before his first year of law school had ended, Hammerstein was asked to write next year's show.

The varsity show of 1917 made clear to everyone once and for all that Oscar Hammerstein II belonged in show business. OSCAR HAMMERSTEIN, 2D, COMEDIAN IN COLUMBIA SHOW, "HOME, JAMES!" proclaimed the *New York Herald* headline. "His performance," wrote their critic, "would have done credit to the best of the Broadway comedians, and shamed not a few." Later, when he was a successful writer, Hammerstein looked back on these first attempts with dismay. "About my own scamy side past. I intend to quote some of my early efforts," he wrote in his book, *Lyrics*, "the main motive being to reassure young writers. Knowing how bad I was at one time, I hope that they will be encouraged."

The year 1917 was an important one in Hammerstein's life. He met his future wife, Myra Finn, a cousin of his now close friend, Richard Rodgers. He tried to enlist in the army—America had entered World War I—but was turned down because he was too thin and underweight. He realized, finally, that he would never be satisfied with law and that what

Richard Rodgers *(second from left)* and Oscar Hammerstein, shown with their wives, attended the movie premiere in 1955 of their hit musical *Oklahoma*. UPI/BETTMANN NEWSPHOTOS.

he really wanted more than anything else in life was to be in the theater.

He decided to go see his uncle Arthur, who was managing his grandfather's opera houses. Arthur had just had a box office success with his production of Victor Herbert's *Naughty Marietta*, and was soon to have another hit with a new work, *The Firefly*, by Rudolf Friml, a brilliant young composer who had emigrated from Czechoslovakia. Oscar

told his uncle that he wanted to learn theater from the bottom up and that he wanted to become a playwright. Arthur reminded his nephew of the promise he had made to his father never to seek a livelihood in the theater. "It's in my blood," Oscar insisted, "and, furthermore, I need the money now that I'm getting married."

"But how can I face the memory of your father?" Arthur answered. Still,

Oscar was adamant. What a loss, he argued, if a Hammerstein, the third generation of Hammersteins in the theater, were not at least given a chance.

Uncle Arthur gave in, though still burdened with having betrayed his dead brother's wishes. He hired Oscar as an assistant stage manager for twenty dollars a week to work on the Broadway hit musical *You're in Love*. Oscar rolled up his sleeves and eagerly went to work setting up the stage, hauling props from one scene to the next, moving scenery, handling lights—learning everything there was to know about stage production. It wasn't long before Arthur realized just how talented his nephew was, and so he hired Oscar on permanently as production stage manager for a new upcoming show, comedian Ed Wynn's *Sometime* with music by Friml.

Oscar went on to do five more Broadway productions. During rehearsal, he stood by in the wings with the playbook, "listening to the authors and actors, and drinking in as much as I could at close range. I was an office boy and playreader by day, stage manager by night, and an eager kibbitzer at the rehearsals of the new shows." By 1919 Oscar had been made general stage manager of his uncle's shows and was responsible for supervising all of the road company's performances. Unknown to his uncle he had also been writing his own lyrics and librettos. And he was once asked to write a last-minute addition to a musical being rushed into production. "Boy, does that stink!" he said years later when looking over these hastily written, amateurish lyrics.

Now that even Uncle Arthur was on his side, Oscar thought about what he wanted to do in the theater. The famous stage and, later, movie actress Mae West had told him one day backstage, "Listen, get out of this crazy business and go back to your law career. The theater ain't for you, kid. You got too much class!" But there was no possibility of that now; the theater was in his blood.

But did he want to act? No; that was fun, all right, but that wasn't it. And being a stage manager just wasn't enough either. What he really wanted to do was write. It was Uncle Arthur who gave him his first real chance. He had read a story that touched him and suggested to his nephew that he might try making it into a play, if he liked. "Liked!" Oscar recalled later. "I would have liked the telephone book if it would get me a production."

The Light—Oscar later always referred to it as "The light that failed"—closed after only seven performances. Although Oscar Hammerstein I made one of his rare appearances in public to attend the dress rehearsal of his grandson's play, and had assured the young writer that he had written a good play, the production was a disaster. Under the headline THE LIGHT IS NOT DESTINED TO SHINE VERY BRILLIANTLY: CRUDE PRODUCTION OF A MODERN DRAMA BY OSCAR HAMMERSTEIN, 2D, FAILS TO INTEREST the play was pronounced deadly dull and absurd.

But Hammerstein didn't have to await the next day's newspapers to know what had happened.

> When I went into the Saturday matinee, I knew I had a big flop. There must have been twenty people in the Schubert theatre that day. When the ingenue came on, one of her lines was, "Everything is falling down around me . . ." and at that precise moment her petticoat started falling down. I didn't wait for the yell that followed. I just ran out of the theatre, went into the park, and sat on a bench. While I was sitting there, an idea came to me for a new show. So I started writing it.

Hammerstein was already demonstrating one of the most important qualities of any creative person: resilience. "I am never discouraged," he once remarked. "I don't believe in discouragement. When I had a failure, I refused to be cast down."

Just two months later, Oscar saw his grandfather for the last time. They could not talk or share in last sentiments; the old man lay dying in a coma. Oscar recalled walking out of the hospital and being surprised most of all that he had absolutely no feelings toward his grandfather, no resentful memories, no sense of being free of him, no feelings of grief. His grandfather had died and somehow, strangely, it didn't matter.

As he read the editorials, tributes, and obituaries, he realized he was coming to know Oscar I for the first time. He realized, too, that he missed him and wanted to know more about him. He sought out the old man's friends just to hear their often fond and sometimes bitter reminiscences of his grandfather. It was time to find the real Oscar Hammerstein I and maybe, then, better understand himself.

> Perhaps for the first time it seemed safe to try. He couldn't hurt me now. He couldn't humiliate me. The fears and resentments of this remote "old man," developed in my childhood, were no longer a block to our union. It is ironic and sad and strange that I did not begin to understand or like my grandfather until the day of his death. But he was a strange man and so, perhaps, am I.

In 1923, when he was twenty-eight years old, Hammerstein had his first hit show, *Wildflower*. Musicals were becoming popular entertainment in the early twenties. Americans were both weary from years of horrible war and optimistic or, at least, guardedly hopeful, that permanent peace was at hand. They wanted to be entertained, to hear lilting songs and be made to laugh. They wanted more and more musical comedies. The "musical" had not yet assumed any kind of form or style. It had grown out of early vaudeville and was a hodge-podge of songs and dances, slapstick comedy, farce, parody, pretty girls, juggling acts, melodrama, operetta, what have you. The story was of little importance, serving only as the slightest excuse for a string of songs and dances—a bit of story, a song and dance, a bit of story, a song, a bit of story—that's the way it went.

But Hammerstein had a different vision of the musical, just beginning to take shape in his first hits. His biographer, Hugh Fordin, describes what was happening:

> As Oscar practiced his craft in the early years, he stayed in touch, as he always would, with popular taste and interest. But even as he mastered the existing structure of the musical, a determination grew in him to bring the elements together in a relationship that would make songs an integral part of the story and make both express something more real and more expressive of human life and emotion. This determination, shown only haltingly and infrequently at first, would eventually change the structure of the American musical.

Jan Clayton and John Raitt *(center)* starred in the original production of *Carousel*. PHOTOFEST. PHOTOGRAPH BY RICHARD TUCKER—GRAPHIC HOUSE.

Hammerstein finally succeeded with the story that all Americans seem to take to their hearts, *Oklahoma!* "Plots are generally a nuisance in musical comedies," a critic wrote, "but the narrative line in *Oklahoma!* is arresting and even dramatic." Hammerstein and his old school buddy Richard Rodgers, now a team, received the Pulitzer prize for *Oklahoma!*

The teams of Hammerstein and Jerome Kern and Rodgers and Hammerstein had produced musicals filled with songs

Yul Brynner and Gertrude Lawrence dance in the popular Rodgers and Hammerstein musical *The King and I*. PHOTOFEST. PHOTO-GRAPH BY VANDAMM.

that Americans sang and listened to on phonograph records. There was *Desert Song* (1926) and *Show Boat* (1926), which threatened to run forever.

Uncle Arthur had kept up with all of his nephew's shows and after seeing *Show Boat* told a friend: "Tonight I've seen the perfect show. My decision to take Oscar into show business has been justified. Tonight I knew I did right by Willie after all, even though I broke my word. I'm a happy man."

Oklahoma! was followed in the same year by *Carmen Jones* (1943), a modernized version of Bizet's *Carmen*, with an all-black cast. Here, Hammerstein always believed, he was at his best ever, crafting his most beautiful lyrics. The critics were delighted with his transposition of a story from Spain a century before to contemporary United States.

Generations of Americans grew up with the hits that followed in theaters all over the country, among them a non-musical play, *I Remember Mama* (1944), *Carousel* (1945), *South Pacific* (1949), *The King and I* (1951), *Flower Drum Song* (1958), and *The Sound of Music* (1959), his last. In his last weeks, when he was very ill and knew he was dying, he gave Mary Martin, the star of *South Pacific*, the sketch of a new verse torn from one of his worksheets. He placed it in her hand, saying, "Don't look at it now. Look at it later."

A song is no song
Till you sing it
A bell is no bell
Till you ring it
And love in your heart
Isn't put there to stay
Love isn't love
Till you give it away.

Lorraine Hansberry

1930–1965 African-American playwright, poet, and writer

When Lorraine Hansberry's *A Raisin in the Sun* opened in New York on March 11, 1959, the play became a landmark in American theater. It would be the first of many firsts. It was the first play written by an African-American woman ever to be produced on Broadway. It was the first appearance of the young black actor Sidney Poitier. A month after the play's opening, Hansberry became the first black playwright and the youngest ever—she was twenty-nine years old—to win the Drama Critics Circle Award for The Best Play of the Year. She was named by a *Variety* poll as the "most promising playwright of the season." Critics and black audiences alike considered it the first time the life and concerns of African Americans had been portrayed realistically and thoughtfully on the stage.

Lorraine Vivian Hansberry was born in Chicago, Illinois, on May 19, 1930, the youngest of four children. Her mother was a teacher and a leader in Chicago's Southside black community. Nannie Perry Hansberry was born in Tennessee to parents who had been born into slavery. Lorraine remembers, as a little girl, driving south to visit her mother's birthplace. As they drove, Nannie would relate the story of her parents, "how her father had run away and hidden from his master in those very hills when he was a little boy. She said that his mother had wandered among the wooded slopes in the moonlight and left food for him in secret places."

Sidney Poitier *(left)* and Claudia McNeil *(second from left)* starred in the 1959 production of *A Raisin in the Sun.* PHOTOFEST.

Her father, Carl Hansberry, was a prosperous real estate broker who also founded one of the first banks in Chicago that would serve blacks. He was active in the NAACP Urban League and ran for Congress. In her autobiography Hansberry remembers her father as a bright and commanding presence in her life,

a man who always seemed to be doing something brilliant and/or unusual. . . .

He digested the laws of the State of Illinois and put them into little booklets. He invented complicated little pumps and railroad devices. He could talk at length on American history and private enterprise (to which he utterly subscribed). And he carried his head in such a way that I was certain that there was nothing he was afraid of.

Carl and Nannie created a comfortable, nurturing home for their children.

But Lorraine remembers something more than just physical comfort:

> We were also vaguely taught certain vague absolutes: that we were better than no one but infinitely superior to everyone; that we were the products of the proudest and most mistreated of the races of man; that there was something enormously difficult about life; that one *succeeded* as a matter of course. Life was not a struggle—it was something that one *did*. And whatever you did, you did it well.

Hansberry grew up with the belief that "the only sinful people in the world were dull people." Her home was a center of African-American cultural and political thought, and Lorraine grew up overhearing and taking part in discussions about all the important issues facing her people in the thirties and forties. There was her uncle, William Leo Hansberry, a distinguished professor at Howard University, and one of the world's foremost scholars on ancient Africa. Among his students were Nnamdi Azikewe, the first president of Nigeria; Kwame Nkrumah, the prime minister of Ghana; and others who would become leaders of newly emerging African countries.

Other frequent visitors included many of the most distinguished African Americans of the day: Walter White, writer and NAACP secretary; the actor and singer Paul Robeson; jazz great Duke Ellington; world heavyweight boxing champion Joe Louis; and Jesse Owens, who broke world records in track at the 1936 Olympics.

With all this, Hansberry recalls also a childhood filled with horseplay, giggles, laughter, and fun. As the youngest child, whose brothers and sisters were seven to twelve years older, she learned to play alone.

> My childhood Southside summers were the ordinary city kind, full of the street games. . . . I remember skinny little Southside bodies by the fives and tens of us panting the delicious hours away:
> "May I?"
> And the voice of authority: "Yes you may—you may take one giant step."
> One drew in all one's breath and tightened one's fist and pulled the small body against the heavens, stretching, straining all the muscles in the legs to make— one giant step. Evenings were spent mainly on the back porches where screen doors slammed in the darkness with those really very special summertime sounds.

The honesty that would color all of Hansberry's writings came out of her childhood experiences in Chicago, a sharply segregated and divided city. She wrote:

All travelers to my city should ride the elevated trains that race along the back ways of Chicago. The lives you can look into!

I think you could find the tempo of my people on their back porches. The honesty of their living is there in the shabbiness. Scrubbed porches that sag and look their danger. Dirty gray wood steps. And always a line of white and pink clothes scrubbed so well, waving in the dirty wind of the city.

My people are poor. And they are tired. And they are determined to live.

Our Southside is a place apart: each piece of our living is a protest.

But Lorraine did not grow up in shabbiness. In fact, her father's wealth—but only in comparison to his neighbors'—was a constant embarrassment to her and, worse, it separated her from her people. Because Nannie dressed her daughter well—she believed as many of her generation did that one must always dress to make a good impression—Lorraine suffered the taunts and slaps of the poorer children. "My mother sent me to kindergarten in white fur in the middle of the depression; the kids beat me up; and I think it was from that moment I became—a rebel."

Little did they realize how much the little "rich" girl envied them, envied their independence, that they went places by themselves, had learned adult things on the streets, envied the symbol of their independence—"Children who, above all, had their own door keys: gleaming yellow metal, hung proudly, in her eyes, on a string around the neck!" Lorraine took to wearing any key, a skate key, a lost key she found on the street, just to be like them. Of course, the key didn't make her like them and the other kids knew it too.

Although he could afford private schools for his children, Carl Hansberry chose to send them to public schools, what Lorraine would call "Jim Crow schools." Betsy Ross Elementary was a ghetto school, a school designed for children who didn't matter. The school was so crowded that she went only half days.

I was given, during the grade school years, one-half the amount of education prescribed by the Board of Education of my city. This was so because the children of the Chicago ghetto were jammed into a segregated school system. I am a product of that system and one result is that—to this day—I cannot count properly. . . . This is what is meant when we speak of scars, the marks that the ghettoized child carries through life. To be imprisoned in the ghetto is to be forgotten—or deliberately cheated of one's birthright—at best.

The very home and parents that gave Lorraine so much comfort was also a place of constant danger. To be black and political in America was then—as it always has been—dangerous. In 1938, when Lorraine was just eight years old, Carl Hansberry deliberately moved his family into a restricted neighborhood. It was a time when the "better" neighborhoods of Chicago were posted with signs warning that Negroes and Jews were not allowed. Hansberry's intent was to test real estate covenants—clauses in sales and rental agreements—that barred certain races or religions or ethnic groups from buying a house or renting an apartment. Hansberry, using up most of his savings, pursued his lawsuit and his appeals through the Illinois courts, but lost. Then, in 1940, Hansberry, with the help of an NAACP legal team, won a landmark decision in the U.S. Supreme Court, which ruled that restrictive covenants were unconstitutional (*Hansberry v. Lee*). Despite the ruling, covenants continued in practice up into the 1960s, and the Hansberry family was evicted from their home.

While they lived in the disputed house, the family endured hellish hostility from white neighbors and howling mobs that surrounded them day and night. Bricks, rocks, and chunks of concrete smashed through all the windows and into every room as Nannie bravely shielded her children inside. Lorraine was almost killed by a brick.

"My memories of this 'correct' way of fighting white supremacy in America," Lorraine later wrote in a letter in defense of civil disobedience (1964), "include being spat at, cursed and pummeled in the daily trek to and from school. And I also remember my desperate and courageous mother, patrolling our house all night with a loaded German luger [pistol], doggedly guarding her four children, while my father fought the respectable part of the battle in the Washington Court."

Though she was behind in her math, Lorraine was way ahead in her reading. She was already writing, keeping extensive journals, and, in the Englewood High School yearbook, expressing her ambition "to be a journalist." These were years of turmoil, of riots and warfare between students of segregated and white schools. As she watched the confrontations, she gained respect for black students who were not taking it any longer but fighting back—*They had fought back!*—and that she would never forget. Still, from her father and mother she had learned that her way was not to fight, but to excel, to win by being the best you could be and, in that way, raise up yourself and your people.

Hansberry was elected president of the debating society and she read and read—Shakespeare, especially her favorites: *The Tempest*, *Othello*, and

Hamlet. "Rollicking times, Shakespeare has given me," she wrote in her notebooks. "I love to laugh and his humor is that of everyday; of every man's foible at no man's expense. Language. At 13 a difficult and alien tedium, those Elizabethan cadences; but soon a balm, a thrilling source of contact with life." Hansberry was falling under the spell of "theater magic," as she called it. "I was intrigued by the theatre. Mine was the same old story—sort of hanging around little acting groups, and developing the feeling that the theatre embraces everything I like all at one time."

The excitement of high school would be tempered by the tragedy of her father's death. Distraught from the long court battles, Carl Hansberry had become emotionally and physically ill. He had lost faith in America. After the trauma he and his family suffered at the hands of the mob, no longer could he tell himself or his children that this was a land of opportunity no matter what your color, nor could he envision a future for his children that would be much better.

During Lorraine's sophomore year in high school, he went to Mexico, intent on relocating his family there to escape and save them from the violence of racism. It was there that he died. "Daddy felt he still didn't have his freedom in this country." Later, reflecting on his leaving, she realized why, in spite of all she suffered, she would not leave: "One of the reasons I feel so free is that I feel I belong to a world majority, and a very assertive one."

After graduating from high school, Hansberry attended the University of Wisconsin, studying art, literature, drama, and stage design. Sometime during her childhood, perhaps because of her uncle, she had developed an interest in Africa, searching through magazines and books for any photographs she could find. She looked into Zulu, Kikuyu, and Masai faces and recognized herself in them. She embraced Africa as her homeland and in college read everything about Africa she could find— Jomo Kenyatta's *Facing Mt. Kenya*, Basil Davidson's *Lost Cities of Africa*, and W. E. B. Du Bois's *Black Folk Then and Now*. She took a seminar on African history with Professor Du Bois and later used much that she learned to give historical accuracy and background to her plays about African Americans. Africa and the black struggle for liberation became the theme for *Les Blancs* (1964), making Hansberry one of the first Americans to envision and describe African independence movements. Her husband, Robert Nemiroff, recalls: "In 1951 Lorraine Hansberry was a young woman on fire with black liberation not only here but in Africa."

It was while she was at Wisconsin that Hansberry first attended performances of plays by Ibsen and Strindberg. But the play that would have the most powerful and lasting influence over her was *Juno and the Paycock*. The setting was Ireland, but Hansberry realized for the first time that there isn't just one setting for injustice and pain.

> I remember rather clearly that my coming had been an accident. Also that I sat close to the stage. . . . The woman's voice, the howl, the shriek of misery fitted to a wail of poetry that consumed all my senses and all my awareness of human pain, endurance and the futility of it. . . . The wail rose and hummed through the tenement, through Dublin, through Ireland itself and then mingled with seas and became something born of the Irish wail that was all of us. I remember sitting there stunned with a melody that I thought might have been sung in a different meter. The play was *Juno*, the writer Sean O'Casey—but the melody was one that I had known for a very long time.
>
> I was seventeen and I did not think then of *writing* the melody as *I* knew it—in a different key; but I believe it entered my consciousness and stayed there.

Hansberry stayed at Wisconsin only two years. She was bright and intensely intellectual, but despite all she had absorbed from her parents, she was beginning to have doubts about being only an intellectual. Another side of her—the take action, do something, speak out, make a difference part of her—was beginning to emerge. There was a moment in college when it happened, during a talk by one of the most prominent and visionary architects of the century.

> I shall never forget when Frank Lloyd Wright came and spoke at the University. . . . He attacked almost everything—and, foremost among them . . . the nature of education saying that we put in so many fine plums and get out so many fine prunes. Everyone laughed—the faculty nervously I guess; but the students cheered. . . . I left the University shortly after to pursue an education of another kind.

Later, in her play *Les Blancs*, one of the characters expresses what must have been going through her mind in college:

> . . . one day, sitting on a bench in Hyde Park—watching the pigeons, naturally—it came to me as it must to all men: I won't come this way again. Enough time will pass and it will be over for me on this little planet! And so I'd better do the things I mean to do.

Though writing had intruded on her thoughts, Hansberry continued to pursue her interest in art, studying painting in Mexico and then, in New York City, jewelry making and photography. She also took a course in short story writing at the New School for Social Research and began working at *Freedom*, a black magazine published by Paul Robeson. While on the staff of *Freedom* she wrote articles about child labor, African independence movements, and the stereotyped roles still being given blacks on TV. She moved to Harlem and became active in peace and freedom movements. Hansberry marched on picket lines and spoke on street corners about black social, economic, and political liberation.

During what she later called these "erratic" times, she worked on and off as a clerk in a department store, waitress, hostess, typist, a cashier in a restaurant, and as an aide to a theatrical producer, and began work on three plays. She attended an International Peace Conference in Montevideo, Uruguay, representing Paul Robeson, who was denied a passport by the State Department; and she traveled throughout South America. She married Robert Nemiroff, a New York University student and aspiring writer who would soon write a hit song and become her partner in her new life as playwright.

That chapter began one evening in 1957 when, at a party at their house,

Hansberry read an unfinished play she was working on to her husband, his collaborator on a hit song, and another friend, a music publisher. The friends were so impressed with *A Raisin in the Sun* that they decided they would raise the money and produce the play. Sidney Poitier was given the lead role, and the director was to be Lloyd Richards, a talented young black actor.

The night before the opening in New Haven, Hansberry sat in her hotel room reflecting on the hard work that had gone into her first play and wrote home:

> Mama, it is a play that tells the truth about people. Negroes and life and I think it will help a lot of people to understand how we are just as complicated as they are—and just as mixed up—but above all, that we have among our miserable and downtrodden ranks—people who are the very essence of human dignity. That is what, after all the laughter and tears, the play is supposed to say. I hope it will make you very proud.

Hansberry had learned that telling the truth is what good, meaningful art is all about. Later, while working on *A Raisin in the Sun*, she acknowledged her debt to O'Casey and the dawning that came that evening in the University of Wisconsin theater.

I love Sean O'Casey. This, to me, is the playwright of the twentieth century accepting and using the most obvious instruments of Shakespeare, which is the human personality in its totality. O'Casey never fools you about the Irish, you see . . . the Irish drunkard, the Irish braggart, the Irish liar . . . and the genuine heroism which must naturally emerge when you tell the truth about people. This, to me, is the height of artistic perception and is the most rewarding kind of thing that can happen in drama, because when you believe people so completely—because *everybody* has their drunkards and their braggarts and their cowards, you know—then you also believe them in their moments of heroic assertion: you don't doubt them.

Lorraine Hansberry around the time *A Raisin in the Sun* was produced. SPRINGER/ BETTMANN FILM ARCHIVE.

A Raisin in the Sun became an instant success in New Haven and Philadelphia, and then went on to Chicago before opening at the Ethel Barrymore Theatre in New York. The critics realized the talent that had suddenly appeared in their midst. The *New York Times* critic Brooks Atkinson, one of the most influential in the whole country, admired Hansberry's pluck for taking on serious issues without making it boring. "She has told the inner as well as the outer truth about a Negro family in Chicago," he wrote. "The play has vigor as well as veracity and is likely to destroy the complacency of anyone who sees it." The critic of the *New York Herald Tribune* called it "an impressive first play, beautifully acted . . . [with] relieving and wonderfully caustic comedy."

It must have been most satisfying to the young playwright to have audiences and critics get the point. "The thing I tried to show," Hansberry explained in an interview, "was the many gradations in even one Negro family, the clash of the old and new, but most of all the unbelievable courage of the Negro people." She told how she had taken the title of the play from a poem,

"Harlem," by the African-American writer Langston Hughes:

> What happens to a dream deferred?
> Does it dry up
> Like a raisin in the sun?
> Or fester like a sore—
> And then run?
> Does it stink like rotten meat?
> Or crust and sugar over—
> Like a syrupy sweet?
> Maybe it just sags
> Like a heavy load.
> *Or does it explode?*

The whole world, not just Americans, took this play to their hearts. *A Raisin in the Sun* would eventually be translated into more than thirty languages and appear on the stages of as many countries, including Czechoslovakia, East Germany, England, France, Kenya, Mongolia, the Soviet Union, China, and Japan. It was made into a film (1961) and, after Hansberry's death, a Tony Award–winning musical. The play brought a flood of letters, including one: "I'm a white native Georgian and I thought it was a wonderful play—and most informative from a Negro's viewpoint." Hansberry had begun to do the things she meant to do.

More than those of any other dramatist, Hansberry's plays began changing the way we looked at oppressed people. Before *A Raisin in the Sun* there had been plays like *Uncle Tom's Cabin* and, one Hansberry particularly deplored, *Porgy and Bess*, both written, she admitted, with good intentions. But "we've had great wounds from good intentions. Even the most sympathetic novel for the Negro . . . happens to have been built around the most offensive character in American literature—who is Uncle Tom. That doesn't mean we Negroes don't understand Harriet Beecher Stowe's motives."

Lorraine Hansberry died of cancer at thirty-four. Yet she accomplished more than others have in lives twice as long—five plays, more than sixty magazine and newspaper articles, speeches, and poems. Her words accompany the hundreds of photographs in *The Movement*, a powerful photographic documentary of the Civil Rights movement. Always the activist as well as an artist, she spoke at civil rights rallies, schools, and universities, and she marched in demonstrations.

Even after her death, Hansberry spoke out, in a biographical play, *To Be Young, Gifted and Black* (1967–68), adapted from her writings by Robert Nemiroff and performed on radio and hundreds of college campuses and communities all over America. When, toward the end of her life, she was asked why many black writers are so young, she answered: "Maybe because we have so much to say, we start earlier."

Sean O'Casey

1880–1964 Irish playwright

He was born John Casey in working-class Dublin, Ireland, the youngest of a large brood of children, thirteen in all. Eight had died in infancy, "for at that time," O'Casey wrote later, "the death-rate in Dublin was as high as in the plague-spots of Asia." His father, Michael Casey, a clerk, died when John was only six, and the family began a life of poverty in dreary Dublin tenements. From this beginning emerged Ireland's most important modern dramatist. "A proud rebel," one of his biographers describes him, "with a mighty rage for life who in the midst of tragic surroundings made himself a great comic artist." His language added a glorious new chapter to our tradition, and his plays opened a new chapter in the history of the theater.

O'Casey tells us something about the tenements in which he lived, not in his autobiography, but in his plays. He would write not about the famous, but about the poor, proud lives of working-class people like himself. Here he sets the scene for Act I of the play that made him a playwright, *Juno and the Paycock.* It will do fine as the setting for the first act of O'Casey's life:

The living room of a two-room tenancy occupied by the Boyle family in a tenement house in Dublin. Left, a door leading to another part of the house; left of door a window looking into the street; at back a dresser; farther to the right at back, a window looking into the back of the house. . . . Farther to the right is a small bed partly concealed by cretonne hangings strung on a twine. To the right is the fireplace. . . . Beside the fireplace is a box containing coal. On the mantleshelf is an alarm clock lying on its face. In a corner near the window looking into the back is a galvanized bath. A table and some chairs. On the table are breakfast things for one. A teapot is on the hob and a frying-pan stands inside the fender. There are a few books on the dresser and on the table. Leaning against the dresser is a long-handled shovel—the kind invariably used by labourers when turning concrete or mixing mortar.

Michael Casey had no money to leave his son, but the boy did inherit his father's love of reading and learning. O'Casey recalled:

> A little feared by all who knew him, having a sometime gentle, sometime fierce habit of criticism; and famed by all as one who spat out his thoughts into the middle of a body's face. A scholar he was to all, who was for ever poring over deep books, with a fine knowledge of Latin, and a keen desire that others should love learning for its own sake, as he did.

O'Casey became a lifelong student like his father, and remarked to someone when he was well over eighty, "I am a student still."

Susan Archer Casey was a strong woman who kept her family together no matter how dreadful life became for them. "Susan, ragged dame of dames," O'Casey later wrote of her, "so quietly, so desperately courageous. Life couldn't get rid of her till she died. She went on going forward to the end, ignoring every jar, every misfortune, looking ahead as if she saw a great hope in the distance."

Like his father before him, O'Casey would not get much schooling. Most working-class children got some formal schooling in those times, leaving school usually at fourteen to go to work. But at the age of five John had gotten a terrible eye disease that persisted the rest of his life.

Years and years of treatment followed. The boy would not be blind, the doctors assured his parents, but getting well would be a long process.

The time came when Johnny could lift the bandages and look at the blue sky without any pain. He could see! In his autobiography O'Casey described the elation of Johnny Casside, his fictional self. He spent hours just looking, taking joy at the world around him. The colors, such wonderful colors, doorsteps painted bright red or blue, the baker's carts, one green, the other a reddish brown, pulled by trotting horses, and the milk carts with polished brass spouts. A band came down the street wearing blue uniforms braided with red and green, and the brass bugles sparkled in the sun.

John was enrolled in the Infants' Class (kindergarten) and was taught by his sister Bella. Throughout his few years of school, old friends remembered, his attendance was poor and often he came to school with his eyes bandaged. He was teased constantly by his classmates, who often played cruel tricks on him, but he played games with them as best he could and eventually won their respect.

Although he had more schooling than he later admitted to, his eyesight was so poor that O'Casey remembers getting through school without learning to read. You can imagine the twinkle in his eyes when he tells of passing all three of his annual examinations in reading with honors! It seems that he had a prodigious memory. His mother and sister would read to him long passages from the Bible and school primers at home and then, at the end of the term, when he was examined at school by the inspector, he could recite everything he had heard by rote, all the time moving his eyes across the page, pretending he was actually reading.

Like most working-class children of the day, O'Casey left school and went to work. For much of his life—O'Casey did not become a playwright until his mid-forties—he worked as a laborer, first as a stockboy and then, briefly, delivering newspapers. He worked for nine years

for the Great Northern Railway carrying tools and mixing mortar as a bricklayer's assistant, twelve hours a day, six days a week. From this experience came O'Casey's lifelong connection with working men and women and his commitment to their cause. These were the people he would always consider "his people," his friends, and, even as a famous dramatist, his class. Their dreams, toil, suffering, and simple pleasures became the subject of his plays.

His identification with the people of Ireland made O'Casey a political activist as well. In his early twenties he joined and worked for the Irish Transport and General Workers' Union founded by James Larkin, a labor leader who inspired Irish workers to unite and fight their deplorable working and living conditions. O'Casey's first published writings appeared in the labor periodicals. He became active as well in the Irish Republican Brotherhood, committed to ending England's centuries-old control of Ireland, and became the secretary of the Irish Citizens' Army when it was founded in 1913. As a youth O'Casey had worked as one of the "faceless volunteers" delivering the magazine *Irish Freedom*. He learned to speak, read, and write Gaelic, the language of ancient Ireland, and taught it in a slum school run by the Gaelic League. He learned to play the Celtic bagpipes and help found the St. Lawrence O'Toole Pipes Band. And he rid his name of all traces of the English oppressor, becoming Sean O'Cathasaigh.

Despite his poor sight and troublesome eyeglasses, O'Casey read and read and read. From his meager salary as a stockboy and as a laborer, he managed to set aside a little money to buy books from the bookstalls he frequented around Dublin. He recalled the excitement of seeing a book he wanted and hoping it would still be there by the time he had saved enough money to buy it.

For weeks he'd watched the lovely book in its blue and gilt binding in the little bookcase at the back of the open-air bookstall at Hanna's shop; for ever fearing that by the time he got the money the book would be gone. Every evening, going home from work, he'd gone out of his way to make sure the book was still there. It was there yesterday, and it was bound to be there today.

As a youngster just learning to read, O'Casey liked to read the Bible, not because he was religious, but because he like the stories and the old language. And he read Shakespeare. Oh, how he loved the excitement of those early times, reading again and again his Globe Edition of Shakespeare until the old book was falling to bits.

As an adult, his eyes continued to trouble him and he had horrible pain. Still, he read and collected books hungrily. Among his favorites were Charles Dickens, Sir Walter Scott, Balzac, and Victor Hugo. He read Dumas's and Sheridan's plays, and the Americans James Fenimore Cooper and Jack London. He bought beautifully bound volumes of Byron, Shelley, Keats, and Tennyson, and a very special book, *Milton's Works*—"a blind man seeing more than a man with many eyes." All were lined up, looking grand, on the top shelf of his old dresser.

O'Casey was, as he says, "touched by the theater" when he was about ten years old. That's when he began accompanying his older brother, Archie, to his rehearsals at a local amateur theatrical company. Later, he and Archie founded the Townshend Dramatic Society. They had rented an unused stable, taken out all the stalls, whitewashed the walls, and made a stage at one end and a few benches from old timbers found up in a loft. Old secondhand lanterns fitted with cardboard shades served as footlights. A tattered red cloth was made into a curtain which could be raised up and lowered and lovely sets were fashioned from old cloth thrown away by the Queen's Theatre. The brothers drew an audience of forty or fifty who each paid about two cents to get in.

They were, together, an entire theater

company. Archie played the Duke of Gloucester to Johnny's Henry IV. After a quick costume change, they returned as Brutus and Mark Antony in *Julius Caesar*, then back behind the curtain again to return as Cromwell and Cardinal Wolsey in scenes from *King Henry the Eighth*. Archie in his red gown and floppy cardinal's hat and Johnny in dark blue tights, yellow buskins, and green silk cape. The audience sat in stony silence throughout the whole evening with nary a hiss nor a cheer, except for Johnny and Archie's friends, who cheered loudly and shouted out to the actors.

Johnny began to live theater. He was on or down in front of the stage whenever he wasn't at work. Archie played small parts in Irish plays at the Mechanics' Theatre in Abbey Street and gave his little brother free passes. The boy would sit in the very first bench down in the pit watching Charlie Sullivan and Tommie Talton, two of Ireland's very best actors of the time. When he wasn't in a theater he dreamed of plays and the stage, and of someday becoming a professional actor. Little did he realize, as he sat entranced one day with Sullivan's acting in the Irish play *Arrah na Pogue*, that he was very soon to get his chance. A messenger appeared at his side and shook him to attention, handing him a note marked *Urgent*.

The note was from Tommie Talton. What could it be? Johnny wondered. Perhaps they wanted him to put up some bills advertising *The Shaughraun* playing at the Mechanics' Theatre, and he could earn a few pennies. He ran to the actor's fine house and stood before the door all too aware of his threadbare clothes and run-down, scuffed boots. He reached for the heavy brass knocker and tapped ever so quietly.

A small woman came to the door, expecting the youngster and happy to see him. She took him into a room filled with beautiful furniture, blue vases, and everywhere cut crystal, which caught the gleam of the dancing flames in the great fireplace. Before he knew it the great actor was in the room, sitting down next to him, talking to him as if he knew him and they were old friends. O'Casey would never forget what happened:

—Well, Johnny, me lad o'gold, he said intimately, as he slid into a chair beside the fire, and began on the egg, while Johnny munched a junk of buttered toast and sipped from a cup of tea, you know that tonight's Charlie's benefit performance? Well, Cleggett, who plays Father Dolan, 's gone and got ill; none o' the rest know the part, so we're in a devil of a hole. We want you to fill the part for us, me lad.

—An' well he'll fill it, too, murmured Mrs. Talton.

—Aw, no, no; indeed I couldn't, exclaimed Johnny excitedly; but the thrill of the cheering audience went through his beating heart.

—You're goin' to do it, said Tom emphatically. Haven't I seen you doin' the parlour scene to Archie's Conn, an' the one in Ballyragget House to Archie's Kinchella, to the manner born, too? Besides, you know the whole part, don't you?

—Yes, I know it all, said Johnny; the whole play, I know it nearly all.

Tommie jumped up, wiping bits of crumbs from his mouth, his eyes ashine, showing a problem solved.

—Me sowl man, he said heartily; now, mother, turning to Mrs. Talton, measure him so that you can stitch enough tucks in Father Dolan's togs to fit him fair.

Johnny and Tommie rushed out to catch a tram to the theater for a hurried rehearsal. After a break for supper, Johnny returned to the theater and Tommie made him up. It was an evening O'Casey would never forget.

Johnny stepped through the door into the glare, the white light, the dazzling place of play, sensing, though he didn't see, the vast gathering of watchers hidden in the gloom, waiting, wondering, pitching their tents of thought with the players in the pool of light that showed another world of good and bad, gay and glum; knowing and simple people.

At the age of forty-three O'Casey was still working as a manual laborer, but he had decided to write a play. It would be produced by Dublin's Abbey Theatre, which had been founded by the Irish poet and dramatist William Butler Yeats. After three one-act plays were rejected, his first full-length play, *The Shadow of the Gunman*, was produced at the Abbey in April 1923. A year later his second and perhaps best-known play, *Juno and the Paycock*, was presented at the Abbey. When he received his share from the two plays, twenty-five pounds—about what a laborer earned in a year—he gave up his work and, at the age of forty-four, decided to try earning his living writing. In 1926, the Abbey produced his third play, *The Plough and the Stars*, whose title was taken from the symbols on the Irish Citizens' Army flag. His new name began to appear on the stage bills—Sean O'Casey.

It's one of those ironies that with all his love for Ireland and his lifelong devotion to Irish causes, especially the plight of the working class and the struggle for independence, O'Casey's plays were not appreciated by his countrymen. His characters and plots were not what Dublin audiences were used to. Instead of the conventional sentimental and idealized view of Irish life, O'Casey's characters were real people, with all their strengths and flaws. There are none of the bigger-than-life heroes Irish audiences loved in his plays. His men are not derring-do fighters, unfurling nationalist banners amidst furious battles, but real men, sometimes cowardly, sometimes besotted, or sad and weary, broken by their endless labors. His women emerge as strong characters, holding their families together in poverty and chaos, suffering the loss of their husbands and children.

Irish audiences recoiled at the blunt realism of the characters, plots, and scenes. Some of the actors were offended by the parts O'Casey asked them to play. Critics called them the "sewage school of drama." During the fourth performance of *The Plough and the Stars* a riot broke out in the audience. Recalling a similar incident during a play by Irish playwright William Synge, William Butler Yeats came to the front of the stage and raised his hands to quiet the din. "You have disgraced yourselves again. . . . Dublin has once more rocked the cradle of genius. From such a scene in this theatre went forth the fame of Synge. Equally the fame of O'Casey is born here tonight."

O'Casey was not yet known to American audiences, but at least one actor living in America appreciated O'Casey's work. Eileen Carey, an Irish actress modeling and performing in musical comedies in New York,

Sean O'Casey *(right)* shown in 1934 with Norman MacDermott, producer of O'Casey's play *Within the Gates.* UPI/BETTMAN.

discovered him. She recalled in her memoir, *Sean*:

One miserable day, glum and cold, the girl I had understudied in *American Born* handed me a play to read. "Can you speak with a brogue?" she asked. No, I told her, explaining that though Irish by birth I had been brought up in England. Nevertheless, she left the play with me and I found that I was reading *Juno and the Paycock*, a tragedy by the Irish dramatist, Sean O'Casey. Forgetting everything else, I

Sean O'Casey and his bride, Eileen K. Carey, following their wedding in 1927. HULTON DEUTSCH
COLLECTION LIMITED.

read it straight to the end, profoundly
moved. Suddenly I became as happy as
I had been miserable; overcome with
excitement, I wished above all else to
meet the dramatist himself.

Carey soon met O'Casey. He offered
her the part as Nora Clitheroe in *The
Plough and the Stars* to open in ten days.
And not long after that he asked her to
be his wife. They were married in 1927.

Sadly, O'Casey decided he would have
to leave Ireland. He could not be free
to write as he wished there. His vision
for the theater—"I am out to destroy
the accepted naturalistic presentation
of character"—could not be realized
in Dublin, so set in its ways, and at
the Abbey. He had been to London to
accept the Hawthornden Prize of one
hundred pounds for *Juno*, and decided
to move there.

O'Casey continued writing in England but his concerns and themes were the same—the struggles of workers to find a better life and the cruel hypocrisy of the government and established church— themes he would write about, in fact, for the rest of his life. *The Rose and Crown* (1952) he dedicated "To the Young of All lands, All Colours, All creeds:

> Shadows of beauty,
> Shadows of power;
> Rise to your duty—
> This is the hour!"

The controversy continued as well. When he was asked to submit a play for an annual festival of plays and music in Dublin, he sent *The Drums of Father Ned*. But the Archbishop of Dublin refused to open the festival with the customary Votive Mass if O'Casey's play was performed. O'Casey withdrew the play. In support of O'Casey, Samuel Beckett withdrew three of his plays from the festival as well. "Where are all the indomitable Irish," O'Casey wrote to the *Irish Times*, "about whom the poet sang? Gone to cover? Looks like there isn't an arm or a leg of them left. They have left for other lands to get outside of the ecclesiastical iron curtain."

Then, Yeats's refusal to produce *The Silver Tassie*, an unsentimental story of infantrymen in World War I that would not glorify war as was necessary for successful theater then, was the last straw. O'Casey banned the performance of all his plays in Ireland. *The Drums of Father Ned* had its American premiere in 1959, produced by an amateur company at Purdue University in West Lafayette, Indiana.

Sean O'Casey lived into his eighties and completed his last piece of writing just days before he died. His friends speak of his kindness, rollicking good humor, his courtesy, and that wonderful brogue; O'Casey's friend and critic John Trewin describes it as "the Dublin voice that curled into every crevice of every phrase."

His biographer Brooks Atkinson sums up Sean O'Casey's life so:

> Over the forty six years of his literary career the quality of his writing was uneven. Although he wrote the most glorious English of his era—the English nearest in color and strength to the Elizabethan—the content did not always support the imagery. But he was creative and imaginative and he was spiritually alive until the last moment. He had the moral courage of an idealist. Whatever his religious ideas may have been, I think God had reason to be proud of Sean O'Casey.

Eugene O'Neill

1888–1953 American playwright

Sometime in the spring of 1910, a young man appears on Boston's Mystic wharf and lingers day after day, sitting among coils of rope, fishing nets, and wooden crates stenciled with the names of far-off places, watching the four-masted clipper ships put out to sea, to ports all over the world. His heart is filled with the stories and adventures of Joseph Conrad and Jack London, one-time sailors who later wrote novels about life at sea. He overhears the talk of sailors coming ashore from newly arrived vessels, speaking foreign languages or heavily accented English. Now and then, he approaches them, asking where they've been and where they're going, what kind of ship they're sailing, and what it's like to be a sailor, to spend months at sea without sight of land, and

what they had found out there, just over the horizon.

At twenty-two, Eugene O'Neill has already tasted adventure. He had sailed to Honduras the year before, to find gold. What he found was a hellish world of insects and malaria, which forced him to return. As he sits on the wharf looking out on the water, he wants to be there, but more urgently, he wants not to be here. It's not that he hasn't experienced life; it's that he's already experienced too much of life.

He's gone to private boarding schools and failed at college. He's already read a lifetime of books. His brother Jamie has introduced him to the poetry of Wilde, Swinburne, Rossetti, Dowson, Kipling, and Omar Khayyam. He's lived on his own—supported by his wealthy father—

and he's begun writing poetry. He's attended the theater, worked backstage with his actor father, and discovered there a new, revolutionary voice, Henrik Ibsen. He's too young to realize it yet, or maybe, just maybe, he has an inkling of the idea that he'll write plays someday. Just before going away to Honduras, two weeks before his twenty-first birthday, he secretly entered into a marriage that is already failing, and he's thinking about getting a divorce; he's just discovered he has a son. At twenty-two he already drinks too much.

One day O'Neill found that he'd signed up on the crew of a Norwegian bark, a tall, graceful, three-masted, square rigger, with a cargo of lumber bound for Buenos Aires. The *Charles Racine* was two hundred feet long with a thirty-eight-and-a-half foot beam and a crew of thirty-five men. "It happened quite naturally," he recalled later, "as a consequence of what was really inside me—what I really wanted, I suppose. I struck up one day by the wharf in Boston with a bunch of sailors, mostly Norwegians and Swedes. I wanted to ship with somebody and they took me that afternoon to the captain. Signed up and the next thing we knew we were off." The crew assigned him the rating of gunman, a step above deck boy.

A little scared, O'Neill went back to tell his father what he had done and found, to his surprise, that his father was happy for him and even staked him to his gear for the voyage. He shipped as an ordinary sailor and, though bound for Argentina, his secret hope was eventually to reach China. It was a voyage of sixty-five stormy days, but O'Neill felt he belonged on that deck rolling under his feet and in the rigging, a hundred and fifty feet above. He wrote a poem on that voyage that begins, "Weary am I of the tumult, sick of the staring crowd / Pining for the wild sea places where the soul may think aloud" and ends "And at last be free, on the open sea, with the trade wind in our hair." He sailed the high seas for a little more than a year, but in that time he worked, drank, and caroused with the characters and lived the scenes for a dozen plays. Like his heroes Conrad and London, O'Neill had found a life to write about.

Eugene Gladstone O'Neill was born in New York City on October 16, 1888. His father was a celebrated actor. James O'Neill had originated and then played the lead in *The Count of Monte Cristo* six thousand times! And many of those times little Eugene was in the wings watching his father. Eugene's mother was Mary Ellen Quinlan, a devout Irish Catholic who disapproved of her husband's profession but followed him wherever he went. Ella struggled with the constant conflict between her pure religious nature and the worldly life she was forced to endure with her husband. Even if there hadn't been the stage in young Eugene's childhood, the conflict and tensions and resentments, spoken and unspoken, between Ella and James, would have provided the boy enough drama to last a lifetime.

The two could not have been more different. Ella had come from a middle-class family, pampered and spoiled, educated and cultured. She was very shy and reserved, which most people took for aloofness. She was also exceptionally well educated for a young woman of her day. Her father, Thomas Quinlan, a prosperous newsdealer, believed that his daughter should be educated and go on to college. She attended St. Mary's, at that time associated with a boys' school that would become Notre Dame University in Indiana. St. Mary's was the only college in America at the time that would admit women to liberal arts courses, and so in addition to religious instruction she also studied English, rhetoric, philosophy, astronomy, and French. Ella's love was the piano and she dreamed of becoming a concert pianist. She studied music theory, composition, and piano technique. At St. Mary's, too, were not only Catholic but also Protestant and Jewish students whose parents wanted a liberal arts

education for their daughters. Ella, then, was as cosmopolitan as she was educated. She never became the concert pianist of her dreams. She graduated with honors, received a gold medal for her accomplishments in music, and two years later met and fell in love with a dashing, talented young actor, James O'Neill.

James was gregarious, outgoing, and social, and was loved by all who knew him. He had had no schooling and had grown up in the theater; his father, the first James O'Neill, had been a popular actor of his day. Though the second James was not as well educated as his wife, his travels and the people he met in the theater had made him far more worldly. And he was considered an accomplished actor. He had played Shakespeare with Edwin Booth, his idol, who was considered by many the greatest American actor of his day. As a newspaper article summed up James's development as an actor: "Most of all did he become the pattern of Edwin Booth. So keenly did he study Booth that he copied even his defects in mannerisms. He dressed like him, posed like him, and finally came to speak like him."

Ella suffered her husband's outgoing, merry, boisterous rough-and-tumble theater life and silently resented him for it. James suffered and resented Ella's pride and her disdain and contempt for his life. He resented, also, his wife's superiority by birth, background, and education, a fact Ella never let him forget.

Eugene grew up with parents who engaged in constant, recurring cycles of punishment, then reconciliation, then more punishment, then another reconciliation, again and again. (When he was fourteen, Eugene learned from his brother, Jamie, that their mother had been a morphine addict for years.) They could not give each other happiness but neither could they leave each other alone.

Neither of them, apparently, was capable of closeness with their children. Although O'Neill never spoke directly to us about his parents, he does speak about them through his characters and plays. In *The Great God Brown*, written a few years after the death of his parents, O'Neill speaks through a character based largely on himself.

What aliens we were to each other! When [my father] lay dead, his face looked so familiar that I wondered where I had met that man before. Only at the second of my conception. After that, we grew hostile with concealed shame. And my mother? I remember a sweet, strange girl, with affectionate, bewildered eyes as if God had locked her in a dark closet without any explanation.

Shortly after his mother's death, O'Neill told a friend that for many years his mother actually lived in a room from which she seldom ventured.

O'Neill's plays are autobiographical and so, while he may not be able to speak or even to understand his feelings and the workings of his mind, he reveals it through the characters and situations of his plays. There's little controversy about this. In *Long Day's Journey into Night*, one of the most autobiographical of O'Neill's plays, the couple's names are James and Mary Tyrone (a name that, O'Neill knew from his interest in Gaelic history, is derived from the name of his earliest known ancestor, Owen). It is through these thinly disguised characters that O'Neill reveals the most intimate details of the lives of his parents, his brother, Jamie, and himself.

It is from Mary Tyrone that we learn of the great guilt that burdened Eugene from the day of his birth. "You were born afraid," Mary tells her third-born son in the play. "Because I was so afraid to bring you into the world . . . afraid all the time I carried you. I knew something terrible would happen . . . I should never have borne [you]. It would have been better for [your] sake." Eugene was the third son—another son, Edmund, had died of measles as an infant—and whether or not Ella actually said this to Eugene, he believed it. He carried all his

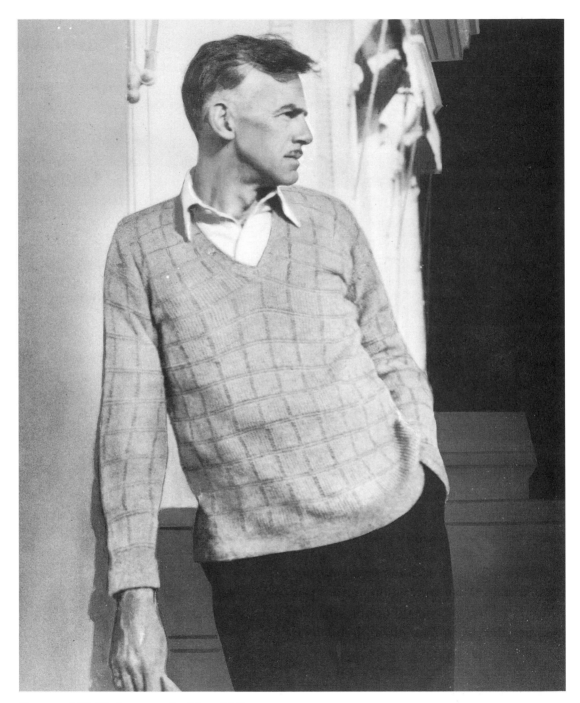

Eugene O'Neill photographed in middle age. EVERETT COLLECTION.

life the guilt of Edmund's death for which, of course, he had no responsibility. He carried, too, the guilt of his mother's addiction, believing all along that it was his birth that had caused it. And, like many children, Eugene possibly held himself responsible for the unhappiness between his parents. None of this is to be dismissed as conjecture; O'Neill went through life carrying the burdens of Ella's guilt, resentment, and anger.

Eugene O'Neill was born in a comfortable family hotel which once stood at Broadway and Forty-third Street in New York. Ella had gone there while James played *Monte Cristo* in New Jersey. In later life, O'Neill looked back nostalgically on what was then a residential neighborhood. For years, until it was torn down in 1940, O'Neill would return to the Barret House, sometimes to show his friends where he was born.

O'Neill followed his father around on tour and spent summers "at home" in New London, Connecticut, where James had bought a house. He had no love for the theater then. "My early experience with the theatre through my father really made me revolt against it. As a boy I saw so much of the old, ranting, artificial romantic stuff that I always had a sort of contempt for the theatre." When he was six, Eugene was sent to boarding school at Mount St. Vincent on the

Hudson until he was twelve, when he was sent to the Betts Academy at Stamford, Connecticut, a preparatory school, and then at eighteen, Princeton University. "In all those years," a friend of the family recalls, "he had almost no home life at all. The nearest approach to it was when, occasionally in the summer, the O'Neill family stayed at New London. . . . But nine-tenths of the boy's time was spent in hotels and schools."

Another New Londoner who remembers O'Neill as a boy recalls that he was "always the gloomy one, always the tragedian, always thinkin'. My God, when he looked at you he seemed to be lookin' right through you, right into your soul. He never said much and then spoke softly when he did speak. Brilliant he was too, always readin' books. We're all Irish around here and knew the type. He was a Black Irishman." O'Neill himself acknowledged his Irish heritage. "One thing that explains more than anything about me," he once told his own son, "is the fact that I'm Irish. And, strangely enough, it is something that all the writers who have attempted to explain me and my work have overlooked."

School reinforced the boy's feelings of isolation and of not belonging. Those years in Catholic boarding schools he referred to as his "rigid Christian exile," and rather than confirm his faith, school destroyed it. He was away from everyone now: his mother and father, his beloved childhood nurse, Sarah, and his brother, Jamie. The only thing he seemed to have in life was his dog, a large odoriferous hound he had named Perfumery, who was not allowed at school. O'Neill begged and begged his teachers to let him have Perfumery at school, and finally he was given permission. A priest who was touched by the boy's sadness arranged to have a doghouse built. Excited, anticipating his reunion with his old buddy, O'Neill wrote his cousin to ask her to ship Perfumery to school. The day before the letter arrived, Perfumery was killed under the wheels of a carriage. Now, the boy had nobody.

O'Neill was destined for Princeton or Yale, and he chose the former. Some would say that he was not college material, but we have to understand that in those days private universities were filled with the sons of the wealthy who were not necessarily interested in learning. The teaching was often uninspired and there was little in the courses about contemporary issues and writers and artists of the day. O'Neill referred to it as "professional dry rot." Shakespeare, who O'Neill later discovered and read with pleasure on his own, was presented at Princeton in a way that intimidated students. "I was afraid of him."

"Wilde, Conrad and London were much nearer to me than Shakespeare at that time," he recalled. "And so, later, was Ibsen. . . . I needed no professor to tell me that Ibsen, as dramatist, knew whereof he spoke. I found him for myself outside of college grounds and hours. If I had met him inside, I might still be a stranger to Ibsen." During his first year in college, O'Neill went to see an Ibsen play for the first time. It was *Hedda Gabler* at the Bijou Theatre in New York, played by the great actress Alla Nazimova, discovering "an entire new world of the drama for me. It gave me my first conception of a modern theatre where truth might live." He returned to see the play on ten successive nights.

Princeton decided it didn't like Eugene O'Neill either; he was suspended after a spree of vandalism, but then decided just to quit. It was not the end of his education, however; it was another beginning. For the next two years, until he sailed away seeking gold and riches in Honduras, O'Neill lived with friends in New York and began to write poetry. It was also when he discovered Benjamin R. Tucker's The Unique Book Shop. Tucker had been an anarchist since he was eighteen, a journalist, an agitator, and now in his later years editor of the anarchist publication *Liberty*. The hours spent browsing through The Unique Book Shop, talking with Tucker and meeting other anarchists who frequented the shop, provided O'Neill with a rich education unobtainable at Princeton or anywhere else, for that matter.

He also returned frequently to his birthplace, Times Square, and the two dozen theaters nearby. Here he saw plays by Booth Tarkington and Somerset Maugham, and the great actress Ethel Barrymore. He deliberately avoided seeing James O'Neill in *Monte Cristo*, which had returned yet another time—he had had enough of that—but did go to see musicals by Victor Herbert and George M. Cohan, and the Ziegfeld *Follies*. It was also the year that the old dreams of going to sea became more urgent. It was time to be moving on. He sailed for Honduras, a year later to Argentina, and, for his last voyage, O'Neill sailed from New York to Southampton, England.

O'Neill was happier at sea than he was, perhaps, at any other time in his life. There he found a real world not like the insincere and fake world of the city. "I look on a sailor man as my particular brother," he told an interviewer not long after his first voyage. "I liked [sailors] better than I did men of my own kind. They were sincere, loyal, generous. You have heard people use the expression: 'He would give away his shirt.' I've known men who actually did give away

their shirts. I've seen them give their own clothes to stowaways."

He also found a freedom all but impossible to find anywhere else and adventure as well. Always, at sea, he was being tested. O'Neill thrilled at the climb up the rigging to the royal and gallant sails 150 feet above the deck, the mast swaying back and forth, pitching forward and back, the wind roaring in his ears. It seemed as if he could see the whole world up there and the sky—the sky and the clouds were so close.

Writers need to be good listeners and observers, and O'Neill sat for countless hours just listening to the sailors spin their yarns. He noted every detail of the ship, learning new tasks every day on his climb from ordinary to able-bodied seaman. His first major play, *Bound East for Cardiff*, was also his first sea drama. Over his lifetime O'Neill would write more than forty plays, thirteen of which would be set all or in part aboard ship, and another six include sea characters, plays with titles like *Thirst*, *Warnings*, *Fog*, *Atlantic Queen*, *The Rope*, and *Beyond the Horizon*.

O'Neill's return to New York from his adventures at sea began years of unhappiness, tragedy, and a writing life. He took a room at Jimmy the Priest's, a waterfront saloon and rooming house where he could stay in touch with his sailor brothers. He discovered the Irish

A theater poster advertises O'Neill's *Long Day's Journey into Night*. PHOTOFEST.

playwright John Millington Synge, especially his play *Riders to the Sea*. "I first saw the possibilities for dramatic realism," he recalled, "when I witnessed a performance of the Irish Players in new York. [They] gave me a glimpse of my opportunity. The first year they came over here [1911] I went to see everything they did. I thought then and still think that they demonstrated the possibilities of naturalistic acting better than any other company."

A year later, still depressed over his family and only an impenetrable blackness ahead of him, O'Neill attempted suicide, but was saved by his friends. He was diagnosed as having tuberculosis—an often fatal disease in those days—and was sent to a sanitarium. Here, he used his time to read dramatic literature, the Greek and Elizabethan classics, and discovered the work of the man he considered "the greatest of all modern dramatists," the Swedish writer August Strindberg. In a flash O'Neill's life changed.

> It was reading his plays when I first started to write, back in the winter of 1913–1914, that, above all, first gave me the vision of what modern drama could be, and first inspired me with the urge to write for the theatre myself. If there is anything of lasting worth in my work, it is due to that original impulse from him, which has continued as my inspiration down all the years since then.

In a burst of energy O'Neill completed eight one-act plays and two longer plays in less than two years.

So it was that, arising from near death and terrible illness, O'Neill began to write plays. In just six years he received his first Pulitzer prize for *Beyond the*

Horizon (1920) and two years later a second for *Anna Christie.* In 1928, he received a third, for *Strange Interlude.* It was also the first drama to reach the best-seller lists. O'Neill was also awarded the Nobel prize in literature in 1936. Another play, *The Iceman Cometh* (1946), became best known to American audiences in its film version.

But of all his plays, O'Neill would have considered most important among them *Long Day's Journey into Night,* "a play of old sorrow," he said, "written in tears and blood." It was his longest journey, back to his roots, examining the lives of his father, mother, and brother with, as he put it, "deep pity and understanding and forgiveness."

O'Neill was now fifty-one, palsied, weakened by a disease doctors were never able to name. He felt an urgency to write about his life and the parents he at once loved and hated. "He explained to me that he *had* to write the play," his wife recalled. "He had to write it because it was a thing that haunted him and he had to forgive his family and himself." It was not out of bitterness and darkness that he wrote; he was seeking understanding. "I love life," he said. "But I don't love life because it is pretty. Prettiness is only clothes deep. I am a truer lover than that. I love it naked. There is beauty to me even in its ugliness. In fact, I deny the ugliness entirely, for its vices are often nobler than its virtues, and nearly always closer to a revelation."

"In power and insight," drama critic Robert Brustein writes, "O'Neill remains unsurpassed among American dramatists, and, of course, it is doubtful if, without him, there would have been an American drama at all." When the American novelist Sinclair Lewis received the Nobel prize, he spoke of every writer's debt to Eugene O'Neill. He had transformed the theater utterly, "from a false world of neat and competent trickery to a world of splendor, fear and greatness. . . . He had seen life as something not to be neatly arranged in a study, but as terrifying, magnificent and often quite horrible, a thing akin to a tornado, an earthquake or a devastating fire."

George Bernard Shaw

1856–1950 British dramatist, novelist, music critic, and essayist

Bernard Shaw, as he was known, was a literary rebel who created a shockingly new art of drama in the 1890s. For the next half century he was regarded, all over the world, as the preeminent modern playwright. Whether he was "much loved," as is said of some writers, is a measure that cannot be used for someone like Shaw. We can say, however, that he moved people with his powerful ideas and social views and angered others with the same. But those who admire Shaw and those who detest him would agree, if about nothing else, that he had a revolutionary effect on the theater, indeed on all of English-speaking culture. He learned his craft in the wake of Ibsen's world-shaking theater of realism and led the way for a new generation of Irish writers, including James Joyce, John Synge, Sean O'Casey, and Samuel Beckett, who immeasurably enriched modern English literature and drama. More than any other dramatist, Shaw, the man, as much as his writing, is one of the most interesting and controversial figures of modern times.

Like most famous people, Shaw's beginnings gave no clues to his eventual influence in the world of ideas. He was not gentle with people who displeased him, even when they happened to be his own family. "I am pure Dublin," he wrote. "We are a family of Pooh Bahs—snobs to the backbone. Drink and lunacy are minor specialties." Shaw's father and three uncles were alcoholics. "They avoided observation whilst drinking," Shaw remembers, but "their excesses rendered them wretched. They appreciated music, books and acting, but had not the energy to cultivate these tastes and never took the initiative in visiting any place of entertainment." He also remembered the first time he became aware of his father's drinking and coming to tell his mother in a shocked, disbelieving tone, "Mama: I think Papa is drunk." And she replied, "When is he anything else?" The sentiments, the sarcasm and irony, and the wicked way with words is pure Shaw. And now you know what you're in for.

Shaw left us a collection of autobiographical writings, "confessions" he called them, from scattered sources. He warns us to be careful, however.

> All autobiographies are lies. I do not mean unconscious, unintentional lies: I mean deliberate lies. No man is bad enough to tell the truth about himself during his lifetime, involving, as it must, the truth about his family and his friends and colleagues. And no man is good enough to tell the truth to posterity in a document which he suppresses until there is nobody left alive to contradict him.

Still, he admits, "the best authority on Shaw is Shaw."

George Bernard Shaw was born of Protestant parents in Dublin, Ireland. His mother was Bessie Gurly. He wrote:

> Bessie was taught how to dress correctly, to sit motionless and straight; how to breathe, pronounce French, convey orders to servants. She was taught how *not* to play the pianoforte with such entire success that she has never been able to play since with any freedom or skill.

But Bessie loved music and was a talented singer.

His father, George Carr Shaw, was a partner in the firm of Clibborn & Shaw, corn merchants. "My father married in his middle age; and the union produced three children: the eldest Lucinda Frances (Lucy), Elinor Agnes (Aggie or Yuppy), and finally a son George (Sonny): in short, myself."

Shaw never could understand why his mother married his father, but then there was little he could understand, except their profound unhappiness. So painful was Shaw's childhood that he could not look at it directly and so learned to view it through what one biographer calls "the spectacles of paradox." A paradox is a contradictory, absurd statement that also speaks the truth, and it was the way that Shaw learned to look at life, as when he comments, "The fact that I am still alive at seventy-eight and a half I probably owe largely to her [Bessie's] complete neglect of me during my infancy, because if she had attempted to take care of me her stupendous ladylike ignorance would certainly have killed me."

Shaw counted himself among the "halfeducated." It wasn't that he wasn't interested in learning; it was that, as many children have discovered, interesting subjects are often taught poorly. Among the worst tortures for young Shaw was language instruction; it was hopeless. Latin was unbearable because no one bothered to explain to children why it was so important that they learn a dead language.

Shaw was moved from school to school each time it was discovered that he wasn't learning anything. Finally, the school he was attending, his "last school prison," was closed. "I decided, at thirteen or thereabouts, that for the moment I must go into business and earn some money and begin to be a grown-up man." He was hired as a junior clerk in an estate office.

Despite his inability to learn in school, Shaw was well educated. He had no access to libraries and no money to buy books. But he read everything. He loved Shelley; "I read him, prose and verse, from beginning to end." He read, all on his own, *The Arabian Nights*, *The Pilgrim's Progress*, and *The Ancient Mariner*. He read George Eliot, Shakespeare, and Dickens among others; Lewe's *Life of Goethe*; and *Faust*. For a

time he entered into Dickens's world, escaping his own, finding in *Great Expectations* and *A Tale of Two Cities* characters "more real than reality and more vivid than life." Some Shakespeare plays he knew by heart. He loved music and was able to borrow books from a Dublin musician. And he loved art, which he discovered at the National Gallery. "Here boys are permitted to prowl. I prowled. . . . Let me add a word of gratitude to that cherished asylum of my boyhood, the National Gallery of Ireland."

At a very young age Shaw became aware of English class consciousness. Later, in his twenties, he became a socialist, a political conviction that shaped the ideas and themes of his writing and his plays throughout his life. Though all English children are at a very young age made aware of their social class—who their inferiors and who their betters are—young Shaw saw through the system and its evil and condemned it with all his might. Class distinctions became especially clear when he left school and went to work, where university graduates were addressed as "Mister" while he was just plain "Shaw." There was unimaginable wealth in England at that time, but most people lived in unimaginable poverty. The rich lived in palaces and had private tailors and yachts. The poor in the cities lived in slum tenements or, in the country, mud-floored cabins with their livestock. He became incensed at the social injustices all around him.

At the age of twenty, Shaw left Dublin for London, where his mother was now living. She had left Ireland—and more to the point, her husband—taking her two daughters to study music and was now teaching music herself. Shaw arrived untrained for any kind of job, almost hopelessly rustic in manners, and painfully shy.

At this time, Shaw's ambition was to become a painter, but he soon realized he had not the talent and that it would distract him from his real love, literature. For the next ten years, he lived in his mother's house, surrounded by piles of manuscripts for novels rejected by publishers and unsuccessful job applications. He continued to read widely and was paid for a series of articles on music appearing in *The Hornet*, a satirical weekly review, and he found a job with the Edison Telephone Company. These, as he described them to a friend, were his "desperate days."

Desperate as they may have been, they were also fruitful. In the years 1873 to 1883 he wrote his five novels: *Immaturity, The Irrational Knot, Love Among the Artists, An Unsocial Socialist*, and *Cashel Byron's Profession*. This last book came from Shaw's interest in pugilism at a time in his life when he was taking boxing lessons at the London Athletic Club. It turned out to be a popular book, which made Shaw wonder if he would ever be a "good" writer.

During these years Shaw joined some of the many philosophical and debating societies. He enjoyed the complete freedom of discussion impossible to find anywhere else in British life. It was at one of these, The Zetetical Society, that the shy young man got up and spoke in public for the very first time in his life.

> I could not hold my tongue. I started up and said something in the debate, and then, feeling that I had made a fool of myself, as in fact I had, I was so ashamed that I vowed I would join the Society; go every week; speak in every debate; and become a speaker or perish in the attempt. I carried out this resolution. I suffered agonies that no one suspected.

Shaw also joined the New Shakespeare Society, the Dialectical Society, and the Fabian Society. It was at one of these meetings that he heard a lecture on socialism by the American Henry George.

> I knew he was an American because . . . he spoke of Liberty, Justice, Truth, Natural Law, and other strange eighteenth century superstitions; and because he explained with great simplicity

George Bernard Shaw photographed at the age of thirty-six. THE BETTMANN
ARCHIVE.

and sincerity the views of the Creator, who had gone completely out of fashion in London in the previous decade and had not been heard of since.

In this wonderfully humorous way, Shaw was expressing how impressed he was with George. The speech changed the direction of his life. Shaw went on to become a spokesman for his new cause on London street corners and curbstones and, later, in his new writings. "I was thus swept into the Great Socialist Revival of 1883."

Now the young writer was finding a voice, and a way of expressing political beliefs he had always felt in his heart but had never known how to express. And he was finding friends. He met William Morris, the celebrated poet and artist-craftsman who he came to know as a man of deep social and ethical convictions. Shaw's novels, which at that time remained unpublished, languishing on his shelves, found the approval of the editors of socialist newspapers and magazines he met and so appeared for the first time in print in *To-Day* and *The World*. In this way, they attracted the attention of publishers and eventually appeared as books.

In 1889 a new newspaper appeared, *The Star*, and Shaw was asked to be the music critic. He wrote marvelously funny reviews under the pseudonym Corno di Basseto, or basset horn, an obsolete kind of clarinet. It was not a very pleasant instrument and its use in the orchestra was short-lived; as Shaw said, "The devil himself could not make a basset horn sparkle." He became music critic to *The World* as well and in 1895 was asked to be drama critic for *The Saturday Review*.

Shaw appeared never to take anything too seriously, a strange attitude in an age when most people, especially literary and cultured people, took everything entirely too seriously. This was part of the reason for his success as a critic. Another was that Shaw was himself an amateur and, therefore, better able to explain music to audiences who loved to listen to music but were not themselves professional musicians. He taught himself to play not by practicing scales for endless hours, but by choosing a piece he loved, a very difficult piece like the overture to the opera *Don Giovanni*, and then trying to play it. "When I look back on all the banging, whistling, roaring, and growling inflicted on nervous neighbors during this process of education," he recalled, "I am consumed with useless remorse."

The music establishment was incensed at Shaw's appointment as critic. He was told by a music authority of the day that "I knew nothing about it; that nobody had ever seen me in really decent society; that I moved amidst cranks, Bohemians, unbelievers, agitators, and—generally speaking—riff-raff of all sorts." Shaw, of course, rather than taking this as an insult, was quite proud.

Shaw was in his thirties when he began writing for the stage. A lot of things had been working up to this step, but one of the most influential was his discovery of the Norwegian dramatist Henrik Ibsen. What a revelation that must have been, reading Ibsen's poems and then his plays for the first time. Shaw felt as though he knew Ibsen, that here was another person in the world like himself. He recalls sitting in the audience watching Ibsen's *The Wild Duck* unfold:

> To sit there getting deeper and deeper in that Ekdal home, and getting deeper and deeper into your own life all the time, until you forget you are in a theatre; to look on with horror and pity at a profound tragedy, shaking with laughter all the time at an irresistible comedy; to go out, not from a diversion, but from an experience deeper than real life ever brings to most men, or often brings to any man: that is what The Wild Duck was like last Monday at the Globe.

Excited by Ibsen's new theater, Shaw wrote and produced his first play,

Widowers' Houses, set in the slums. His characters were real, if somewhat stereotyped—too real for London audiences. They hooted at the play and louder at the playwright when he got up on the stage to face them after the final scene. Oscar Wilde liked this first effort—"I admire the horrible flesh and blood of your creatures"—but the critics did not. Still, Shaw was satisfied: "I had not achieved a success; but I had provoked an uproar; and the sensation was so agreeable that I resolved to try again." He began work on his second play, *The Philanderer*.

For his third play, Shaw took on society as Ibsen had, and was about to shake it to its very roots. What's more, he now confronted for the first time a most dreaded aspect of British culture, the terrible power of the Censor, the power to examine all works of art and determine whether they can be made public. For the subject of *Mrs. Warren's Profession* Shaw chose one of the most vicious aspects of capitalism—prostitution. The subject was unacceptable on the stage even though, in the best of Shavian paradox, the word was never spoken. Actually, its existence was never confronted or even acknowledged. Shaw had to fight in order to have rehearsals. Although managers eagerly awaited this play and anticipated its performance, they canceled out, realizing that if they did allow it on the stage, they would have their licenses revoked and be forced to close their doors.

The play was denounced in advance of its opening. That, no doubt, thrilled Shaw, but he was not alone in this. The supporters and investors in the play did not leave Shaw in the face of possible censorship but stayed with him. The Stage Society vowed to give battle at all cost to prevent the play's suppression. And the actors themselves made the play their mission, determined to bring *Mrs. Warren's Profession* to life no matter what the dangers and annoyances.

The problem wasn't "sex." As Shaw put it, "Prostitution is not a question of sex; it is a question of money." Prostitution was one of the largest and most lucrative businesses in London. It involved government and wealthy businessmen both as investors and clients. It involved police bribery at the highest levels. It touched on repressive attitudes toward women, especially poor women. The issue cut across the whole fabric of Victorian English life. It was, as Shaw was the first to say publicly, white slavery.

Taking the side of women in the issue, Shaw's point was that all that was necessary to reduce prostitution was to raise women's wages. Decades ahead of his time, Shaw was actually using *Mrs. Warren's Profession* as a call for social

Katharine Cornell plays the title role in George Bernard Shaw's *Saint Joan*. PHOTOFEST. PHOTOGRAPH BY VANDAMM.

George Bernard Shaw photographed outside of his home, Shaw's Corner, near London, where he died at the age of ninety-four. The house has been preserved as a memorial to him.
HULTON DEUTSCH COLLECTION LIMITED.

reform, including a living wage for women, "a minimum wage law," and "provisions for the unemployed." But the English did not want to hear this and, because they expected to be entertained at the theater, they especially did not want to hear it coming from the stage.

Shaw was perhaps more proud of that opening night than of anything else he had ever done. Everyone was under a tremendous strain.

Nevertheless, there was no hesitation behind the curtain. When it went up at last, a stage much too small for the company was revealed to an audience much too small for the audience. But the players, though it was impossible for them to forget their own discomfort, at once made the spectators forget theirs. It certainly was a model audience, responsible from the first line to the last; and it got no less than it deserved in return.

This had been a private performance. Another thirty years would pass before *Mrs. Warren's Profession* would appear in public in London. When the play was first performed in New York, the police stormed the theater and arrested the entire company. The judge held over the case until he could read the play, and when he resumed the proceedings he seemed, to Shaw, disappointed. He said that he had read the play and had found nothing objectionable and so acquitted all the defendants.

Later, back in England, Shaw appeared before the Lord Chamberlain and argued his case admirably: "I have suffered both in pocket and reputation by the action of the Lord Chamberlain," he told the committee.

I am not an ordinary playwright in general practice. I am a specialist in im-moral and heretical plays. My reputation has been gained by my persistent struggle to force the public to reconsider its morals. In particular, I regard much current morality as to economic and sexual relations as disastrously wrong; and I regard certain doctrines of the Christian religion as understood in England today with abhorrence. . . . I

object to censorship not merely because it hinders me individually, but on public grounds.

Eventually, Shaw won for himself and all of England's artists; the ban was lifted and the play licensed.

Over the years, several of Shaw's many plays have dropped out of the theater repertory, but others have deservedly become standards. Most notable is *Arms and the Man* (1894), in which Shaw attempted to show people the horrors of war as experienced by soldiers. It was unspeakable at the time that soldiers should be represented in any way other than in the most heroic terms. The public's images of war had come from a few idealists' etchings and paintings and glorious episodes on the stage. Shaw depicted not ideal soldiers, but real ones.

The Devil's Disciple (1896) was set in the American Revolution (and was made into a film in 1959 with Laurence Olivier in the role of General Burgoyne). In 1899 Shaw wrote *Captain Brassbound's Conversion* for actress Ellen Terry. *Man and Superman* (1903) startled audiences with its frank and realistic discussion of the relations between men and women. *Major Barbara* (1905) is a sympathetic play about the Salvation Army. Still others performed frequently on the American stage are *Androcles and the*

Lion (1911), *Pygmalion* (1912), and *Saint Joan* (1924). Shaw was awarded the 1925 Nobel prize in literature, but he refused to accept the prize money.

Bernard Shaw, his plays, and his ideas have enthralled audiences and stirred controversy for well over a century now. As with any writer, he is best understood and appreciated by reading his writings and going to see his plays. If you do that, you will discover the real Shaw. Or will you? He once wrote:

The celebrated G. B. S. is about as real as a pantomime ostrich. But . . . I have played my game with conscience. I have never pretended that G. B. S. was real: I have over and over again taken him to pieces before the audience to shew the trick of him. And even those who in spite of that cannot escape from the illusion, regard G. B. S. as a freak. The whole point of the creature is that he is unique, fantastic, unrepresentative, inimitable, impossible, undesirable on any large scale, hopelessly unnatural, and void of real passion. Clearly such a monster could do no harm, even were his example evil (which it never is).

Luis Miguel Valdez

1940– Actor, poet, playwright, filmmaker, and founder of
El Teatro Campesino

Row upon row of vines heavy with bunches of purple grapes stretch to the horizons of California's San Joaquin Valley. It is almost dusk and the blazing ball of the sun is low in the sky, but the air is still stifling hot. It's the end of a long workday that began at dawn this morning. And now lines of straw-hat-shaded workers, brown from the hot sun and their Indian ancestry, make their way wearily back to the cars and pickup trucks strung out along the shoulders of Highway 99. Suddenly the scene comes alive with laughter, singing, the staccato rhythms of Spanish voices, guitars, and *corridos*, popular ballads. And there, under a little grove of trees in the only shade for miles around, is an ancient flatbed truck and, alongside, rows of folding chairs beginning to fill up with a crowd of dusty *campesinos*, farmworkers, men and women of all ages and small children who harvest our food. Above them stretches a banner proclaiming *El Teatro Campesino*, The Farmworkers' Theater.

Up on the flatbed, four workers strumming guitars sing in front of a bright yellow-and-orange Aztec sun painted on a simple backdrop. The song is about the children who are never in one place long enough to go to school. It's about the little ones with old faces who travel endlessly from field to field, from harvest to harvest, who spend their days stooped in the dust picking grapes or onions or lettuce. It's about children who do not know a carefree moment or the joys of childhood, only that tomorrow or the next day they will be in the back of a rusty old pickup truck, enclosed in a cage of chicken wire, little migrant birds off to they don't know where:

Children are on the road in summers,
winters and springs, crossing states
    and counties
and cities that are foreign. Like
    swallows come
down from the heavens they give
    themselves
flight to their true desires.

The song was written by a young Chicano poet, Luis Valdez, who explains what these people are doing here: "The last divine Aztec Emperor Cuauhtémoc was murdered and his descendants were put to work in the fields. We are still there, in the fields of America."

So it is that the proud people of a once great civilization are among us, doing the work no one else will do for wages few would even consider in this rich country. They are *Chicanos*, Mexicans born on either side of the border, and they are migrants, workers who follow the harvest. The year is 1965, and for the first time they have a leader, César Chávez, whose organization, the United Farmworkers' Union, speaks for them. The cry in their throats this summer is *¡Huelga!* "Strike!" *¡Ya basta!* "We've had it!" And the hope in their

hearts is a living wage; clean, safe housing for their families; schools for their children; and, above all, respect.

Teatro Campesino is a vital part of this movement. It is not a visiting theater from a nearby city, where theaters usually are, but their theater, the workers' theater. These musicians, the playwrights, actors, stagehands, set painters, and mask makers are all *campesinos*. The flatbed of the truck is their stage. The playwright who organized and energized Teatro Campesino is not a famous actor or producer from New York, but one of them, a *campesino* who has worked alongside them in the fields, suffered with them the insults and indifference. And he's here this evening— he's always here—climbing up on the flatbed stage to begin the performance.

Luis Miguel Valdez was born in Delano, California, on June 26, 1940. At the age of six, when his small hands were strong enough to pull the bunches of grapes from the vines, he was taken into the fields by his parents. He grew up in the vineyards and orchards and the farmworkers' camps. He can recall a few bright moments in his young life, bittersweet memories, the songs and dancing in the *cantinas*, the closeness of the Chicano community. He liked to build cardboard stages for the puppets he had made and put on plays for his family and friends. It is the nature of his people

Luis Valdez photographed in 1981. EVERETT COLLECTION.

that even in the hardest and poorest of times there is always time for family. Like the other children, young Luis's work was needed to earn extra money so that the family could make it through the winter months when there would be no work, no pay.

Though the farm owners made fortunes, the farmworkers came away often with not enough money to make it through the winter. Later, the *campesino* actors of El Teatro created a character whose hat and shirt were covered with dollar bills; "I am summer," the actor announces. And Valdez recalls what this all meant.

I can remember my family going north toward the prune and apricot orchards. My image was of leaves and fruit clustered on the trees, and all of this flowing into flows of dollar bills. . . . It's a vision of paradise; you're going there—the promised land—you're getting there finally. Then reality creeps in again, and you end up with less money than you started with. But the dream is always there, the dream that you are going to get rich quick.

Twenty-five years later, little had changed since Valdez's childhood. The workers still lived in squalor, in shacks without clean water, toilets, sewers, electricity, or cookstoves. There was hardly a moment without hunger. Many families lived in tents or makeshift lean-tos, or slept under the open sky, or in the back of their cars and trucks. Even if the companies provided some housing, the workers were not allowed to stay there over the winter but were forced to move on. Some returned to Mexico, but most just made do somehow until the spring, when their labor would be needed again.

Actually, something had changed—the farmworkers' lives had gotten worse. Even their communities had been taken away from them. Delano was, in Valdez's childhood, a Mexican town, a home away from home.

As a kid I can remember that Delano was a very different sort of town than it is now. There was a street several blocks long that had Mexican shops, a Mexican show, a Mexican dance hall. There were Mexican things for sale, Mexican candy, Mexican clothes, Mexican food. It was a place full of character—Mexican character

And then! Then! Six or seven years ago our whole section of town was ripped away. The freeway came through like a surgical knife and cut out the very heart of our side of Delano. Urban renewal? [Valdez laughs bitterly.] For whom?

A lot of people were upset. They had taken away our towns, our personality. It's not surprising that this town exploded and became the heart of *Huelga*.

They filled our hearts with emptiness. There is contempt for Mexican things in the Valley.

When he was fourteen, Valdez fled from the endless, stupefying life of the fields, searching for something, anything better. He went to the cities and found a growing number of restless young Chicanos who were leaving the little towns, hitchhiking to anywhere as long as it was away, joining the Army, looking for jobs, just wandering, disappearing into the crowded *barrios* of Los Angeles and other big cities, trying to shake off the stigma of the "dumb Mex."

Valdez wandered too, but rather than getting lost, he continued his education as best he could and earned a scholarship to San Jose State University. Here he began writing plays and dreamed of having his own theater company some day, a company of actors who would do plays about Chicanos for Chicano audiences. While he was at San Jose State, Valdez wrote and produced his first two plays, *The Theft*, a one-act play about a young Chicano, and *The Shrunken Head of Pancho Villa*, a fantastical play about a farm family's struggle for economic and cultural survival.

The university, however, was not a comfortable place for a young man of Valdez's background and dreams, and he suffered what he called "cultural schizophrenia." He could not be who he was. His education was forcing him to be someone else, someone he knew he could not be. "This is a society largely hostile to our cultural values. There is nothing poetic about the United States. No depth, no faith, no allowance for human contradictions, no soul, no mariachi, no chili sauce, no *pulque*, no mysticism."

Valdez came under two important influences on his odyssey. First, he discovered the powerful, lyrical verse of the early twentieth-century Spanish poet and playwright Federico Garcia Lorca. The themes, sounds, and rhythms of Lorca's verse are a blend of the language, folk songs, stories, and traditions of the Spanish peasants. Because he wrote about the peasants in their language, Lorca did not want his plays performed just in the big cities like Madrid and Barcelona, but out in the villages, where there were people who were too poor to travel to the city, people who had never seen a play before. So Lorca assembled a small company of actors and traveled from village to village, into the remotest mountains and river valleys, performing his plays on the back of a truck. Lorca confirmed Valdez's belief in the language and folkways of his people, strengthening his resolve to write Chicano plays about Chicano life. And he was taken with the idea of Lorca's truck.

Then, in 1964, Valdez joined the San Francisco Mime Troupe. This was theater as he had never seen it before, funny, energetic, captivating, and involving. They often performed in parks for free. Their audiences were people right off the street who had gathered at the first sounds of music from the little band of players and the dancing that introduced every performance. Their themes were the important themes of the day—war and peace, government corruption, racism, oppression, poverty, police brutality. They wrote their own plays but also adapted classical plays for modern, especially young audiences. The actors sometimes spoke to the audience directly, came down off the stage, and moved among them and involved them in the action of the play. The Mime Troupe's style and techniques were reminiscent of the old Italian *commedia dell'arte* tradition, complete with slapstick farce, harlequins, exaggerated body language and comical gestures, leaping clowns, masks, and large signs identifying characters. The actors sketched out the story beforehand, but then, once on stage, improvised the lines and action, making it up as they went along, making the plays even livelier and ensuring that no two performances were ever alike.

Lorca's truck and the improvisational style of the Mime Troupe came together in Valdez's mind, and the idea of El Teatro Campesino was born. It was now 1965. *La Huelga*, the grape pickers' strike, had hit like a flash of lightning and rolled across the valley like a summer thunderstorm. Half a century of apathy and bitterness suddenly exploded into rage. Valdez enjoyed his playing with the Mime Troupe, but his people and their struggle called him back. "Moving back to Delano," he recalls, "was a real, commonsensical act for me. I cannot begin to explain how much it was like 'coming home.' Without sentiment, you understand, only clear-headed *doing*."

Valdez found things very different from when he had left years before. Everywhere, now, there was singing. There had been no singing in the vineyards when Valdez was a boy, only sullen silence. But now in the fields and along the dirt roads the *campesinos* marched to *Huelga* every morning at dawn singing. It was like old Mexico, the parades and the fiestas of the saints. People on the picket lines carried their own paintings of the Virgin and handwritten quotes from the Bible and they sang from their hearts, songs they use to sing only in church and in the *cantinas*. The union had organized choruses, one for the adults and one for the children.

The Farmworkers' Union newspaper, *El Malcriado* ("The Mischievous One"), included, besides news of the strike, poems, stories, and essays written by the *campesinos.* Valdez was overwhelmed, ecstatic. "You can see a new spirit in the people," he wrote. "Where they were shy and retiring and frightened about American society, now they're expressive, courageous, and determined. The farm worker who has never said anything is now speaking." Valdez set about organizing El Teatro Campesino.

El Teatro's actors, Valdez envisioned, would be the farmworkers themselves, the vineyards and the truck the stage, and the plays the improvisations of the *campesinos.* Because he was working with people who had no experience in the theater—had never even seen a play—he had to start with the basics of stage direction, voice projection, beginning acting. Strong voices were essential if the actors were to be heard. The plays would not be performed usually in a quiet theater but outdoors, where the farmowners often honked car horns, played loud music, and did anything they could to disrupt the performances.

Valdez conceived of the play as an *acto.* "We could have called them 'skits,'" he later explained, "but we lived and talked in San Jauquín Spanish (with a strong Tejano [Texan] influence), so we needed a name that made sense to the Raza." *Acto,* in standard Spanish, means an "act," or an "action," and, in a theatrical sense, the "act" of a play. But in El Teatro the word took on a new meaning.

Acto, rather than being a part of a play, became a complete statement, a little play in itself.

Meeting with a group of striking farmworkers, Valdez brought El Teatro alive from its very first moments. He asked for anyone in the audience who would like to come up front and show what happened to them on the picket line today. Two *campesinos* stepped up and Valdez hung signs around their necks that identified them as *huelgistas,* strikers. Then he asked for a third volunteer to play a strikebreaker. There was silence; no one wanted to be the despised strikebreaker, but then a young farmworker volunteered, and around his neck Valdez placed a sign reading *esquirol* ("squirrel," the *campesino* term for a "scab"). "Now show us what happened today on the picket line," Valdez told the three farmworkers. Without prompting, the two "strikers" began shouting at the "scab," imploring him not to cross their lines, but instead to join them. The "scab," staying true to his character, shouted back at them what he had actually heard on the lines that day, and soon everyone in the audience was taking part. "I'll play the *esquirol* this time," someone shouted. "I want to be the *huelgista,*" came another offer from the back of the room, and soon a group of farmworkers, tired from a day of confrontations on the picket line, began to shape an *acto.*

Then, with his back to the group, Valdez pulled a piglike mask over his head and, spinning around, confronted his audience. This figure didn't need a sign around his neck; he was recognized immediately. *El Patrocinto!* "The boss," everyone jeered, the wealthy grower who refused to negotiate with the union. "Who wants to play *El Patrocinto*?" Valdez asked, and from the audience, hopping up on the stage came another worker eager to portray the despised boss. He put on the mask and when he turned his face to the audience, the pig mask seemed to come alive. He strutted back and forth in front of the crowd, mimicking the boss's walk, pointing at this worker and that one. "Y'all stop that laughing!" he shouted in a Texas drawl, and the crowd erupted in a roar of laughter.

Masks are an old tradition in theater, going back to plays of ancient Greece and even further back, before recorded history. Most recently it came out of the *commedia dell'arte* of Italy, the French *Comédie Française*, the theater of Jean-Louis Barrault, and the San Francisco Mime Troupe. For centuries Mexicans wore masks in the Corpus Christi play and other sacred performances, and there is in Mexico to this day the craft of mask making. The mask, lifeless in itself, is magic in the way it comes alive on the wearer.

Jorge A. Huerta, who writes about Chicano theater, explains how Valdez understood this magic and how it helped otherwise shy workers, who had never gotten up on a stage, to perform.

Valdez the actor had learned to bring a character to life through the use of a comic mask and the body movement necessary to animate the false face. He also understood that the mask was a form of protection for the wearer, separating him or her from the character assumed. . . . The instant anyone put it on, the howls of laughter showered the actor with a sort of approval, and he could relax, knowing that the spectators were not laughing at him but at what he represented.

It was late and the farmworkers reluctantly left and drifted out into the night; El Teatro Campesino had begun.

The next day several *campesinos* approached Valdez, wanting to help. Among them would be the first authors and actors of El Teatro's first *actos*, the first stagehands and set designers, the first costume makers and sign painters, the first musicians and singers and poets. Among them, too, were El Teatro's first "star" performers. There was Felipe Cantu, a grape picker and father of seven children who had worked, he said, as everything from "a policeman to a clown." To Valdez he "resembles a Mexican version of [silent film comedian] Ben Turpin. He speaks no English, but his wild, extravagant Cantinflas-like comic style needs no words." (Cantinflas was called Mexico's Charlie Chaplin.) Agustin Lira, just twenty, suddenly appeared out of the ranks of *huelgistas* and became El Teatro's first guitarist. Soon Valdez discovered that there was more in this intense, sensitive young *campesino* than beautiful music. Lira was a poet who wrote some of El Teatro's first songs— fiery, passionate songs like "Yo no Le Tengo Miedo a Nada" (I Am not Afraid of Anything), and "Ser Como el Aire Libre" (To Be Free as the Wind), which tell stories of the migrants:

> When I was little,
> My mother said,
> Don't get in trouble.
> Now that I am grown up,
> These words pain me,
> For life is long,
> And I go through it crying.

Errol Franklin, a Native American from Cheyenne, Wyoming, was hired as an *esquirol*, but when he saw the determination of the *huelgistas* he decided not only that he wouldn't cross their lines but would join them. Franklin was a lean, powerful, wiry guy who had worked as cowboy, horse breaker,

Luis Valdez portrayed an elderly migrant worker in his play *El Corrido*. EVERETT COLLECTION.

fisherman, apple picker, short-order cook, and longshoreman. He became El Teatro's mask maker and, during performances, the stage cop. Valdez knew he had succeeded in making El Teatro truly a *campesino* theater, because from the very beginning they had taken it over and made it their own.

Valdez readily admits that he did not invent the *acto*, but that he got the idea from Bertolt Brecht's *Lehrstucke*, or "learning pieces." But the *acto* was more than just a learning piece. It was shaped by Valdez and his *campesino* company into a medium for Mechicanos to express their concerns in the language of the fields and barrios. The *actos* were written and produced not by a playwright, but a true collective of *campesinos* with Valdez's guidance.

Like Brecht, Valdez also saw in theater a higher purpose than entertainment or even enlightenment; theater could move people to act, to better their lives and the lives of others. "In a Mexican way," Valdez wrote, "we have discovered what Brecht is all about. If you want unbourgeois theater, find unbourgeois people to do it." Anybody could write an *acto*. As El Teatro began to evolve, Valdez formulated five goals of the *acto*:

Inspire the audience to social action
Illuminate specific points about social problems
Satirize the opposition
Show or hint at a solution
Express what people are thinking

Satire was an important part of the *acto*, but not for its own sake. "We use comedy," Valdez explains, "because it stems from a necessary situation—the necessity of lifting the morale of our strikers. . . . This leads us into satire and the underlying tragedy of it all—the fact that human beings have been wasted in farm labor for generations."

El Teatro performed not only for the tens of thousands of farmworkers living in camps, at the edges of the fields, along the roadsides, and under bridges, but also followed them on their migrations up and down California's fertile Central Valley. Valdez was interested in change, not in creating Great Art. "We are not aspiring to Broadway," he once told an interviewer. "We aspire to build a theatre among our people. That's the whole bit about El Teatro. We are not a theater *for* farm workers; farm workers *are* our theatre. Besides, we are trying to build something bigger than a theatre."

The something bigger turned out to be a cultural center, returning to a people the culture that had been taken from them. "The Mexican American farm worker in the Southwest has long been denied the tools of [his] cultural expression," Valdez says. "El Centro Campesino Cultural is an attempt to hand over these tools—the tools of the arts—directly to the Spanish-speaking people of the Southwest."

Soon El Teatro found a broader audience. They were invited to perform at Stanford University, and Valdez seized on the invitation as an opportunity to bring the farmworkers' struggle to campuses, churches, community halls, and the cities. El Teatro became known to more people than they ever dreamed of and, less than a year after they began, they were written up in the *San Fran-*

cisco Chronicle: "It's vital, earthy, and vividly alive theater . . . an impressive demonstration of what can be done when men work together in a common cause."

El Teatro began touring nationally and internationally, bringing attention to the cause of not only Chicanos but exploited farm labor everywhere. In 1968, El Teatro was awarded an Obie and, the following year, invited to the Théâtre des Nations at Nancy, France. In 1978, *Zoot Suit*, the play for which Valdez is perhaps best known—after his motion picture *La Bamba*—broke all records for a Los Angeles run. A second production in New York became the first Chicano play on Broadway.

Valdez went on to write and direct *Corridos* (1980), a performance of *actos* and dances set to Mexican folk ballads, and *I Don't Have to Show You No Stinking Badges* (1986), coproduced with the Los Angeles Theatre Center.

El Teatro Campesino is still alive and well, and Valdez continues to find new ways to tell the story of his people. "There are beautiful things in our lives," he says. "We have had them in our past and we will have them again. We will create our own 'flowers and songs.'"

Tennessee Williams

1911–1983 American playwright

A painfully shy, withdrawn young woman sits in candlelight, playing with tiny glass animals while she "entertains" the one gentleman caller she will ever know. A beautiful, mentally unbalanced woman comes to live with her sister and brutal brother-in-law, with catastrophic results. A strong, fiery-spirited woman takes on her estranged husband's powerful family in an effort to win back his love. A former Southern belle dresses for a dinner in a gown thirty years old, reminiscing about her lost youth in a scene both hilariously funny and pathetically sad.

These haunting scenes have entered our theatrical world forever, and their characters' names—Blanche DuBois, Amanda Wingfield, Maggie the Cat— have become household words, thanks to the pen of "America's poet playwright," Tennessee Williams. During his lifetime, many considered him the foremost playwright in the country, if not the world. His timeless plays enjoy continual popularity; at any time somewhere in the world you are likely to find several of his plays being produced, in any of a dozen different languages. Most of his major works have been turned into successful motion pictures, and colleges offer whole courses on his writings in their theater departments.

Some authorities would place him side by side with Eugene O'Neill in importance as an American playwright. Other people have said that, yes, O'Neill was the father of American drama and the first of our world-renowned playwrights, but Williams's writing, word for word, is actually better. Certainly, no one before or since has written plays so filled with poetic imagery. For although he wrote mainly for the theater, at heart Tennessee Williams was a poet. And if his plays tend to focus on certain human frailties and problems, it is understandable. His own life was a wild ride of tangled personal relationships, years-long struggle for recognition, battles with shyness and loneliness, which he fought with drugs and alcohol, and at the center, a heartbreaking family tragedy. Through it all, his writing was his strength, his anchor, and ultimately, his life.

Thomas Lanier Williams was born on March 26, 1911, in Columbus, Mississippi, near the place where another Southern writer, William Faulkner, was born. Throughout his life he kept a soft Mississippi drawl, even though his family left the state when he was eight years old. He spent most of his youth in Missouri, mainly in St. Louis. But his early days in the deep South left such an impression on him that he returned to it again and again for material for his writings. Why, then, isn't he called Mississippi or Missouri Williams? When he was searching for a pen name, having decided that using his full name was a bit old-fashioned and Thomas Williams was just too common, he struck on Tennessee, which had a much better sound to it than the others. Besides, his family

had roots there; his grandfather on his father's side spent years and most of the family fortune trying unsuccessfully to get himself elected governor of Tennessee. The struggle left Tennessee's own father financially and emotionally poor, a situation that was to have an immense impact on both the life and the plays of Tennessee Williams.

It was his mother's side of the family that had the most influence on young Tom, as he was called. His mother, Edwina Dakin, was a beautiful girl who, like Amanda Wingfield, her counterpart in one of Williams's greatest plays, had many "gentlemen callers." Her own mother, Rose, whom everyone called "Grand," was a strong-willed, beautiful, and talented woman who practiced every day on the violin and piano. She gave lessons on these instruments throughout her life, and with the money she earned, she helped support her young grandson as he struggled to become a successful writer.

Edwina had married Cornelius Coffin Williams, a man whose family lines and importance impressed her. It was not a happy marriage, and at times Cornelius, who was an alcoholic and possessed a hot temper, could become violent. He was a traveling shoe salesman, often gone for weeks at a time, driving around the South with samples in his car. In his absence, Edwina went to live with her parents at the Episcopal Rectory in Columbus. The first Williams child was a girl, Tom's sister, Rose. She was high-spirited and a natural leader, showing no signs of the terrible mental problems that lay ahead of her. Tom was two years younger, and later, Dakin, their younger brother, would be born in St. Louis.

Tom's early years were spent surrounded mostly by women, his father being on the road. They were happy years, by his own account, pursuing simple pleasures. He played with Rose, sailed paper boats, kept pet rabbits, cut paper dolls from mail-order catalogs, and delighted in the stories told him by the children's young, pretty black nurse, Ozzie. Ozzie would sit by the children's bedside in the evening and entertain them with tales of bears, foxes, and rabbits. Although he was quite shy, Tom himself began telling stories when he was very young. His favorite subjects were animals. Once he related a story of a hero, himself, being chased by increasingly larger animals. The story got more and more exciting until Tom finally cried out, "It's gettin' so scary I'm scared myself!"

When Tom was five years old, his grandfather, the Reverend Mr. Dakin, was transferred by the bishop to the little town of Clarksdale, in the western part of the state. Edwina and the children followed. Ozzie had failed to return after picking cotton for her brothers one day—no one knew why. Edwina was left to raise the children herself, as Cornelius was absent so much of the time.

Soon after this move to Clarksdale, Tom nearly died of a terrible illness, which his mother thought was diphtheria. There was no hospital nearby, so Edwina cared for him herself. She kept him close to her for several nights, changing ice packs on his throat and trying to relieve his fever. Later, she was told by the doctors that she had saved his life. One morning, examining his throat, she noticed that his tonsils, which had been swollen from the disease, had simply vanished. She panicked and summoned a befuddled doctor, who examined Tom and confirmed this medically marvelous occurrence—Tom had swallowed his own tonsils! For the rest of her life, Tom's mother attributed most of his various physical problems to this unlikely event.

Tom was sick for over a year, and was a changed boy when it was over. The disease, whatever it was, affected his kidneys and his legs, paralyzing them for months. He was so weak he had to push himself along the floor, and later rode about in a little "Irish Mail" wagon. His eyesight was damaged and remained poor for the rest of his life.

And he was a different child in other ways as well. He had been a very active little boy, almost a bully and always a ringleader, but after his sickness Tom was much more passive, withdrawn, and shy, and spent much more time alone, reading or playing imaginary games. He later wrote that all of the care and attention from his mother seemed to have made him a "hybrid"—a "sissy," as he called himself. His sister, Rose, had also suffered an attack of diphtheria, but she seemed to have been much less harmed by it.

As Tom was recovering, a momentous change was about to unfold for the family. His father, Cornelius, having proven himself a success as a traveling shoe salesman, was promoted by his company to an executive position at the St. Louis offices of the International Shoe Company. This meant that the Williamses would be making a home of their own, away from Clarksdale and the Dakins. They moved into a dark, drab, ugly apartment in St. Louis. Edwina was expecting her last child, Tom's younger brother, Dakin.

Life changed drastically for the boy. Gone were the sweet, tranquil days with "Grand" and "Grandfads" and the friends he'd known. Now, he and Rose had to make new friends, a difficult task, as they discovered. In Mississippi, they had been the grandchildren of the Episcopal minister and had been considered among the "best people" in town. Now, in St. Louis, many of the neighboring children went to private schools, so that Tom and Rose only saw them at Sunday school. They were looked down on and considered "white trash." Their Mississippi accents didn't help. Tom did manage to befriend a little girl two years younger than he, Hazel Kramer. Plump, redheaded Hazel remained a close friend and childhood sweetheart for years. Williams later called her "the greatest love, outside the family, of my life," this despite the fact that virtually all of his later relationships were with men.

Edwina moved the family to a brighter and sunnier home, but in so doing left behind old friends. The children had to begin all over again. Rose and Tom drew closer together, "aliens in an alien world," as their mother called them. Edwina was not helpful in encouraging their friendships. She saw all of Rose's friends as a "bad moral influence" and all of Tom's friends as "too rough." It was a difficult time for the two children, but not always terrible. Their new town had lovely parks, and many ponds, lakes, and pagodas left over from the St. Louis World's Fair of 1904. Edwina would take the children there and to the zoo and Botanical Gardens for picnics. Tom learned to be a good swimmer, the only sport besides bicycling he ever enjoyed.

Later in his adult life, Williams always tried to live where he could swim every day for health and relaxation.

Tom could now walk again, but could not run and was not much of an athlete at school. This further antagonized his father, who took to teasing him and calling him "Miss Nancy." Life with Cornelius at home was terribly hard for the children and their mother. Used to his freedom on the road as a salesman, Cornelius felt trapped by his desk job, his family, and his life. He was loud, belligerent, prone to drinking bouts and gambling. There were long, noisy, and sometimes violent scenes and arguments between their parents that Tom and Rose were witness to. Tom, about to enter adolescence, badly needed an outlet for his inner storm of troubles, fears, and feelings.

When he was eleven, a seemingly small but momentous occurrence changed Tom's life. His mother took ten dollars from the household spending money and bought him a secondhand typewriter. It was large and clumsy and sounded like a threshing machine, but Tom was delighted with it and spent hours banging away on the keys.

At eleven, Tom entered a writing contest offered by a flour company. He wrote a wonderful composition praising crisp, brown muffins. He didn't win the contest. Then, at age twelve, he wrote his first literary piece. Told by his teacher to look around the classroom at the pictures on the wall and choose one to write about, he chose a picture of the Lady of Shalott, the legendary lady drifting down a river in her boat. He read his paper before the whole class, and it was much appreciated. "From that time on," he was later to say, "I knew I was going to be a writer."

His first known published works are two poems written for his junior high newspaper. One poem, called "Nature's Thanksgiving," describes the woods in autumn. The other poem, "Old Things," is about the worn but beautiful contents of an old attic. Each of these poems is surprisingly mature and well written for one so young. Tom was in the ninth grade at the time. Tom—or rather, Tennessee—wrote poetry all his life, and poetry runs through all of his plays. You could say he was a poet who wrote for the theater and not be far wrong.

In the summer of 1928, when Tom was seventeen, he went with his grandfather Dakin on a trip to Europe. While in Paris, he experienced a strange and terrifying psychological crisis that had nothing to do with the trip or his companions. He describes it in his *Memoirs* in this way:

It began when I was walking alone down a boulevard in Paris. . . . Abruptly, it occurred to me that the process of thought was a terrifyingly complex mystery of human life. I felt myself walking faster and faster as if trying to outpace this idea. It was already turning into a phobia. As I walked faster I began to sweat and my heart began to accelerate, and by the time I reached the [hotel] where our party was staying, I was a trembling, sweat-drenched wreck . . .

The phobia stayed with him for over a month and grew worse, until he was convinced that he was going mad. One day while visiting a cathedral, he found himself in a panic. He knelt to pray, and then, as he puts it, a miracle occurred: "It was as if an impalpable hand were placed upon my head, and at the instant of that touch, the phobia was lifted away as lightly as a snowflake though it had weighed on my head like a skull-breaking block of iron." This episode made Tom an unashamed believer in God; he would remain so for the rest of his life.

For a week he felt wonderful, and began at last to enjoy his European tour. But then his phobia began to return. This time, in Amsterdam, he exorcized his fears by writing a short poem:

Strangers pass me on the street
in endless throngs: their marching feet,
sound with a sameness in my ears

that dulls my senses, soothes my fears,
I hear their laughter and their sighs,
I look into their myriad eyes:
then all at once my hot woe
cools like a cinder dropped on snow.

That little bit of verse with its recognition of being one among many of my kind—a most important recognition, perhaps the most important of all, at least in the quest for balance of mind—that recognition of being a member of multiple humanity with its multiple needs, problems and emotions, not a unique creature but one, only one among the multitude of its fellows, yes, I suspect it's the most important recognition for us all to reach now.

He saw this second gentle lesson, in the form of an inspiration for a poem, as coming from the same divine source as the first saving touch. It was a profound period in his young life. Perhaps this crisis, beginning with overwhelming terror and ending with a sense of salvation and his common link to all humanity, was the wellspring for the thread of truth that runs through all of his plays, even the very unrealistic ones. It is perhaps this truth, which shows us how we are all linked together, how one person's sufferings affect us all, that Williams's audiences recognize and are touched by, sometimes without their even being aware of it. Possibly, this mystical experience was the beginning of his greatness.

After his trip, Tom returned for his final semester of high school. By now, he was writing constantly, for one thing or another. Often he would enter advertising contests. He sold his first short story—a lurid tale of ancient Egypt, filled with murder, revenge, and suicide—to *Weird Tales*, a popular pulp magazine. This piece, "The Vengeance of Nitrocris," earned him thirty-five dollars, his first big writing money. Tom "wrote" his first play at a summer camp amateur night, rewriting Shakespeare's *Romeo and Juliet*, making all of the poetry rhyme. It was a bold experiment for a teenager.

Tom set off for college in the fateful year of 1929, the beginning of the Great Depression. There was no money to be had for his education. Fortunately, Grand came through with a thousand dollars in tuition money, so off Tom went to the University of Missouri, in Columbia.

One sad result of this departure for college was his breakup with Hazel Kramer. The two, children when they met, had been sweethearts all through high school. Cornelius disapproved of the idea of Tom marrying early, and with his influence (Hazel's grandfather worked for him) persuaded the Kramer family to send Hazel to Wisconsin for college. Tom, in a panic, proposed to her in writing on the day he arrived at the university. But no answer was forthcoming, and shortly thereafter, Hazel found a new boyfriend. She later was unhappily married, divorced, and died mysteriously in Mexico. Williams never asked another woman to marry him, and never quite forgave his father for their breakup. Would he and Hazel have married if this forced parting had not occurred, and would his whole life have been different? No one knows, but Tom's brother, Dakin, in his biography of his famous brother, admitted his belief that it might have turned out differently.

In college, Williams entered the Missouri School of Journalism. He intended to become a journalist after graduation. When he wasn't studying or playing pranks on his fraternity brothers, Williams was busy writing. His first serious play, *Beauty Is the Word*, was written in his freshman year and was the first freshman play to be given honorable mention in the Dramatic Arts Contest. He signed his work at the time with his full name, Thomas Lanier Williams. The play has never been produced.

At first, Tom's grades were high and he worked to keep them that way, but over time he began to fall behind in some courses as he concentrated more and more on his writing and less on his studies. He did well in English and one or two other subjects, but flunked out of Reserve Officers' Training Corps (which had been a requirement), and did poorly in most of his other subjects. As far as his father was concerned, failing ROTC proved that his son "was no good at college." So after Williams's third year at Columbia, the first of three universities he was to attend, Cornelius announced that he could no longer afford to send him to school. He was forced to drop out.

Cornelius found his son employment at the Continental Shoe Company. This job was to last from 1931, when Williams was twenty, to 1934. The job, which he thoroughly hated, brought him sixty-five dollars a month. He was given tedious, arduous, and menial tasks that called on no part of his intelligence or imagination. Every morning he had to dust hundreds of pairs of shoes in the company's sample rooms, then spend hours typing up factory orders. In the afternoons he would carry huge packing crates of shoes across town to different stores. Still, he made friends at his job, and would spend hours in whispered conversations about stage shows, good movies, and radio shows he had enjoyed. In the evenings Williams kept at his writing, staying up late into the night. Sometimes his mother would find him in the morning sprawled fully clothed across his bed, where he had finally thrown himself in exhaustion.

He was writing both poems and short stories, usually turning out one story a week. He had worked out a pattern for his free time. Saturday afternoons were always the same: a trip to the library in downtown St. Louis, where he would read all afternoon; a thirty-five-cent lunch at his favorite restaurant; and a long ride home on the streetcar, while he polished the week's story in his head. Sundays were devoted to finishing up the story. Then he'd mail each piece off to *Story* magazine, hoping for publication. At first the editors sent personal notes of criticism, which he found encouraging. But soon he began to receive back nothing but rejection forms.

Weekdays Williams worked on poetry, some of which he later admitted was very bad indeed. Some of these poems were published by the local newspaper. His stories, which he was able to spend more time on, are much better, and many of these are preserved in the archives of the University of Texas. One short story, "Stella for Star," was awarded first prize in an amateur writing contest sponsored by the St. Louis Writers' Guild.

In the spring of 1934, Williams developed a heart condition, which troubled him for the rest of his life. At times he was able to ignore it, and at other times would become obsessed with fear and worry by it. The problem was probably made worse by his heavy smoking, but whatever the cause, he suffered two separate attacks of palpitations and was admitted to a hospital for observation. He remained in the cardiac ward for over a week. Shortly after his return home Williams, with huge relief, submitted his resignation to the Continental Shoe Company. It was politely accepted.

It was after his return from the hospital that Williams first admitted to himself that Rose was obviously suffering from some form of grave mental disturbance. For years, the family had refused to accept the situation, but now her symptoms could no longer be ignored. Williams later admitted that he and Rose were closer to each other than is usual for brother and sister. Over the years, Tom's love for Rose and his guilt and torment over her illness were the source of both his deepest anguish and inspiration for his writing. At this point, Williams left once more to attend Iowa University. Grand had come through with some money and he was anxious to be off. He never saw the really frightful part of Rose's psychotic episodes, as did the rest of the family. To Williams, her condition was heartbreaking and dreadful, but also somehow bittersweet in its tragedy.

Rose was observed for several months while the family debated a course of action. In crisis, they succumbed to the doctors' suggestion that Rose be "treated" with a new, barely tested form of brain surgery. She underwent a lobotomy. It was a tragic mistake. The wild, explosive, and dangerous behavior was gone, but also gone was the Rose her brother knew and loved. In her place was a placid, mindless stranger who barely talked sense to him. He would forever be haunted by this loss of his sister, worse than any physical death.

In 1938 Williams received his B.A. from the University of Iowa. He had spent his time there feverishly writing stories and plays, a few of which were produced locally or broadcast on the radio. After graduating, Williams sent a huge bundle of his plays to the Theatre Guild in New York. He had joined the Dramatists' Guild in New York, with the hope that one of his plays would eventually be produced on Broadway.

Most of the next year he spent as a penniless drifter, living now in New Orleans, now in Los Angeles, even spending some months in Mexico. He lived off handouts from his mother and grandmother, and took odd jobs that barely kept him alive. He worked as a shoe salesman, a theater usher, a waiter, an elevator operator, a squab picker. For a while he bicycled twenty-four miles a

Tennessee Williams sails for Morocco in 1948. THE BETTMANN ARCHIVE.

day between jobs. Through it all, his real work was his writing, and at this he was tireless, usually rising very early in the morning to write for six to eight hours a day. He literally starved for days at a time.

Finally, the hard work and his untiring faith in his writing brought him recognition. In 1939 Tennessee, as he now called himself, received a Rockefeller grant of $1,000, a fortune to him. It was paid out at a hundred dollars a month, and kept his writing going now in relative comfort. He was approached by various theatrical agents, and he chose one of them, Audrey Wood, to represent his work. Her job was to sell his plays to Broadway producers. Her tremendous energy matched his, and their partnership was to last almost thirty years.

In 1940 it appeared that Williams's break was coming at last. The Theatre Guild produced his play *Battle of Angels*, but the plot, about a young stranger who takes the women of a small town by storm, was considered too racy by the proper Boston audience at its premiere, and it failed. Somewhat daunted but still determined, Williams continued to move about, now in New York, now on Cape Cod, even at times back under the unhappy parental roof. It was there, during the early years of World War II, that Tom took up

an old manuscript and began to rework it into what would become his masterpiece.

It had several working titles—*Portrait of a Girl in Glass* was one, *If You Breathe, They Break* another. But Williams finally settled on the title *The Gentleman Caller*. The play is Tennessee's most autobiographical work, and the main characters are clearly based on himself, his mother, Edwina, and to a lesser extent, his sister, Rose. He wasn't sure just how the play would turn out, but he called it a "memory play," and writing it was a painful experience for him.

Williams wasn't able to stand living with his troubled family for long, and fortunately was offered a six-month contract as a Hollywood script writer. His salary was very good, but he was unhappy writing for anyone but himself, and was actually relieved when his contract was not renewed. He was now thirty-two, penniless, seemingly unable to hold a job, though greatly respected by a few people who knew his work. A few believers were trying to get his plays produced, but time was catching at him, and he had begun to feel like an utter failure.

Then, quite suddenly, after all the years of struggle and starving and accepting bad jobs and humiliating handouts, it happened. Tennessee had finished *The Gentleman Caller*, now retitled *The Glass Menagerie*, and had taken it back to New York. He presented it to his agent, Audrey Wood. She showed it to Eddie Dowling, an independent producer, who was struck by the haunting, simple beauty of the play. He found a financial backer for it, and Dowling himself wanted to take the central role of Tom. For the part of Amanda, the character based on Edwina Williams, the actress Laurette Taylor came out of her self-imposed retirement, while the brilliant young actor Julie Haydon took the part of Laura, a touching, gentle depiction of Rose as Tennessee liked to remember her.

The play opened in Chicago on an icy December 26, 1944. There had been a tryout and the audience seemed to like the play, but no one knew exactly how it would be received. *The Glass Menagerie*, filled with bittersweet poetry, is about a young man, Tom, remembering the family he has left behind—his charming, domineering mother, Amanda, who lives in the past of her Southern girlhood; and his sister, Laura, crippled and painfully shy, hiding from the world, playing with her collection of glass animals. In the course of the play, Tom, at his mother's insistence, brings home a "gentleman caller" for Laura, but Amanda's plans come to nothing. The play ends with the departure of the

Jessica Tandy played Amanda in the 1983 Broadway production of *The Glass Menagerie*. PHOTOFEST.

gentleman caller, and Tom, turning away from the memory, says, "Blow out your candles, Laura—and so, good-bye." And the curtain falls.

And as the curtain fell on December 26, 1944, at the Chicago Civic Theater, there was, for one moment, not a single sound. Edwina Williams, who was there for the opening night, feared that the audience had not liked it. But then the applause came like the breaking of a huge wave, growing louder and louder, crashing up over the footlights. One critic returned to see the play three times in three days.

It was no surprise, then, that *The Glass Menagerie* was an instant hit when it opened in March of 1945 on Broadway. Not only did the audience like it, they had been told they would like it and had come prepared to like it. The lines at the box office stretched for a city block. Never again would Williams know what it was to starve. And he immediately set about repaying the kindnesses of his friends and family. Within days, he set up an account whereby his mother, who had always believed in and supported him, would receive half of all royalties the play earned. With this she was to live in comfort for the rest of her life. Rose was similarly provided for; Williams bought her a lovely cottage at a private sanitarium, and set up a trust for her lifetime. He was generous with his newfound wealth, helping many struggling artists.

Williams never quite got used to fame and fortune, and forever remained obsessed about his work. Play after play, hit after hit followed *Menagerie,* including *A Streetcar Named Desire* and *Cat on a Hot Tin Roof,* which won the author Pulitizer prizes. Tennessee Williams, when he died in 1983, had become a household word. On the day following his death, the *New York Times* ran an editorial entitled "Remembering Magic," noting that "Tennessee Williams . . . left many mourners: strangers who for forty years depended on him for the most magical evenings in American theatre." His magic lives on in the beautiful poetry of his words.

PART IV

MODERN
ACTORS

Jean-Louis Barrault

1910– French mime, actor, producer, and director

"A theatre stage has always made me think of a conjurer's box," wrote Jean-Louis Barrault.

> A theatre stage has always made me think of a mysterious cube, ten metres a side, a sort of dark room where enchantment reigns.
> Let us imagine it: a box, the magic room, the cube.
> At the moment it is empty. A block of frozen silence, full of potentialities.
> Soon the silence is gently ruffled, as water is rippled by the passing of an invisible fish.

A figure appears, his dark eyes flash under high, arched brows, and bright red lips move magically on his white white face. Instantly, we are enchanted by his movements. It is Barrault, Barrault of a thousand faces, master of the silent art.

Jean-Louis Barrault is one of the most talented of a very special group of actors, the mime. He apprenticed in the old French tradition, the Comédie Française. Then he went on to create new techniques of acting and some of the most innovative and exciting theater of the twentieth century. His stagecraft is a medley of the spoken word, mime, dance, and music. He first became known to Americans as Baptiste in the magical, one-of-a-kind film *Children of Paradise* (1945). But he has played hundreds of roles, founded theaters in France, and become an inspiration to actors all over the world.

Jean-Louis was born on September 8,

Jean-Louis Barrault in the costume and makeup of a mime. EVERETT COLLECTION.

1910, in Le Vésinet, a suburb of Paris. He recalls in his memoirs:

> My father, Jules Barrault, was a young chemist there. His dispensary was a modest one, and he made both ends meet by working at a lunatic asylum in the neighbourhood. . . . His real love was politics: he was a socialist. . . . Deep down in him he felt as a poet, which made him faint at the sight of blood when an injured man was brought into his shop. He was thirty-four, and had only eight more years to live.

Before his father, there had been several generations of winegrower Barraults tending their vineyards outside their little village. "For three centuries wine has flowed in our veins. I feel I am a peasant. . . . my hands are more like great paws."

Barrault's mother, Marcelle Hélène Valette, was born "in the heart of Paris." Her father had a small candle shop and was a thrifty, businesslike man who memorized Latin quotations so that he could drop them here and there in his conversations with his wealthy customers. He was a proud man who sent his children to the best schools. But in the Paris of those days, the children of shopkeepers were not allowed to forget who they were. At the convent school, "my mother, poor thing, had to learn the hard way, what are called class distinctions. The daughter of this *bourgeois gentilhomme* [gentleman shopkeeper] was made to suffer the worst humiliations at the hands of the nobility, and this marked her for life. . . . Still, my mother did receive a particularly refined education (although having suffered so much from it, she became the opposite of stuck-up)."

Jean-Louis suffered more than remembered his early years. His brother, Max, had come first and now his mother hoped for a daughter. Undeterred by the birth of a second son, she simply called Jean-Louis her "little girl." His brother called him Nénetté, after a popular girl doll.

One of Jean-Louis's earliest memories was when he was four, when one night, in his little bed, he was awakened by a raspy beard brushing against his face and a kiss—his father saying farewell. It was August 1914, the Great War had begun and Jules Barrault had been called into the army. He was a stretcher bearer in the front lines while, at home, Marcelle ran the chemist's shop.

Jean-Louis recalled occasional visits with his father in his barracks and in the gloomy hospital. He remembers, too, his father's premonitions of death.

> Summer came; he took us on leave. . . . He talked to me—I think for the first time—as a little man. I hope I too took

him seriously. . . . We visited the vineyards. We took part in the vintage. When night came, we would lie, snuggling against him, on the wall of that terrace where I still never lie down without a shiver. He talked to us about the stars, life, love, his approaching death, and our mother, whom he loved. There are two lines by him which stay in my memory:

> My heart's an old man sitting on
> a hill
> Looking down at the road by which
> he came. . . .

That is himself at that moment: he was forty-two. Those nights at Beauregard when I was eight! . . . Jules Barrault died on 16 October 1918.

Two years later Jean-Louis's mother remarried. He was happy for her (though his older brother, Max, refused to go to the wedding). But he missed his father and fell into a deep loneliness that never went away. "A child who loses his father when he is eight," Barrault wrote many years later, "is in danger of being an orphan till he dies. . . . A corner of our being will suffer loneliness for life, and be nervous and fear-ridden."

Jean-Louis, Max, Marcelle, and her new husband, Louis, moved in with Marcelle's parents. There was no money and her father had taken them in, but it was not happy under his roof. Dependent on the old man as they were, they

had to endure his lectures and sermons, his scoldings, and fits of temper. This is where Jean-Louis passed into adolescence, into the craziness of the years after the war, the twenties. He recalls a kaleidoscope of sounds and images—seeing his first automobiles, listening to early radio broadcasts on a crystal set through little black earphones, jazz, ragtime, dancing the Charleston—"I was a champion"—Lindbergh's flight, and African art—"I was present at the postwar whirlwind."

Because of his frail health Louis was advised to leave the city. He took Marcelle back to the old country home to live, and Jean-Louis—now fourteen—stayed in Paris with his uncle Bob. Bob had been crippled in the war and now had a wholesale flower business. He was a talented painter and encouraged his nephew to paint and draw in pastels. Was this, Jean-Louis began to wonder, his life's work? Or would it be his mother's first love, the theater? "I was from now on, secretly, at grips with two vocations."

Barrault was an excellent study and passed through the six forms of grammar school and into the *collège*, or secondary school, ahead of the other students. But, as he admits, he was not well behaved. He spent a lot of time in the hall, having been thrown out of class. He would steal a janitor's broom, rig it above the classroom door, make a loud noise, and then wait for the teacher to burst through the door and be clobbered by the falling broom.

Barrault loved mathematics more than any other subject, which seems strange for a boy so artistic, but he had found a surprise in solid geometry. Here he was taking a figure which existed on one plane—a flat sheet of paper—and creating from it a three-dimensional object, a thing. "Oh yes!—it is exactly like taking a text printed on paper and making of it a show. This poetry of space was leading me on. But I was not yet aware that that is what theatre is."

When not in school, Barrault explored the city or played football (soccer) with his friends in the local park. Bob, who was more like a big brother than an uncle, saw to it that he experienced life beyond school. Together they went to the Louvre, where Jean-Louis delighted in the paintings of the Impressionists and Cubists.

I loved Van Gogh, his tragic life; when I thought of him I would touch my ear. It was still there, but I would have gladly cut it off if that would have made me a hero like him. I loved heroes. Above all, above all I loved the theatre. I was always making up, disguising myself. I learned soliloquies. I thought up subjects. I played whole scenes, with myself as audience.

Uncle Bob read poetry to him and sometimes in the evenings after supper, they made a game of exploring the dictionary, choosing words at random and discovering their meaning and origins.

During the summers Jean-Louis found another love that called to him as strongly as his art and the theater, the country life. He was attracted to the life of the peasant, the shepherds, and the herdsmen; he loved to milk the cows and play with the goats. But most of all, he loved the winegrowers' life. He spent hours watching the nurseryman lovingly pruning the pear trees, and worked long hours in the vineyard. "At fifteen I was capable of doing my day's work as a winegrower. I learned to prune, to dig, to cut back, to tie up [the vines]." When his parents offered him a gift for his excellent work at the *collège*, he asked that they apprentice him to a farmer for the summer, and so they found a farmer nearby who would take him on. His favorite time of the year was September, the time of the harvest and the wine making, and the subtle change of the seasons.

Barrault was becoming closer to the theater, though he rejected its strange, discomforting pull on him. His mother had joined an amateur dramatic society as she had in her younger years—"She acted in comedies and was happy"—and now his brother, Max, had joined too.

For Jean-Louis, however, the theater was still beyond reach, mysterious, something forbidden. He became enchanted with the verse and ballads of the fifteenth-century French poet François Villon. They had a lot in common, Villon and Barrault. Villon had lost his father at an early age, and he too was a prankster, and he loved Paris. He roamed the French countryside and wrote his ballads in the jargon of thieves.

Barrault discovered the acting of Louis Jouvet, who would later become his mentor. However, now sixteen, he was still afraid. When he was offered a chance to meet Jouvet, Barrault refused. "Jouvet frightened me, I didn't dare. Besides, the stage was a scorching thing, like hell. It was too sober for a scamp. And at the same time the stage tempted me. . . . In short, between these aspirations I remained hesitant and timid."

For a while Barrault's practical old grandfather took charge of his life, and apprenticed him to a bookkeeping firm. One day, while on an errand, he decided not to return to the office, and like his poet friend Villon, he took to the road without even going back to collect his pay. He worked for a while with his uncle, selling flowers at Les Halles. "Life in the market was indeed marvelous. There I found my artists." There he could observe people, rub shoulders with them in the cafés, enjoy the twilight. "Les Halles, my first theatre." At nineteen Barrault returned to school, only now as an assistant to the teacher. He soon found teaching insufferable. He was attending the art school at the Louvre, and though he loved the painting and the beautiful mysteries of the museum, he did not feel fulfilled in his art. Later, he recalled this time in his life as the poet Paul Claudel wrote:

> That enormous Past pushing us
>   forwards with an irresistible power
> And in front of us all that enormous
>   Future breathing us in with an
>   irresistible power.

Until now he had worked at life, but now he discovered that one thing was effortless—the theater, which simply breathed him in. He was going to the theater more and more now, the Comédie Française and the plays of leading French dramatists. He saw many of the most talented actors of the day, including a young unknown, Charles Dullin. There was a theater opposite the school where he was teaching, the Théâtre des Arts, and one day, on an impulse, he took a walk-on part. "I prefer to give up trying to understand," he mused later. "What is certain, clear and decisive is that I wanted more and more to go on the stage. I wanted it frantically. . . . I wanted the theatre desperately. All through my life, indeed, I have acted like that, 'desperately.'" And so, in desperation, he sent a letter off to the actor and teacher he so much admired, who had been so much now in his thoughts, Charles Dullin. Let him decide, Barrault thought, if I really belong in the theater.

Barrault received his reply, a "summons" from Dullin for an audition. Barrault had prepared two scenes. Dullin listened and watched with curiosity as Jean-Louis played the several roles in each scene by himself—"whenever I changed character I gave a leap like a goat and addressed the shade I had just left. . . . When I had done, Dullin said in a whisper:

> "Do you really want to go on the stage?"
> "Yes, sir."
> "This is serious! Are you ready to starve?"
> "Yes, sir."
> "Have you anything to live on?"
> "No, sir."

Dullin must indeed have been impressed. He did something he never did, took on Barrault without charging him the school fees, begging him not to tell another soul. Barrault was an avid student. Dullin became Barrault's master and led his young disciple through adventure, madness, youth, and passion. "I was being born for the second time."

Several months of hard work later, Dullin summoned him to his dressing room and once again he was questioned about his commitment to the stage. Barrault was now even more adamant about becoming an actor. "Very well," Dullin abruptly announced, "that's agreed. You are now part of the company. You will get 15 francs a day and as a start you will learn the part of Volpone's servant." So it was that on his twenty-first birthday, Barrault made his debut at the Atelier Theater.

As always with people he admired and respected, Barrault trembled and blushed and made his worst mistakes in Dullin's presence. Then, one day, Barrault stammered out his fear of disappointing his teacher. Dullin said: "You want to do too well. That's why you do badly." Now, because he had finally confessed his fears in all frankness, there was a new, deeper bond between the young actor and his teacher. From this experience and from his own years of teaching Barrault concluded: "A master is a good master only so far as the pupil lets him be a good master. The nourishment he brings you depends on the nourishment you let him bring. It is the pupil who brings out the richness of the master."

It was during those very early days of acting that Barrault learned something else, too.

I made a horrible discovery: stage fright. On stage I was afraid I would faint. The presence of the audience terrified me. In *Volpone* I could feel my body becoming as thin as a halberd; my wig seemed to be perched on a broomhandle. My saliva dried up, my mouth was like a stone, my heart was beating like a drum and everything began to whirl around. That is forty years ago, and I confess it is not very different now. I haven't made much progress. . . . I only act decently when I am very tired, when I no longer have the strength to feel stage fright, as though in a dream.

Barrault's salary was too little for food and rent, and so, as a favor, Dullin let him camp at the Atelier. One night, after everyone had gone off for the night, he decided to sleep on the stage, in Volpone's bed, which remained there after the last act. He opened the curtain so that now he confronted the terrifying, mysterious emptiness of the hall.

The silence of the whole theatre possessed me. . . . I was very near to being afraid and I went and cowered in bed . . . Volpone's bed. . . . There I dreamed and remembered. . . . It was in this theatre that my childhood dream was being realised. I was living the art of the Theatre . . . and I perceived during that night of initiation that the whole art of the Theatre is to make the *Silence* vibrate.

"Dullin's teaching," recalled Barrault, "was based on the essential importance of *living a situation sincerely*. The exercises he taught us were practically always *exercises in sincerity*." Another essential part of Dullin's training was to draw attention to the actor's body and give it expression. And it was here that Barrault received his first lesson in mime from another master, Étienne Decroux. "Miming enthralled me from the first moment, and I was the more passionately interested in it as for the first time I began to see what it meant to have a *gift*."

Barrault continued to study with Dullin and Decroux, at the same time exploring the techniques of mime on his own. He would choose a movement to study—walking, for instance—and become totally engrossed in it, looking at walking, the musculature of walking, the little idiosyncrasies in each of our walks. Rather than focus on the legs or the feet, which only move the body along, Barrault discovered, it is the body that makes the walk, what he calls the "moving WHOLE."

Throughout all this, Barrault was a working actor and was dreaming about producing his own kind of theater. In 1934 he became absorbed in a book lent to him by a friend, *As I Lay Dying*, by William Faulkner. To Barrault the book seemed a study in silence. There was very little dialogue; the characters didn't talk much, only when they were alone; and the main character spoke mostly to himself, in a monologue. It was the story of a wild young man taming a wild horse, and it was the breaking and training of that horse in mime that enthralled Barrault. He would do it, except for a couple of short monologues, in *silence*. But as the rehearsals went on, the actors dropped out one by one; none could see Barrault's vision.

Theater people joked about it; indeed, Charles Dullin, who appeared at the dress rehearsal, apologized to his student for not being able to come to the performance; it would be, he said, "too painful."

Finally, it was the night of the performance. Scenes were rewritten at the last minute. The few actors who stayed on— Barrault now had to play two parts, the boy and his mother, sometimes in the same scene—agreed to go through with it.

The crowd that night laughed and jeered fully ten minutes before the play began, rose to a deafening tumult as the curtain went up, and got rowdier when the actors appeared, stomping, yelling laughing uproariously. And then:

> At the training of the horse silence fell. I felt it for the first time, congealing the audience. . . . Holding both the audience and my horse by an imaginary bridle, I . . .

Jean-Louis Barrault with his wife, the actress Madeleine Renaud. UPI/BETTMAN.

ended with a gallop that shook the whole stage, the horse plunging, rearing, arching on its hind legs, and then a rapid exit at the gallop. The rest of the performance passed off amid silence and interest.

There were long periods, some more than twenty minutes, when Barrault acted in silence. "The only noise I allowed myself was the rhythm trodden on the boards by my bare feet, the wizard beating of my heart, and a whole poetry of breathing. It was theatre in its primitive state."

In the audience that night was the French dramatist Antonin Artaud, who was creating a new kind of visual theater of his own. "Just breathing alone," he had written, "provides a whole laboratory of magic." He wrote:

> There is in J.-L. Barrault's play, a marvellous sort of centaur-horse, and great was our emotion on its appearance, as if J.-L. Barrault had brought magic into our lives. . . . It is here, in this enchanted world, that Jean-Louis Barrault performs the antics of an untamed horse and that suddenly one is amazed to see him actually turn into a horse. . . . Victoriously he demonstrates the importance of gesture and movement in space. He gives back to theatrical perspective a place it should never have lost. He fills the stage with pathos and with life.

Louis Jouvet, whose acting schedule would not allow him to come to a performance, asked Barrault if he could please have an extra matinee. Charles Dullin came to see it after all, and wrote appreciatively of it.

Barrault went on to write, adapt, and produce scores of plays, from Aeschylus, Molière, Racine, Shakespeare, and Chekhov to the new writers of his own generation, Albert Camus, Jean Anouilh, Jean Cocteau, André Gide, and Paul Claudel, among others. Each he did with renewed creativity and freshness, always trying to bring new dimensions to the theater. Each required taking the greatest risks. "The theatre," he said, "is first and foremost an art in motion. Everything must always be wiped out, forgotten, so that we can start again."

Ethel Barrymore

1879–1959 First Lady of the American theater

She first appeared on the stage in 1891, when she was twelve; her last public performance was on television, in 1955—sixty-four years of acting in the theater, on the radio, and before movie and television cameras.

She was a member of a royal family of actors, the Barrymores. They were all actors—her brothers, Lionel and John; their father, Maurice; and their mother, Georgie Drew Barrymore, a witty, captivating comedienne. John Drew Barrymore was their celebrated uncle, whose mother, Louisa Lane Drew—John, Lionel, and Ethel's grandmother—was not only a beloved actress but also manager of the Arch Street Theatre in Philadelphia for nearly a quarter of a century. So when Ethel was born, on April 15, 1879—her father named her for

his favorite character, Ethel, in William Makepeace Thackeray's novel *The Newcombes*—there was little doubt that she would be anything but an actor in the Barrymore tradition, which meant a great actor.

It's not clear how many generations of Drews and Barrymores back through the ages appeared on the stage. Ethel begins her own autobiography with her great-grandmother, Grandma Kinloch, who came to America from England. "Mrs. Eliza Kinloch, a Sweet Singer of Ballads," as one of her programs announces, introduced her own daughter to the theater at a young age. Louisa Lane (Ethel never understood why they all had different names—"I never dared ask") made her debut, according to the family story, at a year old, as a crying baby. She debuted on the New York stage at eight. She went on to play Shakespeare and, as Ethel says, all of the classics. Sometime in this busy career she met John Drew, a brilliant and popular Irish actor, whom she married. They soon had four children, among them Georgie, Ethel's mother.

As a young woman, Georgie played small parts in her mother's Arch Street Theatre, and it was there that she met a young English actor, Herbert Maurice Blythe. Blythe had been born into a very proper upper middle-class Victorian family, sent to Harrow, a proper preparatory school, and then to Cambridge University for a very proper education. He became a champion amateur boxer—later in her life, Ethel became a boxing fan—and studied for a career in law. "Then came upon the scene two villains—or angels," as Ethel describes it, "who told him it would be years before he would get a brief, and—'Look at him! And listen to that voice!—the stage!' He was flattered and delighted, and broke it to his family." They were horrified. But he struck a bargain with them. To spare them the embarrassment of having an actor in the family, he would change his name and go to America. Then, if he didn't succeed, he promised to come home and resume his law career.

At twenty-seven and for the first time in New York, Maurice Blythe Barrymore, as he now called himself, landed a role as Laertes in Edwin Booth's *Hamlet*. He fell in with another actor playing Rosencrantz, John Drew. John invited the young Englishman to come home with him for a weekend in Philadelphia, where he met Mrs. Drew and their daughter, Georgie.

What a magic flame was lighted that Sunday in a small house in Philadelphia!—that lovely fair-gallant girl and that overwhelming and unpredictable Briton, my mother and father to be. I don't know how many Sunday visits before they were engaged . . . I should think not many. And then they were married.

The young couple moved in with the Drews, and so it was in the house in Philadelphia that Ethel and her brothers were born—"it was unthinkable that her daughter's children should be born anywhere else. . . . That house was our home as little children. In fact, it was the only home we ever knew together."

"I thought that house in Twelfth Street was enormous—with large rooms and cavernous halls and most alarming echoes. . . . There was a sturdy solemnity about the place which made me seem very tiny." Ethel was a shy little girl in a household that included her two brothers, her parents, her aunt Tibby, her grandmother, Mummum (emphasis on the last syllable), and her great-grandmother, Grandma Kinloch.

I was brought up in the interim of busy lives, lives of the theater, where children had to be set aside and cared for by others, so my most vivid memories of the beginning are naturally those connected with the rare times when the family were together. If I speak of my elders a great deal in these early years it is, first of all, because I had a remarkable grandmother and because my parents had a romantic glamour about them which appealed to a child.

Perhaps more than any other person in her life, Ethel was inspired by her grandmother, Mummum. "I never met anyone who had quite the amazing force without effort that my grandmother possessed," she wrote later. Louisa was an amazing woman, for any age, but especially in her own, when women's lives were so restricted. She was active in the theater for seventy years, both as actress and manager of what she rightly called "Mrs. John Drew's Arch Street Theatre." The same year she took over the theater—redecorating, straightening out the finances, and putting together a company of actors—Louisa performed in forty-two roles! Mrs. John Drew brought to her stage many of the finest actors in the world, among them Edwin Forest, whose pictures Ethel remembers on Mummum's piano at home. Ethel often accompanied her grandmother in her carriage to the theater,

and "when she reached her office she would go over books, listen to reports, sign documents and inspect things with the regal manner which betokens state affairs."

As close as she was to Mummum, Ethel had a loving but distant connection with her mother and father. The children were cared for mostly by a nanny. Ethel remembers that her father "had a really startling beauty," that he was charming and seldom serious about anything, that he often told them bedtime stories, but that she had no real sense of him as a father. Of her mother she knew little. Georgie had been on the stage since she was fifteen when she acted opposite her own mother in a play called *The Ladies Battle*. The relationship between Georgie and her mother had also been unnaturally austere and formal. Georgie was lauded as "the most accomplished comedienne of her time," and Ethel remembers her mother's unerring sense of comic timing, but they were not close. She wrote later:

> I often wonder what those days would have been had I really known my mother well. I have only intermittent pictures of her—a tall, fair, slender girl with blue eyes. I looked at her in worship and in silence, longing to talk with her, but fearing, out of the very shyness of my nature, to speak to her.

In 1882, when she was three, Ethel left her comfortable home in Philadelphia to go on her first tour—actually, it was her father's tour. Maurice had begun acting with the famous Polish actress Helena Modjeska, famous for being the first Nora of Ibsen's *A Doll's House* in the United States. As young as she was, Ethel always remembered the excitement of being taken to a private railway car in which they would tour. What she remembered most, though, was being welcomed by "what I now know to be the most charming and entrancing woman I was ever to meet. . . . Madame Modjeska was stamped on my mind and heart indelibly for my life, and my gratitude is unbounded."

Their relationship was more than that of dreamy-eyed little girl and a renowned, worldly actress from Warsaw. Modjeska had lost a daughter, her only child, when she was very young, and now she was drawn to Ethel as the daughter she had lost. Ethel adored her. Modjeska would take her and Lionel out for tea and little cakes and give them parties in her hotel suite, serving them Polish sweets she had enjoyed as a child. Ethel was allowed behind the scenes to watch her father and Madame Modjeska play Romeo and Juliet, but that she would see again and again. Most important, on this trip, she seemed to have two mothers, two beautiful ladies who loved her, but one, especially, who showered her with attention and affection.

The tour with Madame Modjeska would be the first of many for Ethel. They returned to Mummum's house and soon left for England. Maurice acted in new plays by Oscar Wilde and the French dramatist Victorien Sardou. The children spent days in the parks and the British Museum with their nanny, Polly, so beautiful, Ethel remembered, for her "crinkly red hair." Their home became a gathering place for artists, writers, and actors, and the children got used to meeting and talking with Oscar Wilde or the famous actress Ellen Terry or some other interesting person. Ethel remembered these always as the happiest of times, especially when Maurice took her and Lionel to see the pantomime at Drury Lane or the zoo in Hyde Park.

Everything about those two years was magical. Those London days are clear and shiny in my mind. Our house was in St. John's Wood Road, with a garden surrounded by a tall brick wall. From our nursery at the back of the house on the third floor we could see Lord's cricket ground where all the most famous matches were played. We used to borrow father's field glasses and try to watch the matches. We had a lovely big garden and a great many animals— dogs and monkeys. Papa loved monkeys and birds.

The return to Mummum's house, complete with monkeys, birds, and Polly, meant a new life now that Ethel was older—six—and it was her time to go to school. She was enrolled in the Academy of Notre Dame, a convent boarding school in Philadelphia, where she was known to students and the sisters alike as "Little Ethel." She amused the other girls with her English accent and enjoyed her life there, though now she saw her mother and father only occasionally, on weekends and summer vacations. Lionel was gone from her life too, far away at a boarding school for boys outside New York City. But she worked hard and dreamed of becoming a pianist. She became an accomplished musician during her school years and won a silver medal for her playing of a Beethoven sonata.

Ethel's greatest fear was reciting in front of the class and having to memorize:

In the classrooms I suffered much because of my shyness. Whenever we were told to memorize anything for our English class and had to stand up and say it the next day, I had my full quota of torture. The ease with which so many of the children rattled off Shakespeare was a constant source of wonderment to me.

But one of her classmates remembers it differently: Ethel "could memorize to beat the band. Boy, could she reel off Longfellow!"

Ethel had always had the security of knowing that her parents were there for her, and when they were away on tour as they were more and more now, there was always Mummum and the house on Twelfth Street. But while she was away at school, life as she had known it for so long began to change. Grandma Kinloch had died and, a year later, Aunt Tibby.

Then, in 1892, after thirty-one years as its manager and hundreds of roles on its stage, Mrs. John Drew left the Arch Street Theatre. She was seventy-two. Louisa was leaving behind more than just a theater; she had lost her spiritual home. With tears streaming down her cheeks, the beloved actress stepped out to the footlights to speak to the audience that had just applauded her performance so warmly, not realizing it was her last. "This week has been a very happy one for me," she told them, her voice breaking. "The only drawback was, it was the last. To hear these walls resound with applause for simply acting and nothing more, the acting of an old comedy, merely acting, is something to make an actor's heart almost burst with joy. I thank you sincerely. . . ."

With all of her children settled in schools, Georgie had returned to the stage, bringing down houses from New York to San Francisco with her sparkling wit and gifted sense of the comic. The only cloud over her life now was a troubling cough, and her doctor advised her to return to California, to the warmth of Santa Barbara. She took Ethel out of school, and together they went off to the sunshine.

Georgie seemed happy and seemed, too, to be healing. (Actually, she was suppressing her worsening cough so as not to alarm her daughter.) Then it happened so suddenly. Ethel was strolling home from church one morning:

> I saw a girl running toward me. It was Mabel, the mayor's daughter. She called to me "Oh Ethel! Hurry home, your mother has had a hemorrhage." I got home just before she died. She didn't know me. She was thirty-four and a great and gallant lady, my beloved mother whom I hardly knew.

It was up to Ethel now to pack all the beautiful clothes her mother had laid out, to make all the arrangements with the undertaker and the railroad, and to accompany her mother's body back to Philadelphia. Somewhere on that eight-day journey, sitting all the while in her long black dress, Ethel realized, "Next month I'll be fourteen."

Unlike many actors' children, Ethel had not been immediately attracted to the stage. She was terribly shy, terrified of having to memorize her part, and was dreaming of becoming a pianist and giving concerts all over the world. (She would continue playing the piano for herself and her friends all her life and be complimented as an accomplished pianist.) She and her brothers had put on their own plays and she had been given minor roles in her parents' and uncle John Barrymore's plays, but she had been allowed a normal life, as normal as the life of the daughter of actors could be.

But everything was different now. Louisa Drew's long tenure with the theater had ended and Georgie was dead. "Suddenly there was no money," Ethel recalled, "no Arch Street Theatre, no house, and I must earn my living. No one talked about it; no one talked about it at all, ever." Ethel was on her way to Montreal with Mummum to play in Richard Brinsley Sheridan's *The Rivals*. At fifteen, Ethel Barrymore's acting career was still slowly, haltingly about to begin.

Ethel's first role was the part of Julia, given to her because it was inconsequential and easily removed if she did badly. She had very little time to learn her lines, but that was theater life, and she'd better get used to it. "On the stage that first night before an audience I was naturally terrified. . . . But there I was, on stage with Mummum and Uncle Sidney, and so began an apprenticeship which was to last for more than half a century." So strong was the Barrymore/ Drew acting tradition in the family that her grandmother just assumed that Ethel too had it in her blood.

> I don't remember being told anything by anyone. Once when I did ask Mummum something about acting, she lifted her eyebrows and said, "You should know that without being told." It always seemed to be taken for granted that I would know what to do without being told. Of course I didn't. Luckily the parts given to me were tiny, so I didn't ruin anything.

The work with Mummum was only occasional, and to fill the spaces in between Ethel went looking for work. These were the months Ethel called "a time of searching," when any job would do. "Day after day I kept on going to agencies and various offices and came home without the faintest sign of an engagement or even hope of one." But if she was discouraged and out of work, John Barrymore, her "Uncle Jack," was not. With the help of his new manager, Charles Frohman, John was becoming a star, and he had not forgotten his niece. More out of wanting to help than any faith in her talents, John got her a small walk-on part and so, in performance after performance of *The Bauble Shop*, Ethel walked on stage carrying a tray, without a word.

The director faced a crisis when the lead actress refused to leave with the company on tour. And Ethel recalls what happened. "I was barely sixteen and the author, Henry Arthur Jones, had described Lady Kate Fennell in the program as 'A Woman of the World, of 45,' some maniac suggested that I be given a trial in the part." The "maniac" was her uncle Jack. She went onstage in the older actress's sophisticated dress and, "feeling very terrified and perhaps a little ridiculous," played the part. Terrified or not, she must have done well, because she went on to play the role in Boston, Philadelphia, Chicago, and St. Louis. In Chicago she was actually noticed by a critic, who described her as "an opalescent dream named Ethel Barrymore that came on and played Lady Kate." She recalled in her memoirs, "I hadn't the faintest idea what that word meant and had to ask Uncle Jack. I was delighted to find it meant something pleasant."

Although her formal education was over—Ethel never returned to school— she read and read everything she could get her hands on and "at least two Dickens books every year." Alexandre Dumas was another one of her favorites, as well as Edgar Allen Poe and a new writer named Rudyard Kipling. She went through periods of fascination with a single author, devouring everything he

Ethel Barrymore as Rosemary. PHOTOFEST.

wrote—Thomas Hardy, Turgenev, William James, Robert Louis Stevenson, and Mark Twain. She loved the poetry of Keats and Shelley, and read all of Walt Whitman and Shakespeare.

It was probably the reading that kept her together during the years of hunger, the cold, discomfort, and loneliness of shabby hotels and rooms. As difficult as these years were, though, Ethel never lost her love of travel. "I never know what some people mean when they complain about the rigors of the road," the veteran actor told an interviewer late in her life. "Lord, they must be very faded lilies indeed if they mind touring! Oh, I look forward to it—the drafty dressing rooms, the rats, everything! It's all part of it."

Although modest about her acting, Ethel's first appearance with John Barrymore must have been something, because soon she was being called on to take roles. She had considerable success with audiences and critics in a play called *Rosemary*, and then a dream came true. Her favorite actor, her "matinee crush" as she called him, was William Gillette, who she went to see every Thursday in his hit play *Secret Service*. Ethel dreamed of meeting him—she had bought his photograph— but those hopes were dashed when she and Uncle Jack went on to St. Louis. Then, one evening, Uncle Jack called her into his dressing room and handed her a telegram he had received, and she read:

WOULD ETHEL LIKE TO GO TO LONDON WITH GILLETTE IN SECRET SERVICE?

Ethel was offered only a small part and understudy, but she was thrilled and soon found herself in London. Once again the young actress was called out from the wings to take the part of the leading lady, who had just fainted and was being carried off to the hospital. Instantly, Ethel stepped into the role and was noticed by all of London. Soon she was meeting and receiving the compliments of the Duke of York, playwright Bernard Shaw, and one of her favorite writers, Henry James, among many other admirers. Still, when the play closed, Ethel found herself without work—she had marvelous letters of introduction, but was too timid to use them—and faced having to leave her beloved London. What happened next is so magical that Ethel has to tell it herself to be believed. She was packing her clothes in her trunk, crying, wiping her eyes, trying to keep the tears from staining her dresses . . . "And a hansom cab stopped at the door with a note for me. It read: 'Dear little Bullfinch: [That was the name [she] called me because she thought I looked like one.] I hear you're going back to America.

Ethel Barrymore *(second from left)* with her sons, Samuel Colt *(left)* and John Drew Colt *(right)* and her daughter, Ethel Barrymore Colt. PHOTOFEST.

Come down to the theatre tonight to say goodbye to Sir Henry and me. Ellen Terry."

Ellen Terry and Sir Henry Irving were the leading actors of their day. Ethel quickly bathed her red eyes, dressed, and went immediately to the theater to Ellen Terry's dressing room. Terry wished her well and insisted, as terrified as Ethel was, that she must go say goodbye to Sir Henry. "So I went to Sir Henry's dressing room and he said, 'So you want to go back to America?'

"'No Sir Henry,' I said, 'I don't, but I can't find anything to do.'

"And he said: 'How would you like to stay here and be our little leading lady!'"

Ethel Barrymore went on to act almost without rest, year after year, hundreds of roles, on Broadway, in all the great cities of the world, in small towns all over America from Maine to California. She played in everything, from drawing-room comedies such as Somerset Maugham's *The Constant Wife* to serious roles such as Nora in Ibsen's *A Doll's House* to Shakespeare— *Hamlet, The Merchant of Venice*, and *Romeo and Juliet*. She acted in one play, *The Corn Is Green* (1940), through three hundred performances. "I like it better than anything I've ever done," she said. "It has everything in it I care about." Late in life, when she was in her sixties, she began a new career in movies, making three or four a year during her first five years in Hollywood. Ethel won an Oscar for her role in Clifford Odet's *None But the Lonely Heart* and Academy Award nominations for other films. Somehow in her busy career she was married to Russell Griswold Colt and raised three children, all of whom have appeared on the stage. And though she never cared for the title, Ethel had truly become the First Lady of the American theater.

Katharine Hepburn remembers visit-

Ethel Barrymore in her famous role as a Welsh schoolteacher in *The Corn Is Green*.
UPI/BETTMANN NEWSPHOTOS.

ing Ethel Barrymore in the last year of her life, bringing her a book or flowers. She was bedridden, and very ill.

She was *beautiful* to look at. . . . and eyes that, well, scared you to death sometimes, and at other times I'd look and think, "Where have you been and what are the lives you have seen, and what really goes on in your mind?"—because although she was a great actress and a great personality and had known everyone in the world, she had a very odd look about her. She was religious. She never talked too much about it, but I think she had great faith in—something. . . . I don't know what the dickens it was. A kind of faith in life, I think. She made you feel that there was something about the human race that was thrilling.

Ethel Barrymore would choose to close with her most famous line:

"That's all there is, there isn't any more."

Helen Hayes

1900–1993 American actress of the stage, screen, radio, and television

"It's because I'm pigeon-toed, you know, that I'm an actress at all." That's how Helen Hayes explains the beginnings of her lifelong career. "When I was five—that would be 1905—my mother sent me to Miss Minnie Hawkes' dancing school to see if my feet couldn't be taught to conduct themselves in parallel lines. That seems to have been accomplished." The little five-year-old who walked funny grew up to become one of the most loved actresses of all time, generally acclaimed the First Actress of the American Stage. Hayes entertained millions of Americans on tour, in summer theaters, on radio, and in the movies. She was one of only two actresses in the history of the American stage to have a theater named after her, the Helen Hayes Theatre in New

York, in celebration of her fiftieth anniversary on the stage. (The other was Ethel Barrymore.)

Helen Hayes Brown was born on October 10, 1900, in Washington, D.C. "Our family background was lower middle-class and quite conventional," Hayes wrote in her autobiography. "We were plain simple folk." Her father, Francis Van Arnum Brown, was a manager and salesman for a wholesale butcher whose mother had opposed his marriage to the lively, attractive Catherine Estelle Hayes, nicknamed Essie. "Grandma Brown felt that Frank, one of five sons, married beneath him; the bride's family were poor Irish immigrants, while the Browns, whose forebears came to America before the Revolution, were solidly middle-class.

The Hayeses, to Grandma Brown, were 'scamp' Irish, too wild and unstable."

Grandma Brown was right; the two were a mismatch from the beginning. Francis was a homebody, satisfied with his job and the quiet routines of household and family. He wanted to have children right away. Essie, however, longed to escape her inevitable role of mother and housewife, to her mind as emotionally restrictive as life with her father had been. She scrimped and saved every penny for tuition to study acting at the Robert Downey School only to find that she was pregnant—"I was an accident," Helen always knew. Essie continued as long as she could as the comedienne in The Liberty Belles touring company.

Essie loved the stage and as a child had been encouraged by her mother to perform. She told her daughter later:

I had a great sense of mimicry and amused my brothers and sisters with a perfect imitation of the star in the afternoon's play. Because of this my mother thought I would be an actress some day and I, flattered by this thought, made up my mind I would be. Years later, I was to find out the difference between an imitation and a God-given gift.

Essie, resigned to her role as wife and mother, helped her daughter Helen become the actress she had dreamed of being.

Essie had always attended theater with her mother, a gray-haired, rough-hewn farm woman. Now she would include her daughter on their adventures. "Graddy," as Helen called her grandmother, "loved the theatre and would scrimp and save in order to buy gallery tickets for plays presented in Washington by touring companies. Among the great actors we saw was Sarah Bernhardt, who performed in French. We didn't know a word of French, but Graddy claimed she could understand most everything because of Bernhardt's broad gestures and intonation."

Hayes enjoyed a happy childhood. After the death of Grandfather Hayes, who little Helen never knew—"His main dream in life was to translate Shakespeare into Gaelic"—Graddy had bought a farm outside the city, where the whole extended family lived, including Aunt Mamie, her husband, and their two children. Hayes recalls:

We were an assorted lot of cousins, aunts and uncles. There was plenty of companionship for playing in the farmyard, tending the vegetable garden, roaming the fields and woods, and sharing huge holiday dinners on Thanksgiving and Christmas, when we exchanged homemade presents which we children put more zeal than skill into.

Helen's father was a busy, practical man with little time for the likes of theater, but he enjoyed being with little Helen in his own way. He was a placid, portly man who was always gentle, preferring the quiet of the garden to the bright lights and hubbub of the theater crowd. He took her instead to a baseball game or to the amusement park to ride the Ferris wheel or to the Washington Monument to hear the U.S. Marine Band conducted by John Philip Sousa.

Helen's earliest memory of going to the theater with her mother was to see Franz Lehar's operetta *The Merry Widow*, which she preferred to Shakespeare then. When she did go to see Shakespeare at a very young age, she of course found it difficult to follow the plot and understand Elizabethan English. Once, when they went to see *Hamlet*, Hayes had an experience which would shape her social conscience for the rest of her life.

> During the play, I nudged Mother a couple of times and asked her to explain what they were saying. "Helen," she whispered, "I'll tell you afterward."
>
> "I can't enjoy it if I don't know what it's about," I replied, beginning to whimper. The action was leading into Hamlet's soliloquy and I was completely confused. As I began to fuss, a deep, resonant voice from the row behind said quietly, "He is wondering whether he should continue to live or end his life."
>
> I turned around and was face to face with a black man who, from then on, whispered in my ear, helping me through my first *Hamlet*.

From this, her first meeting with an African American, Hayes felt all her life the injustice of segregation and racism. Later, when as a famous actress she was in Washington to perform, she discovered that though there were black actors among the cast, blacks were not allowed in Washington theaters. At first she refused to go on stage but relented at the urging of the producer. She told the local newspapers, however, that she was on stage under protest and pointed out the disgrace of segregated theaters in the nation's capital.

> I urged all actors who were members of Actors Equity [the actors union] to refuse to play in Washington until the theatres were integrated. At this, the manager of the National Theatre threatened to close, saying he would not be responsible for the bloodshed if he allowed blacks in. I persisted in my battle. Friends in Washington were heartsick and begged me to stop making such a row, but I never gave up. Today, of course, this seems like ancient history.

Like most children, Hayes began attending school at age five, the Holy Cross Academy, and later the Sacred

Heart Academy. Essie had left the church against her husband's wishes—that was another source of conflict between Helen's parents—but both mother and daughter felt parochial school was a safe haven. Helen loved the nuns, and at one time in her life dreamed of becoming one herself. She enjoyed a secure, happy time among her school friends and the nuns who took to the little girl.

Helen was small for her age and was that way all her life. When later in her career she played the queen in *Mary of Scotland*, she was described as Broadway's shortest leading actress portraying six-feet-tall Mary, history's tallest queen. Theater audiences who thrilled to her performance of the tall, stately queen couldn't believe that she was only five feet tall and weighed but 105 pounds.

While attending Holy Cross, Hayes had her first acting experience debuting as Peaseblossom, one of Titania's fairies in Shakespeare's *A Midsummer Night's Dream*. She was not immediately recognizable as a great actress in the making. In one of her first performances she forgot her dance routine and walked off the stage, having confronted for the first time an immense sea of faces out in the audience looking at her alone. But then she had another opportunity when, at nine years of age, as a little Dutch girl, she touched the audience deeply with the tears in her voice and sobs as she sang about her sweetheart going off to America and leaving her alone on the shore of the Zuider Zee. Essie had directed her daughter right down to the last gesture of dabbing her nose with a corner of her apron at the very end of the song.

Little Helen got to live her mother's dream, a dream seemingly unattainable in Essie's own life but still possible for her daughter. We might find fault with Essie's motives, but the results were that Helen grew up in a rich cultural life. Hayes's biographer, Kenneth Barrow, describes Essie's living through her daughter:

> She didn't as such point Helen in the direction she felt she ought to take but rather took her by the hand and led the way. Thus the worlds of art and music, the opera and the drama were opened up to the child who might have passed her entire childhood and youth in complete ignorance that such things existed. The reason Essie took her to the art gallery and opera house was because she imagined that the fashionable lived their lives that way. She probably seldom saw the paintings she was looking at or heard the music which surrounded her, but she was able to see exactly who was there and how they were dressed. Helen, on the other hand, *saw* the paintings and *heard* the music.

What Essie wanted more than anything was for her daughter to become middle class. "My darling mother," Helen recalled later, "would never admit that her class was wild, scamp, working-class Irish."

Helen was fortunate to have other encouraging and supportive adults in her life. She would never forget Martha Clark, her teacher at Central High, who took her to the theater whenever she could get tickets to a new show. Helen's dancing teacher, Minnie Hawke, believed in her, too, and encouraged her to perform and dream about a life on the stage. It was at Miss Minnie's school that Hayes was noticed and got her first offer for work on the stage. She was playing a Gibson girl, a sophisticated, world-weary woman. As Helen strolled off the stage, in the walk her mother had taught her, the audience burst into cheers and applause, demanding seven or eight bows. In the audience that afternoon, tears of joy rolling down his cheeks, was Lew Fields, of the popular vaudeville team Weber and Fields, who produced and starred in many loved musical comedies. "He must have been amused by my act, for he sent a note to the manager, saying that if my parents wanted a stage career for me, he would like to see them about it in his office in New York." For Hayes's parents it was too much too soon for a little girl.

Though Father took parental pride in this tribute, he wasn't really interested. But Mother was delighted. To her it seemed that destiny in the person of Lew Fields had come and tapped me on the shoulder. But she wisely decided that at the age of six I was too young to brave New York.

Hayes did continue acting. She joined a Washington acting company, the Columbia Players, and made her professional debut as Prince Charles. Fred Burger, the producer who had given Helen's mother her first chance on the stage, now wanted Helen for a child's part in his production of *The Prince Chap*.

> He asked Mother to let me play the role. As extra bait he offered her a part too, and she agreed. I remember playing a boy in an uncomfortable corduroy suit with a stiff collar and tie, but on the plus side, I appeared with my mother, just as years later my daughter, Mary, made her debut acting with me in summer stock.

Hayes went on to act with this group in *The Prince and the Pauper* and *Little Lord Fauntleroy*, all boy's parts.

When she was nine, she gave her first performance in New York, at the Herald Square Theatre, as Little Mime in a Lew Fields production of the Victor Herbert musical *Old Dutch*. Her mother had

Helen Hayes at the age of ten in her first New York performance, in *Old Dutch*. PHOTOFEST.

taken her to Fields's office to remind him of his offer. Fields remembered little Helen and offered her a contract. Her salary was to be fifty dollars a week, a handsome sum in those days, and rehearsals would start in six weeks. As it turned out, Helen not only got her first salary from Fields, but her stage name as well.

As Mr. Fields raised his pen to sign the contract, he inquired of my mother, "What is the little girl's name?"

"Helen Hayes Brown."

"That's too long for a theatre marquee," Fields answered. "We'll call her Helen Hayes."

Hayes looked back on that six weeks as the longest of her life, and she would never forget that first night, November 22, 1909.

What an opening night it was! All the flowers that had been sent to the cast were arrayed along the walls of the lobby, placed in fragrant tiers almost to the ceiling. . . . It was like a fairyland, and Mother and I watched from the secrecy of the box office until we had to scamper backstage for the opening curtain.

From that very first performance, I was hooked on the theatre. Everything was intriguing: the costumes, the scenery and lights, the festively dressed people out front. The actors and crew were my playmates, and the backstage area was my special, magical playground. It was all make-believe, but I didn't pine for an ordinary existence as other child actors did. Of course I'd already had some experience in stock, but it was nothing like a Broadway production.

Hayes learned a lot these first months in the theater; she was observant, quick to pick up her roles, and always looking to the older, more experienced actors for new techniques.

From Mr. Fields I learned that there were three key words for success in the theatre: discipline, discipline, discipline. Mother added bits of practical advice offered by cast members, such as: "Let the writers write, the directors direct, and you stick to what you know best. That's acting." Another proverb passed along from an old vaudevillian was: "Always leave them wanting more."

Hayes went on that season to play other child parts and then returned to the Columbia Players. All the time she continued to study, either in school or at home.

Helen's father remained supportive of his daughter and his wife, though he himself had no interest in the arts.

My father was bewildered by my mother's love of the theatre and her ambition for me. But he was a good-natured man and indulged her whims. I suppose he thought this was just a whim, and we'd soon come home with nothing gained but a look at New York.

Those magical first days in the theater with all the backstage goings-on, the glamour, excitement, great stars, and appreciative audiences ended for a time when Hayes reached the age of twelve. It is an awkward age for some young actresses when they have become too old for a child's role and yet are not quite old enough to act the role of an adult. Reluctantly, Helen and her mother returned to Washington and a husband and father who missed them and was overjoyed at their return. In celebration of their return, Francis bought a new house. Helen, still very young to be away from home so long, missed her father too and looked forward to the family being reunited again. Of course, she knew in her heart that she would return to the stage—it was in her blood now—but it also seemed like a good time to return to school and to take up everyday life where she had left off.

Helen's mother, it was soon clear, was not happy to be home. Indeed, she missed the theater and wished to be back there. Essie did her best to readjust, but she was visited again by suffocating feelings of being trapped, needing desperately to be free. She began dealing with her boredom, unhappiness, and frustration by drinking. It was a new and trying chapter in Helen's life, one that would turn her into an adult very quickly.

For years, I couldn't admit that my mother was an alcoholic. Our family kept the problem hushed up, as families did in those days. But in time, the roles of Mother and myself were reversed: I became the mother, taking care of her, undressing her and putting her to bed. The first time that happened, I had just turned twelve. . . . It was a difficult life, but perhaps coping with Mother strengthened me.

Hayes was home two years when she was called back to Broadway, but this time it was different. She would be not in a musical but a serious play staged by Charles Frohman, one of the most respected producers of the day. The play was *The Prodigal Husband*, a romantic comedy from France, and Hayes would be acting with the elegant John Drew, a spellbinding actor, who became a mentor to Helen. When the play went on tour by train, Drew gave the young actress French lessons and, during stopovers, took her to museums and galleries. Later, when the tour ended, Drew gave Helen a beautifully illustrated biography of Joan of Arc, which she kept and treasured her whole life.

Helen Hayes with her husband, playwright Charles MacArthur, and their daughter, Mary. PHOTOFEST.

The Prodigal Husband was a weak play and it soon closed. Still, it was Helen Hayes's first dramatic appearance in a young woman's role and an important step in her stage career.

Four years later, when she performed on Broadway in *Dear Brutus*, the critics hailed her acting. The playwright Maxwell Anderson felt that "nobody else ever touched *Dear Brutus* with such a wistful beauty as she gave it." Hayes had become a professional actress and began performing play after play, year after

year. She did mostly contemporary plays but also starred in theater classics like *She Stoops to Conquer* and George Bernard Shaw's *Caesar and Cleopatra*.

In 1928 she performed one of her most memorable roles, Maggie Wylie in *What Every Woman Knows*. As a critic put it then, "In consenting to play the part of Maggie Wylie in the revival of *What Every Woman Knows*, Miss Hayes 'came of age' in the theatre. She was no longer Helen Hayes, the ingénue, or player limited to flapper parts, but Helen Hayes the character actress."

That same year she married playwright Charles G. MacArthur and the year after left acting briefly to have her daughter, Mary. Like Helen and Essie, mother and daughter would someday act together.

When Hayes returned to the theater, she was given a play by Maxwell Anderson, who had so much admired her performance in *Dear Brutus*. It was *Mary of Scotland*, the play in which she acted Mary Stuart. Anderson had been in a quandary about giving her the part because she was so short. Then he met her and decided that it was better to have the best possible actress in the role than the tallest. Hayes had a way of thinking herself tall, she once said, and so was able to convince the audience that she was tall. Hayes made the role her own, and for years Americans thought of Helen Hayes as Mary Stuart. Her biographer, Kenneth Barrow, quoted Helen's story about how she made the role so touching and real to her audiences even after 248 performances on Broadway, a story which also reveals the techniques of a great actress.

When I was preparing to play Mary I was taken by a friend to the Morgan Library where I was allowed to hold in my hands and read several letters actually written by Mary. One in particular had been sent to Queen Elizabeth shortly before her execution begging for a chance to speak to her face to face. Although they met in Maxwell Anderson's play they never met in life. "Dear Cousin," the letter began. Reading that long letter one can see the gradual deterioration of her handwriting. At its close she apologizes to her "gracious cousin" explaining that the prison was so cold her fingers couldn't get a proper grip on the pen. At every performance during the entire run of the play I saw that line in my mind's eye, and it somehow made me feel the poor queen's suffering much more poignantly than all the dialogue in Maxwell Anderson's eloquent script.

Hayes seemed to be specially cut out to perform the roles of historical women. Her most brilliant performance, some say of her entire career, was in the role of Queen Victoria in Laurence

Helen Hayes in her famous role as Queen Victoria in *Victoria Regina*. PHOTOFEST.

Housman's *Victoria Regina* (1935). The play ran in New York 123 weeks, and on its tour of forty-three U.S. cities it broke box office records. In all, Hayes acted the role of Queen Victoria—living eighty years in two and a half hours—969 times. Once again, Maxwell Anderson was moved to praise her: "She gave us such moving young grace and such heartbreak in the final scenes that many count *Victoria Regina* their happiest experience in all modern theatre." It was in the thirties, also, that

Hayes began appearing frequently in Shakespearean roles, such as Viola in *Twelfth Night* and Portia in *The Merchant of Venice.*

Hayes appeared on the stage her whole life, but she also enjoyed and experimented with other dramatic forms, especially film and radio. She began in radio in the 1930s appearing with Orson Welles. Then she produced and acted in her own radio series, the *Helen Hayes Theatre of the Air,* and was voted radio's best actress in 1940. She starred in CBS's *Electric Theatre* and put on a series of radio plays by the Helen Hayes Drama Group. In the early days of television, she brought her performance of *Dear Brutus* to the TV screen, to another generation who had not seen her on the stage. Hayes was considered a true professional, an actor's actor by her fellow players.

In all, Helen Hayes was a remarkable woman, acting with a passion, living almost her entire life in the theater, but never entirely *for* the theater. She was happy being first a daughter and then wife, mother to Mary and James, and grandmother to her own family. She had no use for fame and would not want to be counted among the celebrities of her time, though she deserved to be among the very finest of them. She said to biographer Barrow in her later years, toward the end:

There was a time when I thought the theatre and all its absorbing work had deprived me of other things in life. I have learned I was wrong.

I look back on my career with gratitude. If my stage-struck mother hadn't catapulted me into the theatre I'd never have had the opportunity to encounter all the richness in my life—my husband Charlie MacArthur, all the people I've known, the world I've inhabited as an actor. But as for the actual work, I don't think I was ever really happy acting. I lived in deathly fear, wondering if I could make it and after I got to be famous, the expectations got worse. . . . The one thing I can remember vividly is the struggle for perfection—the perfection that always eluded me, but lured me on.

Laurence Olivier

1907–1989 English stage, film, and television actor, director, and producer

At sixteen many boys and their fathers are not very close. Young men at that age are supremely self-centered, having reached an age when they feel they know all there is to know about life. Many fathers are also self-centered, too concerned about their life and work to think about what's in a young boy's heart.

That's what Laurence Olivier thought about his father, a high Anglican clergyman. One sad evening, after his older brother had left for India, perhaps forever, Laurence wondered out loud about his future. "I asked my father how soon I might reckon on being allowed to follow Dickie to India," Olivier recalls in his autobiography. The expected answer was that young Olivier would become a minister, like him.

My father's answer was so astonishing that it gave me a deep shock: "Don't be such a fool; you're not going to India, you're going on the stage."

"Am I?" I stammered lamely.

"Well, of course you are," he said; and as he went on I realized not only that he had been thinking of me quite deeply, which was something I had long before decided he never did, but that he had been following these thoughts through in pleasingly creative and caring ways.

Though Gerard Olivier could not possibly have guessed then, he was making it possible for his son to become one of the most brilliant, certainly the most versatile actor in the history of the theater. Before his long acting career would come to an end, he would perform 121 roles on the stage in Shakespeare and Sheridan, Ibsen and Chekhov, Shaw and O'Casey, Ionesco and Anouilh, Coward and O'Neill and Williams. He would star in 57 films, including *Wuthering Heights, Rebecca, The Entertainer*, and *The Boys from Brazil*, and he would direct several films of his own, among them *Henry V, Richard III*, and *The Prince and the Showgirl*. He is considered the first director to film Shakespeare successfully. Included in his nineteen portrayals on television are Big Daddy in *Cat on a Hot Tin Roof*, Shylock in *The Merchant of Venice*, Lear in *King Lear*, and James Tyrone in *Long Day's Journey into Night*.

He created his own theater, The National Theatre. He was the youngest actor to be knighted and the first to become a lord. As the writer J. B. Priestley described him: "No English actor, living or dead, can begin to compete with him. A Garrick, a Kean, a Henry Irving, merely enjoyed a small local reputation when compared with his. His career has been fantastic, as if a young actor had been visited by a wild dream."

Olivier had been on the stage since he was seven when, at the All Saints Church Choir School, he played Brutus in Shakespeare's *Julius Ceasar*. In succeeding years he played two female roles, Maria in *Twelfth Night* and Katherina in *The Taming of the Shrew*.

His performances were notable, even years later. "Anything [Larry] did was always well above boys' standards," recalled one of Olivier's teachers. "I really think his Brutus was amazingly mature and very moving. Later of course his Katherina was equally brilliant in quite another way and was seen by hundreds in the Memorial Theatre at Stratford."

The school's theater class was of interest to newspaper critics. A critic from the *Daily Telegraph*, who admitted to his readers going to *The Taming of the Shrew* that afternoon out of boredom, suddenly sat up when Olivier appeared. "The boy who took the part of Kate," he reported, "made a fine, bold, black-eyed hussy badly in need of taming. I cannot remember seeing any actress in the part who looked it better." The critic from the *Times* expressed "wonder at lines so well and clearly spoken," and declared that Olivier's performance had "a fire of its own."

Of all the praise Olivier received as a youngster there was one incident that must have touched him deeply. Many distinguished people attended the All Saints productions and on one occasion the audience included Ellen Terry, called the First Lady of the English theater. Terry had begun acting at the age of ten and now, almost sixty, she must have watched the performances with deep nostalgia and appreciation.

Among Laurence Olivier's famous roles was that of Shakespeare's King Henry V in this film production. HULTON DEUTSCH COLLECTION LIMITED.

Dutifully, she went backstage after the performance to praise and encourage the company of young actors. But she had special words for the timid, awkward, bony little eleven-year-old who played Brutus. She actually returned for the next evening's performance apparently just to see Olivier again, and then wrote in her diary: "The small boy who played Brutus is already a great actor."

Olivier was unaware of the honor he had received. The boy was pleased, of course, that this elderly actress had liked his playing, but he had no idea who Ellen Terry was and so had no measure of the praise. It was when he returned home for the Christmas holidays that his mother made him realize that he had received not just praise but praise from England's greatest actress. She also told him about someone else who had been in the audience, Sir Johnston Forbes-Robertson, an artist, theater manager, and celebrated actor. After the performance he introduced himself to Laurence's parents, exclaiming, "My dear fellow, your son *is* Brutus."

In Shakespeare's day male actors played women's parts because women were not permitted to perform in public. This was true in many countries—China and Japan, for example—where there has been a long tradition of female impersonators in the theater. This would also be true for boys' schools like the one Olivier attended, simply because there were no girls to play female roles in the student theatrical productions (and in girls' schools, girls would have to play the male roles).

It was customary—indeed, it was considered an important part of a young actor's training—for girls to play the parts of boys, and boys the roles of girls. There was nothing strange, then, about a young male actor appearing dressed as and playing the role of a woman. Olivier was an accomplished player of female roles. He remembers that Reverend Geoffrey Heald, who directed the plays, "injected into my consciousness a conviction that I was, in fact, being a woman."

When Ellen Terry saw young Olivier as Katherina, she remarked that she had never seen the shrew acted better "by any woman but Ada Rehan," an American actress much admired in England. The actress Sybil Thorndike also sensed the genius in the boy's acting: "I saw Larry in all those productions at All Saints and most of all I was impressed by his Kate. . . . His Shrew was really wonderful—the best Kate I ever saw." Surely, Terry must have been struck by the irony of the evening. She had begun her career as a boy, playing parts like the young Duke of York in Shakespeare's *Richard III*, Mamillius in *The Winter's Tale*, and Puck in *A Midsummer Night's Dream*. Now, here she was watching another young actor, Olivier, beginning his career as a girl.

What was it these accomplished actors saw in the young Olivier? His biographer Thomas Kiernan relates:

On stage he had an eerie authority that immediately drew one's eyes to him. Most of the boys in *Julius Ceasar* were clearly amateurs. I mean, when they didn't have lines to say they stood around like statues watching whoever else was speaking, or else they engaged in obviously stagey side business. But not Olivier. There was something in the way he handled himself, even when he was not engaged in the central action, that made you feel that here was no amateur. Of course, you knew that you were watching an eleven-year-old. But somehow he transported his character out of boyhood into a semblance of actual manhood. He did it with gestures, movement, even standing in repose. And with his eyes. For all of Larry's physical imperfections, he possessed the most compelling eyes.

Whenever the topic of genius comes up there is always the question, where did it come from? Since Olivier was born and grew up in a time of awareness of psychology, there's more discussion of this than with earlier actors. Kenneth Tynan, a longtime friend, thinks he knows. From his father Olivier inherited what Tynan calls "exterior gifts"—his voice, appearance, risk taking, innovation. These alone would have made him a competent but not an inspired actor. Olivier told Tynan in an interview:

> My father was an effective preacher, and as a boy, sitting in the choir watching him and others in the pulpit, I was fascinated by the way a sermon was delivered. Those preachers knew when to drop the voice, when to bellow about the perils of hellfire, when to slip in a gag, when suddenly to wax sentimental, when to turn solemn, when to pronounce the blessing. The quick changes in mood and manner absorbed me, and I have never forgotten them.

"What served to ignite and transform all those traits into something unique," suggests Tynan, "were his interior gifts, which are what I believe he got from his mother. By these I mean his perception, his instinctive intelligence, his intuition for the absolutely right gesture and movement, his ability to plumb character, his powers of observation and mimicry, his clearly feminine sensitivity and emotional expanse."

Agnes Crookenden Olivier was to everyone who knew her a warmhearted, intelligent, humorous woman from a cultured, educated family. "My mother was lovely," Olivier wrote in his autobiography. "There is no photograph of her I have ever seen that has revealed this in anything like its true measure. She was also undeniably a favorite among her own generation, gifted with a delightful wit and serenely high spirits." It was Agnes who encouraged her son to read until he was almost an adult reader at eight. She had him recite passages from Shakespeare, Marlowe, and other English playwrights, making it all the more real to the boy by setting the scene and telling the story of the play.

When Laurence was eight, his older brother built him a small curtained stage on which he performed plays, sometimes with his brother and sister. Agnes encouraged her son's passion for playacting, Olivier remembers.

> Although the whole family would be present at my little theatricals, I played shamelessly to my mother. She would mouth the words with me, and whenever I stumbled she would urge me on,

applauding deliriously when I got it right and suffocating me with hugs at the end. Soon she started to invite other people in to watch me perform—neighborhood ladies, relatives and the like. And it was always the same at the end—much applause, most of it polite, I'm sure, and a great deal of hugging and "Isn't-he-darling" sort of praise. I suppose you could say that I decided at a very early age that acting was for me.

Agnes introduced her son to acting and was his first drama coach; she lived through his growth and success. "Mummy was just everything to Larry," his older sister, Sybille, recalled, "she adored Larry. He was hers."

In 1920, when Olivier was thirteen years old, his mother suddenly developed a brain tumor. The last time the boy saw his mother was a day when he had been allowed to leave school to be at her bedside. As was the custom, Larry was not told how serious his mother's condition was nor that she might die. So he just left her as he usually did after a weekend visit and returned to school, not realizing that he would never see her again. He felt "utter desolation" over his mother's death. Over and over again, it came back to him how he had not even said good-bye to her. Olivier told friends, "I often think, and say, that perhaps I've never

got over it." He had even thought of drowning himself in the Thames River.

Out of his grief and the overwhelming pain of loss came a passion that his friends feel drove Olivier for the rest of his life. During the last moments Larry and his mother were together, she had kissed him good-bye and then, before letting him go, held him to her and whispered, "Darling Larry, no matter what your father says, be an actor. Be a great actor for me."

Olivier returned to All Saints after his mother's death a changed boy. He had lost his closest friend, the only person on the whole earth who, he felt, loved and cared about him. His emotions were frozen, he told his friend Kenneth Tynan. "I was a sailing ship adrift, lying dead in the water, masts buckled and sails in tatters, at the mercy of the ocean's currents."

Now his behavior puzzled and sometimes rankled his schoolmates too young to understand what was going on in the boy's mind and heart. One of them, Laurence Naismith, who also became an actor, remembers the change that came over his closest friend almost overnight.

Larry was capable of alternating bouts of almost hysterical good cheer and despondence, mixed further with frequent expressions of rude behavior. He went through a period when he was an inveterate show-off. At times he was an immature clod who conducted himself in the most boorish way. At other times he would deport himself in a elegant manner that was well beyond his years. He kept us all off balance in our attitudes toward him. As I remember it, he had no close friends throughout his stay. No one could trust him to be constant. He would be your great pal one day, and then turn around and rather compulsively try to humiliate you the next.

Agnes remained in her son's heart, so present that he actually became her. Olivier's first roles, women's roles, which brought him so much praise and offered so much promise of a great actor in the making, seemed still to be coached and encouraged in her loving way by Agnes. Sybille Olivier did not see her brother act the role of Katherina, "but I understand he modeled his character on Mother, and that it was this that enabled him to come across so well as a woman." Olivier's acting must have been astounding—and unnerving—for Sybille remembers also her father's reaction.

He had to get up and leave, so shaken was he to see Larry recreating Mother down to the last detail. Father, of course, misunderstood. He castigated Larry for his "sacrilege" in bringing mother back to life, so to speak, and for supposedly "exploiting" her memory. He forbade Larry ever to act again. . . .

Gerard never really understood his son; after all, he had never understood his wife, and now Larry had turned out to be every bit like his mother! It's hard to tell whether he actually began understanding his son's love of the stage or whether—and this seems more the case—Olivier just overwhelmed his father.

Olivier was sent to a different school, St. Edward's School, Oxford, to get him away from acting. He was forbidden from taking part in dramatics. The headmaster called in the unhappy, lackluster student for a talk and pried out of him his unhappiness, his inability to compete on the playing field, and his love of acting, which was now forbidden him. The headmaster interceded, cleverly suggesting to Reverend Olivier that dramatic skills would better prepare the boy for his ministerial training. It was a ploy. Reverend Heald confided to Larry that when the time came he would recommend him for a scholarship.

Olivier also got some unexpected help from his father's fiancée, his future stepmother. All she knew about the boy was from Gerard's laments about how poorly he was doing at school and what a disappointment he was at sports, and what a sullen, uncooperative child he was at home. Gerard took her to see Olivier's performance as Puck, and she understood immediately. "My goodness," she scolded Gerard, "he's a natural actor. That's what he should be—not a cricketer, not a preacher. Why, with a little training he could really become something in the theatre."

So it was, that at the age of seventeen, Olivier was given a day off from school and was heading for London, where he would try out for a scholarship at Miss Fogerty's Central School of Speech Training and Dramatic Art, one of the only two acting colleges in all of England. Elsie Fogerty didn't need to read the letters of recommendation from the headmaster and family friends. She watched the boy mount the stage, saw his pale, placid face suddenly light up. Then she heard his voice, clear, without distracting regional peculiarities. Olivier's voice, trained by years of choir singing, was lyrical, resonating from the chest rather than the thin voice from the throat.

His wild gestures and posturing—which, in the role of Puck, had charmed his audiences—were trite. But Fogerty saw through that, listening instead to a voice just made for Shakespeare or Shaw. Olivier recalled in his autobiography:

When it was over I was beckoned down to sit with Miss Fogerty at her table. She obviously found my efforts commendable enough, because without any beating about the bush she informed me that the scholarship was mine. Before I left she gave me one unforgettable, very special word of advice, which has been imprinted forever in my memory. During my recitation I had noticed her shading her eyes top and bottom in order to peer at me with greater intensity. She now leant towards me and said, "You have weaknesses . . . *here,*" and placed the tip of her little finger on my forehead against the base of my remarkably low hairline, and slid it down to rest in the deep hollow of my brow line and the top of my nose. I felt immediately the wisdom of this pronouncement. There was obviously some shyness behind my gaze.

Olivier joyfully entered actor's training, which consisted of rigorous classes in movement, voice, diction, makeup, fencing, gymnastics, stage and set design, lighting, making scenery, and history of the theater. Ringing in his mind was Fogerty's oft-repeated slogan "Breath, note, tone, word," a formula that strengthened his voice. He spent evenings in his tiny room in front of the mirror experimenting with makeup. On the very few occasions when he would have a little extra money, the young actor went to the theater. His scholarship was fifty pounds a year, less than seventy cents a day in American money. Another student in training with Olivier remembered that "he changed very rapidly during the first few months. When we first saw him he was nervous, shy, withdrawn. But he got hold of the place very fast, and in no time he was king of the roost."

Olivier became bored with the classes and left Fogerty's to take on roles in second-rate theaters in which he played badly, mostly just acting the cut-up. When he was fired, his father heard of it and asked their friend Sybil Thorndike to talk to the boy. Thorndike took Olivier in hand swiftly and firmly, probably, he recognized later, saving his career. "You have it in you to become a fine actor," she told him, but "you must decide what it is you want to be. A dilettante, such as I understand you are busy being now with all your friends? Or a true man of the theatre? If you choose the former, then be gone with you. If the latter, then we can help you."

The help Thorndike offered was work in her husband's London production of Shakespeare's *Henry VIII*. "I will give you some understudy work," Lewis Casson told him, "and an assistant stage manager's job for the season—three pounds a week. If you behave yourself and do your work well, I might even give you a small part in each play."

Olivier accepted and applied himself seriously. The jobs gave him his first real experience with theater and an opportunity to work with experienced, professional actors. And he was also learning to be responsible and disciplined. He was given small parts as servants in each play, but his real work was assistant stage manager—skills he would need to call on later in life when he mounted his own productions.

Olivier set out to find acting jobs on his own, but to no avail. He turned once again to his mentor, Sybil Thorndike, who recommended him to a friend at the Birmingham Repertory Theatre, which was, in 1926, a celebrated innovative theater putting on experimental plays and training young actors. Olivier was given a small role, which, though unnoticed by the critics, impressed the director, who asked him to become a permanent member of the Birmingham. He would be in a new play and have an opportunity to work with rising stars of the stage like Cedric Hardwicke and Ralph Richardson. Olivier still had not settled down—he was, remember, now all of nineteen. Hardwicke remembered him at the Birmingham as a "noisy young actor—yet there was something about him that told you that once he got control of himself he would amount to something fine on the stage." Another Birmingham actor remembers, "The boy was a natural and no one had to look at him more than once to realize it."

Olivier was finding that control. Part of the problem, he confided later, was that he was scared and felt so far out of his element. The irony was that he clowned and overacted to get attention, but he had gotten everyone's attention just by walking out on the stage. Olivier pleaded with the director for a role in one of the London productions. He was given a small role in an avant-garde American play, *The Adding Machine* by Elmer Rice, which required him to speak with a distinct New York accent. The first thing Olivier did was work on his voice, which, with its upper-class affectations, was unsuitable for the part. It's very difficult for English actors to learn American accents, but Olivier's efforts were successful.

The critics lambasted the play and the performers because of their accents, but one of London's leading critics singled out Olivier for having "by far and away the best Americanese." The critic from the London *Observer* said that "Mr. Laurence Olivier as the young man who accompanies Judy O'Grady into the graveyard gave a very good performance indeed—the best, I think, in the play. He had little to do, but he acted."

That same year he played the title role in Chekhov's *Uncle Vanya* and Malcolm in *Macbeth*. Jessica Tandy, then a young actress, recalled being startled when Olivier appeared on the stage.

"One left the theatre with an exhilarating feeling of having seen the beginnings of an actor of enormous potential."

Olivier was now, at nineteen, firmly established as an actor. With that confidence, he wished for a chance to prove himself as a leading man. The next play was to be a revival of *Harold*, poet Alfred Lord Tennyson's play written in the style of Shakespeare. *Harold* was considered a gloomy, ponderous play— it had never been staged before. Henry Irving, the illustrious actor of the 1800s, considered it "quite impossible." Olivier knew he was not being considered for the part. The director had said the role called for an experienced, romantic lead, and the search was on for an actor outside of the Birmingham's company. But still Olivier got a script for *Harold*, and while performing in *Macbeth* and rehearsing for the next play, Shaw's *Back to Methusela*, he started learning a few of the title character's speeches.

It was a few days before *Back to Methusela* was to open when the author, George Bernard Shaw, and the director chosen for *Harold* appeared to watch a dress rehearsal. Olivier appeared on the stage dressed as Marcellus, but instead of speaking the lines of his character, he broke into a speech from *Harold*.

The first reaction was outrage at what everyone thought was another one of Olivier's pranks. But then everyone became fascinated with what was happening. Here was Olivier, dressed as Marcellus, moving about the set for *Methusela*, speaking the lines of the last Saxon king of England. Biographer Thomas Kiernan describes what happened.

> When he had finished, silence descended on the theatre as Shaw, Jackson and Ayliff looked at each other and the actors on the stage milled about in confusion. Shaw, familiar with Tennyson's play, called up to Olivier, who was edging his way offstage in embarrassment. "Young man, you mispronounced the word 'deleterious.'" With that the tension was broken, and after everyone had a laugh the *Methusela* rehearsal resumed. Afterward, Shaw and Jackson went backstage and confronted the contrite Olivier. "It's all right," Shaw said to him. "I've recommended to Sir Barry that you play Harold. He agrees. Now, I trust, you will return your full attention to Marcellus for the next month."

Harold was an immense step in Olivier's career. Yet he got the role by taking frightening risks—to anyone but Olivier, that is. His gutsy "audition" on the set of *Methusela* was just the beginning.

Olivier was showing now that he was not afraid of hard work. The role of Harold required learning three thousand lines. While playing Marcellus evenings and rehearsing *Harold* mornings and afternoons, Olivier learned his lines and countless cues—in less than a week. Ralph Richardson, another of Olivier's mentors and also one of this century's greatest actors, once remarked that "it's often jokingly said, but true, the first mark of a good repertory actor is his ability to memorize his part in no time. In this respect alone Larry was a genius—better than any of the rest of us."

Predictably, the critics did not like the play, but Olivier was praised for his role—"easily the best actor in the entire cast," one said.

There would be still much to learn in so long a career and life. Olivier took his next role in *Bird in Hand*, not because the play offered any challenges but because he could work with the actress Jill Esmond, with whom he had fallen in love. That's a long story—they would eventually marry—but the importance of Esmond in Olivier's life was her knowledge of technique and theater tradition. She had come from a theater family and then studied four years at the Royal Academy of Dramatic Arts. And she became Olivier's teacher, some say the most influential in his long career.

Until now, Olivier had been succeeding largely on his own natural gifts, his presence and striking manner. But it was Esmond who showed him how to

Sir Laurence Olivier with his third wife, the actress Joan Plowright, in 1966. PHOTOFEST.

would be good experience for him. Now, in his early twenties, the pieces of the intricate puzzle that would become Laurence Olivier were falling into place. The young actor had found his wings, and he was ready to fly.

In his long career Olivier played 194 stage, screen, and television roles. But apparently many of his great roles were played offstage. When his wife of later years, Joan Plowright, was asked how she knew when her husband was acting, she answered: "Larry? Oh, he's acting all the time." Olivier himself said once, "I am far from sure when I am acting and when I am not. For what is good acting but convincing lying?"

It seems that Olivier couldn't help but act. During a rehearsal at the Old Vic a drunken stagehand became disruptive and had to be thrown out of the theater amidst much yelling and shoving. The screaming went on outside until suddenly a familiar grin flashed across the face of the "stagehand." "Just practicing, don'tcha know," said Olivier.

In another instance a group of tourists being shown around the new Chichester Festival Theatre became annoyed at a man who constantly grumbled loudly that it was all a waste of public money. Finally, someone suggested angrily that he quiet down and take his complaints to the theater's artistic director. Off came the disguise,

refine these, to make them work even better. They worked together on researching roles—she got him to look at portraits of people whose lives he would try to portray on the stage, and learn something of their characters—how to observe people. From her he learned more subtle gestures and movements and how to combine these with vocal intonation in a way that heightened his natural stage presence. And she steered him toward roles she knew and there stood the director himself, Sir Laurence Olivier.

Until the end of his life, Olivier thought and worked out every detail of his craft. Of all the Olivier stories, one of the most telling is about his performance as Othello one evening at the National Theatre in 1965, when he was almost sixty. So powerful was this particular evening's performance, that the audience jumped to their feet cheering and his fellow actors formed a line and applauded him all the way to his dressing room. He stormed past them, grim faced, slamming the door behind him. Worried that something was amiss, one of the cast called through the door, "What's the matter, Larry? It was great!" From inside came the master actor's reply: "I know it was great, dammit, but I don't know how I did it. So how can I be sure of doing it again?"

The great impersonator, like all great artists, never grew stale in his roles or ceased to learn something new. After all, he is one of the few actors who has worked brilliantly in three media—stage, screen, and television. But there was an endearing part of the old actor that had not really changed since his early days. Elsie Fogerty had pointed out to her new acting pupil that first day a weakness in his face, a weakness young Olivier knew was there and acknowledged the rest of his life. To act he

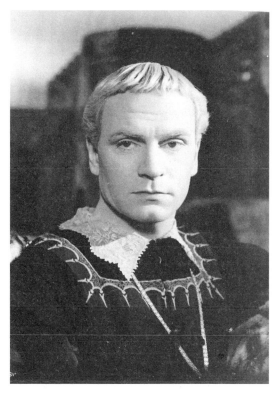

Laurence Olivier in one of his best-known roles, Hamlet. EVERETT COLLECTION.

needed makeup; indeed, a false nose, a smile, or a motion was often the very thing upon which Olivier built up an entire persona for his character.

Olivier and his old friend Ralph Richardson shared a vision over their many years together, a national theater for England. That vision became reality in 1963, and Olivier was chosen as its director. Here, for the first time, would be an opportunity for an actor of tremendous stature to design and direct his own theater. When the plans were made public, Olivier received a lot of criticism for selecting his talent from the new theaters rather than those with Shakespearean repertories. Olivier answered that the National was to be a theater of the future, best served by those with vision. "If this is going to work," he answered his critics, "we will need new ideas, blood, new approaches. Anyone who thinks our goal is to keep repeating the classics is wrong. We will do our share of classics, but the National is for everyone in England. It is especially for new writers as well as old, for new actors as well as old, for new directors as well as old." The program of the National's first year made Olivier's point—Paul Scofield, considered Olivier's successor, would play in Shakespeare's *Coriolanus* and Sir Laurence would play Nathan Detroit in *Guys and Dolls*.

That was Olivier's last word on the theater. But how did he, Laurence Olivier, want to be remembered? "God help me if I'm turned into some kind of institution, some monument. Let them say, if they have to say anything: 'Here lies Laurence Olivier. He was funny.'"

Paul Robeson

1898–1976 African-American concert artist and actor of stage and screen

In every generation there are men and women who are outstanding in their fields as athletes or scholars, musicians or actors, professionals or political activists and heroes to young people and adults alike. There are those who stand before us as symbols of excellence. And there are those who use their talents to better the lives of others.

Paul Robeson was not one of these—he was all of them. He was the second African American to be named all-American in college football. He was a "four letter man," starring also in college baseball, basketball, and track; in all he won twelve letters. At the same time he excelled in academics—graduating Phi Beta Kappa, the highest academic honor, and first in his graduating class—becoming the third African American to graduate from Columbia Law School. He went on to careers as a lawyer and professional football star.

From there he became the Paul Robeson we know best, a folklorist and singer who brought back black spirituals for the first time to concert stages around the world, and the first African-American actor to attain international prominence as a star of stage and screen. Along the way, he learned to speak and write a score of languages, including Chinese, Gaelic, Russian, Arabic, and several from Africa. The honors did not end with his death. In 1995, Robeson was elected to the Football Hall of Fame. He was the son of a slave.

Paul Bustill Robeson was born the youngest of five children in Princeton, New Jersey, on April 9, 1898. His father,

William Robeson, was born in slavery in North Carolina. William grew up in the traditions of his people, the Ibo of Nigeria. In 1860, when he was fifteen, William escaped, made his way north into Pennsylvania, and served in the Union Army. Twice during the Civil War he managed to make it back through Confederate lines to visit his mother. After the war he attended elementary school and, earning his way as a farmworker, studied theology at Lincoln University, a school for blacks near Philadelphia, receiving his degree in 1876. While in college, William met Maria Louisa Bustill, a young teacher who would become his wife and Paul's mother.

Maria, too, grew up steeped in the lore and traditions of her people, the Bantu. Among her ancestors—several who had intermarried with Delaware Indians—were Cyrus Bustill, who had helped found the Free African Society, and Joseph Cassey Bustill, who was a leader in the Underground Railroad. Another of her people helped found the Philadelphia Female Anti-Slavery Society, and her sister wrote for several newspapers. Maria was remembered by her friends as a brilliant woman, well read, who wrote poetry and many of her husband's sermons. She was there to start her son off on a life of learning and accomplishment, but died, as many women did in those days, of burns from a cookstove. Paul was six then, and carried through life loving impressions of her. To his last days, he recalled vivid memories of her funeral, his "Aunt Gertrude taking him by the hand, and leading him to the modest coffin, in the little parlor at 13 Green St.—to take one last, but never forgotten look at his beautiful, sweet, generous-hearted Mother."

Paul and his sister and brothers would be raised by their father, in poverty but always with dignity. When Reverend Robeson lost his ministerial position, he went to work as a coachman and a teamster. "Never once," Paul recalled, "did he complain of the poverty and misfortune of those years." The family "home" was now the attic of the grocery store where Reverend Robeson found some work. Somehow he was able to find the time to gather together a congregation and even build a small church for his flock. As he looked after their spiritual needs, they shared with the family any extra vegetables, peanuts, and cornmeal they had and took care of the children when the reverend had to be away from home.

Paul missed his mother and was often alone, "but what I most remember from my youngest days was an abiding sense of comfort and security." Paul later told his granddaughter:

I marvel that there is no hint of servility in my father's makeup. Just as in youth he had refused to remain a slave, so in all the years of his manhood he disdained to be an Uncle Tom. From him we learned, and never doubted it, that the Negro was in every way the equal to the white man. And we fiercely resolved to prove it.

William saw to it that his children were thoroughly educated at home before they went off to school, and he especially trained Paul from an early age in oratory skills. Reverend Robeson preached and spoke in what Paul recalled as "the greatest speaking voice I ever heard . . . a deep, sonorous basso, richly melodic and refined, vibrant with the love and compassion which filled him." He gave his son speeches to memorize, going over each line with him word by word, "dwelling on the choice of a word, the turn of a phrase, or the potency of inflection." Then, each evening, Paul would deliver the speech they had prepared together, his father listening carefully, offering stern but loving criticism. Early on, Paul was developing his own beautiful baritone voice. After Paul's speech, father and son would sometimes play checkers or just sit and talk, the reverend sharing with his son stories of his childhood as a slave. On Sundays, after church, the family would gather around their father to share with one another what they had done and learned that week.

Paul was devoted to his father, and the two, given the fifty-three-year difference in their ages, were very close. Much of Paul's hard work was to please his father and so, too, he was usually an obedient child. There was one time when he wasn't, and that one time was so painful that often throughout his life, even well into his later years, there was a story he told again and again about his father. Robeson's biographer, Martin Bauml Duberman, records it:

> I remember once he told me to do something which I did not do and he said "come here." I ran away. He ran after me. I darted across the road. He followed, stumbled and fell. I was horrified. I hurried back and helped "Pop" to his feet. He had knocked out one of his most needed teeth. I shall never forget my feeling. It has remained ever present, and I sometimes experience horror, shame, ingratitude, selfishness all over again, for I loved my "Pop" like no one in all the world. . . . Never in all my life afterwards, and this happened in 1908, when I was ten, did he have to admonish me again.

Reverend Robeson was a loving but demanding father, expecting nothing less from his children than perfection. Once, in school, when Paul got seven

A's and one *B*, his father asked him to account for the *B*. The children were expected to go to church, to share in the chores, and to be not just good, but excellent students. William, the oldest son, became a physician; Paul gives him credit for teaching him how to study. Another brother, Benjamin, became a minister like his father. His sister, Marian, followed in her mother's footsteps to become a teacher. His brother Reeve he remembers as "restless, rebellious," and a brawler, but he too had a lesson for Paul. "His example explains much of my militancy. He was always 'scoffing at convention, defiant of the white man's law,' and often told me, 'Don't ever take it from them, Laddie—always be a man—never bend the knee.'"

Paul would have to call on Reeve's strength and advice his entire life. From his very beginnings he experienced segregation and bigotry. The towns in New Jersey in which young Robeson grew up were as segregated as the deep South. Whites were middle class and well-to-do; blacks were servants and laborers. Segregation laws applied to schools, transportation, restaurants, and hotels. Black workers were excluded from trade unions. Black travelers were denied access to white hotels (though the staffs were all black).

During the first sixteen years of Paul's life, more than eleven hundred blacks were lynched, tortured, mutilated, hanged, or burned at the stake in America. Legally, blacks could vote, but intimidation and threats of violence from groups like the Ku Klux Klan kept them away from the polls. Presidents Taft, Theodore Roosevelt, and Wilson (who was born in the South) saw to it that blacks were denied federal jobs and that they remained in their "place."

But Paul and his family also grew up in a time of some promise. Booker T. Washington, and W. E. B. DuBois and the National Association for the Advancement of Colored People were speaking, sometimes militantly, but usually cautiously, for black rights. Paul attended "colored school," but he also attended unsegregated schools like Somerville High, where teachers and students were supportive and Paul was allowed a serious education. His fellow white students recalled later that they were not aware of any prejudice or antiblack feelings—in school, at least. Paul himself recalls that he was welcome and encouraged to participate in sports, to sing, and to debate on the school team. He acted the role of Mark Antony in Shakespeare's *Julius Caesar* with white classmates before an appreciative audience that was mostly white. One of his teachers noted the remarkable voice Reverend Robeson had trained in his son, and invited him to sing bass—the only bass—in the school chorus.

But Somerville was a little oasis of racial harmony; other towns were not that way. When Paul played away from home he was twice deliberately injured by opposing players laying for him, and often played baseball to shouts of "Nigger!" coming out of the stands. Even the apparent racial harmony at Somerville High was not all that it appeared to be to white students, and Paul was never allowed to forget for a moment that he was black, apart from white society. Although some teachers encouraged him to attend social events, "there was always the feeling," he recalled later, "that—well, something unpleasant might happen." Some students and teachers remarked that Paul was such a popular boy and so well liked precisely because he knew his "place." The praise of one of Paul's teachers sums it up: "He is the most remarkable boy I have ever taught, a perfect prince. Still, I can't forget that he is a Negro."

Paul felt deeply all of the subtle racism but kept quiet. It was the way his father had brought him up. He was told over and over to "act right," to avoid showing any hint of arrogance or even triumph. "Above all," he had learned from childhood, "do nothing to give them cause to fear you, for then the oppressing hand, which might at times ease up a little, will surely become a fist to knock you down again."

To be this way required incredible self-control, looking straight ahead toward his goal, not allowing himself to be pulled into the fray, no matter how much his sense of justice and fairness made him want to. It was an uncomfortable balancing act, the way black people had learned to cope. Today, we might put it this way: You need to be proud of yourself and your people, and assert yourself to get the education and things from life you deserve, but avoid all confrontation or even calling attention to yourself. It was a difficult strategy for survival, and an impossible way to live. Paul seethed constantly, and admitted that thinking back over these years always "aroused intense fury and conflict" within him.

In 1915, at the age of seventeen, Robeson took a statewide examination for a scholarship to Rutgers University. Reverend Robeson preferred that his son go to an all-black college as he had done, but Paul's mind was made up. He won a four-year scholarship and Reverend Robeson was secretly relieved; he had not the money to pay Paul's tuition to a black college.

That fall, Paul entered Rutgers and showed up to try out for a football team that had never had a black player. The coach had seen him play at Somerville, was impressed, and had welcomed him to try out. At six feet two inches, Robeson towered above his teammates and outweighed them by twenty pounds or more. But several of them would do their best to see that he would not make the team. The first day of scrimmage they piled on him, breaking his nose and spraining his shoulder. It took him ten days to recover.

"It was tough going. I didn't know whether I could take any more," Robeson recalled. But he remembered what his father had told him. "When I was out on the football field, or in a classroom, or anywhere else, I was not just there on my own. I was the representative of a lot of Negro boys who wanted to play football, and wanted to go to college, and, as their representative, I had to show that I could take whatever was handed out."

So Paul returned, this time to have a player deliberately and brutally stomp on his hand. Robeson's biographer, Martin Duberman, describes what happened next.

On the next play, as the first-string backfield came toward him, Robeson, enraged with pain, swept out his massive arms, brought down three men, grabbed the ball carrier, and raised him over his head—"I was going to smash him so hard to the ground that I'd break him right in two"—and was stopped by a nick-in-time yell from Coach Sanford. Robeson was never again roughed up— that is, by his *own* teammates. Sanford, a white New Englander committed to racial equality as well as football prowess, issued a double-barreled communiqué: Robey had made the team, and any player who tried to injure him would be dropped from it.

Robeson continued to suffer injustices in college, but he excelled at his studies, graduated with honors, and gave a brilliant valedictory speech, "The New Idealism," encouraging blacks toward self-reliance, self-respect, industry, and perseverance. He went on to four years at Columbia Law School, financing his studies playing professional football on weekends—a thousand dollars a game—coaching at his father's alma mater, Lincoln University, and tutoring Coach Sanford's son in Latin.

It was while at Columbia, too, that Robeson had his first experiences on the stage. He agreed reluctantly—just as a lark—to act in a play by the Amateur Players at the Harlem YWCA. The other players had to waylay him and then drag him to rehearsals. No critics were there to record the performance, but someone else was. Robeson recalled:

Well, it happened that Eugene O'Neill, the American dramatist, was in the house. He came round to see me afterwards and told me I should act and that I should play the part of Emperor Jones in his great play which was to be produced in London. I laughed at the idea, though, of course, I appreciated his interest, and went back to my law work.

His mind had been for so long focused on a career in law, and he hadn't even considered until now the possibility of being an actor.

Besides, he had new responsibilities. He and Eslanda Cardozo Goode, "Essie," had just married and were starting out in their life together. Essie was working as a hospital laboratory technician to help Paul through law school. An actor's life, at this time in his career, seemed just too uncertain.

Robeson had impressed everyone who had seen or heard about his first amateur attempts and so he was soon asked again. Essie encouraged her husband toward acting, and so it was with her enthusiastic support that he said yes to the next offer, the lead male role in a new play, *Taboo*—though he insisted on continuing his studies at the same time. Robeson was coached by Charles Gilpin, the most accomplished black actor of his day, and the first Emperor Jones.

The play turned out to be a flop, but the critics did notice Robeson, especially his "rich, mellow" voice and the way he dominated the stage with his presence. By now Essie was convinced of her husband's singing and acting skills. She had sat in on every rehearsal, going over his lines with him. She found money in her small salary to buy them tickets to New York shows. Yes, she understood Robeson's need for security, for prominence in a profession that he might open up for the first time to blacks; she understood his drive to be the best he could be. And, yes, he would be a good attorney, but she believed with all her heart that he could be a great actor.

While performing in *Taboo*, Robeson was asked to join the black quartet The Four Harmony Kings, then singing in the Broadway smash hit *Shuffle Along*, the first all-black musical in many years. Their bass had left suddenly, and Robeson agreed to fill in. Robeson impressed pianist Eubie Blake, the show's composer and conductor. "That boy will bear watching," he told his show-business friends. Robeson's solo, "Old Black Joe," brought wild applause and quickly became the audience's favorite. This was too much even for Robeson to ignore. When he was offered his role in a London production of *Taboo*—now renamed *Voodoo*—he said yes. Now he would have the chance to play opposite one of the legendary stars of the English stage, Mrs. Patrick Campbell. When Robeson sailed for England in July 1922, he was determined to return to complete his last year in law school.

Robeson returned from London to hard times. Essie had been ill, and there were huge medical bills. His occasional singing and acting engagements were not enough. He again played pro football, worked as a postal clerk, and even considered an offer to be a prizefighter.

He did receive his law degree in February 1923. He accepted an offer from a Rutgers alumnus, Louis William Stotesbury, to join the prestigious law firm of Stotesbury and Miner. Robeson would be the first African American ever in the firm, and one of only a handful in the entire country. Even black-owned businesses refused to hire their own people as attorneys. Despite Stotesbury's good intentions, it didn't work out. The firm's clients made hostile comments about Robeson and then things turned ugly. When Robeson called for a stenographer to take down a brief, she refused—"I never take dictation from a nigger," she told him, and stormed out of the office. Stotesbury believed in his young protégé and offered to open a branch of the firm in Harlem with Robeson in charge. But the two agreed that America was not yet ready for a black lawyer. Law, it was now clear to Robeson, was a dead end.

For all the disappointment and anguish, it turned out to be a pivotal moment in Robeson's life. For the very first time, rather than waiting for theater companies to find him, he actively sought acting roles. He hadn't been forgotten at the Provincetown Players, a company closely associated with Eugene O'Neill, and soon came a note from its director: "I want very much to talk with you about Eugene O'Neill's new play, which we will give in February. Have you a phone?" Robeson read and auditioned before the Players for a part in *All God's Chillun Got Wings*. Sixty years later, Bess Rockmore, assistant to the director, still recalled Robeson's reading as though it were yesterday.

> All I remember is the audition—and this marvelous, incredible voice. . . . I can tell you, he was a most impressive personality. Even in those days, he was flabbergastingly impressive. . . . He was built so beautifully. He moved so gracefully. . . . something unavoidably present about him.

Robeson was offered the part, and O'Neill wrote to a friend:

> I've corralled a young fellow with considerable experience, wonderful presence and voice, full of ambition and a damn fine man personally, with real brains—not a "ham." This guy deserves his chance, and I don't believe he'll lose his head if he makes a hit—as surely he will, for he's read the play for me and

I'm sure he'll be bigger than Gilpin was even at the start.

Essie was there for her husband again when he most needed her support. Together they read over the play and reread and discussed its every detail. Essie recalled how he "fell to work in earnest, put his whole heart and soul into memorizing his part; for days and nights eating, sleeping, walking, talking, he would be learning his lines." Robeson and Essie worked over the script phrase by phrase, changing emphasis here, increasing intensity there, "digging down to the meaning of every single comma." After a period of seemingly pointless drifting, their lives became full again. They attended plays on and off Broadway, lectures by African-American leaders, and meetings of the NAACP. While studying the script and waiting for rehearsals of *Chillun* to begin, Robeson joined an all-black cast in a revival of *Roseanne*, the story of a black preacher in the South.

O'Neill and *Chillun*'s director, Jimmy Light, worked with their new star, helping him to refine and polish his craft. But Light never told Robeson what to do or how to do it. His way was to help an actor find himself in the part.

The new young black actor went on to do *Emperor Jones* in New York and London, and it was in this play that

Paul Robeson as Emperor Jones. THE BETTMANN ARCHIVE.

"another" Paul Robeson appeared, the singer. His granddaughter relates how it happened: "A scene in the play called for him to exit whistling. Never able to whistle, Paul sang a spiritual. The majesty of his voice struck the audience like thunder." Jimmy Light was ecstatic and Robeson began singing lessons. He encouraged the actor to get together with his friend Larry Brown, an accompanist and acknowledged historian of African-American folk music, and give a recital.

In May 1925, they did just that at the

Greenwich Village Theatre, and a prominent music critic wrote:

> All those who listened last night to the first concert in this country made entirely of Negro music . . . may have been present at a turning point, one of those thin points in time in which a star is born and not yet visible—the first appearance of this folk wealth to be made without deference or apology. Paul Robeson's voice is difficult to describe. It is a voice in which deep bells ring.

Paul, Larry Brown, and Essie—she'd left her job at the lab to be their manager—set off on tour. American audiences were hearing for the first time African-American music and song, not just in Harlem or in the black neighborhoods of the cities, but in the best concert halls. During the performance, Robeson would explain to the audience how the spirituals they were singing "portray the hopes of our people who faced the hardships of slavery. . . . They sang to forget the chains and misery. The sorrow will one day turn to joy. All that breaks the heart and oppresses the soul will one day give way to peace and understanding, and every man will be free. That is the interpretation of a true Negro spiritual."

Robeson was surprised at the way Americans took his people's spirituals to heart, but even more so at the reaction of audiences in London and Moscow. He was now becoming more famous as a singer than as an actor, and his next hit was in Jerome Kern and Oscar Hammerstein's musical *Show Boat*. He was now known to millions of Americans who hadn't seen him on the stage—perhaps still is—for his rendition of the song "Ol' Man River." Like *Emperor Jones*, this show was a hit in London, and English audiences welcomed Robeson warmly. In England, unlike in America, blacks could stay in hotels and be served in restaurants. (In New York, Robeson would not be served in any restaurant outside of Harlem except in Pennsylvania Station.) In London, the Robesons were welcomed into all of the fine restaurants in the theater district. For the first time they did not feel the sting of racism. "Here in London," Essie wrote home, they "could, as respectable human beings, dine at any public place."

So welcome did the Robesons feel in London, that they decided to move there. Robeson had become disillusioned with American society, the last straw being the racist attacks on him personally and on *Chillun*. He told an interviewer from a London newspaper:

> I have had great difficulty in making films in America. There is the possibility that Southern audiences might object to me, not as a film actor, but as a

Paul Robeson traveling in England in 1935. HULTON DEUTSCH COLLECTION LIMITED.

film *star*. They would resent that a Negro was enjoying the social and economic advantages of the star's position. Again, in certain towns it is impossible for me to sing, because the municipal authorities refuse to "hire the hall."

Even in Russia the Robesons found more tolerance than in America. They were welcomed as celebrities, taken to concerts, and spent Christmas with the Soviet Foreign Minister. (Through all their travels, the American embassy ignored them.) Robeson met the famous Russian film director Sergei Eisenstein and told him, in his perfect Russian: "I hesitated to come; I listened to what everybody had to say but I didn't think this would be any different from any other place. But—maybe you'll understand—I feel like a human being for the first time since I grew up. Here I am not a Negro but a human being. . . . Here, for the first time in my life, I walk in full human dignity."

It was in London that Robeson gave his first performance in Shakespeare's *Othello*. He had always looked forward to tragic roles, but he saw them as needing maturity. Early in his career he told an interviewer: "When a Negro does any good work as an actor every one begins to talk of Othello. Of course, I think about Othello, but as a sort of culmination." There had not been a black Othello—only white actors in black face—since Ira Aldridge had played the role in the 1860s. Now he would act with England's beloved Peggy Ashcroft.

In preparation, Robeson studied other works of Shakespeare with a scholar's eye for detail and immersed himself in English as spoken in the 1600s. Susan Robeson writes about her grandfather:

> Paul related to *Othello* as no White actor could. His interpretation was revolutionary, yet true to Shakespeare. Paul viewed Othello as a Black man of noble ancestry, alone in a hostile and alien White society. Feeling his honor betrayed, Othello kills—not out of jealousy, but from the deeper roots of cultural and racial integrity. The interpretation surprised the British public; it sent shock waves through America.

Robeson returned to America to begin his acting anew, singing and working for his people's causes. He starred in Eugene O'Neill's *The Hairy Ape* and several movies, including a film version of *Emperor Jones*, which he felt presented his people's struggle with realism and with dignity. Eventually, Robeson gave up on Hollywood, feeling that it was impossible to make films, in America at least, that accomplished what he hoped for: "In my music, my plays, my films I want always to carry this central idea: to be African."

Robeson thought radio a better

medium for actors. He made frequent appearances on radio and more than three hundred recordings, including "Ballad for Americans," by Earl Robinson, which became, some said, our unofficial national anthem. The ballad includes the lines: "Man in white skin can never be free / While his black brother is in slavery."

He became more of an activist, urging blacks to join the United Automobile Workers of America. In 1941 he sued a restaurant for refusing service to blacks. He was the first concert artist of his stature to perform in prisons, and in 1943 met with the baseball commissioner, speaking as a black athlete, to ask that Jackie Robinson be allowed to play major league baseball.

In 1943 Robeson performed *Othello*, breaking all Broadway records for a Shakespearean production—296 consecutive performances. "One of the most memorable events in the history of the theatre," one critic wrote. "There has never been and never will be a finer rendition of this particular tragedy. It is unbelievably magnificent."

Throughout his life, Paul Robeson was punished for his beliefs at the same time that he gave the people of the world the most stunning, moving performances we have ever known. He stood bravely before his attackers because he knew for what and for whom he stood—for any

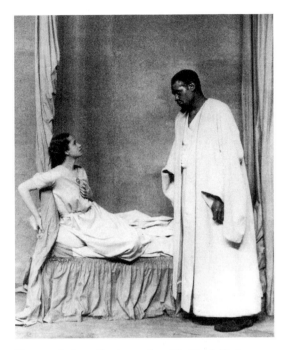

Peggy Ashcroft starred with Paul Robeson in the London production of Shakespeare's *Othello*. UPI/BETTMANN.

oppressed people anywhere in the world. He said this at an antifascist rally:

> The artist must elect to fight for freedom or for slavery. I have made my choice. I had no alternative. The history of the capitalist era is characterized by the degradation of my people: despoiled of their lands, their culture destroyed . . . denied equal protection of the law, and deprived their rightful place in the respect of their fellows.
>
> Not through blind faith or coercion, but conscious of my course, I take my place with you.

Ethel Waters

1896–1977 African-American actress and singer

As a theater actress, nightclub singer, vaudeville performer, and, later in her life, as an evangelist, Ethel Waters touched the lives and hearts of more people than any other performer of her day. Most Americans knew her in her nightclub, radio, and television roles. She made hundreds of records, best known among them songs like "Dinah," "Stormy Weather," and "Having a Heat Wave." Today, they are all sought by collectors.

But she was considered by the most influential entertainment critics as one of the top-ranking actresses in the world, along with Katherine Cornell, Lynn Fontanne, and Helen Hayes. She also received the highest praise of other entertainers, among them Oscar Hammerstein, Judith Anderson, Dorothy Gish, and Tallulah Bankhead, who described one of her performances as "a profound emotional experience which any playgoer would be poorer for missing. It seems indeed to be such a magnificent example of great acting, simply, deeply felt, moving on a plane of complete reality. . . ." She was among the first African Americans to be given serious dramatic stage and screen roles, and with her brilliant performances led the way for a new generation of black actors.

Waters's beginnings did not seem to hold promise of greatness. In her autobiography, *His Eye Is on the Sparrow*, she wrote:

> I was never a child.
> I never was coddled, or liked, or understood by my family.
> I never felt I belonged.

I was always an outsider.

I was born out of wedlock, but that had nothing to do with all this. To people like mine a thing like that just didn't mean much.

Nobody brought me up.

I just ran wild as a little girl.

Some of the problem, she always felt, was her mixed blood, her light skin, which drew taunts and abuse from other black children. Her great-grandmother had been a slave, but fair skinned. Her great-grandfather was from India. Sally, her grandmother, was the first in her family to be schooled, and was remembered as an intelligent woman who raised her four children, including Ethel's mother, Louisa, or "Vi," alone. Ethel was born when Vi was only twelve. She never knew her father, John Waters, or anything about him, for that matter, except that his mother was her "white grandmother." Ethel was rejected by her mother, who wanted nothing to do with her after her birth, and so she was raised by her grandmother, Sally, and her sisters and brother. "My whole childhood was almost like a series of one-night stands," Waters remembered later. "I was shuttled about among relatives, boarded out, continually being moved around to Camden, Chester and Philadelphia homes."

"Mom," as Ethel called her grandmother, was seldom around, having to work long hours as a maid. Still, "she, Mom, was the greatest influence of my childhood. What she wanted to do, and desperately, was to save me from the vice, lust and drinking that was all about me—and to keep me whole and unharmed as a human being." Sally worked her life away trying to provide a better one for her children. Because she worked for more well-to-do people, she saw how it was possible to live better and she wanted the kind of home they had for her own children.

But it remained always just a dream. "Again and again," Ethel recalls, "the pathetic little homes she set up for us broke up. There was only Mom to keep them going, and her work kept her away too much of the time for that." Ethel slept on the floor, or on chairs put together, a broken-down couch, or even an ironing board, anywhere she could find. As a child of four Ethel was tall and already curious and talkative, and she was placed early in kindergarten. She remembered her teachers always commenting on how cute and sweet she was, but they didn't really know her. "I might have looked angelic, but what came out of my mouth would have shocked any New York cab driver."

As a child Waters also learned to sing, as many African Americans did to soothe the pain and suffering of their lives. She was enthralled by the songs and stories she heard all around her; everyone in her family, it seemed, sang.

I'd ask one of them, "Tell me a story," when I was little, and they'd sing it. Later, when I sang those same old songs, both folk songs and popular numbers, on the stage or on the radio, they gained nationwide attention. In 1949, when I appeared on the Tex and Jinx program, I sang some of those songs, humming the parts where I didn't remember the lines. I got letters from people all over the country who sent me the words I'd forgotten. They'd remembered the old songs all those years and kept them in their minds like treasures.

Families got together in those days to sing, and there were always neighbors who could play the banjo, mandolin, or guitar. Waters remembers, too, the hurdy-gurdy man who played his old street organ at the curbside for pennies, and all the children would gather around and sing to the music. At the age of five, Ethel made her first public appearance in a children's program put on in church. "I was billed as Baby Star," she recalled proudly in her later years. "In my act I had to recite a short piece and also sing a little song which went like this:

I am dying for some one to love me,
Some one to call my own.
Some one to stay with me all the time
For I am tired of living alone.

Again and again I was called back for encores. I was a sensational success."

Probably few who sat in that audience understood how real was Ethel's cry for love.

A bunch of us would often sleep all night out on the street, over the warm iron gratings of bakeries and laundries. Our families didn't care where we were, and these nesting places, when you put your coat under you, were no more uncomfortable than the broken-down beds with treacherous springs or the bug-infested pallets we had at home.

The streets were Ethel's home, and they were also her introduction to human nature.

I was not yet six years old when we moved [to Clinton Street] and seven when we left, but I had one hell of a time for myself in that plague spot of vice and crime. I came to know well the street whores, the ladies in the sporting houses, their pimps, pickpockets, shoplifters, and other thieves who lived all around us. . . . It was they who taught us how to steal.

What Waters stole was food for herself and her family. Mom stole, too, from the kitchens in which she worked as cook or maid, but it was not enough to keep her family fed. Often Ethel would be given a supper of whatever was left over from lunch in one of the many bars up and down the street. Sometimes she would be fed by the sisters at the convent school she attended, but she refused anything she suspected was charity. After their offers of food were refused, the sisters learned to invent errands for Ethel to do, for only as recompense for work done would the proud little girl accept a meal. She learned to steal vegetables from the sidewalk food stands while the owners were inside. Then as now there was an entire world of poverty living on the streets, but as terrifying as it might seem, Waters and her little friends were fearless. She had become, as she put it, a "wised-up child," and felt confident that she could handle any and every danger that awaited them in the streets and alleys of Philadelphia: "My vile tongue was my shield, my toughness my armor."

It was on the streets that Waters discovered the stage. "The shows were vaudeville, put on in the little store-front theaters along South Street. These were the nickelodeons and had tiny stages and folding chairs. Admission cost ten cents, with a few front rows at twenty-five cents. I always stayed to see these shows over and over again, until the manager put me out." Then she would go home or to her friends gathered on the street and imitate the songs and acts she saw on the stage. Ethel was learning about something else on the streets. Everywhere around her were people ravaged by opium, cocaine, morphine, and heroin.

At the age of nine, Waters found what she would always remember as her first permanent home, the Catholic school. From eight in the morning until two, every day now, there was a bright, clean, safe place for her to be where she felt loved and cared for. The sisters and the priest all counseled her, encouraged her to break away from the life she had been leading. No one punished her or called her names. Here she found peace. "I would leave the school full of hope and feeling exalted. Then I had to go home." And home was always the same, the drunkenness, violence, and cursing. Ethel's mother and her aunts despised Catholicism and, eventually, they took her out of the convent school, though she returned whenever she could and was certain her family wouldn't find out. At eleven, Ethel was back in public school and working afternoons as a cleaning woman for seventy-five cents a week. She had acquired a deep faith. "At home I talk a great deal to Jesus. Often he is my only playmate."

At thirteen Waters found herself in a marriage she did not want, set up by her mother, to a man twice her age. After a year of abuse she stood up to her husband and left. As she put it: "At thirteen I was married, and at fourteen I was separated and on my own. I had a certain amount of battle cry in me." She went to work as a chambermaid and a waitress, jobs she enjoyed, and she always did the best she could. More than the job, she enjoyed having the same work every day and with the same people. She was now earning $3.50 a week. She earned another $1.75 by taking some of the guests' laundry home.

That might have been her life were it not for two friends who talked her into going on stage to sing at a local nightclub, Jack's Rathskeller. Young people came from all over Philadelphia to perform in competition that night. It was Ethel's birthday and she sang—and shimmied—her heart out. It turned out that along with the amateur contestants appeared also some well-known professional musicians, blues and jazz bands, and the vaudeville team Braxton and Nugent. They and the crowd were dazzled by Waters's singing and offered her ten dollars a week to join their act. She felt that she was too young to be on the stage, but her mother agreed to sign a paper swearing that she was twenty-one; she agreed also to hold down

Ethel's job while she was gone, just in case.

Waters had a favorite song that she now wanted to sing for her first appearance at the Lincoln Theatre in Baltimore—"St. Louis Blues." She would have to have permission, though, because in those days song publishers restricted the number of performers who sang their songs. Waters wrote to the copyright owners, Pace and Handy, in Memphis, Tennessee, asking permission to sing the unknown song on the stage. To her surprise she received a letter granting her permission. "That was how I, a seventeen-year-old novice, became the first woman—and the second person—ever to sing professionally that song which is now a classic and, according to many people, the greatest blues ever written."

From the beginning, Waters would have things her way. She would sing "St. Louis Blues" in a low, quiet, soft way that was her style. The problem was that black audiences of the day were used to what she called shouters, Bessie Smith and Ma Rainey. What she wanted to do was not what the audience expected. "I could always riff and jam and growl, but I never had that loud approach." She sang it her way. "And you could have heard a pin drop in that rough, rowdy auditorium out front."

"That first time, when I finished

Ethel Waters as a young actress. THE KOBAL COLLECTION.

singing 'St. Louis Blues,' the money fell like rain on the stage. Nugent had to come on again to get me off or I would have been sitting there yet." Ethel Waters—"Sweet Mama Stringbean" as she was called on the posters outside the theater—was a hit.

She left the troupe and formed her own group with two other women, the Hill sisters. They traveled around the country. Soon, Waters was well known and drawing crowds everywhere the singers appeared. They'd get off the train and there, across the main street, would be a banner advertising: "The Hill Sisters, Featuring Sweet Mama String-bean, Singing 'St. Louis Blues.'" Waters worked hard night after night, sending money home to her mother whenever she could. It was a hard life, but not unlike the one she had known as a child. Later she recalled of these days: "I used to work from nine until unconscious."

The tours continued, now to Pittsburgh, Detroit, Cincinnati and Lima, Ohio; Atlanta, Charleston, Savannah, and all around the United States. She was invited to perform at the famous Cotton Club—home of stars like Duke Ellington and Cab Calloway—and the Plantation Club in New York's Harlem. And she was being offered recording contracts. But even with the fame and the money, the impatient audiences chanting, "Blues! Blues! Come on,

Stringbean, we want your blues!" Waters felt an emptiness deep in her soul—instead of happiness, "only squalor and contentiousness and professional jealousy. I still had no feeling of having roots, of being on a team and belonging to a group. I was still alone and an outcast, even though I was starting to get top billing."

Sweet Mama Stringbean was having adventures she'd never forget, but what she wanted more than anything in the world was what she'd never had—in show business or out of it—"clean surroundings, a decent, quiet place to sleep, some sense of order, and good meals at regular times of the day."

Until now, Waters had performed only in black nightclubs. In her day, audiences did not mix. These were the days before the Civil Rights movement and integration, the teens and twenties, the days of segregation. A few white faces might be seen at Harlem clubs, lovers of jazz and blues who cared about black music. But in the swank clubs and Broadway theater nary a black face was ever seen. Her first appearances on Broadway were in Negro revues, *Africana* (1927), *Blackbirds* (1930), and *Rhapsody in Black* (1932). Waters herself was uncomfortable with even the thought of appearing before white audiences and resisted the idea for a long time.

But she also recognized within herself an ability to change, to take on new challenges. After all, considering all her life had been, what had she to lose? She joined the cast of Irving Berlin's *As Thousands Cheer* with the popular white actors Clifton Webb and Marilyn Miller. "I guess I was facing the most important test of my career," she realized later, "as I started rehearsing for *As Thousands Cheer*." The show was a smash hit and many knew that it was because of Waters. The real test for her came with the summer, when the lead actors went on vacation. That left Waters and Helene Broderick to go it alone, and still the theater filled up every night. For the first time, Waters was receiving top billing with the white stars, and she became the highest-paid woman performer on Broadway.

The first time she performed before a white audience, Waters discovered how different it was from the all-black audiences she knew. She insisted that white people wouldn't understand her or her music. But she agreed to go on mostly to prove her point. The audience applauded enthusiastically at the end of her performance, but Waters was backstage in tears. "What's the matter? What's the matter?" she cried when the producer tried to comfort her. "You know we took the flop of our lives just now. Those people out front applauded us only because they wanted to be polite." Waters was used to black audiences:

> They did whatever they pleased while you were killing yourself on stage. They ran up and down the aisles, yelling greetings to their friends and sometimes having fights. And they brought everything to eat from bananas to yesterday's pork chops. But they were also the most appreciative audiences in the world if they liked you. They'd scream, stomp, and applaud until the whole building shook.

Her audience tonight had "only" applauded her. "They merely clapped their hands. Such restraint is almost a sneer in the colored vaudeville world I came out of." It took her a while to finally realize that she had not failed in front of a white audience. They had loved her. It's just that they had a different way of showing it.

Though she didn't realize it at the time, Waters was the first of what we would call today a "crossover," an artist who introduces the art of one culture to another. Waters's recordings of African-American music and song were probably bought by more whites than blacks. Countless white people enjoyed her movie, radio, and television performances and took her to their hearts. She introduced her bluesy jazzy style, once heard only in black nightclubs, to the cultural mainstream, and made black music American music.

Still another big step in Waters's career came in 1938, when she starred in *Mamba's Daughter*, her first straight dramatic role. The writers of the play changed it to make her role, Hagar, the dominant role. The producers had difficulty finding investors when they explained that Ethel Waters was to be the lead actor. "Ethel Waters, are you kidding?" they asked. "Ethel is a good singer but no actress." But the producers believed in her and found the money they needed to put on the play.

Ethel wanted the part. She had turned down earlier offers: "The characters in them had been either created by white men or by Negro writers who had stopped thinking colored." But this play was different; this was the first role that rang true to her. It was written by a Southern white man and his wife—DuBose and Dorothy Heyward—who had also written the folk opera *Porgy and Bess*. Waters respected DuBose. He was "a man of charm, great talent, absolute integrity, and deep-hearted sympathy for all Negroes." She realized that this was her story.

[It was] a play ripped out of the life I'd always known and was still living. Even when I read it for the first time I understood instinctively that there could be no greater triumph in my professional career than playing Hagar. All my life I had burned to tell the story of my mother's despair and long defeat, of Momweeze being hurt so by a world that then paid her no mind. It was a tragedy and a story of courage, with Hagar, like Momweeze, meeting it all with her heart up, never once doubting her God, and furiously intent on staying a person no matter how tricked and buffeted and besmirched and bruised.

But the role was more than a personal matter to this black actress. "Hagar, fighting on in a world that had wounded her so deeply, was more than my mother to me. She was all Negro women lost and lonely in the white man's antagonistic world."

Mamba's Daughter opened at the venerable old Empire Theatre on January 3, 1939. Waters wrote in her autobiography:

I still remember [it] as the most thrilling and important experience of my life as a performer. And my whole life, too, except for when I found God. I was the first colored woman, the first actress of my race, ever to be starred on Broadway in a dramatic play. . . . And the Empire's star dressing room was mine on that opening night. While the carriage trade was arriving outside, I sat at the dressing table where all the great actresses, past and present, had sat as they made up their faces and wondered what the first-night verdict would be—Maude Adams, Ethel

Barrymore, Helen Hayes, Katherine Cornell, Lynn Fontanne, and all the others, now dead, who had brought the glitter of talent and beauty and grace to that old stage.

The audience that night summoned Waters to seventeen curtain calls. The critics loved her. "In her moments of tenderness," one wrote the next day, "she is heart-wrenching. In her moments of blind passion magnificent." Another said that "in the playing of Ethel Waters, Hagar becomes magnificently like a force of nature." And another: "Ethel Waters established herself as one of the finest actresses, white or black."

In between her stage and nightclub appearances Waters still had energy for another career as a film actress. It had begun in the early forties with performances in *Tales of Manhattan* and *Cairo*. In 1948 she returned to Hollywood to play the grandmother in *Pinky*, a story familiar to her, about a black girl whose light color enables her to pass for white. In 1950 she performed in the play *Member of the Wedding* and later repeated her acclaimed performance on film. Waters would have the opportunity of working with one of the greatest film directors, John Ford, and some of the most talented actors of the day.

Waters had always admired Ford and was honored to be in one of his pictures,

Julie Harris with Ethel Waters in 1950 in Carson McCullers's popular play *Member of the Wedding.* PHOTOFEST.

though she was also frightened to death at the thought of working with him. Not long into shooting the film, however, Ford had to drop out and she found herself working with another of her favorite directors, Elia Kazan. Waters had nothing to fear; she was, by now, a professional. Kazan, himself an actor, respected Waters's intelligence and her natural instinct for the part. Kazan, as a good director should, helped her be her best in it. For Waters it was almost not acting.

"All I had to do to play Granny well was remember my own grandmother, Sally Anderson. The Granny in *Pinky* was much like her, being proud of her blood, hard-working, fierce-tempered, and devoted to her white employers."

The film performance brought praise from the critics—"Ethel Waters endows this gentle lady with tremendous warmth and appeal"—and an award from the Negro Actors Guild of America. She also became the second African American to win an Academy Award nomination for Best Supporting Actress. (The first had been Hattie McDaniel, who received an Oscar for *Gone with the Wind*.)

Sadly, Ethel Waters has been misunderstood and all but ignored by African-American women today. They see her simply as Beulah, the mammy, or in one of her early vaudeville roles that many—blacks and whites— find demeaning, uncomfortable, and embarrassing. But she endowed the black women she played, including Beulah, with warmth and humanity, recognizing their complexity. Waters brought to all of her roles the hard lessons she had learned and humility, the toughness and resilience she possessed in real life. "As a dramatic actress all I've ever done is to remember. When I act I try to express the suffering—or the joy—I've known during my lifetime. Or the sorrow and happiness I've sensed in others."

Despite her talents, Waters was always puzzled that she is considered an artist.

An artist, it seems to me, should be complete mistress of her medium. Many critics have been kind enough to say that about me. But if I was mistress of my medium I wouldn't be so scared each time I walk out in front of an audience. Before each performance I tell myself the same thing: They don't have to like me, those people out there. They are not my friends. My job is to *make* them like me. I have to make these strangers my friends.

Further Reading

Titles marked by an asterisk are most suitable for young readers.

GENERAL

Brown, John Russel, ed. *The Oxford Illustrated History of Theater*. Oxford: Oxford University Press, 1995.

Henderson, Mary C. *Theatre in America*. New York: Abrams, 1986.

Wright, Edward A. *A Primer for Play Goers*. Englewood Cliffs, NJ: Prentice Hall, 1958.

CLASSICAL DRAMATISTS

CHEKHOV

Gillés, Daniel. *Observer without Illusion*. New York: Funk & Wagnalls, 1968.

Gorky, Maxim, Alexander Kuprin, and I. A. Bunin. *Reminiscences of Anton Chekhov*. New York: B. W. Huebsch, 1921.

Hingley, Ronald. *Chekhov: A Biographical and Critical Study*. London: George Allen & Unwin, 1950.

Laffitte, Sophie. *Chekhov: 1860–1904*. London: Angus and Robertson, 1974.

IBSEN

Brustein, Robert. *The Theatre of Revolt*. Boston: Little, Brown, 1964.

Heiberg, Hans. *Ibsen: A Portrait of the Artist*. London: George Allen & Unwin, 1969.

Ibsen, Bergliot. *The Three Ibsens*. New York: American-Scandinavian Foundation, 1952.

Jaeger, Henrik. *Henrik Ibsen: A Critical Biography*. New York: Haskell House, 1972.

Meyer, Michael. *Henrik Ibsen: The Making of a Dramatist 1828–1864*. London: Rupert Hart-Davis, 1967.

MOLIÈRE

Fernandez, Ramon. *Molière: The Man Seen Through the Plays*. New York: Hill and Wang, 1958.

Howarth, W. D. *Molière: A Playwright and His Audience*. Cambridge: Cambridge University Press, 1982.

Lewis, D. B. Wyndham. *Molière: The Comic Mask.* London: Eyre & Spottiswoode, 1959.

SHAKESPEARE

Craig, Hardin, ed. *The Complete Works of Shakespeare.* Chicago: Scott, Foresman, 1951.

Quennell, Peter. *Shakespeare: A Biography.* Cleveland: World, 1963.

Rowse, A. L. *Shakespeare the Man.* New York: Harper & Row, 1973.

*————. *Shakespeare's Self-portrait: Passages from His Work.* London: Macmillan, 1985.

Schoenbaum, S. *William Shakespeare: A Compact Documentary Life.* New York: Oxford University Press, 1977.

ACTORS OF THE EIGHTEENTH AND NINETEENTH CENTURIES

BERNHARDT

*Bernhardt, Sarah. *My Double Life.* London: William Heinemann, 1907.

Gold, Arthur, and Robert Fitzdale. *The Divine Sarah: A Life of Sarah Bernhardt.* New York: Knopf, 1991.

Noble, Iris. *Great Lady of the Theatre: Sarah Bernhardt.* New York: Julian Messner, 1960.

Salmon, Eric, ed. *Bernhardt and the Theatre of Her Time.* (Contributions in Drama and Theatre Series, No. 6.) Westport, CT: Greenwood Press, 1977.

BOOTH

Ruggles, Eleanor. *Prince of Players: Edwin Booth.* New York: W. W. Norton, 1953.

Winter, William. *Life and Art of Edwin Booth.* New York: Macmillan, 1893.

DUSE

Rheinhardt, E. A. *The Life of Eleonora Duse.* London: Martin Secker, 1930.

*Signorelli, Olga. *Eleonora Duse.* London: Thames & Hudson, 1959.

Weaver, William. *Duse: A Biography.* London: Thames & Hudson, 1959.

GARRICK

*Kendall, Alan. *David Garrick.* London: Harrap, 1985.

Price, Cecil. *Theatre in the Age of Garrick.* Oxford: Basil Blackwell, 1973.

Stone, George Winchester Jr., and George M. Kahrl. *David Garrick: A Critical Biography.* Carbondale: Southern Illinois University Press, 1979.

IRVING AND TERRY

Auerbach, Nina. *Ellen Terry, Player in Her Time.* New York: W. W. Norton, 1987.

Bingham, Madeleine. *Henry Irving and the Victorian Theatre.* London: George Allen & Unwin, 1978.

*Cheshire, David F. *Portrait of Ellen Terry.* Oxford: Amber Lane Press, 1989.

Irving, Laurence. *Henry Irving: The Actor and His World.* London: Faber and Faber, 1951.

Saintsbury, H. A., and Cecil Palmer, eds. *We Saw Him Act: A Symposium on the Art of Sir Henry Irving.* New York: Benjamin Blom, 1939.

KEAN

FitzSimons, Raymund. *Edmund Kean: Fire from Heaven.* London: Hamish Hamilton, 1976.

Hillebrand, Harold Newcomb. *Edmund Kean.* New York: Columbia University Press, 1933.

Playfair, Giles. *Kean: The Life and Paradox of the Great Actor*. London: Columbus Books, 1988.

MODERN PLAYWRIGHTS/ SHOWMAKERS

BARAKA

*Baraka, Amiri. *The Autobiography of LeRoi Jones*. New York: Freundlich Books, 1984.

Brown, Lloyd W. *Amiri Baraka*. Boston: Twayne Publishers, 1980.

Lacey, Henry C. *To Raise, Destroy, and Create: The Poetry, Drama, and Fiction of Imamu Amiri Baraka*. Troy, NY: Whitson Publishing, 1981.

Sollors, Werner. *Amiri Baraka/LeRoi Jones: The Quest for a "Populist Modernism."* New York: Columbia University Press, 1978.

BARNUM

*Barnum, P. T. *Struggles and Triumphs: Forty Years' Recollections*. Buffalo, NY: Warren, Johnson & Co., 1872.

Eckley, Wilton. *The American Circus*. Boston: Twayne, 1984.

Wallace, Irving. *The Fabulous Showman: The Life and Times of P. T. Barnum*. New York: Alfred A. Knopf, 1959.

BRECHT

Bartram, Graham, ed. *Brecht in Perspective*. London: Longman, 1982.

*Bentley, Eric. *The Brecht Commentaries: 1943–1980*. London: Eyre Methuen, 1981.

Esslin, Martin. *Brecht: A Choice of Evils*. London: Eyre & Spottiswoode, 1959.

Lyon, James K. *Bertolt Brecht in America*. Princeton, NJ: Princeton University Press, 1980.

HAMMERSTEIN

Fordin, Hugh. *Getting to Know Him*. New York: Random House, 1977.

Sheean, Vincent. *Oscar Hammerstein I*. New York: Simon & Schuster, 1956.

HANSBERRY

Carter, Stephen R. *Hansberry's Drama: Commitment amid Complexity*. Urbana: University of Illinois Press, 1991.

Nemiroff, Robert, ed. *Lorraine Hansberry: The Collected Last Plays*. New York: New American Library, 1983.

*——. *To Be Young, Gifted and Black*. New York: Signet/NAL, 1969.

O'CASEY

Atkinson, Brooks. *The Sean O'Casey Reader*. New York: St. Martin's Press, 1968.

Margulies, Martin B. *The Early Life of Sean O'Casey*. Dublin: The Dolmen Press, 1970.

*O'Casey, Eileen. *Sean*. London: Macmillan, 1971.

O'NEILL

Alexander, Doris. *Eugene O'Neill's Creative Struggle*. University Park: Pennsylvania State University Press, 1992.

*Estrin, Mark W., ed. *Conversations with Eugene O'Neill*. Jackson: University Press of Mississippi, 1990.

Gelb, Arthur and Barbara Gelb. *O'Neill*. New York: Harper & Row, 1962.

SHAW

Holroyd, Michael. *Bernard Shaw*. London: Chatto & Windus, 1988.

Morgan, Magery M. *Bernard Shaw I: 1856–1907*. Windsor, England: Profile Books Ltd., 1982.

*Weintraub, Stanley, ed. *Shaw: An Autobiography*. New York: Weybright and Talley, 1969.

VALDEZ

Bagby, Beth. "El Teatro Campesino; Interviews with Luis Valdez." *Tulane Drama Review*, 11 (Summer 1967), 70–80.

Huerta, Jorge A. *Chicano Theater: Themes and Forms*. Ypsilanti, MI: Billingual Press/Editorial Bilingüe, 1982.

Steiner, Stan. "The Cultural Schizophrenia of Luis Valdez." *Vogue* (March 15, 1969), 112–113, 143–144.

*Valdez, Luis. "The Actos." In *Guerilla Street Theater*. New York: Avon Books, 1973.

WILLIAMS

Williams, Dakin, and Shepherd Mead. *Tennessee Williams: An Intimate Biography*. New York: Arbor House, 1983.

Williams, Tennessee. *Memoirs*. New York: Doubleday, 1975.

MODERN ACTORS

BARRAULT

*Barrault, Jean-Louis. *Memories for Tomorrow*. New York: E. P. Dutton, 1974.

———. *Reflections on the Theatre*. London: Rockliff, 1951.

———. *The Theatre of Jean-Louis Barrault*. New York: Hill and Wang, 1961.

BARRYMORE

Alpert, Hollis. *The Barrymores*. New York: Dial Press, 1964.

*Barrymore, Ethel. *Memories*. New York: Harper, 1955.

Peters, Margot. *The House of Barrymore*. New York: Knopf, 1990.

HAYES

Barrow, Kenneth. *Helen Hayes: First Lady of the American Theatre*. New York: Doubleday, 1985.

*Hayes, Helen. *My Life in Three Acts*. San Diego: Harcourt Brace Jovanovich, 1990.

OLIVIER

Holden, Anthony. *Laurence Olivier*. New York: Atheneum, 1988.

Kiernan, Thomas. *Sir Larry: The Life of Laurence Olivier*. New York: Times Books, 1981.

*Olivier, Laurence. *Confessions of an Actor: An Autobiography*. New York: Simon & Schuster, 1982.

*Tanitch, Robert. *Olivier*. London: Thames and Hudson, 1985.

ROBESON

Duberman, Martin Bauml. *Paul Robeson*. New York: Alfred A. Knopf, 1988.

Foner, Philip S. *Paul Robeson Speaks*. New York: Brunner/Mazel, 1978.

*Robeson, Susan. *The Whole World in His Hands: A Pictorial Biography of Paul Robeson*. Secaucus, NJ: Citadel Press, 1981.

WATERS

*Waters, Ethel, and Charles Samuels. *His Eye Is on the Sparrow*. New York: Da Capo Press, 1989.

*———. *To Me It's Wonderful*. New York: Harper & Row, 1972.

Index

NOTE: *Page numbers for illustrations are in italics.*